SQUAD 13

WORSE THAN DEATH

By D. G. Valdron

FOSSIL COVE PRESS   WINNIPEG, MANITOBA

SQUAD THIRTEEN, Worse than Death
Fossil Cove Publishing, 1301 - 90 Garry Street, Wpg, Man, Can, R3C 4J4

EBook - ISBN: 978-1-998453-34-4
Print Book — ISBN 978-1-998453-19-1 (IngramSpark)

Cover and Interior Art by Nym Productions
Cover design by Dean Naday
Copy Editor Ryan Melnyk

Published by D.G. Valdron, Fossil Cove Publishing,

Text set in Garamond

DEDICATED
To Those Who Helped Make This Real

Dean Naday
Nym Productions
Anna Valdron
Patrick Lowe
Mireille Theriault
Ryan Melnyk

MY SPECIAL THANKS
To each of you who supported this project

Alex McGilvery
R. Graeme Cameron
Sherry Charbonneau
Kat Martens
Krista Ball
Jazz Russell
Bruce Thomson
David Annandale
Ron Hore
Melissa Yi
Y.M. Pang
Sharon Hamilton
Lindsey Watson
Sandra Kasturi
Dan Roop
Ryan Melnyk
Douglas Smith
Michael Barbour
Wes Chee

SQUAD THIRTEEN
Worse than Death

Table of Contents

PROLOGUE WITH A VAMPIRE 1

THE DESERT 11

BRIEFING 23

CENTIPEDES 29

WINDY VALLEY GO-GO 47

HUNGRY HUNGRY HOUNGANS 141

More Books by the Author 291

PROLOGUE WITH A VAMPIRE

The general sits on the park bench in full dress uniform, feeding pigeons. The park is empty. The fountain continues to flow. The artificial pond in the center of the park, surrounded by unused jogging trails and bike paths, is still and without motion. There's not even a ripple.

Outside, the park, there is no traffic at all. The shops are empty, the buildings unoccupied. The town is utterly silent.

The pigeons swarm, a small flock at his feet. They're all so very hungry, food's been sparse. He feeds them from his bag of crumbs, but after a while he runs out. The pigeons stick around for a little while after that, but eventually, one by one, they depart, leaving the General alone. He sighs. He enjoys their company, their motion and sounds, the aliveness they'd brought.

Now departed, he feels like he is in a still life. He waited. That was one thing you learn to do in the military, clear your mind and wait for whatever was coming.

A newspaper blows past. He watches the page flutter on the wind, already yellowing and faded. He doesn't bother to chase or catch it. It would have dated to two weeks ago, when the town went dark.

The shadows grow long. Night is coming. At one point, a stray dog appears, stepping out of some bushes far off. The animal seems healthy, though gaunt. Its ribs are showing. The General and the Dog look at each other for a long moment, then it disappears without ever coming closer.

The sun is setting, The General simply waits.

Then, suddenly, with no sense of abruptness, there is a young woman sitting on the park bench with him. Her skin is pale. She wears a summer dress, floral patterned, with spaghetti straps and visible cleavage, just loose enough to be comfortable but still revealing her shape. The General notes that she isn't wearing a bra, he is vaguely happy that he still notices things like that. She is barefoot, her toes flexing automatically. The paint is chipping from her toenails.

Her smile, when she smiles at him, is brilliant. She's beautiful, she's radiant, she's everything he ever dreamed of. He wants, suddenly, to offer himself up to her, to pledge his undying love.

She knows this, and it pleases her.

WOMAN: Nice night.

GENERAL: I suppose.

WOMAN: I haven't seen you around?

She smiles. Her teeth flash, whiter than ever. She leans forward, extending her hand. He takes it. Her flesh is cold, like all her kind, stiff with rigor and unearthly strength.

ANDY: Hi. I'm Andy, short for Andrea. I'm not going to kill you.

The General nods.

GENERAL: Pleased to meet you, Andy. It's quiet out here.

ANDY: I like it quiet. We don't see many people out, these days. You're not from around here are you?

GENERAL: Just visiting.

ANDY: Really. Do you have family here? Who are they? I can help you find them. What's your name?

Andy digs her toes luxuriously into the grass beneath the bench. The general is in mind of a cat stretching, extending its claws. She yawns and stretches, arching her back to show off her bosom.

GENERAL: No family. I don't remember my name. Protective measure.

Andy barks a laugh. Her lips are red, her teeth a blinding white.

ANDY: So you're just here, sitting in the park, are you? Feeding pigeons?

GENERAL: They seemed pretty hungry. I wish I'd thought to bring more for them.

Andy shrugs, she leans up against, him, feeling his chest as she fingers the decorations of his dress uniform.

ANDY: You're a military man. Ooh, look at all those medals. You must have seen all sorts of action?

The General touches his fingers to one of the medals.

GENERAL: This one's for typing. That one's for attendance.

Andy stares, confused.

ANDY: Is that a joke?

The General watches her.

GENERAL: Do you still have a sense of humour after you turn?

ANDY: I never really thought about it. Maybe. I'm still the same person I was. Turning, you keep what you need, and lose what you don't. I'd turn you, if you wanted, you could be useful. Is that why you're here?

GENERAL: No.

ANDY: I don't think I could, even if you wanted it. There's something wrong with you. I can smell it in your blood.

GENERAL: Cancer.

ANDY: I'm sorry.

The General looks at her with mild surprise.

ANDY: I guess I'm sorry. I don't really care. It's just a thing people say to each other when they don't really care.

She looks up at that moment, mildly surprised. The figure of a man is walking down one of the bicycle paths. He is huge, hulking, dressed in nondescript dark overalls. He is wearing some sort of mask or helmet, obscuring his face. The figure in the distance pays no attention to them, simply continuing on the path, eating up distance with every stride, until it vanishes out of sight.

She saw him, she realizes. But she couldn't sense him. It was as if he wasn't there at all. She frowns. She tries to keep her voice casual, light and friendly, as if it's all just banter.

ANDY: What the hell was that? One of yours?

The General shrugs. The General notes that her eyes had gone red, her nails have lengthened into claws, and her canines are extended, all involuntary reflexes. He waits politely as they recede and she regains control of herself.

Disturbed, she stares at the General, appraising him.

ANDY: You're not dressed for combat.

GENERAL: Nope. Dress uniform, salad and all.

ANDY: Why are you here? To negotiate?

They'd discussed it in their councils, the times and places when the humans would try to negotiate, who they would send, what they would ask for and what offers or threats they might make. They had worked it all out, planning for a big beautiful new world.

They hadn't discussed some random, late middle-aged officer sitting casually on a park bench, feeding pigeons, waiting for them.

GENERAL: A week ago, the town went dark. We got reports from survivors and refugees. Standard practice, we sealed the perimeter.

Andy laughs, it sounds like music to the General.

ANDY: We know about that. It won't hold us. We can go wherever we want, whenever we want.

GENERAL: At night, at least. So anyway, what's the plan here?

ANDY: We're going to take what's ours. We've been hiding in the shadows for too long. We've found a leader, a visionary. Brother Vulk.

GENERAL: The rat-faced bald git? We know that type. Long timers, their minds usually deteriorate to crushed gravel, hiding in basements, eating vermin. So what's the deal? He ate someone with basic cable? Started watching television?

Andy's face stiffens.

ANDY: Don't be disrespectful! You don't know how anything works. You're already slaves, living in a world run by the one per cent. The thing you don't understand, is how utterly mediocre your one per cent is, how incompetent and narrow-minded and self-centered they are. They're wrecking your lives, and they're wrecking the world.

Andy blazes with genuine emotion, the true passion of the enlightened. The General narrows his eyes watching her. She lays a hand on his shoulder, not to attack, but to emphasize her point.

ANDY: You'll see. When we take over, your lives won't change. They'll actually get better. We'll look after you, because you matter to us. We'll heal this world of the scars your leaders have inflicted.

For a moment, the General can almost see it. What would they be, if they didn't have to be monsters? Walking free in the world, casting their glamour, worshiped by those they fed upon? Would they really be worse than what we have now? Maybe they would be better? Maybe they deserve it. The General knows it's mostly her glamour washing over him. But ... maybe?

He shakes his head. He's seen too much...

GENERAL: Farming humans, blood fountains, humane slaughter, all of that. Replacing corporate bloodsuckers with real ones. A future as factory farmed animals, like chickens or cattle.

ANDY: Yes, there'll be some changes. But you won't be cattle, you're being dramatic.

Andy tosses her head, dismissively, and the General is struck by how ridiculous he must sound to her.

ANDY: Can't you see? We'll make a better world... for everyone, not just a predatory, incompetent ruling class, stealing all the wealth for themselves. Do you really think the world is better off ruled by billionaires sucking the planet dry? At least we care.

The General shrugs.

GENERAL: That's out of my pay grade, honestly. What about the people in the town? Are they on board?

Andy looks away, refusing to meet his eyes. The glamour ebbs a little. She uncrosses and then crosses her legs. Her voice is slightly less confident.

ANDY: There are growing pains in making a better world. Sacrifices. Hardships.

GENERAL: Where are they?

Andy shrugs.

ANDY: Holed up in churches. Sanctuaries. Schools and hospitals. Every night they fight us off, every day, they try and break out. But it turns out it's easy to turn refuges into prisons. We could take them if we wanted them, but they're where we want them to be.

GENERAL: The survivors.

He grunts, and looks away from her. Her kind has an unnatural hypnotic quality, he can feel it pulling at his mind. But he is inured, he'd seen and experienced too much. Instead, he glances off into the distance. He noticed a plume of smoke, pale against the night sky, and points.

GENERAL: What's that?

Andy looks, following the direction of his finger. She leans forward, staring hard at the plume, extending her unnatural sentences.

ANDY: Saint Michael's Basilica.... it's on fire! There are hundreds of people packed in there!

The General stares at her.

GENERAL: The next phase?

She glances at him, horrified.

ANDY: What? No! That's not us... Why would we... There must have been an accident. I have family in there.

He can sense her body tensing. He looks away, surveying the skyline.

GENERAL: It's not the only one.

He points out other faint plumes, just beginning, still low and wispy, illuminated pale against the darkness.

Her eyes widen as she focuses.

ANDY: Wait, that's the Synagogue. And the Baptist Church! All those people!

Abruptly, her eyes go red, her fangs extend, fingers turned to claws. She snarls accusingly at him.

ANDY: Are you doing this? Because if you are...

GENERAL: No. It's not me. I'm just here.

He can feel her mind reaching for him. He lets her. He has nothing to hide. What is happening was nothing he can control. He accepts that. Andy's claws retract, the fangs recede.

She swallows, composing herself. He can tell she's worried.

ANDY: All right. If you'll excuse me, I need to go. But don't worry, I'll be back. I'll find you...

Then she stops, confused, as if she's forgotten what she meant to say. She looks down, puzzled. There is something sticking out of her chest, just below her breasts, protruding through her sun dress. She finally identifies it as a large piece of metal, rebar or something. How did it get there?

It is impossible for anything to sneak up on her. She knows this with utter certainty.

The General is watching her. She turns to speak to him, to ask something.

And then, at the last instant, she senses it. Or doesn't sense it. An emptiness behind her, a void, something formless and vacant, but somehow... hungry. Her last thought, is the realization that there is something evil in the world, far worse than anything she's ever imagined.

At that moment, her body explodes into pieces, and disintegrates. In an instant, she's no more than dust.

Johnson steps around from behind the park bench. He's tall, though it's impossible to quantify exactly how tall. Six feet? Six Four? Seven? He's dressed in nondescript working man's clothes, dark gray, heavy, almost like canvas, with protective coat, wearing a welder's hood. The black visor is impenetrable. He moves with supernatural grace.

The General watches him. Once at the beginning, when he started to understand, he used to be afraid. Then wary. Now, he just watches. He knows he might be next, but he's just stopped caring. Being around them does that to you.

Johnson, however, doesn't acknowledge him at all. The hood with its impenetrable black visor swivels back and forth. He seems to select a direction, and then he simply walks that way, moving with graceful, measured strides that impossibly eat up distance.

The General watches until he's out of sight again, and then sighs.

Time to go to work. He stands up, dusts himself off, and heads to the center of town.

By the time the sun rises, everyone and everything in town will be dead. There's nothing he can do about that. There's nothing anyone can do.

They're here now.

THE BEGINNING

Squad Thirteen, Worse than Death – Page 9

THE DESERT

Chapter One

An armoured limousine drives through the desert across an empty dirt road. A cloud of billowing dust rises up behind it. In the distance a series of guard towers loom. As they get closer we see that they're connected by three layers of cyclone fences and barbed wire. Ominous signs appear:

"Trespassers will be executed."

"Minefields Active."

Powerful stadium lights illuminate the landscape beyond.

Cut to the inside of the armoured car. There are two people. The driver is ranked as a General. He's smoking a cigar. He's in his late fifties, prematurely gray and wrinkled. His passenger is a Lieutenant, clean cut, crisp, by the book, female, and stern.

GENERAL: This is all just for show. They throw money at us; we have to spend it on something. Worst goddamned duty in the service as far as I'm concerned, sitting in those towers waiting to be killed. Pushing paper at Checkpoint Charley. The real protection is distance. We've got another sixty miles to go. Sixty miles of the most godforsaken, desolate territory on the face of the earth. No water, no plants, not even a lizard can live here. We made sure of that. We got a geosynchronous satellite up there permanently stationed right over us, watching. I can't tell you what that cost us. A bird flies over this place, we know it. We got traps and deadfalls, minefields everywhere. Set a man down in here, and he's dead within a day.

The Lieutenant looks doubtful.

GENERAL: Distance is what it is. This car is wired to explode if anything happens. Those sons of bitches will have to walk out. They're a lot faster than they look, don't be fooled. But even they, take 'em most of a day to get out this far, takes them even longer to get anywhere. By that time, we can organize a response.

LIEUTENANT: Sounds like a tough set up.

GENERAL: Not tough enough. We almost had a break out in 1999. They decided to go for a walk, the whole bunch of them. Cut right through the fences as if it wasn't there, the minefields, the towers, didn't matter more than swatting flies.

LIEUTENANT: Briefing report says that they're all just psychopathic criminals. But my dossier doesn't tell me anything, just names and bullshit. Like this: "Likes teddy bears." What does that even mean? There's no psychological profiles, no personality assessments, just random notations. I expected the dirty dozen, but this? There are no specialties identified, there's no history for any of them. I can't believe they're regular army.

GENERAL: They're not.

LIEUTENANT: Permission to speak freely, Sir?

GENERAL: There's just us here.

LIEUTENANT: This is fucked, Sir. What the hell am I supposed to be doing?

GENERAL: You lead them, Lieutenant. You take them out into the field, and you maybe try to point them, and then after, you try to get them to stop.

LIEUTENANT: Why me?

GENERAL: You're a woman. You fit a profile.

LIEUTENANT: So... what? They don't kill women?

GENERAL: They kill everyone and everything. Men, women, children, dogs, cattle. There ain't anything they don't kill. But sometimes, it looks like maybe they don't like to kill certain women. Or at least, they don't try as hard. Or maybe they can't. We're not sure.

LIEUTENANT: Who are these men?

GENERAL: They're not men.

LIEUTENANT: Then what? Martians? Aliens? Werewolves? Vampires? Genetic experiments?

GENERAL: No one really knows. They started showing up in the Eighties. Or at least, that's when we started noticing them. Then, the historians poked around, and whatever they are, that goes way back. But we're not sure. We don't know much about them. We know names, but that doesn't tell us anything. We know where each of them came from, sort of. We know what they've done. But what are they? You tell me after you meet them.

LIEUTENANT: What's the point of this?

GENERAL: You know the Iraq War, how Baghdad just fell apart? You heard of the Chinese Border incident? Although we hushed that one up pretty good, come to think of it. That mess in Africa? Scottsboro? That's them. It's what they do. When things are really bad, alien invasion, vampire infestation, zombie outbreak, we send them in. And then...

LIEUTENANT: And then...

GENERAL: And then, Lieutenant? We pray.

LIEUTENANT: That they succeed?

GENERAL: No, Lieutenant. We pray that sooner or later, they stop.

The Lieutenant looks out the window. There's no answer. The car proceeds in silence through the sterile and endless desert. They pass by a human skeleton half buried by the side of the road. The Lieutenant watches it as they go past.

* * *

The building looks like it was a gas station in the 1950's. The old fashioned gas pumps are still there, covered with dust. There is a drive through around the back. The General pulls up to the window. No one appears.

GENERAL: Checkpoint Charlie. The last stop before them.

There's an emphasis on the word 'them.' The Lieutenant doesn't respond. The General fishes out a clipboard and pen from the dash and makes a few notes. They wait. After a few minutes, the General honks the horn. Nothing. The General peers at the clipboard.

GENERAL: They're on a nine day rotation. In, then out. After that, counselling, suicide watch, medication, whatever it takes. They're only six days in, should be fine.

Nothing. Abruptly the General guns the engine, pulls out to the front of the station and parks. For a moment the motor idles, then he shuts it off.

LIEUTENANT: We're not supposed to exit the vehicle, Sir.

GENERAL: Whatever.

He puffs his cigar.

GENERAL: What are they going to do? Court martial us?

The General steps out of the vehicle, and the Lieutenant, impelled by some random feeling of solidarity, gets out with them. They walk over to the bay doors of the old garage. The windows are caked with decades of dust. The General wipes as best he can and stares in. Then he proceeds to the front door. The Lieutenant follows, but as he turns, she glimpses, over his shoulder, four hanging bodies. The General strides through the front door, there's a counter, and beyond it, desks, telephones, piles of paper, all the detritus of a normal office. The General pounds on the counter and bellows.

Eventually an MP comes out from the back. He's got dried blood on his uniform, across his left shoulder, and spattering down the front of his shirt. He's got a crude bandage wrapped inexpertly around his temple. He is dishevelled, shirt untucked, buttons missing, fly unzipped. His eyes are a little wild.

GENERAL: Paperwork.

MP: Ah, yes.

The MP takes the clipboard, and starts leafing through it.

GENERAL: There should be five men on station. Where are the others?

MP: They're around.

GENERAL: I saw them. What happened to you?

MP: Light fixture, Sir.

GENERAL (nodding): They can't take the weight. Maybe you were counting on getting electrocuted?

MP: Belts and suspenders, Sir. Make sure. Important to make sure. They wouldn't let us have guns. Not allowed anything sharp.

The General grunts. The MP stamps a page.

MP: Papers are in order, Sir.

GENERAL: Where were you when we came?

MP: Bathroom, Sir.

The General shook his head.

GENERAL: You're going to wreck the plumbing.

MP: The plumbing doesn't work, Sir. We use a bucket. Nothing works. It's all just here. You can feel it every day. You can feel them from here. Like a stain. Like you're drowning in a stain on the world.

GENERAL: You have three days left, Soldier, before relief.

MP: Yes, Sir.

GENERAL: Until you are relieved, you are not to kill yourself. Do you understand? That is an order.

MP: But General!

GENERAL: THAT'S AN ORDER! Not until you are relieved.

The MP looks like he's about to break down and cry, a tear trickles down his cheek. He trembles, but in the end he salutes.

* * *

The armoured vehicle pulls up on a ramshackle sprawling building. Shingles are peeled off the roof. The windows are broken. A door barely clings to its hinges.

GENERAL: Used to be a residential compound for the Prometheus Project. This is all that's left.

LIEUTENANT: Prometheus?

GENERAL: Classified. Biological warfare. The next generation of superbugs, back when the world was simple and we knew who the bad guys were. Communists, blacks, hippies, that sort. Something got out, everyone died. I hear it was pretty messy. We dropped a neutron bomb to try and sterilize the place. We think we got most of it. At least, it hasn't spread much since then.

LIEUTENANT: So this is a bio-warfare and a radiation hazard zone? And you station men here?

GENERAL: I told you before, they're not men.... We're here.

The vehicle stops in front of the building. A wind stirs through, but there's no motion. The windows are black. There's no sign of life. The General and the Lieutenant step out of the car. The Lieutenant looks around.

LIEUTENANT: No sign of life. Maybe they're all dead, considering the place.

GENERAL: That's one theory to explain them.

He hesitates.

GENERAL: No sense wasting time, let's go in.

The Lieutenant grabs her briefcase. The two proceed into the building. There is a large central hall, possibly a cafeteria. Tables and chairs are shattered or pushed to the side, light fixtures dangle from the ceiling. There are strange red splatters on the floor and walls. The place is empty. The two stand in the centre.

LIEUTENANT: Where are they? They must have heard us coming? Were they informed?

GENERAL: Patience.

From a darkened corridor, there's a series of heavy footsteps approaching closer and closer.

GENERAL: It's them.

The footsteps slow and heavy come louder and louder, but they can't see into the darkness. The Lieutenant draws closer to the General. Movement catches her eye; she looks behind them and screams. A hulking shape looms over them, a pale mannequin's face atop military fatigues. Suddenly they're surrounded by hulking, masked figures all around, bearing primitive weapons. Axes, machetes, knives and clubs. All of them unnaturally still and silent.

GENERAL: Lieutenant, let me introduce you to your command: Michaels, Jackson, Sawyer, Vernon, Hatcher, Beane, Monk, Otis, Ed, and Hatfield. There are more, these are just the ones feeling social today. Can't kill them; so we enlisted them.

The Lieutenant turns around and around, staring at the hulking passive figures, their attention focused on her. As she moves their heads track her.

LIEUTENANT: They're all wearing masks.

GENERAL: Because they're all so damned ugly. Actually, some of them, Michaels, Vernon, they look human. They could pass. But they all like masks, it's some sort of pathology. They cover their faces, even when there's no one to look. It's one of the little mysteries.

The figures begin to gather, closing in on her.

LIEUTENANT: Do they speak?

GENERAL: Sometimes one of them will say a word, so they can speak. But they don't. The best you can hope for mostly is that they'll listen sometimes.

One of them, Vernon, reaches out a hand to touch the Lieutenant's hair. Trying not to show fear she moves away and bumps into Hatcher. She retreats.

LIEUTENANT: Get back! General, tell them to step back!

The figures continue to close in on her.

GENERAL: I said "sometimes" they listen. Sometimes. You're on your own, Lieutenant. Consider this your test.

The Lieutenant continues to back away, turning from one to the other as they close in on her. Then she stops and visibly gathers herself.

LIEUTENANT (Announcing, clear commanding voice): I have something in my briefcase.

They stop, expectant. Not so much dissuaded as curious. A couple of them tilt their heads. Finally, one shrugs and they advance. The Lieutenant holds up her briefcase and snaps the lock, opening it towards her. Again, they hesitate for a second. She spins the briefcase around, so it faces them.

It contains a teddy bear.

LIEUTENANT: I brought this all this way. Who wants it?

She lowers the briefcase, which is otherwise empty, and holds the bear out. A broad heavy shape wearing a leather mask made of human skin, Sawyer, shambles forward. It reaches out.

LIEUTENANT: You want this?

She pulls the bear away from Sawyer. She stares directly at him. Sawyer is still. The others watch. The two stare at each other. Finally, Sawyer nods. The Lieutenant holds the teddy bear out to him. Sawyer takes it, and clutching it to him protectively, shambles off.

Jackson, the largest of them, a hulking brute in some kind of battered sports mask, advances towards her. But suddenly, Michaels the tallest, wearing a corpse mask, is in his path. Jackson pauses and tilts his head. Michaels tilts his head as if in answer. For a second, the moment hangs. And then, as if there was nothing, Jackson and Michaels walk off smoothly in different directions. In an instant, the rest of them have vanished. Not disappeared, but just... it's as if they'd all just casually walked away while she wasn't paying attention. But she had been watching.

GENERAL: Congratulations.

LIEUTENANT: I passed a test?

GENERAL: They let you live. Come on, let's get out of here. The place gives me the creeps.

They walk out to the car. The Lieutenant gets in, slams the door shut, she's shaking visibly.

LIEUTENANT: My god, what are they!

GENERAL: I've got the papers for your first mission here. Read it, we've got the Evac Chopper coming. I'll be driving back.

LIEUTENANT: What are they?

GENERAL: There's some sort of outbreak over on the pacific coast. We've got a perimeter, but nothing we've sent in comes out. You're going to have to take them in.

LIEUTENANT: I SAID WHAT THE HELL ARE THEY???

GENERAL: I DON'T KNOW! NO ONE DOES!

LIEUTENANT: I thought they were going to kill me.

GENERAL: It was possible.

LIEUTENANT: And if they had?

GENERAL: Then I'd have brought someone else and hoped for the best.

LIEUTENANT: I'm not the first am I?

GENERAL: You've got a mission coming up fast. You need to get your head around that.

LIEUTENANT: How many? How many before me?

There was a long pause.

GENERAL: Six.

LIEUTENANT: Six?

The General doesn't reply. The Lieutenant shoves him.

LIEUTENANT: You brought six others? I'm the seventh?

GENERAL: Yes. One at a time.

LIEUTENANT: And?

GENERAL (shrugs): They killed them. Each of them. It wasn't pretty. They like to take their time.

LIEUTENANT: And me...

GENERAL: You were the one. The one we were looking for.

LIEUTENANT: Why?

GENERAL: Because they let you live. You were the one. We don't know why. We don't know how they think. We don't know if they do think. We don't know why they do what they do. We don't know why they kill. We don't know why they let some live. We don't know how to kill them. We don't know how to stop them. If we did, we'd stop them. If we could, we'd kill them. But we can't. We can't even contain them for long. The best we can do is find someone they won't kill on sight and sort of direct them... point them at something that needs killing and then try and get out of the way.

LIEUTENANT: My God.

GENERAL: God has nothing to do with it. Here's how it is, they let you live, so they are yours now, and you are theirs. That's all. Now you've got your mission, get prepared.

LIEUTENANT: What about you? They let you live.

GENERAL: I was the last person they let live, until you came along.

LIEUTENANT: So why me?

The General stares at her. Finally, he looks out the window.

GENERAL: T-Cell Lymphoma. Inoperable. No treatment. I have maybe another month or two.

LIEUTENANT: So... I'm your replacement?

The General nods.

GENERAL: We had to find someone they wouldn't kill. I'm sorry, it's a nightmare. But they're our nightmares, and there's others out there, bad things. We need--

The bulletproof glass on the driver's side shatters, and Michaels and Vernon pull the General, screaming, out through the broken window. He kicks wildly, screaming in terror. The Lieutenant shouts, grabbing his feet. Her face is already flecked with his blood. They drag the General off.

The Lieutenant jumps out of the armoured car, shouting. She pulls her sidearm and empties it into Michaels and Vernon, but they don't seem to notice. She follows a half-dozen steps. As the General vanishes into the darkness of the building, her nerve breaks and she runs back to the car, slamming the door, futilely locking it. Praying to herself.

Inside the building, the General's screams go on and on and on....

On the seat beside her, the mission papers are scattered around.

THE END

BRIEFING

TOP SECRET
TOP SECRET REPORT
LEVEL FIVE SECURITY
SECURITY SEAL SECURITY SEAL SECURITY SEAL SECURITY SEAL

TOP SECRET- SECURITY LEVEL FIVE REQUIRED.

DATE: OCTOBER 25, ████

FROM: DR. ████████████
      OFFICE OF ████████████
      DEPT. OF ████████████████

TO: SEC. ████████████
    GEN. ████████████
    SEN. ████████████
    CC: DR. ████████████
    CC: DR. ████████████

SUBJECT: REPORT ON SSK SQUAD ALPHA- ONE

PART FIVE-A: PROFILE SUMMARY

The Squad consists of a group of paranormal humans or humanoids. Physically, squad members appear to be human males of various configurations, and most are morphologically unremarkable. Some of the squad members diverge considerably, some resembling a cadaver in some stage of decomposition, and some who manifests various bleeding stigmata.

Squad members are unified by an overall profile - all of them wear masks of various types and appear to be psychologically or paranormally affiliated with their masks. The masks appear to serve some form of totemic function.

Despite being apparently human, all squad members feature abnormal strength and endurance and a high degree of resilience to harm - most have been shot multiple times with a variety of ammunition, stabbed, drowned, set on fire, crushed or experienced injury or attack that normal humans would find fatal. In fact, most of them have experienced 'lethal' events - apparently been killed or placed in a deathlike state, sometimes for years at a time, before reanimating or reactivating. A number of unsuccessful attempts have been made to terminate the squad by the military command. This has resulted in little more than reciprocal fatalities up the chain of command. Current policy is to deploy the squad or squad members on appropriate missions.
The squad members are astonishingly stealthy, perhaps paranormally so, and are able to move with such silence that they cannot be detected by sound equipment. They have repeatedly been shown to be able to access and enter places apparently impossible to reach, or approach alert watchers undetected. They are even able to avoid surveillance cameras, despite no indication of awareness of these cameras. This skill is compounded by the paradox that the squad members appear to make no effort to be stealthy.

Behaviourally and psychologically, the Squad members display a consistent profile. They are almost wholly uncommunicative. Only a few of the squad members display any verbal traits at all, and only one seems capable of anything resembling a conversation. Each member of the squad is a relentless killer. Their principal behaviour is stalking and killing, while they often select and pursue targets, they also kill opportunistically. When not engaged in stalking prey, they are relatively quiescent.

Very little is known about the members of the Squad. In some instances, there is biographical information and even official documentation of their early life. However, current studies provide contradictory data. The squad members appear to be both alive and dead, X-rays and ultrasounds report inconsistent results. Even DNA sampling has produced bizarre results. Currently, there is a major effort under way to document and study the squad members, but this has produced little more than theories. It is debateable whether the squad members even have recognizably human cognitive functions.

SIGNED: DR. ▮▮▮▮▮▮▮▮▮▮
        OFFICE OF ▮▮▮▮▮▮▮
        DEPT. OF ▮▮▮▮▮▮▮▮▮▮

CENTIPEDES

Chapter Two

LIEUTENANT (voice over): For no other reason than that they did not kill me on sight; I have been given command of a squad of unstoppable killing machines, deathless masked murderers.

My security clearance tripled overnight. You want to know about the President's prostate exam? What they really had down in Area 51? I could get you that. But for these bastards, I barely rank. The files on the squad have so many black marks all over the pages, it was like reading confetti.

The parts that I could read, the edited mission profiles, were like the nightmares of a psychotic witch doctor. Speculations about zombies, demon gods, avatars of death, alien. Sometimes wild ravings. I checked the General's medical history. He was on so many anti-psychotic medications his piss glowed in the dark. He would ask for electroshock. He fought to get a lobotomy, and got one.

Afterwards, he wrote 'It didn't help.'

Mortality rate is 70% among the support crew, two thirds of that is suicide.

Only one thing is clear: whatever these things are, we have no idea. We don't know what they are, or why they are, or how they do it. We just know what they do. We are like monkeys with atom bombs. All we know is that we have them, and we can point them at things that might or might not be worse.

I have a mission. The parameters are fucked. Just a code name and a set of GPS coordinates. No objectives, no rules of engagement, no support. But I know deep down, that none of that is necessary. Their only rule, their only objective is to kill. No survivors. That was the one constant from every mission.

* * *

The helicopter is insanely loud. Its metallic skeleton, a dragonfly carrying a cargo container. The Lieutenant sits beside the pilot.

LIEUTENANT: Is this the target zone?

PILOT: We've just passed the quarantine perimeter.

LIEUTENANT: Any idea what we are facing? What's the perimeter encountered?

PILOT: No idea. Quarantine perimeter is the zone outside contact. You'd want to talk to field Perimeter.

LIEUTENANT: What do they say?

PILOT: Nothing, they're presumed dead.

LIEUTENANT: Where do we land?

PILOT: We don't land. We just drop the container and they do the rest.

LIEUTENANT: We're not high enough for the container parachute.

PILOT: There's no parachute. They don't like it when we go high.

LIEUTENANT: What?

PILOT: Bombs away.

LIEUTENANT: Wait!

The Pilot pulls a switch, the helicopter jerks as the cargo container lets go, begins tumbling through the air.

LIEUTENANT: Jesus Christ! That's a thousand feet.

PILOT: Yeah, I feel better already. Hey, are you into woodworking?

LIEUTENANT: Fuck! What? Woodworking?

PILOT: Yeah, I do it to relax. Unwind from those things. I just bought this amazing table saw; thirty-two inch blade; got it from a sawmill. Knocked half the teeth out, so it does really rough cuts. Just mangles the wood.

LIEUTENANT: What are you talking about?

PILOT: More and more, I've been thinking how restful it would be to just turn it on and lay my forehead against it. You don't think that's screwy, do you?

LIEUTENANT: What?

Loud noise, metal grinding, a flash of light, a chemical stench like burning hair.

PILOT: We're hit. We're going to--

* * *

The Pilot's head impaled on a metal rod. That's the first thing the Lieutenant sees when she opens her eyes. Apart from the blood and the steel jutting through torn flesh, he looks very peaceful. The second thing she notices is that most of his body is missing. The third is the acid smell of burning rubber and plastic.

She thrashes, afraid to look down and see whether her own body is intact. Restraints bite into her shoulders. She is still wearing her safety belts, still strapped into the crash seat. She releases the buckles, feeling the harness loosen.

She crawls away, staggers to her feet. Everything is intact. Miraculously, she has survived. Helicopter debris surrounds her.

In shock, she looks around, seeing a typical, Norman Rockwell, middle-American town. The streets are empty, except for a man and woman who appear to be impaled on a double headed parking meter.

She stumbles toward them, staring. They are back to back, leaning against each other. Their faces are contorted in rictus of agony and terror. The man's lower body is distended oddly; she thinks she can see the shape of the edge of the parking meter in his body. Their feet do not touch the ground, they dangle in the wind.

LIEUTENANT: What the fuck?

Her gaze drifts to their feet. Lower. There are pools of blood and guts beneath them, the remnants of their ruptured bodies. The blood still drips down.

Still drips.

Dripping.

This happened recently, the Lieutenant thinks. Perhaps minutes before the crash. Beginning nausea is swept away by a surge of terror. The Lieutenant, heart pounding, draws her sidearm and whirls around, circling twice, searching the landscape.

That's when she sees the thing. At first she'd taken it as part of the helicopter debris. But now that she looks.... this thing was part of no machine. The alien quality of it baffles her at first. Shining chitin, segments, claws. Some kind of.... insect. Was this thing the problem? The Mission?

It's dead now.

Mission accomplished?

A skitter behind her.

LIEUTENANT (whispers): Ahh… mission not accomplished.

More of them. Not insects. Their wobbling segmented bodies move towards her.

The Lieutenant is proud of how calm she is in that moment, how analytical she is, as she mentally catalogues a description. Can they see her she wonders? Or perhaps, like certain predators, they only see movement? In which case, being still would be best. Or maybe they see in other terms, see other spectrums? Maybe they see with sonar, or track with scent?

Whatever it is, the two things seem to register her presence. She watches as they stiffen and orient on her. Hundred yard range? Does their perception work beyond that?

They move decisively towards her. The Lieutenant wonders how fast they are at the same time that she turns to run.

* * *

The Lieutenant sprints like the wind, it's the fastest she's ever moved in her life, graceful as a gazelle, sure footed as a mountain goat. The ground is a blur beneath her feet. Some part of her feels elevated, flying on an instantaneous runner's high, every bit of adrenalin surging through her body. She would feel great, if she wasn't shitting her pants in terror.

In that instant as she turns to run, as she breaks into her sprint, she sees them move in her peripheral vision. She knows instantly that on a straight away, they will run her down. So she heads around a corner, leaps a wrecked car, uses that to springboard onto a hanging sign and up on the roof. As she hears them skittering up the side of the building, she's already on to the next building, leaps to a thankfully full dumpster, through an open door, and out the other side.

All it had done was attract more of them. Twistings and turnings, the best run of her life, and every glance from peripheral vision showed another scuttling segmented monstrosity joining the chase. She runs along a brick wall, turns a corner, and leaps into a store window, hoping for a back door, a basement, a heavy door that she could slam, a safe she could lock herself into.

Smack into something solid and unyielding. She almost bounces backward, but something catches her shoulder, steadying her.

LIEUTENANT: Holy shit!

It's one of them. One of the Squad. Her mind seizes up in paralysis. Then the training kicks in.

Sawyer, she remembers from the briefing. This is Sawyer. The heavy set one, sometimes childlike, sometimes aggressively sexual, traces of a potbelly, uniform rotting. His mask is made of human skin, someone's face, carefully tanned and lovingly inverted, and his weapon is a chain saw.

Squad Thirteen, Worse than Death – Page 33

Sawyer stares at her, fascinated. He cocks his head, as if not quite recognizing her.

LIEUTENANT: It's me. Remember the teddy bear? I gave you the teddy bear.

Sawyer cocks his head again the other way.

She feels warmth trickling down her legs, and knows she's peed herself. It doesn't matter. Behind her, she hears the skittering, the things are out there. Sawyer looks up. Then he looks at her. He shakes his head as if to clear it, as if the mystery of her can wait until later.

Almost gently, he moves her out of the way, stepping past her. The things waver uncertainly. She does not turn, merely listens to Sawyer's footsteps as he steps over the store window, glass crunching under his boots. She hears the rev of a chain saw.

She does not look. She doesn't want to see.

There's a lot of noise, she thinks that some of it is the sound of things screaming in high pitched chitin voices.

Then the chain saw shuts off. Patient footsteps walking away.

The Lieutenant is staring. In the mirror of what she now recognizes as a jewelry store, the walls smeared with blood, she sees herself, dressed in flight suit. The shattered remains of her crash helmet clings to her head. Her face is obscured by a mirrored visor.

* * *

CONTROL: Please describe the phenomena.

LIEUTENANT: I saw two people, I think it was a married couple, impaled on a parking meter.

CONTROL: That sounds like Hatfield. Not relevant.

LIEUTENANT: Wait? What? Hatfield?

CONTROL: Have you had direct contact with the phenomena?

LIEUTENANT: The enemy? You mean the things that are trying to kill us?

CONTROL (calm and insistent): Designated term is phenomena.

LIEUTENANT: Okay, the phenomena seem to be giant centipedes. Approximately three to five meters in length, each segment is about a foot to foot and a half, with the upper segments larger. Each segment has one set of claws. It seems to anchor itself and walk about with the first four or five segments, the pincers anchor into the ground. After that it rears up, and the pincers on the upper segments get huge. No apparent head, except that each segment might have two eyes.

CONTROL: We haven't seen that before. Would you say the phenomena is extraterrestrial, extra-dimensional or supernatural?

LIEUTENANT: What the fuck?

CONTROL: Please answer the question.

LIEUTENANT: How should I know?

CONTROL: Any sign of clothing, badges, symbols, tool use, weapons, transport vehicles, any apparent technology at all?

LIEUTENANT: No. No they just run around on their own. Naked. Like M. Night Shyamalan aliens in Signs. Not even pants.

Something bubbles up within the Lieutenant. It could be hysterical laughter. She locks down on it physically.

CONTROL: Probably not extraterrestrial then. Are there any unusual properties? Do they float? Glow? Are they decaying unusually fast?

LIEUTENANT: No, I don't think so. I saw a dismembered specimen. The body parts just seem to sit there.

CONTROL: Sounds like a trans-dimensional incursion. Seems manageable. Any sign of a wormhole?

LIEUTENANT: What?

CONTROL: Don't worry, if you come across it, you'll know what it is. Sit tight, we'll do a sweep when they finish.

LIEUTENANT: In the meantime, what should I do? Should I look for survivors?

CONTROL: There won't be any survivors.

* * *

LIEUTENANT (voice over): This is hell come to earth. I have no idea why I'm here. I have no idea why any of this was happening.

Twenty-three hours ago there was a distress call from the local police, calling for the Army, the National Guard, the Air Force, the Boy Scouts, anyone. That wasn't everything.

Psychics started vomiting blood. People were randomly going catatonic. Animals were tearing themselves apart. In San Francisco, seismometers went wild. NASA's satellites went off their orbits, as if gravity had changed. The message was clear. Something had come into the world. We just didn't know what. By the time we figured out where, the whole town had gone dark.

They cordoned off the town and waited for the refugees. There were none. Local chain of command sent regular troops in. Then they spent a couple of hours listening to them screaming on the radio. Some of them are still screaming.

Then they sent us. They could have dropped a nuke. But they said they wanted to make sure.

* * *

The Lieutenant is hunkered down behind the remains of a wall. With her are two children. She's decided that her mission is to keep them alive. She needs a mission, because if she doesn't have one, and if it's not keeping these kids alive, then she's just here. Seeing the things she's seen, hearing what she's heard, and it's just mindless chaos.

So keep the kids alive, and maybe there's a point to existing.

She lights a match. She's been doing it regularly. The little stick of wood flares brightly like magnesium.

When she reported it, Control told her that the proportion of oxygen in the air was high. The flame is greenish, which she was told is aerosolized copper, which makes no sense. Sometimes its brighter, sometimes its greener. Wherever the things are from, the rules are slightly different there, and they're spilling over into here.

Control keeps telling her to lose the children. She stops listening to orders after a while, though she still reports in.

The boy is thirteen, he's almost catatonic, unresponsive. His eyes are wider than anyone else's she's ever seen in her life. Circles of white, with irises narrowed to pinpricks. In the scant hour she's been with him, she hasn't seen him blink once. But he answers when he's asked a question, and he does what he's told, so she thinks he's not too far gone.

Or maybe he is.

She thinks there's a scream in him. Waiting. She thinks that if it gets out, then he'll just scream for the rest of his life. That's all he'll ever do. That's going to be all that's left of him, just a scream, going on and on.

The girl is better. She's fourteen. She's carrying the Lieutenants sidearm. It seems to make her feel better. Safer. Whatever.

The Lieutenant has an assault rifle. It's not hers. She found it near the ruins of a Marine. She wiped the Marine's bits off it, and it seemed serviceable. There was a finger jammed up in the trigger guard, but she'd managed to work it out. It's useless, she knows, the things eat bullets like they were candy kisses. But like the girl, it makes her feel better.

She wishes she had something sharp, something to pry between the chitinous plates of a centipede. She imagines the sound it would make as she worked the blade in and twisted it. She smiles. She can hear it screaming in her head.

Abruptly, she realizes it's not her imagination. Carefully, motioning the children to silence, she creeps to the edge of the ruined wall.

A centipede is screaming. Alien as it is, she can feel its panic. Raw terror exudes from it, it feels like its fear seeps into her pores, it's so pervasive. It's running, out in the open, its multiple limbs churning.

Michaels is behind it, walking calmly, approaching steadily, his mannequin mask devoid of all expression. His dark overalls are drenched with green gore. It's almost luminous.

It turns to look back, at Michaels, and its mouth parts clatter wildly, she can tell it's a squeal. It turns putting on a new burst of speed as it tries to get away. But its limbs tangle over each other and it stumbles. Michaels keeps coming closer. It scrabbles around a corner, Michaels following.

After a moment, there's a wild chitinous screeching. The sound of air being forced through a hundred spiracles, a chain of hearts bursting like a row of firecrackers, segmented limbs torn loose, plates clattering, alien ganglion lighting up with distilled fear.

She turns to the children.

LIEUTENANT: Time to go.

But she has no idea where. Just away. Away from the monsters, she supposes.

GIRL: Your face.

For a second, the Lieutenant has no idea what she's talking about. But then she flips the reflective visor of her helmet up. It keeps slipping down. She smiles at the children. But they're not reassured.

* * *

As they crawl through the remains of the town, there are bodies everywhere. She's never seen so many bodies in her life. There is nothing natural or peaceful to any of them, they are torn, mutilated, the corpses are posed. A row of heads adorn a picket fence.

Once crossing the street, they pass the body of a little old lady that had been carefully dissected, first clothes cut away, then skin, muscles and bones exquisitely sectioned, intestines and organs laid out. They try not to look, but they can't help it. As they pass, the body turns its head, the jaw works, but there are no lips or tongue. Whatever it wants to say, the Lieutenant can't understand. It doesn't matter anyway.

They startle a small flock of birds which take wing, struggling into the air, then falling to the ground, flopping about. The air is wrong, they can't breathe properly.

An automobile catches fire and burns spontaneously, the flame an intense green. They are coming closer, she thinks. She should turn around, lead them in the opposite direction.

Or maybe it is just getting stronger.

* * *

GENERAL: We had a mission in Bakersfield. No big deal. Nest of Vampires. They went in and cleaned it out, like they always do. They killed everyone, of course. There was a group of survivors holed up in the church, it had gotten that bad. Sawyer took the door down with his chain saw. I remember, he stood there a moment. Then he walked in.

The saw started up again... And there was just screaming and screaming.

The General leans up against a wall casually. He's looking at her, but once in a while, he glances around warily. He seems relaxed, his voice is calm, conversational.

GENERAL: Nothing I could do. Nothing anyone could do. That's just how they are.

The Lieutenant knows the General is dead. She's proud of her sanity, in the middle of this insane slaughterhouse, as the sky above the centre of town seems to turn a different colour, amidst the bodies and the monsters and the screaming, she's sane. The General is dead. He's not quite a hallucination; he's more than a memory. The children pay no attention, so she tries not to.

GENERAL: They killed the vampires of course. They killed everyone. That was what they did. After a while, as it was going on, it was as if some of the vampires were trying to save people. It was strange. It didn't matter, they all died.

The Lieutenant creeps up to a car. There is a large building in front of a park. City Hall. She is surprised, she had expected a church, or perhaps some exotic physics lab or power station. It's hard to imagine an assault from another universe beginning next to a stand filled with tourist brochures.

There is no cover. Green light shines from the windows. Centipedes are scuttling in and out of the building. They seem uncertain and full of nervousness.

GENERAL: I was there of course. I made a mistake. This Nosferatu-looking bastard caught me. Corpse skin, rodent incisors, you know that look that they get when they've been around too long, they forget what being human is, it slips away from them. Nosferatu, and he grabbed me with those spidery claw fingers. I thought I was dead. But all he did was say "What have you done? Do you know what you've done? Do you know what you've done?" Over and over, until Vernon killed him. They kill everyone. No one gets away. Nothing stops them. Nothing matters.

Frustrated, the Lieutenant turns, looking back at the memory.

LIEUTENANT: What's the point? What's the point of this? Why are you here? Why am I here?

The General looks surprised for a moment. Their eyes meet. The children, startled, follow her gaze, but they see nothing.

GENERAL: You're here to witness. That's your job. You want to save someone, but that's not your job. You won't save anyone.

The Lieutenant wants to swear at the General, but then she catches the girl looking at her, watching the one-sided conversation. She freezes.

She realizes the boy is missing.

* * *

The boy steps around the corner. He stops, just at the edge. The Lieutenant watches carefully. The boy went up on his tip toes, and then down flat, his knees bend and straighten. His face has no expression, his eyes wide and staring. He waggles his hips, his arms swinging back and forth. For a moment, he seems to be dancing.

Then his head tilts, his mouth falls open, and blood trickles out. He isn't breathing. He isn't seeing. Vernon, with his doll's mask, steps out, and lets the boy's body slide off the crowbar he'd used to puppet the corpse.

The Lieutenant swears. The girl cowers behind her, but when the Lieutenant reached back to hold her wrist, the girl slips back a little. Vernon, bored, is already moving on. With effort, she lifts the visor of her helmet so the girl can see she's all right.

But she's not. This is hell, and they are in it.

* * *

They are in the City Hall, it's a modest municipal building. The girl clings to her wrist. The interior is a wreck, gutted. The remains of walls and floors poking from the building's shell. There isn't anything there though.

The Lieutenant had expected something, a wormhole, a glowing portal, a gateway into an other universe, but there was... nothing. There isn't even a void or some gaping black hole. It is just a kind of non-descript nothingness, an absence that seemed unremarkable. She can't see into it, but it isn't opaque, or diffuse, it isn't light or dark. It just isn't, or it just is, but in an unintrusive way. A casual observer might glance at it; let their eyes linger for a second, and then turn to focus on anything that might be more interesting to look at, because anything was more interesting.

More interesting, like the centipede parts everywhere she looks. They mingle with rotting human corpses. There was an archeological layering in places, ruined and torn human flesh, bodies so thoroughly dismembered they'd lost all significance. And atop them, segmented limbs, chitinous plates, lumps and strips of green gunk, maggot-like worms, a few still squirming, many curled up and dead, or bleeding green.

Whatever was on the other side, it finds this world sour and hateful, unpalatable and repulsive. It loathes this awful place so cold and dour. But yet it is still unbearably hungry. She can feel the hunger, fathomless, unbearable, tortuous, radiating out from the other side. As awful as her world is, it will have to do. The hunger demands.

They are all there, gathering, Vernon and Michaels, Jackson, Sawyer, Bub, the Smiler, the rest of the men with the masks. Some simply standing, others arriving at their casual unhurried pace.

The girl is gone. What happened to her? The Lieutenant knew she'd been holding onto her wrist, the grip so tight the Lieutenant's flesh had whitened. Had she? Or had she fled? She had been there. But now she wasn't. Had there been a scream?

The Lieutenant is confused. Time isn't right. She slides the visor down on her helmet, presenting a red speckled, cracked, reflecting mirror to the world. Somehow it makes her feel right.

A segmented limb advances from the centre of the room, she can't quite see from where. It is narrow and barbed, twisting back on itself in a mantis like claw. It continues to extend, segment after segment after segment, elbows bending this way and that, dozens of twisting segments long, reaching for the men in the masks.

A hooked claw strikes Jackson shaking his massive form. More claws snake and twitch out to the others. Another twisting segmented limb seems to emerge out of the indistinct, empty center, jerking unevenly towards Michaels, who catches it.

Jackson looks down at the claw embedded in his chest, curious. Cilia sprouting like tendrils from each joint of the segmented arm beat against his body, wrapped against their forms, sensing, tasting, perhaps seeing in some primitive way.

Jackson snaps the claw off and flings it aside, dismissively. The segmented limbs shiver and writhe in confusion, some of them withdrawing.

Michaels hold his limb, his fist wrapping around a chitinous segment. It jerks in his hand, as if trying to free itself, at first tentatively, and then frantically.

The other segmented limbs boil suddenly in flexing convulsive motion. The Lieutenant has the sudden sense that it is trying to get away, as if it is suddenly afraid. As if it has touched something awful.

But it is too late. Michaels holds it in his grip, is walking forward, following it as it shrinks. So is Sawyer, Vernon, all of them walking towards the absence?

Then it is gone. The building is just a gutted ruin, bland in its wreckage. The light is different, normal; even the air is different, the otherworldliness dissipating like mist. The Men in the Masks, or whatever it was that they were, were gone too. Gone to wherever the other side was.

On her earpiece, Control is saying something. It doesn't matter. She walks away.

It's over.

* * *

A couple of days later, the pre-positioned satellite registered activity at the Compound. Seismic sensors register footsteps. The passive devices tick over.

The Men in the Masks are back from wherever they had been. No one knew where that was or how they had returned. They were just there.

* * *

The Lieutenant sits patiently through debriefing several times. Each round, she finds she has less and less to say. Her responses become monosyllabic. Eventually, she decides she is bored and stops speaking.

Sometime after that, she just walks away. She goes home. No one stops her.

Late that night, she can't sleep. She wakes up, wandering aimlessly around her apartment until the battered flight helmet catches her attention. She picks it up, staring at it, noticing the bloodstains, the flecks of green ichor, the dust and scrapes, the crack along the mirrored visor.

She realizes she is standing naked in front of a mirror, holding the helmet. How had she gotten there? She stares at her face, as if she doesn't recognize it. She looks down at the helmet, and stares at her reflection in the mirrored visor. It looks better there, it looks like it belongs.

She lifts the helmet, and lowers it onto her head, the visor falling into place, reflecting into the mirror, reflecting back, emptiness falling.

It is good.

THE END

Squad Thirteen, Worse than Death – Page 45

WINDY VALLEY GO-GO

Chapter Three

EIGHT HOURS BEFORE ZERO

The Lieutenant uses all her strength to smash the sharp flat end of the pry bar into the side of Gordon's head. There's a flickering sensation of resistance, and then it punches through the skull, driving through, the bones making a crumbling crunching sound, followed almost instantly by contact, resistance, and then the bar protrudes out through the other side. It's almost comical.

Gordon's eyes unfocus momentarily, his grip on her throat loosens, and he rears back so that she loses her grip on the metal. Expressions flicker across Gordon's bestial features. Confusion. Astonishment. Curiosity. He's almost distracted from her. His head tilts as if from the unaccustomed weight.

Gordon removes a hand from her throat, his grip eases, and she can draw a ragged breath. He reaches back, fingers tracing the end of the pry bar through his skull, fingertips following the cold metal all the way to his scalp.

GORDON: Nice try free-range, but it don't change nothing. I was trying to be nice, make it easy. Going to eat your face now.

Gordon grins, jaws distending, lips peeling back to expose a mouth of sharp teeth. He leans in, wrapping both hands around her throat, his weight pressing down. His tongue flickers in the jagged cavity of his mouth, lashing against his teeth.

Desperately the Lieutenant flails out with one hand, the other pulling at the grip on her throat. She wraps fingers on the sharp end of the bar, feeling blood and viscous lumps under her fingers. She wraps her fingers around it anyway and pulls hard on it.

Gordon shudders, his grip loses strength again for a moment, allowing a harsh breath. The bar slides forward, and she pulls it towards her, twisting Gordon's head to the side just before his teeth can close on her face. His tongue lashes her teeth.

GORDON: Stop.

His voice is plaintive, as if she's cheating somehow.

With sheer force he pulls back, the bar sliding wetly through his head, lifting and preparing for another lunge. Again, his jaws stretch and he descends, and again, with more confidence, she pulls the bar twisting his head to the side. Gordon grunts in frustration.

GORDON: Stop this now!

He sounds irritated, but a little vague, as if she's distracting him. His hands on her throat loosen slightly. The movement of the bar back and forth through his skull is damaging the creature. His body shudders, the grip flickers. She's able to push one hand away from her throat. His eyes are having trouble focusing, slowly zeroing in on her and then drifting in different directions.

She tries to twist the bar moving it up and down, side to side. There's very little give, perhaps a quarter of an inch. But Gordon's body continues to spasm and weaken. The teeth retract, his face becomes almost human. He looks at her with brief lucidity. He seems uncertain.

GORDON: Do I know you? There's something I need to do, but...

The Lieutenant twists the bar pulling it hard towards her. Gordon's head is yanked to the side, looking up towards the corner of the ceiling.

GORDON: Look a spider web! I've got to clean...

His grip is broken completely, she keeps twisting and pushing. Slowly, she works against the creature, bending him backwards until Gordon is down and on his back. The Lieutenant puts both hands on the outer edges of the bar working it back and forth, gasping with the effort, each movement fiercer, until she feels the bony plates of the skull begin to crack, fracturing apart.

Gordon does nothing but twitch and shudder, the smell of excrement fills the air and a pool of urine thick with a pungent ammonia scent puddles beneath him. And still the Lieutenant works the bar until Gordon's head is a shapeless ruin.

When she finally pulls the bar, it comes out with no resistance. It's red and lumpy and dripping. She tries not to register that as she wraps her hand tight around it and pulls it through to get rid of most of the gore.

Somewhere, she notes, someone is crying. Great racking sobs of terror and exhaustion. It takes her a moment to realize that it's her.

As she stands and staggers back, she sees his chest rise and fall with a deep breath. Astonished, she watches him do it again, and again. Impossibly, Gordon is still breathing. The Lieutenant's heart skips a beat. Then she rams her pry bar through the center of his chest, punching through the sternum, driving it into the spinal column, where it stands upright.

The breathing stops.

The Lieutenant backs up against the bench in front of the wall. Some part of her notes that she's still sobbing, crying like a baby, the sounds of fear and anguish. Her skin is clammy, she's trembling like a leaf. Elevated heart rate. She wonders if she's gone into shock, or some kind of fugue state.

LIEUTENANT: Pull yourself together.

Think. That's one of them. She needs to get out. Get away. There are others. She needs better weapons. That was lucky, she was lucky. Luck doesn't last. Steadying herself against the work bench, she starts to rifle through cabinets, finding the assorted tools and gear of animal husbandry. A pack of cigarettes, a cheap plastic lighter.

So monsters smoke? Who knew?

She glances back.

Gordon is staring at her. His head has turned towards her. Was it like that before? She's not sure. But his eyes are open. Were they open before? There's no expression in his face. But he's watching her. She stops what she's doing, turning to stare at the corpse.

Gordon blinks. Her heart skips a beat. He returns to staring at her.

The Lieutenant watches him for a second. His body is still, but he continues to watch her with a blank uncomprehending stare. His lips move, but he makes no sound. A finger twitches. The pry bar sticking out of his chest wobbles slightly.

The Lieutenant turns back, rifling frantically through the drawers. She finds a metal two liter can with a spout, marked, yellow and red, Axiom Brand Industrial Cleaning Fluid. Along the bottom is marked in bold letters 'CAUTION: HIGHLY FLAMMABLE' accompanied by a little cartoon flame.

Moving quickly the Lieutenant strides towards the body. She pulls the pry bar from the chest. It doesn't come easily. There is a hollow sucking sound. As she looks down, the edges of the wound quiver like lips.

She upends the cleaning fluid into the wound, sticking the spout directly in. The walls of the can flex as if breathing, and there's a soft glug as it empties into the chest cavity. She looks up.

Gordon has turned his head to watch her. There's still no expression, no awareness. But there's something: Curiosity.

GORDON: What are you doing?

A hand flutters, grabbing at her thigh. There's no strength in it, so she knocks it away. Her heart is racing. The cleaning fluid is still glugging, she pulls it from his chest and pushes his head to the side. The hole where she punched through his skull with the pry-bar is already covered over. She pokes the spout in, tearing new skin. The newly forming bone is too soft to offer resistance.

His body spasms once strongly, then again, then in disoriented twitching. His eyes struggle to focus on her, his legs kick gently, his hands reach for her.

GORDON: It's my daughter's birthday. She's....

His eyes drift apart.

GORDON: Television. Grandma likes television. One two... seven... green.

Gordon begins to sing wordlessly, his eyes drifting in different directions. His body squirms, his shoulders writhe as if his body isn't sure what it's supposed to be right this minute – human or monster.

She pulls the cleaning fluid spout out, retreating towards the door. Attracted by movement, his eyes focus on her, his head turns to follow her as she retreats, squirting the remaining cleaning fluid across his body and the floor.

She reaches the door, and pulls out the lighter. He watches her with innocent fascination.

LIEUTENANT: Goodbye, Gordon.

The Lieutenant ignites the lighter and tosses it. She is startled by how quickly the fluid ignites, by how fast the fire races towards the body which is already beginning to regain vestiges of coordination. Then she's out the door. She doesn't wait for the fire reach Gordon's chest cavity, doesn't see it burst open, or the flames crawl into the skull cavity. She doesn't wait for Gordon to die. Either he will or he won't. If he does, there's no point in sticking around. If he doesn't, she needs to be somewhere else.

What's important is to move and move fast. Don't look back. Never look back. She doesn't need to. She already knows there's always something behind her, and it's always gaining.

There are other hands tending Stock. No one looks up at her. The Lieutenant forces herself to walk calmly. The truck is right in front of her. Do not attract attention, she thinks. Walk to the truck, get in, lock the door, as if it's the most ordinary thing in the world.

No keys. She stares dumbly at the gore crusted tire iron in her hand. Had she been carrying it all this time? She lays it on the seat, bends forward and deftly hotwires the old vehicle. She's surprised by how steady and sure she is.

Until she looks down, and there, on the floor of the passenger side of the cab is a helmet. She picks it up. It's a helicopter flight helmet with a crack in the visor. It's hers.

How did it get there?

For a moment, the Lieutenant holds it in her hands, staring in confusion. She's almost afraid of it. But there's something else, it's safety, it's protection. She almost needs to put it on.

That's when she looks up sees it. A tall manlike shape in overalls wearing a corpse mask calmly walking to the door she exited. It's Michaels. The door opens, there's a plume of smoke, and then the figure walks in, calmly shutting the door behind it.

She blinks while staring at the closed door. It doesn't open again. Then she looks around and sees them. Figures walking, nondescript, uninteresting men wearing masks, striding calmly towards their destinations. No one notices them, the Men in the Masks walking through the blind spots in everyone's vision. They're not seen unless they want to be seen. They're not seen until they're ready to kill.

Suddenly, the Lieutenant is terrified, more scared than she has been this whole mission. They're here, several of them, and she knows that before sunrise tomorrow, everyone will be dead. She needs to run. With an effort of will, she puts the helmet down on the seat next to her.

No one is looking. The Lieutenant shifts into reverse, swings around and drives out. There's no reaction. She drives down the compound's dirt road to the gate. For a moment she thinks about gunning the engine and crashing through the gate. But there's a key fob hanging from the rear-view mirror of the pickup truck. She takes and swipes it, the gate opens.

In the rear-view, she sees a plume of smoke going up behind her. Gordon must be catching. A second later fire alarm klaxons are going off. She drives through. Her knuckles are bone white, she's gripping the steering wheel so tightly, her heart is racing, pounding so hard it feels like it will shatter her sternum, her mouth dry as a bone. She continues to drive normally until she reaches the paved main road. Then she guns the engine, tires squealing, gravel flinging and goes for it. Only at that point does she allow herself to breathe.

She's free. Free of the monsters. Free of that nightmarish town. A glance at the dashboard shows a full tank of gas. She intends to drive and leave everything behind, leave the others to the Men in the Masks. They're welcome to each other, maybe they'll kill each other off. Or headquarters can call in a fuel air bomb, or a cluster bomb, or whatever it takes. Napalm the whole valley.

For the first time in a long time, the Lieutenant feels free. She could just keep driving. British Colombia is not too far away. Keep driving, never stop, and just escape. Freedom. Freedom from them. For the rest of her life, keep moving, never looking back, just live.

That's when she sees it up ahead.

The wall of fire.

At first she doesn't quite understand what she's seeing. It's immense, the flames a solid burning wall over a hundred feet tall. The wall seems to extend right across the road.

She slows and stops. A half mile away she gets out of the truck to stare at it, trying to peer a way through. Even from this distance, she can feel the heat of it baking and tightening her skin. There's no way to run it, the gas tank would explode.

The Lieutenant remembers on the radio, reports of a forest fire in the south. She remembers the monster talking about it. They were watching it, to make sure it doesn't get out of hand.

It was moving fast, the wind was towards her, and even in the few seconds she'd left the truck to stare at it, it had crossed half the distance. The air was full of cinders. Dry trees were bursting into flame even before the wall reached them. The trees going up, the fire climbing up dried branches cresting and dancing at the crown.

Except that she was going north. Did she get turned around?

No.

The road signs said north. Fire in the south. Wall of flame in the north.

Them. Of course it's them. Silent, methodical, no one escapes.

No escape. No freedom. No British Colombia.

The Lieutenant sighs loudly, mostly to hear the sound of her own voice. She retrieves the flight helmet from the seat of the truck. Every little bit of protection helps, she tells herself. Simply wearing it though makes her feel safer, like it belongs.

She almost puts it on. Not just yet, she decides.

The fire almost reaches her before she swings the truck around, and heads back to town. She turns on the radio. "Highway to Hell" blared through the speakers. She doesn't laugh.

* * *

TWENTY-THREE HOURS BEFORE ZERO

KEITH: I bet you've seen some shit.

The Lieutenant presses her sunglasses back up her nose, trying to make sense of the map. She wishes there was some place to pull over, but the edge of the road is a sheer drop, on the other side, steep forest. They're not in the mountains, but close enough, and the roads wind in and out along the sides of the foothills.

She peers down the windshield, seeing nothing but the road and endless trees. They haven't seen a road sign in hours. At least the narrow road is paved.

GPS fried half an hour ago. Coincidence?

LIEUTENANT: Why the hell build these roads into the sides of mountains.

KEITH: We're not in the mountains, these are just the foothills.

She stares at him blankly.

LIEUTENANT: I know. I'm just saying it's fucked up.

Keith shrugs at her irritation.

KEITH: You can't build your roads down the valleys, they tried that. Floods, landslides, wash outs. Impassible in the winter, then you come to a hill, no way past. The engineers have to kind of snake their way along the geography.

They're driving in a late model Toyota. Color yellow. Dressing like civilians. She grunts, uninterested in the conversation.

Keith is talkative. The Lieutenant is almost not sure how to deal with it, or what to make of it. It takes her a while to put her finger on it. He's normal. He's human. She's not used to that any more, the thought shocks her a little. She clears her throat to try a normal conversation.

LIEUTENANT: Some. How about you?

KEITH: Two tours in Afghanistan. Did some missions in Chad, See Eye Aye. Central African Republic. Wire work at Guantanamo. Wet work, Myanmar.

She laughs. He's a toy soldier.

LIEUTENANT: That sounds pretty badass... and classified. Are you sure you should be telling me this?

KEITH: I saw your security clearance, you could look up my colonoscopy pictures if you wanted to.

LIEUTENANT: I did. I have it framed. It's in my living room.

Keith's eyes never leave the road, but his lips pull back in a grin.

She hasn't even looked at his file. She should have. She should have gone through the whole mission briefing, the reports. There's a whole due diligence thing when you're in the forces. You do your homework if you want the mission to succeed. But she'd found more and more, it didn't matter. Shit happened.

The road dips. Beside them the tops of transmission towers come into view, slowly rising as they keep pace until finally they rise high above their car. They pass under power lines crossing high in the air and now the transmission towers are above them as they drive, marching steadily upwards. The Lieutenant watches them indifferently. The electrical transmission towers parallel our road, sometimes below them on the slopes, occasionally crossing to roam above their road.

KEITH: I figure you already read my file. But we're on a mission, we should get to know each other. So, as I was saying, you've seen some shit?

She laughs. He's unwilling to let it go. How long has it been since she had a normal conversation? Since anything but the Division, the handlers and them?

LIEUTENANT: I've seen your security clearance too. You're not eligible.

Suddenly she regrets the words. He's not a bad guy. And he's right, they need to rely on each other. She pulls off the sunglasses, chewing on one of the arms.

LIEUTENANT: You're new to the Division aren't you? I bet you've never heard of us? Of Squad 13?

KEITH: Just assigned here a couple of months ago.

That explains it.

LIEUTENANT: Oh really? How'd you end up there?

KEITH: Pissed someone off, I guess.

LIEUTENANT: How are you getting along?

KEITH: Weird. This program is hard core.

LIEUTENANT: Oh?

The Lieutenant's not sure she wants to know, but she encourages him to speak.

KEITH: There's a game some of the lifers play. They take off their shirts and sit facing each other, they light up a couple of cigars.

LIEUTENANT: Ooh, scary!

The attempt at humor falls flat. Keith's eyes are carefully on the road, what he's talking about disturbs him.

KEITH: Then they take turns stubbing them out on each other. They light them again and again, and they stub them out, and light them again. The other guys, they take bets. After a while, the room starts to smell like pork.

She risks a glance at him. He doesn't look at her. His eyes are fixed on the road, staring straight ahead. She notices for the first time his knuckles are white on the steering wheel, gripping far tighter than even the precarious roads justify. The cheer in his voice is fake. Once she looks for it, she can see the tension.

LIEUTENANT: You played?

He shudders. No.

So he isn't that far gone.

LIEUTENANT: But you watched?

KEITH: I threw up. I wanted to stop it, but I just kept watching it. I couldn't...

LIEUTENANT: Couldn't look away? Some little voice, some urge to try it yourself?

He doesn't answer.

LIEUTENANT: Mutilation, including auto-mutilation is against regulations. Disabling injuries will get you automatic discipline no matter how they happen. No court martial, no appeals. Straight down. Do you smoke?

KEITH: No Ma'am.

LIEUTENANT: Don't start. That's an order.

She pauses, thinking, and decides to broach it.

LIEUTENANT: Have you been having nightmares? Bad dreams? Hallucinations? People in shadows? Feelings you're being watched? Impulses to self-harm? Self-mutilation? Depression? Strange feelings? Suicidal impulses?

He is carefully blank.

KEITH: No more than normal.

There is a careful evasion there. She nods. Two months? She's surprised he is holding up. Mortality rate in division is through the roof. Suicide mostly, the lucky ones. Just being connected to them is toxic, it's like their presence erodes the soul. No one gets out alive, not even her.

She chooses her words carefully.

LIEUTENANT: Have you had a conversation with one of the Doctors? There are mood alterers, inhibitors, blockers. There's all kinds of things. All you have to do...

KEITH: Is ask. No questions. I just ask, anything I want, keys to the candy store. I had that conversation. Not yet.

She nods. Things have gotten dark.

The countryside opens up, broadens. They're no longer driving along winding roads on the side of a steep hill. They're slowly descending into a flat broad valley. The Lieutenant relaxes a little, at least here, going off the road won't involve tumbling a hundred yards down and ending up in a ball of flame.

They find they've run out of things to talk about. Keith plays with the radio for a few minutes as he drives, tuning in a station. She just stares out the window.

She checks the rear-view, sees flashing lights. Now where did they come from?

LIEUTENANT: Looks like Smokey is on to us. Time to pull over.

KEITH: Who?

LIEUTENANT: Doesn't anyone watch old movies?

* * *

THIRTY TWO HOURS BEFORE ZERO

The cattle are spooked. Jake is not sure why. There are no predators in Windy Valley, apart from some feral house cats. There hasn't been a bear sighting in fifty years. The last mountain lion was killed in 1922. The wolves didn't survive the 19th century. These species learned a long time ago to steer clear of the valley.

But something's bothering the cattle, they're restless in their stalls, lowing almost constantly. It's loud enough to be disturbing. Now that he's in the barn, he can feel that the animals are at the edge of panic. Their eyes wide and showing whites as he walks past with the shotgun, their movements are twitchy, alert.

Jake hates cows. He hates the look of them, the smell of them, the disgusting way they shit everywhere, the way they chew their cud. The taste of beef revolts him.

But a man has to make a living.

Jake's family has always raised cattle. So he's stuck with them. Sometimes he's fantasized about just locking them in the barn and setting fire to the whole thing. Sit back in a rocking chair, and watch everything burn, listen to the sound of the cows screaming as the flames consume them. But then, the smell of charred beef would be everywhere.

But a man has to make a living.

Not that he didn't try for a transfer. But the Stock trade is all sewed up.

JAKE: 'You're fine where you are,' they say to me. But they don't have to smell you fuckers every day.

It's probably Millie and her friends, spooking the cattle, Jake decides. He's caught the little bastards out here before, tearing up a steer, playing at kid's games. Millie's the Sheriff's daughter and also a spoiled tomboy. Jake hates the disrespectful little shit. The rest of the family is okay, he grew up with the Sheriff. In Windy Valley, you know everyone, the families grow up together.

But Millie's just a little shit, a spoiled brat with no respect for other People's property.

JAKE: That you, Millie? You might as well come out now, girl. You and your friends. Just go on home, and I won't have to tell your Dad about this.

Jake has his shotgun, fully loaded with steel jacketed shot. If the girl's dumb enough to show her face, Jake plans to fire both barrels point blank into her spoiled little face. Teach the little bitch and her shithead friends a lesson. He's got a pocket full of shotgun shells. He may not like the cattle, but they're his cows, and he'll be damned if he stands by while some snot nosed, spoiled brats molest them.

There's a sound behind him, and he whirls, bringing the shotgun around to fire. He hesitates.

A figure steps out of the shadows, but it's not Millie or one of her little friends. This figure is tall and heavy set, wearing baggy ill-fitting clothes, faded by the elements, and looking like they were stolen off a scarecrow, only a protruding pot belly giving shape to the fabric. There's no exposed flesh, even its hands are covered by gardening gloves, reinforcing the sense of it being some kind of scarecrow. The head is just a shapeless burlap sack, with a single hole to see out of. Jake can hear it breathing, an unhealthy, wet rasping sound. The left hand holds an ancient rusty sickle.

Jake eyes the weapon warily. Sharp or not, it's a butt load of tetanus sitting in that piece of antique scrap. He's not concerned, he'll trust his shotgun against it.

But there's something wrong. The dark hole in the burlap sack isn't where an eye should be, not on any human shaped head, and yet Jake senses that the figure is watching him. The longer Jake stares, the more that seems wrong in the figure before him. The proportions increasingly off, the shape under the burlap is unnatural. And more, it's not quite how it was, as if it had shifted when he wasn't looking, but he hasn't taken his eyes off it.

Jake licks his lips, certain that what is before him is no natural creature.

JAKE: What the hell are you doing here?

There's no answer. It simply stands patiently. The hole in the burlap sack is in a different place, off to the left, several inches lower. He can tell it's still watching him through the hole.

JAKE: I got no time for this nonsense. You're spooking the cattle. You're spooking my cows.

Nothing. Jake swallows, his jaws work as if chewing. He turns his head slightly to spit on the floor.

JAKE: There's a covenant. We expect you folks to keep to it. Now get!

The figure raises its rusty sickle high and starts forward. Jake doesn't hesitate, he empties both barrels, the sound shockingly loud. Jake feels the discharge, the shotgun kicking hard in his arms. Stabbing pain in his ears like knitting needles shove into his eardrums, followed by jangling ringing.

Asshole, for making him use the shotgun inside the barn! It'll take the damned cows forever to settle down again. The figure is falling, but without missing a beat, Jake breaches the shotgun, pops the shells, reloads smoothly. The figure falls flat. Jake fires both barrels again. The stabbing pain in his ears is unbearable, he hopes he hasn't damaged his hearing. It would be criminal to have to get a hearing aid, he's not that old.

There's no reaction to the second volley of shots. The figure simply lays where it's fallen. No blood, Jake notes, as he reloads automatically.

Ignoring the ringing in his ears, he watches the body, counting time against his heartbeats. It doesn't move.

Eventually, he steps up to the body, kicks it lightly. Nothing. Inert. Well, that's that.

Jake figures he should call the Sheriff. Charley gets paid for this kind of shit. Jake's just a farmer, this isn't his business. He wonders if he should do it now, or just wait till morning. The Sheriff hates late calls. But the cattle are all stirred up, so there's no rest to be had tonight.

Movement behind him, Jake swings around with the shotgun, but fast as he is, a hand wraps around the barrel and tries to pull it away. Jake curses, refusing to let go, embarrassed at being snuck up on. Fucking ringing in his ears.

This one is tall and skinny, in ragged black robes, wearing an incongruously massive cow skull. It's a lot stronger than it should be given its gaunt frame, and Jake has to struggle to keep the shotgun being torn from him. Jake snarls.

JAKE: Fuck you!

No more playing. He drops his jaws, dislocating as the mandibles fall into their new setting, triggering his mouth full of fangs to surge out. His fingers lock into curves, claws protruding. The vertebra of his spine pop one after the other like a row of firecrackers. Still holding the shotgun, Jake rams his free hand into his victim's chest cavity, feeling a satisfying yielding. The damned Sheriff will have to shovel up the mess, this ain't his problem.

Agony takes his breath away, so fast so intense, Jake's mind whites out. His body goes rigid, the shotgun pulled from his grip. He can't breathe, he forces his alertness, the pain is in his back, ripping across his spine, moving up. He can feel his liver tearing, his intestines cut open, then up into his diaphragm, the ribs cutting apart like breadsticks. Jake knows what's happening, what's doing it, and the word 'tetanus' flashes through his mind, but he struggles to turn anyway.

He's already dropping, spine severed, there's only a glimpse but it's enough. Looming behind him is a figure wearing a burlap sack on its head, the hole almost at the top of the sack, watching him dispassionately. He tries to curse, but the sickle is shredding his lung.

Afterwards, with nothing else to do, there are the cows.

Jake would have enjoyed their screaming.

✳ ✳ ✳

EIGHT HOURS BEFORE ZERO

The phone connection is bad, the line crackles. Gordon and the Lieutenant wait. For a long minute, there is only silence. Then the voice on the phone:

PHONE: Gordon, I'm busy. Just kill her.

The Lieutenant backs up against the wall, holding her bar. Gordon sits at the table, watching her neutrally. Finally he sighs.

GORDON: Might as well get it over with.

He stands and advances on her.

✳ ✳ ✳

TWENTY-TWO HOURS BEFORE ZERO

Sheriff Charles Carnahan, goes by Charley to everyone in town. His father, was Sheriff, and went by that name. Same with his grandfather. Big imposing men who craved respect, everyone was always a little afraid around them.

But he likes to just go by Charley. He's always had respect. 'Charley' makes him feel... liked. Appreciated.

Maybe Kenneth, when his turn, will go by Sheriff. But that's some other day.

Charley watches the yellow Toyota pull over to the side of the road. They're making a point of being obvious. He squints, man and woman inside, relatively young. Feds? Military? Dealers? Civilians? They could be anyone. He's got a feeling about them, he trusts his feelings.

For just a moment, he fantasizes about just walking up to the car and emptying his pistol into their bodies. He could call Nick and his tow truck. It could be like it never happened.

He shakes his head, casting away the mad notion. Do other policemen have these impulses, he wonders?

Instead, he calls Marci on the radio, reads out a plate number and tells her to stand by. Then with a tired sigh, he gets out of the car to do his job.

Charley ambles on over to the car, his gait casual. He keeps his hand away from the gun. He's been to other jurisdictions where policemen approach with their hands on their firearm. He doesn't approve. You have to show trust, there's no need to bring unnecessary tension.

The window rolls down as he approaches. He sees them watching him in the side mirror, they look nervous, or maybe just careful. He bends down, squinting at the couple. Good shape, too good. The man is military, he'd swear on it. Maybe they both are.

CHARLEY: Howdy Folks, welcome to Windy Valley, the County not the town. Town's just up ahead. License and Registration please?

KEITH: Right here, officer.

Charley squints at the woman. Somehow, he can't get a read on her. He's usually good at sizing folk up right away.

CHARLEY: How about you, Ma'am?

He expects a protest or a complaint, but she hands it over without a word. He thanks them politely, and returns to his vehicle to relay the information to Marcia. It comes back clean, as he expected. Of course, it did. He sighs. They're probably exactly what they present as.

He makes the trip back up and returns their identification.

CHARLEY: You know why I stopped you?

KEITH: No, Sir.

Definitely military, Charley decides.

CHARLEY: We got a report of speeder from the last county. Reckless driving. You know, cowboys.

KEITH: Wasn't us, Sir.

CHARLEY: I didn't think so, but I had to check. You know how it is. Where you heading?

KEITH: We're just sightseeing. Traveling through the state. It's our honeymoon.

Charley nods, not believing it for a second. He sighs mentally. Nothing to do but let it all play out. That was something he'd learned in decades of policing, you let things ride, and sooner or later, the truth would out.

CHARLEY: Well, not much up this way. Windy Valley's basically a farming town, crops and cattle. We don't get many visitors, but it's a friendly place and visitors are always welcome.

KEITH: Thank you, Sir.

CHARLEY: You got family around here?

KEITH: No, sir.

CHARLEY: I got to ask, son. Did you serve?

KEITH: Tours in Afghanistan.

Charley smiles, and holds out his hand to shake. Keith's grip when he takes the hand is pleasingly firm.

CHARLEY: I thought so. I got a feel for these things. Thank you for your service. I have to tell you, Emma runs a nice little restaurant, you want to ask for the blueberry pie, the local berries are in season. Palmer's motel is clean if you want to stay a couple of days. Windy Valley's a little slice of paradise buried in these hills.

He hesitates.

CHARLEY: Drive carefully going in, there's a couple of hairpin turns. Last night a transport truck wiped out. Driver got impaled on the steering wheel. Real mess, still haven't got it all cleared.

After that there are casual pleasantries. Charley watches them drive off. He ambles back to his cruiser.

CHARLEY: Marci?

Casually, he fiddles with the USB, jacking the cable into his chest camera, downloading the recording for transmission. Marci's voice crackles over the radio.

MARCI: Yes boss?

CHARLEY: I'm sending you a Vid/Odd file of that couple I stopped. Run it through face recognition, voice prints. Cross reference it all against their ID and do a deep dive this time. Something's not right.

He pauses.

CHARLEY: Then send it out to Donny over at the Seattle office. Tell him to snoop around, but carefully.

MARCI: Can't feed it to Donny until tonight, and it will take a couple of days. He has to be careful. You sure it's worth it?

Donny is Marci's cousin. Back in the days of their one room school, he always looked after her. Now she tries to return the favor. Charley thinks she is over-protective.

CHARLEY: It's probably nothing. But do it anyway.

A chill goes down his spine, and he feels like he's being watched. Charley looks around, but there's nothing.

CHARLEY: How's the morning by the way? Anything else going on before I head in?

Charley steps out of the vehicle, leaving the door open so he can hear the radio. He places his hand carefully on his pistol, looking around.

MARCI: Report from Eldon. He was over at Jake's place. Someone slaughtered all Jake's cattle. Complete mess, just horrible.

Charley nods, unsurprised.

CHARLEY: That's not much of a mystery. Jake finally lost it. I don't know about that man. Crankiest bastard I ever met, hated cows, but wouldn't give them up. Wouldn't socialize, always keeping to himself, harboring whatever secret. Always knew he was going to snap one of these days.

MARCI: Jake is missing too.

CHARLEY: He'll turn up. But put the word out, especially the neighboring places. He can do what he wants with his own cattle, but I don't want some mad cow-killer running around slaughtering other People's cattle, or hell, even other People.

MARCI: What about the Stock farms?

CHARLEY: Especially them. Pass a message. Let them know to watch out for Jake if he shows. Particularly if he's acting squirrely.

MARCI: Another thing, Grandma smashed her television set. She's going to need a new one.

He's carefully surveying the surroundings, scoping three hundred and sixty degrees, just like he was taught. He nods, then realizes she can't see it. Instead he sighs loudly.

CHARLEY: When did this happen?

MARCI: Last night.

Charley swears.

CHARLEY: Marci! What the hell? You know Grandma loves her television. Why'd you wait? We should have had fixed her up right away. Now she's going to be cranky.

MARCI: I didn't hear till this morning. And anyway, she's all right. The boys are keeping her amused. You know how she loves the kids.

CHARLEY: I'll stop by Palmer's Hardware and get her a new one. The boys should be able to hook it up for her.

Charley doesn't mind admitting it, but nowadays, electronics are kind of a mystery to him. A confusing tangle of wires in the back, and an even more arcane set of prompts on screens. When he and Claire bought that stereo system, he'd paid the neighbor's boy to help him set it up.

MARCI: I talked to Jim Palmer, he's got a 65 inch in Stock.

CHARLEY: I know. He ordered it in for me. I guess Grandma can have it.

MARCI: I'm sorry.

Charley shrugs, still distracted. As if he's ever deny Grandma anything.

CHARLEY: It's for Grandma. I'll order in another one. Maybe we should keep a couple in Stock, just to be safe.

MARCI: She likes plasma screens. You know?

CHARLEY: I know.

There is nothing. Charley has to force himself not to bend over to look under the cruiser. Instead, he walks a few feet away, glancing back. All clear.

His feeling have played him wrong. Still, he can't bear to take his hand off his gun. There is a bit of a haze in the southern sky. He can smell just the hint of smoke.

CHARLEY: Those fires in the south, Ikloosipi County, how are they doing?

MARCI: We get regular updates. A bunch of little blazes, so far it's managed.

CHARLEY: Until the wind shifts and it's not, remember the big blaze of fifty-four?

Marci doesn't reply. Charley's not a fireman, but that doesn't stop him from worrying about everything and everyone.

MARCI: You have tea with the ladies auxiliary at lunchtime.

CHARLEY: Tell them I'm busy.

MARCI: I told them you were looking forward to it.

Charley winces.

MARCI: Oh and Millie's birthday is today.

Charley's heart skips a beat, suddenly he feels it slamming against his chest. His mouth goes dry, he feels a sensation akin to panic. Millie's birthday? How had it slipped his mind? Millie would be heartbroken. Claire would kill him.

His mind races. Maybe when he is picking up the flat screen for Grandma, Palmer can help him out. What do little girls like? Money was no object. Get her anything, something expensive. But Claire would know. She'd know it slipped his mind, and he half-assed a gift for his little girl. She'd see right through him. She always could.

MARCI: I talked to Old Lady Bennett. You know her, lives out by herself, raises those miniature horses, size of dogs. She's going to bring some over to the birthday party, and a couple of ponies for rides.

Relief floods Charley, Millie loves horses. She's practically obsessed with them. Back when they redid her bedroom, they ordered all the way to Vancouver for specialty unicorn-themed wallpaper. This will work, he thinks.

MARCI: Also, I talked to Palmer's wife, you drop by, she'll set out an assortment of gifts to choose from, and wrap them for you. Unicorn paper.

Charley's heart swells.

CHARLEY: Marci... I... I... don't what to say. You're a lifesaver.

MARCI: You don't have to say anything, Charley. We all know how hard you work to make sure everyone feels safe. How you look after Grandma for us. You're the beating heart of the town. We all love you.

Charley can feel himself blushing and choking up.

CHARLEY: Well, it's appreciated. Any word on that transport driver that wiped out?

MARCI: Just ID. No sign of drugs or alcohol involved. Abbelair thinks he was taking a curve a little too fast and a line blew. Bad luck. Body was a mess.

CHARLEY: Does he have family? Are they notified?

Charley's gotten to know a lot of truck drivers over his time. They're good folk doing hard jobs. He tries to imagine riding the road, being away from his family again and again. He couldn't do it.

MARCI: Not yet. We're still tracking it down.

CHARLEY: Well, keep on it, everyone has someone who'll miss them. That's about it, signing out.

He listens to the crackle of Marci signing off on the radio. Unconsciously, his hand slips back to his firearm, and he looks around one more time, plagued by the sense of being watched. But there aren't even bears left in these woods. Not for a long time.

Ridiculous to think that someone is watching him, this was a random stop. He followed the yellow Toyota for miles since they entered the valley. There's no way anyone could have been waiting.

He shivers, trying to brush it off. He's going to need to pick up the flat screen for Grandma, then go find Jake before he hurts himself or someone else. And Millie's birthday party, don't forget that. Going to be a full day. Charley gets in his patrol cruiser and drives off. He doesn't look back. There's no need.

As the cruiser vanishes down the road, the bushes along the shoulder part and a figure climbs out onto the road. It's a man, massively obese, wearing only rubber wading boots and torn dirty overalls. The man's flesh is leprous, with an almost graying unhealthy sheen, covered with stiff thick hairs like bristles, and open running sores. It is carrying in its two hands a massive hammer with a long handle and brutal head. The figure wears a decaying pig's head.

Silently, it watches the departing cruiser vanish into the distance. And then, with patient steps, it follows.

* * *

TWENTY-ONE HOURS BEFORE ZERO

With typical small town conscientiousness, there are flares and reflectors set up to warn them from a mile distance. Keith slows down and they get a good look at the twisted wreckage of the semi. The mangled driver's cab is covered with police tape.

KEITH: I guess the driver didn't make it.

The Lieutenant is more interested in the shattered box, bent in half, torn open, one wheel still thrust in the air. The contents have spilled; boxes, it looks like furniture or machine parts? Pink styrofoam packing flakes are everywhere, giving the wreckage an almost festive air, pink Christmas. She tries to match the debris to the estimated volume the hauler was carrying without Keith noticing, but gives it up.

It's probably unrelated. Just a coincidence. Someone was just unlucky. It happens. Or maybe not. After you've been exposed to them, nothing seems accidental. Are they here? This was supposed to be reconnaissance. Check things out, before they come. The Lieutenant checks the rear view.

KEITH: We're clear. Sheriff Charley's not following us.

The Lieutenant nods and pretends that is what she's watching out for.

KEITH: So we play tourists. We go into town, have lunch, and see the sights. There's a motel on the edge of town. We check in till nightfall. We'll have a few hours....

Is he hitting on her? She thinks it over, and decides that she wouldn't mind. The Lieutenant hasn't had much of a social life since she joined the Division.

LIEUTENANT: That's the brief.

KEITH: So do you let me know the mission parameters then?

There's an edge to his voice suddenly. The Lieutenant realizes she has misread him. She tries to mentally flip through his file. Very mission oriented. Very detail minded. Not a lot of trust. She understands that. Going on faith gets you killed.

She thinks about how to handle him. Pull rank? Or play fellow grunt?

LIEUTENANT: You know what I know. Nightfall, we proceed to the entry point, conduct preliminary reconnaissance. Report back. Unless they contact us at the motel, that's all there is.

Keith processes this for a full minute. When he speaks, his voice is flat.

KEITH: I don't like it. They either know something and aren't telling us, or they don't know shit. Either way, it's fucked up. Things go bad when they're fucked up.

LIEUTENANT: Orders.

When he speaks again, the false cheer is back.

KEITH: Is it always like this?

She thinks of them, the silent men in their masks. At least they're not here, not with the two of them this time. The psychic weight of their oppression is absent. They're somewhere else. But they will come. They always come.

LIEUTENANT: Usually it's worse.

Whatever they're going into, it's not as bad as what's going to follow them. But she doesn't tell him that. He'll have to learn himself. If he lives long enough.

* * *

EIGHTEEN HOURS BEFORE ZERO

GENERAL: Nice night.

The Lieutenant looks up. There he is, in uniform, all his salad on display, leaning up against the vending machine. Casual as anything. She peers hard as she can without being obvious, but she can't see through him. There is a light source behind him, so if he's not there, it should be coming through. She glances at his feet, checking out a normal shaped shadow where it ought to be.

For a moment, she thinks about reaching out to touch him, but she didn't quite have the nerve. Since he'd died, she's wound up seeing quite a lot of him.

LIEUTENANT: According to American Werewolf in London, you're supposed to look like a decomposing corpse, worse each time out.

The General laughs.

GENERAL: I don't think it works that way.

LIEUTENANT: So how does it work?

He shrugs. She decides to push.

LIEUTENANT: So what are we looking at here?

GENERAL: What do you mean?

The Lieutenant waves her hand, casually looking around to see if anyone is watching her talk to him, or to empty air. She still doesn't know what the rules are. Maybe other people can see him. Maybe most can't, but special people can. Maybe he's a ghost, or something else. Maybe he's just a brain tumor. The Lieutenant lives in the blank spot on the map.

LIEUTENANT: The usual mission is something dangerous and weird goes down, and then I go in with the boys and everything goes bad. Why is that? Why am I necessary? Why were you necessary? Why don't they just go themselves, and I can just stay home or go for Starbucks?

GENERAL: There appear to be rules. We're necessary, it seems.

LIEUTENANT: Appear to be? Jesus Christ. You've got no clue, do you?

He doesn't answer at first. Just watches. She sighs, letting the flash of anger go. He surprises her then.

GENERAL: You are, we are, some kind of anchor for them, a reference point. Move the reference point, they follow. That's the best guess.

That was actually... useful. Not new, the Lieutenant has read the various speculations in the analysis. There's a lot of analysis of them, who and what they are. Reams and reams of it. It's mostly speculation. It's mostly worthless.

GENERAL: We're all just pieces on a board. We only think we're making the moves.

LIEUTENANT: Wisdom from beyond? Or did you get that out of a fortune cookie?

And back to useless.

LIEUTENANT: What about this mission. This isn't standard. There's no vampire infestation, no alien invasion, no zombie apocalypse or Hellmouth here. .... Is there?

No response.

LIEUTENANT: This is just a quiet little backwater. There's nothing here.

She hesitates.

LIEUTENANT: Is something coming? Something really bad, and we're being pre-positioned? Something about to erupt? Is that it? Or is it already here?

A thought occurs to her.

LIEUTENANT: What about them? Are they already here? Was that wrecked semi we saw coming in, them?

GENERAL: What do you think?

Useless.

He takes off his hat, runs his fingers through his thinning hair. The gesture is so casual and human. He looks around, and takes a deep breath, savoring the night air.

GENERAL: I miss nights like this. Never appreciated them enough. Beautiful country. Except for the ticks. Sometimes the dog would go out, come back full of them. Hated the things, they'd wedge their heads inside the flesh. You couldn't pull them off, you'd just end up tearing off the head and leaving it inside to cause an infection. Imagine that, biting so hard that even when your head comes off and you're still not able to let go. That's persistence.

The Lieutenant holds her breath, attention focused. Is he telling her something? Was this relevant? Some kind of metaphor? A message? Or random babbling? Do ghosts get Alzheimer's? Or was it a brain tumor in her head just triggering meaningless associations. She still wasn't sure.

LIEUTENANT: I lived in the country, I know how. You light a match, put it out, and press it to the tick.

It's not clear whether he hears. He's not looking at her.

GENERAL: Light a match just for a second, press it against the tick. It lets go. Then you get rid of it. Pain in the ass, but necessary.

LIEUTENANT: General?

His gaze shifts, and he's looking directly at her. There's eye contact, and for a moment, she feels that they're connecting, that he's really there.

LIEUTENANT: General, what's going on?

GENERAL: Nothing good.

LIEUTENANT: Screw you. I'm tired of this conversation. You know what I'm going to do?

The general blinks.

GENERAL: What?

LIEUTENANT: I'm going to stop talking to fucking hallucinations that don't know shit. I'm going to get our drinks. Then I'm going to go back and fuck my brains out, we'll do this reconnaissance, and then we get the hell out of this shit town, and leave the Squad to whatever the hell they're going to do here.

The General smiles.

GENERAL: You do that. Give it your best shot.

LIEUTENANT: He's not one of Division's walking dead yet. Maybe we'll run for it. Head up to British Colombia, keep going. You assholes can find yourself another Final Girl.

The smile fades. The General looks sad and wistful.

GENERAL: Sorry, it's a one way trip.

Then he's not there. Not gone, not disappeared, he doesn't vanish, or snap away or fade out of sight. He's just not there. As always, she feels a little awkward.

She grabs her iced tea from the vending machine and walks away, casually swiveling. No one is watching. Time to go back to the hotel, where Keith is undoubtedly field stripping and testing all the gear. There are hours before reconnaissance, maybe they can find another sort of field stripping to practice.

* * *

EIGHTEEN HOURS BEFORE ZERO

Charley is at the fire department along with Abe and half the men of Windy Valley. Only the Stock shifts are exempted. Abe is the Deputy Sheriff, and also the Fire Chief. Windy Valley is a small town, everyone does lots of jobs. Charley helps out at the Post Office.

Abe's older than Charley by forty or fifty years. He's got the stiffness of Charley's father, all that generation has it. Normally, Charley defers to Abe on firefighting, the older man's careful approach is better suited to dealing with blazes. But Abe's not nearly as comfortable with the new technologies, tablets, drones, thermographic and topographic mapping, so Charley picks up the slack.

On a really big blaze, a forest fire, they work together. This is a big one. They are staring at the image on the tablet. Charley's sweating. The situation is bad, bad as he's ever seen.

The image on the tablet is from the drone high above, switched to thermal imaging to penetrate the columns of billowing smoke. There's a feed from the tablet to the big screen television that Abe requisitioned for the fire department. Fifty-five inches, the biggest screen in town, except for the sixty-five inch screen Charley donated to Grandma. It rankles a little bit, the Sheriff has the best television in town, that's the tradition.

Abe said it was for business purposes. Charley notices that the volunteer firemen watch a lot of sports on it. But it's come in useful, with the image up on the big screen the volunteers can follow along.

It's all gone wrong so quickly. The winds must have shifted, the scattered wildfires coalesce, joining together. Suddenly there's a wall of flame a hundred feet high advancing faster than a man can run.

In the heart of the fire, steel melts. Ahead of the fire, full sized trees burst into flame. A fire truck that wasn't pulled back in time detonates, the heat igniting the gas tank.

ABE: Nineteen fifty-four all over again.

CHARLEY: I hope not, we lost the town, remember. Everything burned flat. Took years to rebuild.

The road is impassible. Collateral fires have cut them off from local firefighting agencies. There's an inferno between them and help.

They're on their own.

Charley switches the tablet's image to topographic overlay. That just makes it look worse.

The fire is racing straight towards them like a burning tsunami, a rushing wall of flame. They're at risk to lose the town. He sees that clearly. There's a clear path unless they can stop it. It'll follow the road and slam down.

Charley draws lines on the tablet with his pencil.

CHARLEY: We can build firebreaks here and here. Get some crews out. I'll put in a call to the City, requisition water bombers. We could save the town.

ABE: It'll go past us, could double back.

CHARLEY: Wind's going the other direction. If it changes, we'll have time to build another firebreak.

 Abe grunts.

ABE: Towns can be rebuilt. We should look out for the Stock first.

Charley studies the terrain between the fire and the Stock farm. Mostly it's hillsides with scrub bush. It'll burn, but not well, there's not enough dry brush for fuel to make an uncontrollable blaze. The hollows are marsh – lazy, meandering, water soaked; as long as it doesn't get too hot, they'll just smolder, not burst into flame

CHARLEY: I don't know, I think we're safe enough there.

Abe taps the tablet. There's just one ravine though, lush with trees, old growth and dry. If the blaze gets a toehold there, it'll drive right into the Stock farms, and then it's all over. The Stock will bake or asphyxiate, two centuries worth of patient nurturing gone.

ABE: I don't like it.

CHARLEY: I took care of it.

Luckily, he'd spotted the vulnerability, and he'd sent a crew down to clear the brush. Create a firebreak, they'd stop it there. Save the Stock, save the community. Abe nods.

ABE: Still risky. If the fire breaks through, we could lose the whole herd.

CHARLEY: No matter what we do is risky. You want to do something else?

The older man stares.

ABE: No, you're right. If it goes bad that way, we'll have time to do something. We should try and save the town. I'm going to issue an Evacuation Ready Order, just in case.

CHARLEY: We'll pull through, just like we did back in fifty-four.

Charley touches the tablet screen, it goes dark for a second, and then lights up with thermal imaging. He selects a spot on the screen and expands it.

They go back to work. Charley doesn't even think of the visitors at all. He's got more important things to worry about.

* * *

NINE HOURS BEFORE ZERO

A hatch opens into a nondescript room. The Lieutenant climbs out followed by Gordon. She looks around. The place is dusty, not quite a shed, not quite a workshop. Benches line the walls. There's a dusty ham radio set up in the corner, an old fashioned wall mounted phone.

GORDON: Have a seat at the table.

The Lieutenant complies, she sits and waits. Gordon takes a seat across from her, watching. She meets his eyes. He glances at the iron bar held loosely at her side.

GORDON: I'm letting you keep that little toothpick because you're scared, I can tell. But you don't show it. You're a pretty cool customer. That's almost admirable.

LIEUTENANT: I've seen worse than you.

GORDON: Have you now?

There's no answer. Gordon sighs heavily.

GORDON: We're not bad People.

LIEUTENANT: I saw what I saw down there.

Gordon shrugs. He pulls out a smart phone and lays it on the table.

GORDON: We're going to make a call. It's impossible to get reception down there.

LIEUTENANT: Pizza?

Gordon laughs despite himself, and gives her a thumb's up.

GORDON: You're a pistol all right. If you can lose the attitude, I might get to like you. You're going to tell us everything. Then we talk to your bosses, things get worked out, and you and your little friend go home. Done it before.

LIEUTENANT: What if I don't believe you?

Gordon doesn't reply at first, he just lays his right hand down on the table palm up. The palm broadens, the fingers lengthen into scimitar claws, a massive flat paddle sporting lethal blades several inches long. As they stare, the paddle returns to shape, the claws recede and disappear.

GORDON: I think you'll talk.

* * *

SEVENTEEN HOURS BEFORE ZERO

The Lieutenant is naked, drenched with sweat, riding Keith, thrusting down on top of him. She grunts, teeth bared, enjoying his humanity inside of her.

True to form, he'd had an arsenal laid out on a bedsheet, meticulously disassembled and reassembled. A true Special Forces professional, all preparation and planning.

He'd watched, eyes luminous, as she locked the motel door behind her and stripped off her clothes.

LIEUTENANT: Let's get into character. Just in case anyone suspects our cover.

Keith pulls the sheet around the gear, wrapping it, and pulling it off the bed. Always a professional, she thinks. He pulls off his T-shirt, there's a satisfying amount of muscle underneath.

KEITH: Newlyweds, right. Horny as hell.

LIEUTENANT: Right.

She's crossed the distance, is undoing his jeans. His hands are on her breasts. His hands are warm. He feels so alive. Everything about him is alive, he's skin and pores and hairs, muscle and fat and bone and organs gurgling wetly in a cavity, she can feel his blood pumping faster as his heart speeds up. His erection is in her hand, throbbing. His brain is alight with sizzling neurons, he's panting, sucking oxygen with each bellows inflation of his lungs, exhaling carbon dioxide. His attention is on her. He sees her, hears her.

The Lieutenant wants him so badly, wants to touch him, to be touched, wants to feel him, taste him, eat him.

LIEUTENANT: Look at me. How do I look? See me. Can you see me?

She pushes him back on the bed, staring down at him. His pants are halfway down, his shirt gone. His erection stands straight up, and it's beautiful. She crawls on top of him, stopping only a moment to taste him between her lips, resisting the urge to bite hard, straddles him, and lowers herself down. His cock is like a living flame inside her, rigid and hot.

She rakes her hands down his chest, exulting in his human solidity, the warmth of him. She takes his hands from her hips and presses them hard on her breasts.

Their bodies collide, sweat drips, the pant and moan, and it's all glorious. The Lieutenant moves seamlessly from making love to fucking and then back again. She bites him, licks him as if she can't get enough.

There are orgasms, white hot and intense, and she barely cares about them. She wants him so much. It lasts hours, and in the end, they're lying in bed in soaked, stained sheets on their backs.

The Lieutenant turns her head, watching him in post-coital bliss, his chest heaves as he gasps for breath. He swallows. She stares at his throat, fascinated, watching his trachea move with each breath and swallow, watching the blood pump through arteries so close to the surface. She has the urge to affectionately seize it between her jaws, to bit down until the windpipe collapses, the flesh tears as her teeth sink in.

She looks up at the ceiling. She shouldn't think like that. Just crush it, instead, or put a knife into it.

LIEUTENANT: You know what? Screw reconnaissance, they don't need us. Let's just drive, go up to British Colombia, just keep playing newlyweds and fuck our way across country. Forget division. Forget the Squad.

She hesitates and then whispers, her voice serious. She stares at the ceiling.

LIEUTENANT: We could make a run for it.

KEITH: We have a mission.

LIEUTENANT (deep breathe): Yeah, the mission. Right.

Keith rolls over on his side, facing her. His flaccid penis moves, and she wraps her hand around it, hoping that it'll be ready for another round soon. She could do with another go.

His body is covered with red scratches from her fingernails.

KEITH: You're a lot different than they said you'd be.

She wants to fake a laugh, and ask what they say about her. She doesn't. She simply shrugs.

KEITH: Can I ask a question.

She smiles, it's genuine.

LIEUTENANT: Sure.

KEITH: What's your real name?

The Lieutenant's eyes sparkle, she grins.

LIEUTENANT: Classified.

He laughs. He thinks it's funny.

But the Lieutenant can't remember. She can almost remember, it's on the tip of her tongue. Sounds, she almost has it. Her memories of life before the Squad are indistinct. Fuzzy and vague, like some television program blurry from being copied and recopied endlessly on a VHS tape. Images and sounds, jumbled and nebulous.

 It's probably not important, she thinks. She wonders if maybe, just maybe, it might be a bad sign. No. She's just overthinking.

* * *

FOURTEEN HOURS BEFORE ZERO

They're on the road outside town, both crews, gathered at the turn off. Charley turns off the radio.

CHARLEY: Highway is blocked. The wind's against it, but the trouble is too much brush, too many little gullies and hillocks, it blocks the wind, shoves it around. It's heading towards town.

ABE: We got bulldozers out, we can stop it before it reaches town.

CHARLEY: Maybe. This is a big one. I'm worried about it jumping around. I think maybe we should be protecting the yards. And Grandma.

ABE: You'd risk losing the town?

CHARLEY: You'd risk losing Grandma?

ABE: Don't be crazy. We got Grandma protected. Remember back in the cold war, the fifties, you all thought there was going to be a nuclear war. We fortified Grandma's place. Nothing short of a nuclear bomb is going to touch her. Even if the fire reaches, it'll go right past. She's got deep wells, cooling and filtration systems. She's got an oxygen supply if she needs it. Only thing we need to worry about is she loses cable access.

CHARLEY: That's a big enough worry right there. You know how cranky she gets when cable goes out.

ABE: We'll find her some free range to play with. Or just give her some Stock, she can't tell the difference.

CHARLEY: Oh she can tell. But even if we're not worried about her, the Yards are right in the middle. Fire could wipe us out, burn it all down.

ABE: Cattle are insured.

CHARLEY: Stock aren't.

ABE: So we just rebuild. Remember when we were starting out, that measles outbreak. Almost wiped us out. We rebuilt.

CHARLEY: How are we going to rebuild the Stock in this day and age?

ABE: I don't know. Do a Code Zero. Get everyone out of the country. Go someplace like Guatemala; lot of illegal immigrants trying to get north from there. Set up shop right, a whole bunch could disappear without anyone really knowing where they went. Or maybe Pakistan, life's cheap there. Worse come to worse, we can make a deal, with Cartels or someone. We have allies. There are Covenants.

Charley shudders at the thought of some of the parties they might have to deal with to rebuild Stock. Fundamentally, the People are simple decent folk, wanting only to be left alone to make wholesome sustainable lives. It's a wicked world out there, and he's got no stomach for it.

CHARLEY: I'd rather not have to.

* * *

ELEVEN HOURS BEFORE ZERO

LIEUTENANT: So… you farm people?

GORDON: You could say that.

LIEUTENANT: Why?

GORDON: What do you think? Human flesh is easy to come by? You fuckers watch each other. Some dickless camper goes missing, there's search parties for a week. Kid vanishes, you never stop hearing about it. Someone disappears? There's reports, there's red flags, amber alerts, missing persons, posters on telephone poles and pictures on milk cartons. Too many someones go missing, authorities start to notice, the media starts covering it, there's a serial killer task force, they start collecting data.

GORDON: Maybe we can stretch it out, take homeless folk, drug addicts, illegals, hookers, there's lots of garbage folk that no one watches out for. But even there, take too many and it gets noticed. And who wants to eat garbage folk anyway? Do you know what a meth-head tastes like? Jesus, makes you want to go vegan! Just joking.

LIEUTENANT: I should mention, I do a lot of crystal meth. It's the army. They hand that stuff out like candy. Keeps us on our toes. Also, heroin, mescaline, and junk foods, tons of junk food.

Gordon laughs.

GORDON: Really good free-range, that's different. There's nothing like it. Young, healthy, athletic, sharp. Like you. It makes my mouth water, just thinking about it. Out in the open, stalking, hunting you down. It's amazing, there's nothing like it.

LIEUTENANT: How much of a head start would I get? You know. To make sure it's interesting.

GORDON: You don't rattle at all, do you? I like that. You're all right.

LIEUTENANT: I've seen worse than you. I've worked with worse.

Gordon laughs again. He shoves the Lieutenant gently, causing her to miss a step.

GORDON: I sincerely doubt that. But let's face it, we have to live in the world, and that shit just doesn't fly any more. Forget healthy free-range, you can't even eat a meth-head these days.

LIEUTENANT: Why not?

GORDON: You folk get so excited. Someone gets eaten? Someone goes missing? It's the end of the world. Some hiker gets lost camping, next thing you know, there are search parties. Dogs, helicopters, assholes walking around linking arms, and everyone's yammering on about a serial killer.

LIEUTENANT: What about these people?

GORDON: Not people. Stock. They're born here, they die here, all off the grid. They're completely off the record. No birth certificates, no school records, marriage certificates, no social security numbers, no records at all. They don't exist at all as far as anyone is concerned.

LIEUTENANT: You raise people?

GORDON: I said Stock. There's a difference. They're where they belong. They don't want to be anywhere else.

LIEUTENANT: I don't see it. They're still people. They don't want to be here.

GORDON: They're Stock. Anyway, how do you figure? They're happy here.

LIEUTENANT: You have them in cages.

Gordon laughs.

GORDON: They don't mind. They're barely animals. We restrict language formation, cognitive development, breed for docility. They're just smart enough to be toilet trained and that's all. Vocabulary maybe fifty or a hundred words. Less than a good dog. Used to be over five hundred words, but we work them down. We try to discourage smartness.

LIEUTENANT: You're farming them?

GORDON: Yep. Most of them we pump with hormones so they mature fast, start breeding early. We keep a good eye on them. They're warm, safe, protected, we keep them fed. They're happy. They don't know anything else.

LIEUTENANT: How many?

GORDON: It varies. Six or seven hundred head right now, I think. You're wondering how long we've been doing it, where'd we get the

Stock. Some of the bloodlines go back five generations. Back to the end of the 19th, when there were more and more humans around. We thought that was great. But we kept noticing, sometimes when we took someone, their folks came looking. At first, didn't bother us much, one on one, bare handed, we can handle ourselves. But it's not like the old times, pistol or rifle will put a pretty big hurt on you. Some of those that came looking, they were stone cold killers.

LIEUTENANT: You've been doing this since the 19th century?

GORDON: Think centuries, at least. We've been around a lot longer than that. Before the white man, for sure. Some say that when the Indians came over the Bering Strait, we were already here, waiting for them. But come the 19th century, some of us started to figure out things couldn't keep on the way they were. Writing was on the wall, you know what I mean. So we changed with the times. Some couldn't keep up, much as we tried, we had to end them.

LIEUTENANT: Times change.

GORDON: We're not evil. We're just farmers, simple folk. Fundamentally, we want what everyone wants. Food, shelter, a safe place to raise kids. Windy Valley's a good place. We look after our own, we don't hurt anyone.

LIEUTENANT: Except you eat people.

Gordon shrugs.

GORDON: What do you think you're put on this earth for? You're here to be eaten. By us, by something else. By each other. You live in your big cities, working at shitty jobs, slowly getting your lives drained away until you're a shriveled husk that no one wants. You end up dead of heart attacks or cancer, or dumped into nursing homes to rot away. That's no life, and no death either. You're better off eaten by us, at least you're appreciated.

Gordon waves.

GORDON: The truth is, we give Stock better lives than you give each other. They're healthier, happier, valued. That stuff I see on television, how you treat each other? Disgusting.

LIEUTENANT: Where do I come in?

GORDON: There's powers, we know they're out there. Some official, some not. We stay quiet, we don't bother nobody. We just mind our Stock. We got deals with most of them, or ways to deal.

LIEUTENANT: You don't have deals with mine.

GORDON: I suppose not. Not yet, anyway. We don't rightly know what you are. But we're figuring on you telling us. Then we'll make some calls, send some messages. It'll get sorted out. You'll probably come out okay.

LIEUTENANT: Not so much Keith though.

GORDON: That was his name? He shouldn't have put up a fight.

LIEUTENANT: Too bad.

GORDON: Come right down to it, no one wants trouble. No one ever wants to rock the boat. You figure your President cares about six or seven hundred head of Stock that don't even legally exist? Better to just pretend, ignore, forget. We make a deal. You walk out. As for your boytoy? He'll be put to use.

LIEUTENANT: You'll eat him. If you haven't already.

GORDON: Be a waste, otherwise. Kind of a sin. And honestly, free-range, that's a treat.

LIEUTENANT: So you're Windigo?

Gordon stopped, looking shocked.

GORDON: Jesus Christ! Racist much?

LIEUTENANT: Excuse me?

GORDON: Just because we eat humans, you think we're Windigo? That's pretty fucking narrow-minded. Do you go around calling black folk 'monkeys' too? Have you ever seen a Windigo? No, you haven't. But you're just going to throw the word around.

LIEUTENANT: I should ... apologize?

GORDON: Yes, you should. I mean, I'll overlook it. But don't use that word around others. People here, they will take offense.

LIEUTENANT: So what are you then?

GORDON: We're just the People, the real ones. At least, that's how it comes down from Grandmother.

* * *

THIRTEEN HOURS BEFORE ZERO

LIEUTENANT: This is it?

It's a heavily forested slope. Below them is a shallow stagnant pond. It smells awful, the product of decades of decomposition with nowhere to go. It would have dried out long ago, but a few streams from the hillside supply just enough of a dribble.

Keith hands the Lieutenant the thermal sensor. The place is honeycombed with heat spots, not volcanic, all of them at a mean temperature. They're standing at one of the spots, it's a large concrete pipe, about a foot in diameter, sealed with a loose mesh screen. There's a dozen more just like it.

And a couple of big ones up ahead.

KEITH: Reminds me of some of the old Russian bunker systems I saw in Afghanistan. Heat builds up, you got to vent it somewhere safe.

LIEUTENANT: Going by the smell around here, I don't think it gets a lot of visitors.

KEITH: This is a lot more extensive than anything the Russians built.

LIEUTENANT: The Historical section of the briefing said that there was a silver mine here in the 19th century. It turned into a huge scandal back in the day. Apparently it played out very fast, but there'd been massive investment. It went bankrupt, lots of lawsuits by investors who lost their shirts. Even charges of fraud.

Keith grunts.

LIEUTENANT: But in its time, it would have been state of the art, and extensive. Assume the area was geologically stable, it might have been pretty intact. So suppose someone came along and repurposed it?

KEITH: When?

That was the question. She had no idea. John Birchers in the 50s, hiding out from nuclear war. Some hippy commune in the 70s.

Survivalist preppers in the 90s. Humanity could throw up any number of cults. For all we knew it was a colony of inbred 19th century Mormons on the way to turning into Morlocks, isolated for decades. Those were the safe cautious answers. Which meant they were probably wrong, and whatever it really was, was insane and dangerous.

LIEUTENANT: Who cares? This looks like James Bond shit. We did our reconnaissance, let's get out of here.

KEITH: Amen.

But a second later, there was a flash of light along the ridge. Keith shoves the Lieutenant down on the other side of the pipe, while he takes up the scope. He is Special Forces after all, she lets him take the lead in the field.

LIEUTENANT: Problem? Are they looking for us? Did we get made?

Keith studies them intently through the scope. He adjusted the settings, and peered again. After a moment, he relaxes.

KEITH: That's a four wheel drive pickup. Hunters, I think. They're carrying deer rifles, single shots, not military ordnance. Orange vests. Look out of shape. Poachers. I could probably take them out, if they make us.

LIEUTENANT: Civilians. We're not here to kill civilians.

If they were civilians.

KEITH: I wouldn't enjoy it.

But she notices he wasn't ruling it out. They hold position and watch, as the visitors stumble along. The newcomers flush a couple of deer, the animals running in their direction.

KEITH: They're going to head our way.

LIEUTENANT: Should we get back to our vehicle?

KEITH: Not without them spotting us.

LIEUTENANT: Options.

Keith chews his lip, and glances to the left.

KEITH: The large vent thirty feet up, probably an access of some kind. We could hide in there, wait them out?

LIEUTENANT: I don't like it.

KEITH: Wait in the open, and then what?

There isn't any choice, so they crawl to the entrance, keeping an eye on the oblivious poachers. True to their guesses, it is a camouflaged concrete port, rectangular. A warm but not hot breeze issues from it. They make their way deeper.

KEITH: Watch yourself.

He says it softly, bracing her as she falls the last few feet in the concrete shaft, making sure that she doesn't make noise. The iron rails they climb down are in good shape, but intermittent, with deliberate gaps. There's no time to ponder it though.

They're in some kind of chamber, three tunnels connecting to it. The Lieutenant can't make sense of the geography, the night vision goggles distort everything. Keith is already scoping, approaching and peering into each.

* * *

TWELVE HOURS BEFORE ZERO

The radio burps. Charley curses in frustration, there's always something. His crew are out in the middle of the woods constructing the firebreak. They can smell the smoke already, see the black rim of the horizon. A lightning bolt shoots down in the black rim, a jagged arc of charged electrons coalescing and leaping from the smoke to ground itself.

It looks so far away, but that's deceptive. A forest fire with the wind at its back can move incredibly fast, even racing ahead of the wind. The fire runs so hot trees will burst into flame before it reaches them. Charley's watched trees go up like candles, the fire laddering its way up the branches, to blaze away at the crown. It's a fearsome sight, one that makes you feel small and helpless.

There's something unnatural and implacable about a runaway fire. It's why he prefers police work. More personal, you deal with people. Charley likes people.

He shouldn't even bother with the phone. But he's Charley, so he picks up. Even if he can't deal with it, it's important that the People know he picks up.

CHARLEY: Go ahead.

He hopes that curt acknowledgment conveys the message. This better be important.

It's Marci, of course.

MARCI: Charley, I got Donny on line, he's calling from a safe house, deep encryption.

There's an edge of something in Marci's voice, she's scared. He knows right away, something's wrong. Donny's FBI, if this was normal, he could call directly. Dangerous, he'd call from home. If he's scared, then safe house. There's layers to Windy Valley's secrecy. But encryption on all that?

CHARLEY: Did he tell you what he's got?

MARCI: No, he just wanted me to put you through right away.

The girl is definitely spooked. She and Donny have always been close, she's intuitive about her cousin. It's not going to be good news.

He waves at the crew to continue work without him, and then he walks off a ways for privacy.

CHARLEY: Put him through.

There's a series of clicks, and Donny's voice comes on, slightly distorted by the encryption signatures.

DONNY: Sheriff?

CHARLEY: Just Charley, my Dad was the Sheriff.

Mentally, Charley kicks himself. He's said it for decades, until the cliché has worn smooth and become annoying. He's heard People recite it when they don't think he's listening. Old habits are hard to break.

CHARLEY: You got some news?

DONNY: Yeah, that couple you asked me to check out. It checks out, I dug deep, and it all came up, totally normal.

Yeah. Donny wouldn't be calling to tell him everything's all right.

CHARLEY: Except?

DONNY: So I dug deeper, and sure enough, it's a cover. Military Intelligence, covert-ops. It looked solid. So I dug deeper and...

CHARLEY: And?

DONNY: Nothing. Vacuum. There was nothing there, just a void.

Charley felt a chill. That meant that someone, some parties had infiltrated Military Intelligence with fake identities, used them like finger puppets for a mission outside their jurisdiction. And they, Military Intelligence, had just rolled over like dogs wanting their tummies scratched.

That was bad news.

CHARLEY: I appreciate your letting us know. Anything else?

DONNY: Yeah, I checked around the Covenants, either no one knew anything, or they're scared. There's a rumor going around that there's something bad out there, something really bad. Like disappearing into a black hole bad, nothing escapes. This isn't the normal dark, this is something else. I don't think we can deal with this.

Charley felt a chill go down his spine. He doesn't need this shit, not right now. Not with the whole countryside ready to go up like a string of firecrackers.

CHARLEY: I see.

DONNY: I sent you a file, not much, just whatever bits and pieces I could scrape up, raw data, no analysis. Nothing directly on them, just... wherever they show up, it's either bad already, or it turns bad. But take a look.

CHARLEY: Okay, thanks.

DONNY: One more thing... I think I triggered something just by looking. I'm burned. I can't talk about it, but I need to go to ground. You won't hear from me for a while.

CHARLEY: Thanks for letting us know. Recommendation for our visitors?

DONNY: Erase them. Wherever, whatever they're coming from, there's no talking to it.

The line went dead.

Charley thought for a moment. Then he called back to Marci, she'd put the word out. The visitors would be dead by morning.

He didn't believe in unnecessary killing. Always better to talk things out, make a deal.

Out of diligence he opened Donny's file on the phone and scrolled through it quickly for a few minutes. Gibberish. A bunch of places that disappeared from maps, oblique references to massacres, bizarre crimes. Spook stuff. He couldn't make heads or tails of it, and didn't have the patience or time to go through it carefully.

If this was anyone but Donny, he'd have dismissed it. But Donny was level headed, the boy didn't spook. But he hadn't just been spooked. The boy was scared. That warranted taking seriously.

But some things out there in the world, there was no way around it but to show some teeth. The People had never run across anything they couldn't handle. But if finally, this was it, well, they'd planned for that too.

They owed it to Grandma.

Charley thought for a moment about putting the phone on silent. But he was too conscientious to ever do that. Instead, he just put it away and went back to the crew.

There was work to be done. They had a town, hell, they had a way of life, to save.

* * *

TWELVE HOURS BEFORE ZERO

The monsters come out of nowhere, vaguely human shaped but with distorted faces, distended jaws full of razor teeth, their arms and legs unnaturally long, hands clawed. Keith has his pistol out and empties it into the face of the first attacker, downing it even as they take him down.

Another comes at the Lieutenant, she aims low, center of mass, and then lower, shooting at the juncture of the hips, just as it grabs her arm. It screeches in agony, hurling her away. She rolls with it, coming up on her feet and emptying the pistol into the skull of one of Keith's attackers. Automatically she reloads, as they turn towards.

Keith, on his back, kicks upward smashing a monster's jaw shut with the heel of his boot. His pistol is spinning away, torn from his grip by the monsters. But his combat knife is in his hand.

KEITH: Goddamit, run!

Two of the monsters turn towards her, hideous in the distortions of the night vision goggles. Keith sinks his knifc into one of their calves. They all turn back to him.

KEITH: Dammit!

The Lieutenant runs. Keith's dead, or he's going to be, and it's time to move. She's trying to remember the twists and turns back to the hatch. If she can get to it, seal it, there's a chance to get the hell out and call in reinforcements.

This place is a maze, it was left, left, right then left. Behind her, she can still hear Keith shrieking, an uninhibited screaming that freezes her blood, beneath it, meaty sounds of flesh and organs rupturing, the monsters roaring.

But she seems to have been forgotten for a second. Nothing is after her. She keeps moving as Keith is torn to pieces.

Was it a trap all along? They'd made their to the target site, identified thermal vents, and that should have been it. Get out and report. But then poachers had showed up, and they'd retreated to one of the vents to wait them out as they'd approached. Then noises, retreating deeper, until they were picking their way through an empty maze of tunnels left over from a derelict 19th century silver mine.

Or maybe guided deeper.

Up ahead: Growling.

The Lieutenant flattens herself against the wall of the tunnel, getting as close to the corner as she can.

The creature doesn't see her, its coming around so fast. There's a glimpse of something monstrous, then it's gone. She retreats back into the shadows, listening to receding footfalls.

Nowhere to go but deeper.

* * *

ELEVEN HOURS BEFORE ZERO

The Lieutenant is looking at an underground hanger, hiding behind pallets of crates just off one of the entrances. A forklift sits a few feet away, the keys visible in it. She's trying to comprehend the vastness. The space is immense, the construction is brutal, steel and fluted concrete arches, probably dating back to the early Cold War, or maybe the World War II. It's a James Bond sort of space, she thinks.

The space has been jury rigged and retrofitted, there are cables and pipes everywhere. Piles of crates, clear spaces. Loudspeakers play inexplicably soft classical music. She's looking for CCTV cameras, detectors, but the lights have been set to low, making everything indistinct. Hanger is filled with large cages, two rows of them, surrounded by catwalks, pipes running to and from them. It reminds her of the utilitarian set up of a factory farm.

Against her better judgment, she makes her way to one of the cages. Attracted by her motion, there's a rustle, figures stand up and approach the bars. Faces look out at her.

The Lieutenant stares. Naked men and women stare back, dozens of them, hundreds. She whispers.

LIEUTENANT: What the hell?

The voice comes from behind her.

GORDON: Stock.

The Lieutenant jumps and spins. Gordon holds up a cattle prod.

GORDON: Easy now. We've been watching you on closed circuit for a while. Just making sure you don't hurt the Stock or tamper or anything.

He waves the cattle prod towards her.

GORDON: You don't want to go the way of the other one. I don't know if you recognize this, we use it to keep Stock from getting out of hand. It can hurt you, stun you, kill you. My call. But we don't want to upset the Stock, so let's both keep it peaceful, you come along with me.

The Lieutenant stares at the prod. Gordon touches a stud and sparks fly between the contact points. The Lieutenant drops her pistol, there are no more bullets left anyway. She holds up her hands.

LIEUTENANT: Whatever you say.

GORDON: Smart one. Smarter than the other one at least. We tracked both incursions. Your friend was a real troublemaker.

The Lieutenant's expression doesn't change, but she notes the words. Both incursions? She and Keith came in together.

LIEUTENANT: What happened to him?

GORDON: We had to take care of him quick. He made it necessary.

She doesn't follow it up.

LIEUTENANT: So how does this play out?

GORDON: Take you back, away from the Stock. No need to upset the Stock. They get excited, they start shitting themselves. It turns into a real mess. The Stock don't know no better, but you have to clean it up or it causes problems. Not healthy, you know.

LIEUTENANT: Sounds awful.

GORDON: It is. I wouldn't look forward to trying to clean it.

LIEUTENANT: So you're going to kill me out of sight? I'm not thrilled.

GORDON: Don't be dramatic. I ask you questions, you answer, then my People talk to your people, it gets worked out. You go home and eventually you bother someone else.

LIEUTENANT: Sounds simple when you put it like that.

GORDON: You'd be surprised. This isn't the first time. It always gets worked out.

LIEUTENANT: Well, we wouldn't want to upset the Stock.

GORDON: I appreciate your understanding.

LIEUTENANT: You're all going to die.

GORDON: Yeah, we've heard that. But somehow, everyone always makes a deal.

* * *

NINE HOURS BEFORE ZERO

Sheriff Charley listens to the voice over the phone. It's the woman in the yellow Toyota from yesterday; the reception is bad, the voice is distorted as it always is around the Stock barns. He's not surprised, there was something off about them. Especially her. The man had been a standard military grunt, a bit full of it, Special Forces probably. But she'd radiated a subliminal wrongness that bothered him more each time he thought about her.

He wonders where her male friend is, probably dead. The boy was a soldier, probably would kick up a fuss, and the Stock handlers were nothing if not efficient.

Girls were more docile.

He really doesn't want to deal with this shit right now.

LIEUTENANT: I'm the final girl.

He's never heard that term before. Gordon saves him from having to ask.

GORDON: I don't know what that is?

When she replies, there's something dead in her voice.

LIEUTENANT: Tell me something, have you ever heard of a quiet out of the way place somewhere? People gathered together for something, a summer camp, a party, maybe a vacation or a retreat... and then, people started dying? Horrible deaths, mutilation, pain. They just got picked off one by one, by some stranger in a mask or a hood. They try to run, they try to hide, to fight, but nothing works. The man in the mask just kills them all one by one. Nothing they can do. The man in the mask disappears. Then, a while later, months, years even, it all happens again. The same man in the mask back again.

Charley has seen terrible things, and he's done far worse. He tries not to let it bother him. He's a family man, you do what you need to do to protect your family, your community, and then you try not to think about it too much.

For the first time in his life, his blood is running cold, he feels chills up his spine.

The fires are blazing, trees are going up like candles. The firebreaks aren't working, the water bombers are futile. They've lost a bulldozer to the advancing flame, and they're in retreat. They're not giving up, they're not close to giving up. But he's worried that they may have to evacuate the town, half the farms in the valley are at risk.

Even hundreds of yards away, he can feel the heat of the blaze, the crawling puckering on his skin.

But right now, his blood is running ice cold as he listens to the calm dead voice on the phone.

GORDON: If there's no survivors how do they know what happened?

Gordon, the amiable dunce, doesn't get it.

CHARLEY: Because sometimes there's a survivor to tell the tale, a final girl. I know the case. Up southwest, by Blue Mountain, back in the seventies.

Charley doesn't just know the case. He was part of it, back in the day, under a younger identity. The Blue Mountain case had made waves, there'd been a regional law enforcement task force put together to investigate. He'd been on the team, going over the kills, examining the site.

He and some other investigators had traveled up to Blue Mountain to poke around. At one point, alone, he'd stopped to prowl through an abandoned village, no more than a cluster of rotting tar-paper shacks falling in on themselves, everything overgrown with weeds and tall grass. And a scarecrow on a cross pole, all rags and burlap and straw, mounted there for no good reason.

That's when he'd felt it, an awareness of something, a presence, or perhaps an absence like a black hole, a dark emptiness that nevertheless had its own sucking gravity. There had been something somewhere in that empty village, it had been slumbering, dormant, whatever it was had been aware of him. Barely aware, like a sleeper staring blearily through half closed eyes.

But for the first and only time in his life, he had been afraid.

He'd gotten back in his vehicle and driven away, unwilling to look back, or even think about it. Some things out there could hear you, if you thought about them.

He made the mistake of confessing that to Abe, the old man's never quite let it go. It comes up at odd moments, usually gently. But Abe wasn't there, he didn't feel what Charley felt.

He'd gotten out of there. He put his time in on the task force sorting through paperwork that came to nothing. He hadn't been a bit surprised when the killings started up again.

To his dying day, he'll swear that scarecrow was watching him.

LIEUTENANT: Yes. Blue Mountain. The Scarecrow, McKay. But that's not the only one. It started in the seventies, in Texas, at a cabin in the Ozarks, an abandoned theme park outside Atlantic City, a summer camp in the woods, a retreat... more and more places. Men in Masks appearing, killing, and then vanishing until it was time to kill again. More and more of them.

His heart was pounding. The phone felt clumsy in his grip. Charley realized that his hands had unconsciously morphed into claws, he was standing inches taller, his shirt on the verge of splitting up the back as his dorsal spines began to protrude. With an effort of will, he forced himself back into human shape. He swallowed saliva, making sure that if he needed to speak his throat was wet enough to make human sounds.

LIEUTENANT: Eventually, someone noticed. Started putting the pieces together, and at first they tried to stop it. But how do you stop smoke? It was different places, different men, different masks. No way to predict it. And even if you caught one, it didn't stop, the minute you turned your back… they'd be gone.

Bad timing, Charley thought. He was dealing with real smoke, and real fire, not this weird voodoo shit. Fuck Gordon for calling instead of just putting the girl on ice until things got sorted out.

LIEUTENANT: So they did something else. They recruited them, brought them together, all those Men in Masks. They use them to… solve problems. They come and they kill, they can't be killed, they can't be stopped or reasoned with. You can't beat them or negotiate with them. They're coming. I was sent to scout, just in case.

Charley's head is spinning with the sheer insanity of what she is saying. Decades later that near encounter with whatever had been up in Blue Mountain continued to give him nightmares. He couldn't imagine gathering a multitude of those things together, the awful consequences of such a concentration of dark madness.

How could anyone, how could humans, be so foolish as to bring those things together? The awful, abyssal implications were terrifying. His flesh writhed under his skin, instinctively trying to reshape itself for threat.

Firefighters were running past him. He struggled to grin and wave encouragingly at them, offering a thumbs up. It was difficult to concentrate, the enormity of what she was saying overwhelmed him.

GORDON: Sounds like bullshit to me.

LIEUTENANT: You're all going to die.

There's something disturbing in the flat, matter of fact way she says it. In the complete lack of affect, as if she was just commenting on the weather, or asking what was on television.

GORDON: You too sweetheart.

LIEUTENANT: There's worse things than dying. There are worse things than you. And they're coming.

Charley's head is spinning. He forces himself to concentrate. Whatever was out there, however bad it was, it wasn't here yet. Set priorities. He had a fire to fight. When that was done, they'd figure out how to deal with this.

PHONE: Gordon, we're busy here. Just kill her.

* * *

NINE HOURS BEFORE ZERO

ABE: Would you look at that?

Three figures are walking towards them, past a fire truck. One is a huge, morbidly obese man, his flesh thick with hair and corruption, wearing what appears to be a decomposing pig's head. The other is a figure clad in impossibly heavy clothing, wearing a welder's mask, and carrying a heavy tank on his back, leading to a hose and lever and awkwardly welded pipe in his hands. Fire drips liquidly from the tip of the metal pipe.

ABE: Is that motherfucker carrying a flame thrower?

Abe's voice is full of disbelief. Who carries a flame thrower around in the middle of a forest fire? Besides, the device is like no conventional flamethrower he's ever seen, it looks amateur and cobbled together.

But that's a distraction. There's a third one that leaves them cold despite the heat.

This one is tall, cadaverously tall, over seven feet, but somehow impossibly thin, as if under its swirling black robes it was nothing but sticks, or perhaps bones. It wears a cattle skull.

There's something else though. They feel... wrong. Their unnaturalness radiates off them in waves, like they're broadcasting emptiness, spreading vacuum. There's a negative energy to them that sets his hackles rising. It makes his flesh want to shift on its own volition.

The whole crew sees them now, everyone stepping back as if awestruck.

ABE: Dickie? Paulette? If you please, children. In your own time, but do it now.

Dickie and Paulette have the rifles. People aren't worried about being in the woods. Even a grizzly's no match for one of the People, and it's been a long time since a grizzly was foolish enough to come to these parts.

But in a forest fire, everything's on the run, maddened with flames, some of them already horribly burned and injured. So they'd brought a couple of rifles so as to make sure any troublesome or suffering creatures were humanely dealt with.

The two sprint for their packs. Paulette, she's a twin, big as her brother, and they're both huge, reaches her's first, swings around smoothly with the unnatural speed and accuracy of their kind, and puts three shots, one after the other, into the heads of the walkers.

As they stagger, Dickie puts three more shots into their chests. Paulette is already calmly reloading as they go down, the sound of the shots ringing in their sensitive ears, sending stabs of pain into the crew, but they barely notice.

Abe is thinking ahead: Approach them carefully, like he was in a horror movie, empty a few more magazines just to be sure, dismember the bodies. That would take precious time from firefighting, and likely a temporary measure, but one damned thing at a time.

Then it all goes wrong. Two of them go down, just as expected. Abe takes satisfaction from that, he remembers the transcript from the Blue Mountain survivor. Whatever they are, they could be hurt, they could be stopped.

One doesn't. The tall one in the ragged black robes and the cattle skull. It just stands there. Paulette puts two more bullets in that cattle skull, bone chips flying everywhere, but it doesn't react. Instead it seems to glance at its companions, one to the other, as if annoyed with their frivolity.

As if on cue, the obese figure wearing the pig's head sits up smoothly and climbs to its feet. The other one with the homemade flamethrower laboriously climbs up. Dickie puts two more shots in them, but it does no good.

Abe feels himself growing taller, heavier, his jaw dislocating and needle teeth protruding, his hands lengthening as they reshape into scimitar claws. He knows, without looking, that the other men are changing as well, some of them rip their clothes in their haste.

Carefully Dickie holsters his gun, he's not concerned that it hasn't had much effect. Bullets don't mean shit to the People either, or a lot of special folk. But he replaces it carefully, because it's an expensive weapon, and needs care, and he'll be damned if he lets it fall in the dirt. Paulette is doing the same.

Abe points a long claw.

ABE: Someone go and kill those fuckers.

Almost as one, with a pack-like coordination that does Abe proud. The People still have the old hunter's blood in them after all - the crew shifts, their forms changing, growing more savage and ferocious, they weave in and out of each other's path, choosing their targets, coordinating their attacks with an intuition bordering on psychic.

Beside him, Paulette launches into a loping run, heading for the obese man wearing the pig's head. Charley can't figure how the man can see out of that thing, and the smell of its decomposing flesh must be something else. But the man heavy as he is, is light on his feet and meet's Paulette's charge head on.

Even for the People, Paulette's full shifted form is awesome to behold. But the pig-man stops her dead, and for a moment, they grapple. Abe is diving in to help her, ready to tear the pig-man's head off from behind.

That's when the flame thrower catches him, and after that, there's nothing but white hot agony, until whatever light that is his identity finally goes out.

* * *

SEVEN HOURS BEFORE ZERO

Lucky's been working the Stockyards all his life. His name is Simon, but he prefers Lucky. His family grew up next to Jake, but they weren't as well off. His Dad never had the patience for cattle, so they made their living with odd jobs.

He remembers when he and Jake were young, he'd make extra money helping out on Jake's farm. Then the two youths would take their money and strut about down in the town, ordering milkshakes at the diner, with a little helping of blood to smooth it out. Then they'd go down to the pharmacy and buy girly magazines, especially Playboy, and look at the pictures, and discuss the articles like real urbanites.

They watched the moon landing together, at Sheriff Charley's house - that was when television was a big deal, the Sheriff had the best television in town, so a bunch of the town's youth crowded in with their little American flags to watch.

Afterwards, he and Jake were in charge of the celebratory fireworks. They were only stupid kids, of course, so they blew half their fingers off - luckily they grow back. Everyone said the fireworks were the best ever though, so it was worth it.

Lucky eventually got a job with the Stock, it was a big deal for his family. He and Jake grew distant. Jake got the reputation of being a bit funny in the head. Lucky couldn't blame him, if he had to work with cows all day, he'd go mental himself. But he always felt close to Jake, he made a point of visiting Jake at all the holidays, staying until the cow stink got too much.

Lucky's not surprised that Jake finally lost it and slaughtered all the cows. He's only surprised that it took so long. He's been worrying over his friend since he heard. The minute he's off shift, he's going to go looking for Jake.

But it's been a strange night. The Stock are restless, skittish. Prone to screaming fits and flinging poop. They're riled up, not sleeping proper.

Some of the males have been attacking females, he's had to go into the pens to separate them, and take a couple of the breeders to the Vet station. A pregnant mare looks like she might miscarry. Simon's angry about that, you're not supposed to get attached, but everyone who works with Stock, they get to have their favorites. They get to know the good ones and the troublemakers. The mare should never have been in that pen, if she miscarries, Simon's going to do some gelding, and do it the old fashioned way.

Then there were the incursions. He was on the crew that took down the first one. Full of piss and vinegar that free-range, decided to make a fight of it. Bad choice. Lucky got stitched up in the gut, Royal got it in the face. They're going to get all kinds of shit for killing the free-range. Particularly since that suck-up, Gordon, caught up to the second incursion, brought her in nice and easy, like she was Stock herself.

But something's wrong. It's night shift, so there's not many on duty. Chigger took off early, and they were short-handed to start with. Simon's restless, so he prowls the pens, doing his best to move quietly, he doesn't need more caterwauling than they're already doing.

His nostrils flair, he catches a whiff of smoke. Fire down here? Impossible. Maybe the air intakes are sucking up soot from the forest fires down south. That could be what's riling up the Stock, humans are more sensitive than you think. Some scoff, old wives tale, but Lucky's seen some things, there's more to Stock than you'd want to admit.

He makes a note to check the scrubbers, or at least to get the next shift to check them. Running the Stockyard's a lot more complicated than cows. Sad to admit it, but much as Jake wanted it, he just wasn't good enough for the Stock farm. No patience.

Suddenly, all the Stock are screaming. It happens, one starts, it sets off the others and spreads until they're all doing it, all of them screaming for no reason. No one is quite sure why. Generally, it eventually settles down. But it's a pain in the ass.

But this is different. Buried in the cacophony of screaming are the shrill notes of genuine terror and pain. There's a stink of fear. You get that sometimes, one of the males turns savage. A few years back, a small group of males backed up, went feral, started attacking everyone in the pen. They'd had to put them all down, euthanize some of the victims.

Lucky was around for that, he remembers what it was like. This is worse. His legs lengthen, his tarsals stretch as he begins to lope on the balls of his feet. It's bad policy to shape shift around Stock, it upsets them. But H Block is way over on south side and he needs to get there fast.

Then two things happen. The first is that he's astonished to see Stock running free, a lot of them. They're not even paying attention, just running in panic. He almost stops to corral them, but clearly, it's part of whatever's going on in H Block, and that's the priority.

The other thing is that there's a lot of smoke, way more than can be accounted. There's a fire inside the Stock pens, which is plainly impossible. Normally, that would be cause for panic. But now he's smelling blood. A lot of it. Some of the fleeing Stock running past are bloody, some wounded.

Lucky puts on a burst of speed, and then stops. H Block is a charnel house. The pens are torn wide open, dead and mutilated Stock are everywhere, he's stepping through pools of blood, picking his way across viscera. This isn't a slaughterhouse, this is more like an explosion. Some of the bodies have been literally torn to pieces.

Leaning up against one of the cages is a scarecrow. Lucky almost mistakes it for Stock, but Stock goes naked. Then he takes it for an intruder for a split second, but his senses tell him it's just rags and burlap and straw, there's nothing alive in it. He dismisses it, with the question – Who would bring a scarecrow down here? And why? A pointless distraction?

As the thoughts flicker through his mind, it turns its head to look at him. Suddenly, he feels something, an empty, hollow attention.

Out of the pen steps a man, except that it's not a man. It's a tall cadaverous figure in tight fitting leather and latex, his body covered in straps, wearing a gas mask. The few spots of exposed flesh are leprous, with visibly weeping sores and ulcers. One arm is wrapped in a heavy gauntlet of thick cow hide, covered in studs and spikes, with lengths of long razored chains depending from each finger.

It glances at Lucky once, as if dismissing him as unimportant. Instead, it drags one of the Stock, a large muscular male, by the hair, pulling him without effort. Almost tenderly, it presses its gauntleted hand against his chest, the lengths of razored chain draping almost tenderly over the shivering human.

Then it yanks, and instantly, the cowering man explodes, dismembered in a fountain of blood and viscera. Limbs fall away, intestines and organs leap into the air. The head flies off and rolls towards Lucky. He sees it blinking, the eyes momentarily focusing on him.

The thing beckons with its free hand. Lucky steps back, swearing, the curses lost and garbled as his body shifts involuntarily. It waits, shrugs, and then selects another victim among the cowering survivors.

Beyond it, Lucky notes thick black smoke pouring out of the air intake. He coughs. How is that even possible? He wonders. He coughs again. The smoke smells fresh, with a taint of burning meat in it. Somehow there's a fire at the filtration systems.

Alarm klaxons sound over his head, his radio buzzes in emergency; confused voices sounding over it. Where the hell is Gordon? He wonders. Gordon should be handling all of this. He reaches out, but he can't feel him through the static of human lives and human terror.

The thing ignores the sound, another victim ruptures, and Lucky is splattered with blood even as he backs away. Where is everyone? He thinks desperately. No way is he taking on whatever these things are by himself. Get the others, take them down together. But there's a fire, where is it? He feels overwhelmed. The fire, that's more important, if it's not stopped, if they don't shut off the intake, the whole herd will be lost. Whatever these things are, it'll keep. He backs away, turning to run.

And that's when the razored chains, impossibly long, wrap around his neck, yanking him backwards. As he lands heavily, claws pulling at the chains, he looks up at the gas mask, and for a minute, he glimpses what's behind the glass eyeholes of the mask.

Lucky screams.

* * *

FOUR HOURS BEFORE ZERO

The Lieutenant is driving blind. Smoke is everywhere, the truck cabin reeks of it. She has her headlights on, although visibility is still good. She keeps an eye on the horizons, trying to gauge how close the billowing clouds of black smoke are, watching for the telltale illumination from below, embers floating in the air.

The fires have complicated her escape. She has no intention of going back the way she came, anything that takes her towards the Stockyards. She's well aware of what's waiting for her.

As she drives back, she takes the first dirt road off the main highway that she comes across.

She curses. The briefing report carried a map of all the logging roads and trails in Windy Valley. She'd done no more than glance at it indifferently, trusting to GPS. She regrets that now. She can only trust that the pickup truck is good for the roads as she bounces around.

Time and again, she finds herself on a road leading into the encroaching fire, forcing her to reverse course, turn around and look for a new way out.

She climbs higher, up the hills. There's more bare rock here, she drives past gray outcrops of naked stone. The trees are smaller, more scattered, struggling to extract sustenance from the thin soil and naked rock. If she can't fully escape the fire, maybe she can find someplace where it doesn't have so much fuel to burn and work her way past it.

The fire is far behind. As the truck climbs again, she can see it in her rear-view, in the valley below. A cloud of smoke, desultory individual blazes in patches, biding their time until the wall of flame finally reaches them. She turns a corner through the brush, and is astounded to find herself facing a paved road and a sign.

"LOOKOUT POINT TOURIST CENTER" accompanied by an arrow pointing the way. A smaller sign beneath reads "Weddings, Traditional Ceremonies, Picnics, Family Occasions."

The Lieutenant stares for a moment, chewing her lip. Along the paved road, there are a series of wooden telephone poles, a single power-line. Presumably carrying electricity to the Tourist Center?

The Lieutenant chews her lip. Sooner or later the fires are going to catch up, she needs a way out. Perhaps they'll have maps of the trails, or a phone.

The flight helmet is on the seat beside her. She can feel it beckoning, offering safety and clarity.

She steps on the gas, following the direction of the sign.

The Tourist Center, when she finally comes to it, turns out to be a house-sized wood frame building, set into the side of the hill. There's a cheerful sign, a roughly trimmed lawn and shrubs, picnic tables and parking lot, with trails extending off in all directions. She parks and steps out.

There's a good view of the valley spread out below her, the farms below, looking manicured, and even the town, a cluster of houses and modest commercial buildings.

There's no one around.

The Lieutenant slips the tire iron through a belt loop in her jeans and approaches the Tourist building. She hesitates at the huge double doors, easily eight feet in height.

Then she sighs and pushes in.

Whatever she expected, she finds herself disappointed. It's like every other Tourist Center she's seen in her life. The glass display cases, the shelves of brochures, a counter, a small seating area next to a collection of vending machines.

There's a phone. Carefully, she picks it up and listens.

From behind the counter, a young girl steps out from behind some doors. She smiles, displaying perfect white teeth. She has long blond hair, and a black 'tourist staff' vest over a red angora sweater with black jeans and high top runners. She wears a badge that says "Hi, I'm Amy."

AMY: I'm sorry, the phone is only for official use.

She pauses, smiling brightly.

AMY: Are you here to see Grandma?

* * *

THREE HOURS BEFORE ZERO

It looks like a teenage girl. The Lieutenant isn't fooled, she clutches the pry bar tightly, and wishes for her pistol.

The girl-thing smiles brightly.

AMY: Hi, I'm Amy! Are you here to see Grandmother? Of course you are.

Amy pauses.

AMY: But not right now though. She's watching Wheel of Fortune, it's one of her favorites. She likes the original guy.

Amy makes a face.

AMY: Not so much the new one.

The Lieutenant simply stares at her, waiting for something. For the girl to change into a monster. But she doesn't. She simply stares.

AMY: Are you hungry? Can I get you something to drink? Some water? While you wait? Or if you'd like, we could peek in on Grandmother, I'm sure she wouldn't mind, as long as we don't distract her.

The Lieutenant swallows.

LIEUTENANT: Grandmother? Who? Who is Grandmother?

Amy smiles brightly.

AMY: Grandmother... is... Grandmother. It's hard to explain, maybe I should show you.

She glances down at the metal pry bar.

AMY: Oh you won't need that!

LIEUTENANT: I think I'll keep it. It makes me feel warm and cozy, you know. Like a teddy bear.

Amy shrugs.

LIEUTENANT: Lead the way.

Amy turns and beckons, leading down a large cavernous tunnel. The Lieutenant notes that work has been done, much of the tunnel is natural stone, but parts of it have been reinforced. A series of lights are strung along the roof of the tunnel providing illumination.

A series of plywood boards form a designated walkway, and the lieutenant notices the tracks of wheels worn into the wood. There's a handrail bolted into the wall of the cavern. Along the floor on the opposite corner, cables are running down into the descent.

Amy notices her looking at them.

AMY: We run electricity down there, and cable television of course, and fresh water. We've got wells and a generator, just in case, but that's for emergencies.

At a large steel door, the Lieutenant stops.

LIEUTENANT: What's behind that door?

For the first time, Amy's friendly smile loses some of its wattage.

AMY: Oh you don't want to see that, trust me. Come on, Grandma's just down this way.

The Lieutenant hesitates. Her fingers tighten on the tire iron. In her mind's eye, she knows what's behind the steel door. Rows and rows of refrigerated human corpses, dressed, butchered, hanging on hooks. That or something worse.

Amy waves.

AMY: Come on.

LIEUTENANT: I know you're not human.

Amy simply rolls her eyes.

LIEUTENANT: Are you going to change?

AMY: Are you kidding? Why would I want to stretch out my favorite top? Look, do you want to see Grandma or not? If you don't, we can go back up front and wait. I can fix you something to eat. It's really not going to make a difference.

The Lieutenant mulls it over.

LIEUTENANT: I think I'd like to see the old girl.

Amy's smile is bright.

* * *

THREE HOURS BEFORE ZERO

CHARLEY: What the living hell?

His blood runs cold, and he stares in disbelief as one of his firemen, Pauly, plays with a little man, the two of them dancing around.

The little man wears a dapper white suit with wide lapels and big gold buttons, like some child's idea of a snappy dresser. He can't be more than five feet tall. He wears a clumsily painted ceramic devil's mask, the sort of thing you'd find in an elementary school craft's class, and he wields a short hooked knife in one gloved hand.

It would be comical, Pauly, even unshifted, is huge, just like his sister, and quick. No way but that Pauly should take the little man in a flash.

But Charley can feel something radiating off the little devil man. It's not exactly what he felt that time out in the Blue Mountains, it's not the same creature. It's different, mischievous, energetic. What he felt then was sullen and brooding. But this, whatever it is, is close, the same thing, just dressed up different.

Charley looks around. The other men and women are staring transfixed. They're almost hypnotized, their eyes glassy, jaws slack. He wonders if they feel the black radiation? The sucking void that comes off the little devil man? Or is there some kind of spell?

Pauly grunts with frustration, swinging wildly. The little devil man skips out of the way. Pauly grows taller, his skull lengthens and jaw protrudes, shark teeth emerging. The loose shirt is stretching at its seams, and Pauly's forearms grow as his claws lengthen. He swings again, and the little devil man just bows out of the way, the arms swinging wide for balance, and just coincidentally, the knife slashes across Pauly's belly.

Pauly bellows, as if it's hurting far worse than it should. Pauly is the same age as Charley. Back in the thirties, growing up, they used to play that children's game where they'd throw hatchets at each other. He remembers laughing hysterically with Pauly when a lucky throw got him right in the center of the forehead so his eyes crossed. Now, it looks like he's really hurting.

CHARLEY: Pauly, stop fucking around and kill that thing!

Charley glances around and snarls at the other men. His anger causes them to shift uncomfortably, eroding whatever spell is under way. He yells.

CHARLEY: And the rest of you assholes, what are you doing, standing there with your dicks in your hands?

The sound distracts the dancing devil figure, Pauly smashes him into the ground with a blow that makes his teeth ache.

But somehow, the devil-masked man is up again, climbing easily up Pauly with a smooth nonchalance that makes it look like it's simply walking up stairs. As it reaches Pauly's head, its hooked knife swirls in a twirling motion like a magician's flourish, or like a man peeling an apple in one long slice.

There's a gurgling sound, Charley has the sense that Pauly tried to scream. Pauly is dropping, and with a casual gesture, the devil-man unwinds Pauly's face from around his head in a long ribbon. Charley hears someone screaming and hopes it's not him.

Pauly is falling bonelessly now, Charley knows he's dead. The dapper devil steps nimbly onto the ground. The top of Pauly's white skull pops off and his brain falls out. The dapper devil catches it in one gloved hand, but it slips, and for a moment, it bounces from hand to hand until it plops on the grass.

The dapper devil shrugs and puts its palms out, as if to say 'oh well,' and then morphs the gesture to 'Jazz Hands.' It straightens up and bows with an elaborate flourish.

Charley stares, frozen, not quite believing what he's just seen. The rest of the crew are quiet, similarly aghast. Someone vomits. Charley can feel, beneath the false levity, a sense of absolute danger. There's something obscene about it, something unnatural and transgressive. Charley tamps down the worms of fear and calls up rage and hatred at this awful thing that has so callously mutilated his friend. There was no need for it, no need to make a show. He whispers:

CHARLEY: Shotgun.

The stance of the dapper devil shifts. Charley feels a row of spines come out, pushing against the back of his shirt. His hands lengthen, his teeth start to protrude, he's inches taller already. The dapper devil extends a hand, palm up, the fingers flex. 'Try me.'

Charley draws and puts a bullet right in the forehead of the devil mask. Shocked, the thing staggers back. Charley puts two more bullets in the mask. The thing falls, and Charley walks up to it with a measured stride, calmly firing into the body. Nine, ten, eleven... then the clip is emptied. With smooth movements, practiced for years in front of a mirror, Charley drops the empty clip, slides a new one into place and keeps on firing all without breaking stride.

Then he's practically standing over the thing, carefully putting shots in the knees, the elbows, wrists, and ankles. He drops and replaces another clip, and walks bullets up and down through the torso, stitching the length of the spinal column, targeting heart, kidney, throat.

Empty again, he only carries two spare clips. Who could imagine needing more?

He calls out again.

CHARLEY: Shotgun goddamnit!

And suddenly one is in his hands. He empties it into the dapper devil's face, till the mask is just fragments of cheap ceramic in red pulp, the body literally in pieces.

CHARLEY: And fuck you.

Charley spits on it.

VOICE: What the living fuck was that?

Charley turns, identifying the voice. Nathan, one of the young ones. Some punk kid who'd rather play video games in the basement than get a real job. He looks around, the other members of the crew are just as shell shocked. Then he looks around again, clear everywhere, there's no way to get close without being seen. His anger, once banked, won't rest.

CHARLEY: Can anyone tell me how that little fucker walked right up in the middle of us and carved up Pauly... and no one saw him coming? No one noticed? What the fuck is wrong with you People?

They mumble and look ashamed. But Charley is starting to think. Why didn't he notice the bastard? Where had it come from? We're in the middle of the woods.

CHARLEY: You fucking idiots.

But that's only his anger, slowly blowing itself out. What had the girl said? 'You don't see them coming. You only notice when they're already there. When they want you to see.'

That deserted village in Blue Mountain reappears in his mind, so vivid he's almost there. Standing among decaying, falling wooden shacks, grass up to his knees, and this awful sense of a presence, some dark negative energy, a sucking vacuum. The Scarecrow, not alive, not moving, the sense that it was dormant, but somehow still aware, still looking at him.

That's when his phone goes off. He jumps.

* * *

THREE HOURS BEFORE ZERO

The smell hits first, the stench of urine and excrement, of blood and decomposing flesh, and something more, something live and breathing. The Lieutenant hears a giggle, and then a peel of incomprehensible syllables.

Then they turn a corner, and Grandmother comes into view. She's ancient, impossibly ancient, you can tell by her loose papery skin, the spots and wrinkles, the sagging dugs of breasts, and the way the ribs and hip bones stand out. She wears an immense stained diaper. Grandmother is sitting crouched in the midst of a nest of cushions and mattresses, mixed with stained ragged blankets. Even sitting, she's taller than an ordinary man, and despite her skeletal thinness, she's massive. The Lieutenant estimates that the creature would stand at least fifteen feet tall, upright.

Even as gigantic as she is, the proportions are inhuman. Grandmother's arms are long, long like an ape's. The hands are massive scoops with spidery clawed fingers. Her face has only a trace of humanity, more creature than person, with a protruding muzzle filled with long needle teeth, and flattened nose like a gorilla.

Grandmother's attention is focused on a sixty-five inch flat screen television. In a corner of the cavern, a dozen broken television sets are piled. On the television set, a rerun of The Price is Right is playing.

The creature glances at Amy and the Lieutenant with the barest interest. It mumbles another string of nonsense syllables, and then returns to her program. Without looking, she reaches into a fifty gallon drum and plucks a human leg, flicking it against her lips. A wet tongue more like a tentacle studded with white barbs flickers out, lashing away the flesh.

AMY (whispering): Okay, I think that's enough. She really doesn't like to be disturbed when her show is on. We'll come back later.

The Lieutenant can only stare. There's something deeply wrong with the creature. Not wrongness in the sense of an abomination of nature, but something different. It reeks of decrepitude and decay.

And it's senile. The Lieutenant felt that when it glanced at her, felt the weight of its attention, and the broken floating fragments of its mind, as it noticed her for a brief second, reading her, and then drifted, struggling to hold its attention on her, but failing.

The Lieutenant is certain that it had been able to focus on her for more than a second, it would have killed her instantly. But she felt the thought, the impulse slip away as it went back to the television.

Shaking, the Lieutenant allows Amy to lead her back up the tunnels. The girl chatters away.

AMY: She likes her television shows. She really loved Bob Barker. When he was on, sometimes her jaws would go all twitchy, like a cat looking at a bird through a window.

She leans forward, and whispers confidentially.

AMY: She would touch herself too. She really liked Bob Barker!

The Lieutenant shies away from the implications of that.

LIEUTENANT: She was speaking to us. What did she say?

AMY: Oh no one knows. Grandmother's so old, that the last People who understood her language probably died thousands of years ago.

Amy has the enthusiasm of a museum tour guide.

AMY: You know, we record what Grandmother says. We transcribe it. We've taken it to ethnologists and linguists, private commissions, very hush hush. Sometimes they compare it to some tribe living in Tierra del Fuego, or this lost language family in Laos, or this village in Ethiopia where only three old folk are left who speak a language. But nothing really matches. They say it's really old, like practically from before humans even. Isn't that amazing?

The Lieutenant is barely listening.

AMY: I feel so sorry for Grandmother. Imagine how old she must be. The last of her kind by thousands, maybe tens of thousands of years. Just living here, all this time, so lonely. We all love her so much.

It's old. The Lieutenant can tell. It's incredibly old, perhaps older than the human race, perhaps older than human ancestors. She can imagine it walking the earth when hominids were merely upright apes. It's ancient beyond all reckoning, the last of its kind. Its body merely remnants of stringy muscle and leathery flesh, maintained through history only by luck, and by the love and care of endless generations of the People.

They pass by the steel door again. Amy pays no attention to it.

AMY: Grandmother's been here a long time in this cave. We found midden pits, and we've dug bears, elk, deer, saber tooth tigers, even mastodons, all kinds of bones.

She almost feels sorry for it, lost in time, tens of thousands of years past its era, all alone and lonely, last of its kind, slowly disintegrating, decaying fragments of identity, disconnected and floating in that hollowed shell of a body.

AMY: But once humans came here, that's all she would ever eat, no other kinds of bones. She must have been so happy.

Somehow, some quirk of luck and history preserved it.

AMY: We think that's where we came from, she didn't exactly eat every human she caught, not right away.

For a moment, the Lieutenant has an image, that gigantic inhuman horror, withered, skeletal anthropoidal abomination, jamming a terrified warrior between her hips in a crude approximation of coitus. In the Lieutenant's mind's eye, climax is accompanied by biting off the warrior's head, just like a praying mantis. And then, unwillingly, followed by the image of Grandmother stroking a now swollen belly.

Amy's voice takes on a religious pitch, as if she is reciting a sermon she had heard and believed deeply in. The Lieutenant can almost feel the radiant glow.

AMY: We all come from Grandmother. The blood has run thin, but we're hers, and she's ours, and we love her. Now we take care of her.

Amy's back is to the Lieutenant, but she imagines that if she could see the girl's face, it would be beatific.

Instead, the Lieutenant rams the sharp end of her tire iron into the back of the girl's skull with all her might. The blow goes lower than intended, just below the skull. The Lieutenant feels the crunch of bone and cartilage as the iron sheers through vertebra. Amy pitches face forward, like a puppet with all her strings cut, falling on her face, not even raising her hands to guard herself. The Lieutenant puts her weight onto the girl, bearing her down. She keeps pushing the crowbar through her neck until it embeds in the padded flooring of the tunnel.

AMY: Oh! I fell down!"

There's no fear in the girl's voice, only surprise. The Lieutenant steps away, watching her carefully. She does not move.

AMY (nervously): I can't feel my arms or legs. I can't feel anything. This is strange. I think something might be wrong.

Despite herself, the Lieutenant suddenly regrets her action. She knows what the girl really is. She knows it's necessary. But that doesn't help when the monster keeps looking and acting like a normal teenage girl. Finally, she speaks.

LIEUTENANT: I'll go get help.

AMY: Oh. Good, I'll wait here.

For the first time, a note of what might be fear creeps into the girl's voice.

AMY: Please hurry.

The Lieutenant turns back the way they came, tracing the winding tunnel through the cavern.

* * *

TWO AND A HALF HOURS BEFORE ZERO

Charley jumps and curses. Somehow, that breaks the spell. There's a round of nervous laughter. He pulls the phone.

CHARLEY: Sheriff here!

It's Tammy-Todd, Gordon's right hand. She's young, practically a kid, barely in her sixties. But she's got a fell hand with the Stock, they'll eat right out of her hand. She makes a point of helping them with the birthings, when it's time for a slaughter she's got a knack for leading them so they barely make a fuss. He's watched her walk into a pen and calm the lot of them down with just a word. Everyone says Tammy-Todd is something special, one of the ones to watch in the upcoming generation.

She sounds scared.

TAMMY-TODD: Sheriff, we got big problems here, we need help.

Charley's a little irritated. He's still rattled from the dapper devil, he's got a fire to fight or they're going to lose the whole town. The last thing he needs is whining about animal husbandry. The fucking Stock will have to wait their turn, he thinks.

CHARLEY: Tammy-Todd, we're a bit busy right now. Call Gordon, have him come in, doesn't matter if he's off shift, this is his job.

Gordon was on the phone with the woman, he remembers.

CHARLEY: Gordon should be there. Where the fuck is he?

TAMMY-TODD: I DON'T KNOW!

The panic in her voice shuts him up.

TAMMY-TODD: We can't find Gordon. Listen, there's been a fire, fires.

That makes no sense, Charley thinks. None of the blazes are anywhere near. Something very bad is happening.

TAMMY-TODD: It looks like they've been set, and they're pumping smoke into the ventilation, into the pens. The air-exchangers are jammed, we can't stop it.

Charley's blood runs cold. There's stories from way back, back before the People got civilized, of natives sealing the People up in their dens, pumping smoke in, until entire families choked to death. It's like it's happening again. Fuck, they could lose the whole herd!

CHARLEY: Cripes! Tammy-Todd, forget Gordon. What you got to do is evacuate the pens, get as many of them out as you can. Don't even bother to manage them, get them out. Let them run around the valley, who gives a shit. Most will come back when they miss a feeding time, and we can run down the rest.

TAMMY-TODD: We're trying. But there's something else. There's something here with us...

The pause is so natural, Charley waits a beat for her to finish the sentence. But there isn't anything, just silence. Charley glances at his phone screen, seconds tick off, the line is still open. The call's not dropped.

He swallows.

CHARLEY: Tammy?

Try again.

CHARLEY: Tammy-Todd? Are you there girl?

Nothing.

Charley listens instead. Not a sound from the phone, and yet, and yet, he has the distinct sense that there's something on the other end of the line, listening. There's no breathing, no heartbeat, no rustle of fabric, or motion. His senses are straining, but there's nothing coming through the phone, except a sense of presence, an awareness, inhuman and malevolent.

The line goes dead. Not call dropped. Hung up from the other end. Something that stayed on the open line just long enough for Charley to realize that there was something there.

CHARLEY: Fuck.

Someone, Davey, pipes up.

DAVEY: Was that Tammy-Todd? Something going on at the Stockyards.

This is happening too fast, Charley thinks. Way too fast. He has the sense of a boulder rolling down the hill toward them, initially far and distant, a slow nothing. A rig going off the road, spilling its contents, a couple of suspicious tourists, Jake going missing and his cows slaughtered. But now it's closing in and picking up speed, and it's monstrous and unstoppable.

NATHAN: Should we send someone to the Stockyard, to check it out?

Charley knows the little shit's motivation, he just wants to get out of firefighting. He's useless here, he'd be useless at the Stockyard.

DAVEY: We got a fire to fight.

There's more conversation, but Charley's not listening. He's going through his phone, tapping every number he's got for the Stockyards and even the individual crew. No one is picking up. Which means it's bad, or....

They're all dead, he thinks suddenly. They're all dead at the Stockyard, Stock, maybe six hundred head dead, the whole night shift crew, maybe the day crew too. All gone. Suddenly, he's absolutely certain of it, so certain his blood is freezing.

Then he rejects it. The Stockyards have been the backbone of the community for well over a century. Even when the fire of Fifty-four came through and destroyed the town, they'd saved the Stockyard.

That big flu, back in the nineteen-twenties, half the Stock died, the whole town had pulled together for that one, everyone doing their share, watching over the Stock, cleaning them by hand when they shit themselves, keeping their fevers down, spoon feeding them by hand when they were too weak to even swallow. They'd saved the herd.

It's not too late, Charley thought, they'd save them. Save some at least. The whole herd couldn't be gone.

CHARLEY: Fuck the fire. Dave, you and Nathan get to the Stockyard, see what's up. The minute you see or hear anything, you report in. I want to know what's going on there.

He thinks momentarily of the dancing devil.

CHARLEY: And don't fuck around. If you see anything strange, any kind of weird fucker, don't engage, just call me.

That gets Nathan's back up.

NATHAN: We can handle ourselves.

CHARLEY: Of course you can, but I don't give a shit. Our needing to know what's going on is more important than you playing footsie. This isn't one of your video games, boy. Can you take an order?

That gets the message through

CHARLEY: You call into Abe's crew, tell them it's off. We're changing strategy. And someone grab Pauly and that little devil shit, we're going to have...

His voice trails off. He's turned to Pauly's corpse. The little dancing devil's exploded corpse should be right next to it in pieces.

It's not there.

He asks the question, even though he knows the answer.

CHARLEY: Did someone move the little shit?

It was in pieces, he'd shot it to pieces. You couldn't even drag it, you'd need a wheelbarrow and a shovel. And it was gone. Just a line of bloody footprints into the grass. Like it just got up and walked...

CHARLEY: Wait... Did someone...? Was anyone looking...? Someone...?

His tongue flexes in his mouth, but the words won't come. Instead, he just grunts.

CHARLEY: Huh?

DALTON: Charley? Abe's crew isn't responding. I've been trying to raise them for the last hour.

Charley blinks.

CHARLEY: You're just telling me now?

DALTON: I figured they were just busy, following the plan. We had a plan, remember?

It feels like a million years ago. The plan: Go out with some crews, knock down a bunch of trees, bulldoze some firebreaks. Save the town. This morning he knew what he was doing. Now he's trapped in some strange netherworld of nameless terrors.

On impulse, he phones the tourist center. Who's on there? Amy.

No pick up. There's always pick up. There's always someone looking after Grandma. The thought something might have happened there sends genuine worms of terror surging through his guts. In panic, he dials Marci. He almost wants to weep with relief when she answers.

CHARLEY: Marci, I can't get through to Amy. You heard anything?

MARCI: I spoke to her a couple of hours ago, everything is fine. Grandma's taking to the new television, likes it just fine.

CHARLEY: Marci, I need you to think on this. You getting any strange reports? Anything odd, anything at all. Reports of funny looking strangers?

MARCI: Nothing Sheriff. I did see something peculiar when I stepped out for coffee. This man in a clown suit, just walking down the middle of the street like nothing. He waved at me.

Charley swallowed. Whatever they were, they were in the town. He looked around, the men, the firefighting crew were all gathered around him, looking serious. None of them had ever seen him this upset. He'd always been friendly, smiling, relaxed Charley, nothing ever bothered him. But they could smell the naked fear coming off him. Some of them were shifting uneasily, talons protruding and receding, jaws distending. A few of them were even tearing their clothes.

He spoke loudly so they could all hear.

CHARLEY: Marci, put the word out. We're evacuating, code zero, time to run.

MARCI: Jesus!

CHARLEY: Serious, Marci. Forget the town, forget the Stock, it's all gone. Code zero.

Some of the men swore. Code zero was as bad as it could get.

CHARLEY: Start the ball rolling. I need to go check on Grandma.

* * *

TWO HOURS BEFORE ZERO

AMY: Hello? Is anyone there?

She still can't move, and she's starting to be genuinely concerned. Amy has never known fear or vulnerability in her life. She doesn't recognize the sensations when she experiences them. But she's beginning to dislike these feelings.

Like all the People, Amy has always effortlessly recovered from any injury, her body rebuilds itself automatically. Except that she still can't feel her arms or legs, or in fact anything below her neck. There's an odor, acrid and smelling of ammonia, and she wonders if her body has pissed itself. She hopes not, that would be embarrassing.

There's something in her neck. She's worked that out. Her body has healed itself, the injury is, all things considered, trivial. But there's still something in her neck and that is blocking the signals preventing them from traveling down her spinal cord. She needs to get it out, and then she's quite certain she'll be fine.

Amy's not sure how it got there, she suspects that the nice lady had something to do with it. Perhaps she should have asked her to stop and examine Amy's neck instead of just going to get help. That might have been all she needed.

She'd remove the obstruction herself, except she can't move.

AMY: Hello? Anyone?

There are footsteps. Someone is coming. Despite not being able to feel her body, Amy feels excitement.

AMY: Hello?

CHARLEY: Amy? What are you doing laying there like a damn fool, girl?

The tone is brusque, but Amy can hear the genuine concern in Charley's voice. As long as she's known him, he's never been anything but good natured.

AMY: I fell down, Sheriff. I can't seem to move my arms or legs. Truth, I can't feel anything below the neck.

CHARLEY: Well of course not, girl. You got yourself a toothpick stuck in your neck. Hold on.

Amy feels a yank, her body rocks, and there's a metallic clang a few feet from her. Suddenly, she can feel again, she takes a deep breath as tissues knit together and sensation returns to fingers and toes. Unsteadily, she crawls to her hands and knees. By the wetness between her legs, she's definitely pissed herself, and her angora top is surely dirty.

She's thankful that Sheriff Charley is too much of a gentleman to notice.

CHARLEY: What happened?

Amy shakes her head.

AMY: I don't rightly know, Sheriff. A free-range came by, so I took her to see Grandma. But Gran was watching television and didn't want to be bothered. So I was going to take her back up and make her something to eat, a sandwich or something.

CHARLEY: And she got you with the toothpick.

Charley helps her up, his head swiveling around. She notices he's upset, but not at her. His nostrils flare, and as he holds her, she can feel the tension in his hands from his claws wanting to sprout.

AMY: I guess so. Sorry.

CHARLEY: This free-range? Is she still around?

Amy shakes her head.

AMY: I can't rightly say.

CHARLEY: Amy, it's bad. We're going to have to get Grandma. We got a fire washing over us, the whole valley is going up.

AMY: This place is fireproof.

CHARLEY: There's something else coming, and it's not good. We're going to evacuate everything. Going down south. Maybe South America. We set it up years ago, if we ever needed it.

Amy feels as if the ground is falling away under her. Windy Valley has been her whole life. She can't imagine anyplace else. Nowhere else would feel right. Even the thought of South America makes her skin crawl. Then she remembers...

AMY: What about the Stock?

Charley looks serious.

CHARLEY: The Stock is gone. We're going to have to start over.

Amy gasps.

The lights go off, and then return, red and blinking.

AMY: Oh darn, the television will have gone off.

CHARLEY: What was she watching?

AMY: The Price is Right, one of the old DVDs.

CHARLEY: With Bob Barker?

AMY: Yeah.

CHARLEY: That's bad, she loves her Bob Barker. She's going to be cranky.

AMY: And Sheriff, she was touching herself.

Charley groans and wipes his brow.

CHARLEY: Worse and worse.

* * *

TWO HOURS BEFORE ZERO

Grandma looks up and snarls, flat nose wrinkling and leathery lips peeling back from row after row of needle teeth. She utters a stream of guttural gibberish, pointing a long bony finger at the flat screen television.

With a furious gesture, she picks it up and hurls it the length of the cavern, where it smashes against the cave wall.

Sheriff Charley and Amy look at each.

CHARLEY: Yep, she's cranky. We need to get her out of here.

AMY: I think I can calm her down.

Amy steps forward, speaking soothingly. The words are almost baby talk, the voice is calm. Amy smiles approaching.

Grandmother huddles down, sitting cross legged, and chutters irritably. She glances at Amy as the girl approaches, and then deliberately looks away, peevishly. She utters a string of nonsense syllables.

Speaking softly, Amy approaches closer.

Lightning quick, Grandma lashes out with an unnaturally long arm, wrapping bony claws around the girl. Before Amy can react, Grandma pulls the girl to her and bites her head off. Amy's skull crunches between Grandma's jaws, her tongue lashing away the flesh as she chews and swallows.

Methodically, Grandma pulls Amy's thrashing limbs off one at a time and pops them in her mouth, rolling them around with her tongue and spitting out the bones. Delicately holding the girl's torso in her paws, she dips her head, extending her tongue into the hole in Amy's neck, and rasping out the internal organs.

Charley is absolutely still as he watches Grandma devour the girl. He waits patiently.

Eventually, Grandma settles down. Her irritated chutters die away, returning to her polysyllabic gibberish. The peevish expression on the monstrous face relaxes, becomes thoughtful. She holds the wrecked body of Amy like a doll. The long rasping tongue moves slowly, rasping away at Amy's innards.

She seems to notice Charley. She extends her arm, holding Amy's dismembered torso out to him, an offering. Charley shakes his head politely.

CHARLEY: I appreciate the kindness, Grandma. But we don't have time for that.

Charley steps forward, looking earnest, carefully maintaining human form. No need to startle the poor old thing. She coos at him. Despite human form, she knows he's one of hers.

CHARLEY: Grandma, I know you can't understand what I'm saying. But maybe you can feel it. I love you. We all love you, and we want to protect you. Something bad is coming, and we need to move you to a safer place.

Grandma stares down at the little man below her. She coos uncertainly. Charley extends his hand out. He shows no fear beyond just the slightest bead of sweat on his forehead.

CHARLEY: You have to come with me, Grandma. Please.

She watches him, eyes thoughtful.

CHARLEY: We'll get you Bob Barker.

Gently, Grandma reaches out with her long arm, laying the tip of a three foot long scimitar claw in Charley's palm. He wraps his hand around it.

Gently, she permits him to lead her away.

* * *

ZERO HOUR

The trail maps the Lieutenant took from the tourist center were worse than useless. The smoke thick now, hanging like a pall over everything. She's gone up and down dirt roads that were barely wide paths, retracing her steps again and again. Twice she got stuck, feeling mounting terror as she had to keep shifting gears before she worked her way free. Each time she gets stuck, there's a better and better chance of dying out here. Glowing embers are floating everywhere.

She stops to drink some water she liberated from the Tourist Center, and lifts the helmet to rinse her burning eyes.

The Lieutenant is wearing the helmet, she tells herself it's for practical reasons. For the little bit of extra protection the visor gives her eyes, for the way the straps allow her to jury rig an ad hoc mask against the smoke.

But really, she's wearing it because somehow it eases her terror. In the last few hours, she's seen an underground Stockade filled with humans that knew no other existence than being raised to be eaten, she's discovered an entire town full of shapeshifting monsters which are probably hunting her right at this moment with ravenous intensity, she's witnessed a fifteen foot tall senile abomination eating human body parts, and on top of all that, she's in the middle of a fucking forest fire, with towering walls of flame closing in no matter what she does.

She needs a weapon. She misses the tire iron, it wasn't much, but there's something comforting about the length of cold iron bar coming to a sharpened edge. She almost wants to go back to the Tourist Center and retrieve it from Amy's corpse, but she has no idea how to find her way back. There's a toolbox in the back of the truck, she has to resist the urge to stop and rifle through it. Maybe there'll be a crowbar or another tire iron.

But the fire is somewhere behind her, moving steadily. A hesitation may be fatal. The Lieutenant keeps driving. She's not exactly going back the way she came, she's not stupid.

The road is narrow here, the hills are steep. On one side, sheer granite rises up sharply, the trees above are barely shrubs, clinging precariously. Below the drop off is sharp, the transmission lines are a hundred yards below the road, a hundred yards out. She doesn't like to look over, the bottom of the valley is far below, everything down there looks like toys.

The Lieutenant doesn't really have a good plan, or much of any plan to speak of. Stay away from the fire, stay away from the monsters, get to high ground, rocky ground, and hope for the best. Just keep driving, and hope she gets somewhere safe before the gas runs out or the fire catches her... or the things.

She's driving much too quickly.

The eighteen wheeler, when it appears, is right on top of her. Instinctively she swerves left. To the right is the big drop. Instead, she careens up the side of the stiff bank. The rig crunches into her stolen truck, the roof collapsing inward. There's a grinding as tons of metal scrape past each other, pushing her vehicle further and further up the steep slope.

Then suddenly the box of the rig is swinging away from her as the whole rig is dragged over the side of the road, plummeting down the hill.

For a second, an unearthly psychic screech pierces her, like a needle through an insect. Her mind locks up, collapses in on itself against the onslaught. A wild succession of incomprehensible images races through her, alien emotions, thoughts, words, and over it all, a wild panic, an animal need to escape that has her thrashing against her seat belt.

She's free falling for a moment, disoriented as the vehicle falls to the road, rolling over on its back.

A boulder tumbles down, crunching into the back end, crushing the rear wheel assembly, sending the stolen truck swinging precariously to the edge.

* * *

ZERO HOUR

Charley's riding shotgun, literally, the ordnance he's carrying across his lap in the passenger seat is military issue, profoundly illegal. He strokes the air cooled barrel, the large canister with the belt feeder beside him.

He doesn't see the lead truck go over, he's too far back in the convoy. But like everyone else, the psychic scream overwhelms him, shattering his mind. He thrashes wildly in his seat, as if afflicted by a seizure, his flesh surging uncontrollably. As he spasms, his claws grip the machine gun, it erupts like a live thing stitching across the windshield and exploding the head of his driver, before his wild spasms bends it in half.

Charley's vaguely aware of the eighteen wheeler going out of control. But he can't focus on it. His mind is full of Grandma's terror. He gets scattered impressions, she's weightless, tumbling in free fall, and it terrifies her. Alongside a frantic gabble of unintelligible words comes a feeling, a desperate need to escape at all costs.

Marci's with her, her fear a lesser broadcast, a whisper carried alongside Grandma's blind panic, almost instantly snuffed. Charley knows that Marci's been torn apart in Grandma's terror, not even noticing. Grandma's tearing at the inside of the box as it tumbles, kicking the wooden frame, glimpses of light from the rents appear tumbling his mind, and a rushing urgency and wild panic.

Some part of him, almost washed away by the overwhelming broadcast of terror as loud in his head as standing next to a jet engine, tries to calm her, tries to plead with her to stay in the box, let it tumble. They'll rescue her, she needs to stay.

But any rationality is washed away as more and more screams, more voices catch and amplify the terror, dozens of sensations, floating, tumbling end over end, the world turning topsy-turvy.

Then Charley's in free fall as his truck goes off the road at full speed, tilting into the air, like an ungainly bird trying to take flight. His last impression as he goes over is the peculiar sight of a pickup truck on its back like a turtle.

All he can hear is Grandma screaming in his head.

* * *

AFTER ZERO HOUR

Charley opens his eyes to silence. For a moment, he's disoriented, hanging on his side, in some sort of cage of twisted metal. His head pains him and he reaches a half clawed paw up to his head, feeling a massive gash, his skull fractured.

His face doesn't feel right, the left side human, the right side twisted and feral, the jaw misshapen, long sharp teeth protruding. That's not how shifting is supposed to go, his brain is damaged. His ears are ringing and it's hard to think.

Even now, his bones are resetting, his body healing, he pushes it, vaguely aware he needs to heal faster. He draws on his strength and tears free of the metal cage wrapped around him, climbing free of the cab of the rig.

The rig? He recognizes it now, he was in an eighteen-wheeler. Not just one, a convoy. Going...

There's an inhuman screaming, a cry of endless anguish and suffering. Charley claps his hands around his ears, staggering, but the shrieking is still overpowering. He doesn't just hear it, he feels it, he feels the subsonic thrum of it in his chest cavity as it washes over his skin like a wave of heat, of pins and needles and ache in his joints. Most of all, it's in his mind, overpowering everything, all the pain and remorse, the ache and loneliness of a lifetime, of a thousand lifetimes, all in this awful ululating wail.

Charley looks up.

Up there, caught between the transmission towers, Grandmother is there, tangled in the electrical wires, dangling. The tension lines are twisted around her neck, strangling her. She struggles and flails, one arm caught on a line. They're sparking, beginning to smoke.

Grandma has been the biggest thing in Charley's life. A great long limbed immensity, twelve or fifteen feet tall, depending on how straight she wanted to stand, a titanic presence. And now she dangles, her impossibly long limbs stretched out as she hangs from the electrical wires.

Her own weight pulls her down. The long hind claws kick the air, a dozen feet up, struggling for purchase. She dances in torment, thrashing above, unable to free herself.

She wails, an ear splitting sound, and from her throat issues a desperate gabble of unearthly words. Charley doesn't know the words, no one does. But he knows what she's saying. Pleading, begging, in awful pain, she doesn't understand what's happened, why this awful thing is happening to her.

As she struggles and thrashes, power surges through her, burning her flesh, stealing her muscles from her and leaving her twitching and jerking helplessly. Thousands of volts are coursing through her body every second, charring pathways through her flesh. Every time she twists in agony, the paths change. She's being burned alive from the inside as she electrocutes.

Grandma is suffering. Charley's god is suffering. For his long life, Grandma has been the constant warm loving presence, a rock of eternity in all their lives, and now she hangs in the sky above him, her massive body suspended, fifteen feet long, stretched out, convulsing, thrashing.

It's almost too much to bear. Her suffering passes through him in waves, but the worst thing is the realization that she suffers, that she can suffer, that this fixture in his life writhes in agony.

Charley's so distracted he almost misses the presence as it lunges, a big man, almost as big as Charley, wearing ragged overalls and a welder's mask, swinging a machete.

He catches the wrist, his hands reshaping into scimitar claws, piercing the other's wrist and forcing fingers open. The machete falls away. Something within him shivers at the touch of the other's flesh, but he ignores the sensation.

CHARLEY (snarling): Oh no you don't!

The words slurring as his jaws lengthen and needle teeth protrude. The figure swings it's free hand, but Charley catches it. The man is strong, but Charley is of the People, and he's far stronger. Growling, he presses the figure backwards pushing it.

Charley lifts up the big man through sheer force, ignoring his kicks and struggles, and brings him down on top of the shattered trunk of a broken pine, impaling it on the naked wood. The figure convulses and goes still, hanging in front of him.

CHARLEY (growls): Fuck you!

He tears the mask away with a scimitar claw, then his breath catches in his throat, his mind blanks, and he steps back freezing in horror.

VOICE (male, in panic): Charley! Grandma's hurting!

Charley's massive head whips around, nictating eyelids blinking. It's Tom, half way shifted himself, his face is caked with blood, but his cheeks are slick with tears as he staggers under Grandma's anguish and pain.

The shock of it brings Charley all the way back. Tom needs him, they all do, Grandma needs him. All he wants to do is curl into a ball and shriek out horror and agony, a conduit for Grandma's pain.

But he's needed. Everyone depends on him.

CHARLEY: We have to save her. We need to get our asses in gear. Get everyone together and we'll go get her down. Get her down before..."

Before she dies. It's literally unthinkable. He can't even voice it in his own thoughts.

Charley blinks. Then he roars, his voice like a lion, the sound echoing off the granite walls of the canyon. Involuntarily, Tom roars back. Then another, and another, dozens of them. The roar is a signal drawing them, uniting them. Even Grandma, hanging and writhing in agony, screaming, coughs a stuttering answer.

Monsters stagger towards him, the remains of the People, shifted and half shifted and human, their skins and forms writhing, all of them twitching and jerking under the psychic onslaught of Grandma's torment.

Charley roars again, forcing himself to be calm and clear. They need him, they need him to lead. These might be all the People left in the world, broken injured, their god in agony. This might be their last stand.

CHARLEY: Get everyone together, find anyone, everyone who can stand. We're going to get her down.

PETE: But the fire...

Pete complains. Charley's never respected Pete, too flighty. Good father though. Wait, Charley thinks, where's my daughter. Where's Millie? He forces himself to stop, there's no time to think of family. Instead, he snaps at the boy.

CHARLEY: Fuck the fire. It's not here yet, we'll deal with...

As he speaks, he glances towards Grandma, and notices something. A figure clinging to one of the adjacent transmission towers, the structure half unmoored, bending from Grandma's weight on the lines, but still standing. A humanoid figure, like a man in a mask...

It's dancing.

A little dapper man in a white suit and a devil mask.

It seems to notice Charley staring at it. It stops and salutes him.

Charley feels something he can't put words to. A kind of noose tightening around his existence, the feel of being trapped in a web or a net. As if they, whoever or whatever they are, have planned it, have set a trap.

But there's more, this is no human agency. This feels too relentless, too inexorable, it's as if something has twisted the strands of fate, the weight and weft of the loom of reality. There's a voice then.

CHARLEY: It's them.

The words comes from somewhere in the gathering, as the People gather, stumbling forward in ones and twos.

Charley grunts.

CHARLEY: They ain't shit. One of them just came at me, and I killed the fucker.

He glances back over to the corpse he impaled on the broken tree.

It's not there. Just like the dancing devil. They play with you, they let you think you killed them, and then they walk away when you're not looking. They like to pretend, to let you think you have a chance.

He snarls then like a caged beast. His head swings from side to side. Around the edges of his vision, men are stepping into view. Strange men, in overalls, in leather, in robes, naked, covered in paint or mud. The fat man wearing the pig's head, the big man in the welder's mask, the tall figure in robes wearing the skull of horse. More. All wearing masks.

The scarecrow… still inert to his senses, but somehow it's walking, and somehow he knows it is looking at him, that it remembers him. His blood chills.

He hears the roar of a chain saw. Somewhere outside his vision, there's the chuff of a flame thrower.

One of them is a boy wearing a towel tied around his neck, and a red knit cap pulled down over his face. Idly, the boy is holding his daughter's severed head.

The Men in Masks have come.

He feels cold. He feels the sensation he'd felt in the Blue Mountains, but crisper, cleaner, more real. He snarls, pushing it away, stoking anger. Grandma needs them.

CHARLEY: Come on fuckers, come on. You think you can take us? You think you can kill Grandma? The People have walked the world before the first human, and we'll walk the world after we eat and shit out the last one of you...

Charley roars and rushes forward. He changes as he rushes forward, each step seeing him taller, more powerful, spines tear through his shirt, his arms and legs stretch out, his jaw distends. Behind him, he feels a stampede, the remaining People following him, the smell, the energy of the change, finally being their true selves, finally raw and honest and ferocious. He roars, and from dozens of throats the People roar with him. He feels powerful and unstoppable...

But only for a moment.

Above them, Grandma screams and writhes as she dangles hanging from the transmission lines, thousands of volts coursing through her body. Her body catches fire, it burns off and on, as her regenerative powers struggle to cope. She bleeds, her life draining away.

Grandma has lived thousands of years, perhaps tens of thousands, her vitality is awesome. For the People, she is something close to a god, something, someone they've loved and worshiped their whole lives, the axis around which their existence turns.

But now she's caught and she can only dangle and writhe and shriek, as bit by bit, her life ebbs. She cries out in her lost ancient language, pleading with spirits and gods long extinct, begging her children to save her.

But of course, they don't. Their blood, her blood in them, rises up, thick in her nostrils. Her heart breaks, as even through her agony, she feels their lights go out, one by one, until she's all alone again.

Even with her unbearable agony, beneath it, she feels her heart break. After all these years, all alone.

She takes a long time to die.

* * *

THREE HOURS AFTER ZERO

Grandma still hangs from the tension wires, but she's no longer struggling. There's no psychic emanation. There's nothing at all, except a charred corpse dangling in the air.

Rather, what's left of her body is a blackened smoking husk, still burning in places. Her claws are gone, bare stumps of arms and legs remain. Only the wind stirs her, rocking the body gently, the slight movement occasionally fracturing some charcoaled remnant of flesh that breaks off and falls away.

Charley crawls inside and out. He drags himself along the ground, charred bits of him falling away. He can't feel his legs much, and he isn't sure that he still has them. He won't look back to see for sure. Turning like that would be more agony than he can bear.

His wounds aren't closing. The cuts and tears and gouges, the ragged gap in his side where the chain saw struck, none of them are closing. Instead, they sag wetly, oozing thick clear fluid polluted with threads of pus.

His flesh twists inside, dorsal spikes rise up out of his back and then sink, his bones shift, his hands lengthen, he grows and shrinks. But it's not enough, he can't maintain one form or another. His body is fighting to stay alive, but it's losing.

Charley drags himself forward a few more feet along the shoulder of the dirt road, and then pauses, panting, gasping for breath.

In his head, Grandma's screams go on and on, the piercing wail of an impossibly ancient being, a withered creature that outlived so many aeons. But the screams are only memories. She's gone, and Charley's heart is heavy, tears leak down the ruins of his face, making tracks in the ash.

Everyone is gone. Marci, Millie, Kate, Gordon even Abe. Hell, he thought Abe would outlive them all, the old bastard. The whole town wiped away. The farms, the Stock, everything.

All gone. All his life, he could feel the presence of his own kind, the flicker of their existence, the quieting of each death, the burst of each new life, and over it, all the loving radiance that had been Grandma. It felt like community, more community than any human could ever know. It had always given him meaning, made him feel like he was part of something greater, something good. But it's gone now.

For the first time in his life, he's alone. It feels empty, like he's at the edge of an endless, bottomless abyss. It feels unbearably lonely. It occurs to him that this is what humans feel their whole life, and for a second, he wants to weep for such sad creatures.

A spasm hits, and he coughs blood all over the gravel. There are black bits mixed in with the red, he sees with his good eye. That's probably not a good sign. He drags in air painfully, the sucking chest wounds inhaling as his lungs expand.

They always leave one, he thinks, those darknesses that masquerade as Men in Masks.

Always one survivor, to tell the tale, to spread the legend, maybe just to carry the nightmare in them like a seed for something darker.

Rested, he lifts his head just enough to clear the gravel, stretches out his arms and pulls himself forward again.

There's something ahead of him. It takes him moments to make it out, as he crawls towards it. Coughing and oozing fluids he painfully drags himself over the ground. It's a woman, sitting on a box of some kind. A crow bar is balanced over her knees. She wears a helicopter flight helmet with a crack across the visor. Some vague part of him wonders at that, why she'd wear such a thing? He recognizes her, the woman from the yellow car.

She turns her head towards him, and he glimpses himself in the reflection of the visor. He looks as bad as he thought. Worse.

She waits, as he crawls towards her. When he's close enough, he swallows blood to moisten his throat to speak.

CHARLEY: It's you. You brought them.

The sitting woman shrugs.

LIEUTENANT: Yes. I suppose I did.

Charley's too exhausted to go further, he lays his head down, resting on the gravel road. Blood trickles from his mouth. His body spasms but he lacks the energy to cough.

CHARLEY: Why?

The Lieutenant stares.

CHARLEY: Why? What did we do? We only wanted to be left alone, to live our lives, to raise our families? Why?

There's no answer. Some part of him wants to grab her, to shake her, to get an answer. But he's too tired. Everything is tired and hurting, he can't find the energy to move again, even his twisting flesh seems exhausted, its pulsing quietly slowing.

He almost doesn't hear her when she speaks.

LIEUTENANT: It's like being a chess piece moving around a checker board. All you see is where they put you.

He thinks of Millie, her sun drenched face, out on the back lawn, smell of freshly cut grass, her mother showing her how to shift. He thinks of Grandma laughing at something she saw on television. But they're fading away, the images growing indistinct.

CHARLEY: We weren't bad people. We didn't deserve... What did we do? Why? Why did you do this...?

They leave one, he thinks. They leave one to tell the story, to spread the dark. The thoughts are indistinct and fading.

It's just not him...

The Lieutenant shrugs, he's barely aware of the play of light and dark near him as the motion shifts her shadow.

LIEUTENANT: Sorry. That's above my pay grade.

But Charley doesn't hear it.

The Lieutenant watches his burnt mutilated body cooling, the eye no longer seeing. Blood and fluids ooze out slowly, but there's no other movement.

The Lieutenant simply sits and waits by Charley's body.

After a couple of hours, a car comes along. It stops

The Lieutenant gets in, and it drives off.

THE END

HUNGRY HUNGRY HOUNGANS

Chapter Four

It is blistering hot. Almost too hot to breathe. Murdoch's clothes are soaked through with sweat. There are no windows in the small room, no furniture to speak of, except the bench bolted into the wall. He's been here suffocating slowly for two days, the single light bulb on all that time. They haven't bothered to feed him.

The room is empty, just featureless concrete walls, clumsily painted over. Murdoch thinks he can make out bloodstains on the wall, showing through the paint, layer after layer of them. How many interrogations do they represent? He imagines the meaty slap of fists against flesh, the heavy thud of kicks. He imagines screams and cries, begging as teeth are pulled out, or water poured down throats, or simply limp forms hanging from hooks.

The door is heavy wood, no window in it. Murdoch tried listening, but there was nothing. He had knelt down to peer under the jamb, but it was covered. He'd tested the door, then hammered at it, then shouted. After a while, he gave up and now he waits.

The door opens, an armed guard walks in and sets a chair down in front of Murdoch. Then he retreats to a corner of the room, ready, keeping his eyes on the prisoner.

Another man walks in, uniformed, an officer. He sits in the chair facing Murdoch. He has no pencil or paper, no recording device. Murdoch doesn't recognize the uniform.

INTERROGATOR: You are CIA, yes?

MURDOCH: Yes.

INTERROGATOR: We have questions.

MURDOCH: I'll tell you everything you want to know. I just don't know if you'll believe it. I don't know if I believe it. No that's not right. I don't want to believe it. But it happened.

INTERROGATOR: At the beginning...

MURDOCH: It starts... with the bar, and the Lieutenant.

* * *

The scent of old decaying blood fills the Lieutenant's nose. A lot of blood has been spilled, gallons and gallons of it, spattering the walls, spattering the ceilings, soaking into the carpet. There's been so much blood in the carpet that it's pooled, unable to dry it's simply congealed and clotted in the air, began to wetly decompose. It's a familiar odour.

LIEUTENANT (voice over): It is a bright sunny day in Miami, Florida. Too sunny, there is something raw and abrasive about the sunshine, a bit too hot, too intense, too much UV. I watch women in bikinis walk by, their skins tanning to leather before my eyes.

She decides she doesn't like Florida, not even a little bit.

LIEUTENANT (voice over): I am standing in a motel room on the outskirts of town. It's a cheap motel, obviously seen better days, not much used now since the bypass came in a few years back. This is probably the busiest it's been for years. There must be over two dozen police cars gathered, plus several coroner's wagons, a few useless ambulances. I saw them all as they drove me in from the airport, so many cars and vehicles that they overrun the parking lot and are forced to park up along the road. Law enforcement officials, paramedics, forensic techs, all bustling around in circles. They remind me of flies endlessly buzzing around a corpse.

Piled up in the corners of the room are the corpses. They've been skinned, no way to tell gender or personality or anything about them. Once people are skinned they become utterly generic.

LIEUTENANT (voice over): Which tells me that it's probably really bad. Not that I care.

She take a deep breath, enjoying it. It's refreshing to be away from the psychic stench of them.

This is like a holiday. Maybe she does like Miami.

One of the forensic technicians taking photographs begins dry heaves and runs out of the room, his little box of yellow numbered cards spilling. The Lieutenant watches the cards fall as the technician rushes past me. He's already vomiting inside his hazmat suit. She think the cards are useless. They'd need thousands to mark all the blood spatters for this room.

She thinks about lunch. Egg salad maybe. They passed by a place at a strip mall on the way in from the airport.

CARTWRIGHT: So what do you make of it? They said you two were specialists?

Cartwright. The Lieutenant likes the name. She's the detective in charge of the scene. Late middle aged, seen it all, likes to pretend she's tough. Probably drinks herself unconscious every night. After this, she'll crawl inside the bottle and not come out. The Lieutenant decide she likes her. Most of the people she works with are careful about not giving their names, it's a superstitious thing. But here it is on the badge.

The Lieutenant's Handler is beside her. She doesn't know him. He hasn't take his sunglasses off. He doesn't want the Lieutenant to see his eyes, another superstition. It won't save him.

It's always a different handler these days. She asked about that. They rotate them. Mental health issues apparently.

CARTWRIGHT: Is it one of them? One of yours?

The question surprises her. Cartwright has heard some things. Learned or guessed. No wonder she drinks.

LIEUTENANT: Not one of ours, they're all accounted for. And it's not one of them. It doesn't feel like it.

CARTWRIGHT: Why?

The Lieutenant shrugs.

LIEUTENANT: Not their style. They hunt, they set up little temples or nests or whatever. But this? This feels like a ritual, gathering all the victims together, preparations, and lots of ceremony. They don't do rituals. Besides, if it was one of them... I'd feel it.

HANDLER: Yeah, you're right.

He surprises her with that. The Handlers try to minimize conversation, any kind of human contact with the Lieutenant. They think it will save them. Probably won't, even without field mortality, the Division's suicide rate is through the roof. There's something corrosive about being around the Squad. But she don't begrudge them the effort. If she had to deal with someone in her line of work she'd probably do the same.

And it's not personal, she knows that, and forgives them. It's not about her.

It's what's always standing in the darkness on the other side of her.

Them.

She yawns.

LIEUTENANT: Then why am I here? You've got real investigators all over the place. Why do we care? Some Hispanics chopped up some other Hispanics. Colorful, but just another day in Miami. Standard police stuff.

HANDLER: Crimson. It's an adulterated blend of cocaine and some designer drug our labs can't identify. Whatever it is, the people involved in it are nasty pieces of work. We have kill sites like this all over the seaboard, from New Orleans to New York. This is recurring.

A pattern. She take another glance around the room, evaluating things with a practised eye, working out the sequence of events.

LIEUTENANT: it's not one of them. But there's something going on if it keeps happening. Ritual killings, everyone's focused on the human skins they nailed to the walls, but that is just an intermediate step, part of the process. The real purpose is whatever they did in the center of the room. They took that with them and dumped the skinned bodies there to cover it up.

CARTWRIGHT: How do you know that?

She shrugs again.

LIEUTENANT: They were skinned on the bed, it's soaked through with blood. They used the bed as a platform, they were doing it carefully. But they didn't care about the bodies, you can see marks around the corners of the room, they just dumped it wherever. They were doing something else.

CARTWRIGHT: I've seen some terrible things. There was a time an unknown perp had bludgeoned four swingers and dumped their bodies in a hot tub in the middle of summer. It was two weeks before the smell had attracted attention and we found the bloated dissolving corpses, the hot tub was rancid human stew, meat was falling off the bones. There was the little girl swallowed by a python and what she'd looked like when they finally caught the animal and slit it open. I've seen murders and mutilation, child abuse cases. I've seen things I can't forget. I see them when I close my eyes. They invade my dreams and I wake up screaming over and over again.

They all stare at her, slightly surprised at the outburst.

CARTWRIGHT: But this? This is the worst I've ever seen. And I see it in the eyes of every attending officer and investigator, a haunted look. Anyone who has been inside of that room is buying themselves years of therapy. Even him.

She gestures at the Handler. Then at the Lieutenant.

CARTWRIGHT: Except you. Straight Army in a civilian crime scene. You're not even blinking. When they told me you were coming in, I asked around. This isn't a regular crime scene, there's all sorts of things going on at levels I never knew existed. They make out like you're some kind of serial killer whisperer.

The Lieutenant holds up her hands.

LIEUTENANT: Something like that, but not in the way you think.

CARTWRIGHT: So what way are you?

LIEUTENANT: I'm nobody. I'm just a tourist. I just come to watch. Ask him.

CARTWRIGHT: What's going on?

*** * ***

LIEUTENANT (voice over): Drug Cartels come and go. For all the money and guns, it's not a business to get old in. It's not like in the movies, mostly it's just greed and brutality. Every now and then someone smart comes along and builds something, but then the violence catches up, they get replaced along the way. Then it just runs on the violence for a while until it falls apart. Medellin, Cali, Sanely, the names aren't even worth remembering…

But Modovar is different. Modovar is like cancer, starting off as some little cell gone wrong, and just slowly eating away until it consumes everything. Modovar is smart, he stays off the radar for a long time, operating through agents and proxies, by the time he starts getting noticed, it's too late…

It gets to the point where he owns half of Colombia and a half dozen other countries, and what he doesn't own either works for him, or is scared shitless of him. He's untouchable…

He's practically a state all by himself. Big enough that the powers that be don't want him to rock the boat. As long as he stays low, does business quietly and doesn't make waves… they'll leave him alone.

But of course, people like Modovar, they never do that, they never stay quiet.

Crimson starts showing up. Not as a main drug, a specialty product, available only to the right people for the right purposes. There's no market for it, no demand. It just shows up, trickling through the channels. Don't mind me, I'm just a perfectly ordinary drug, pay no attention…

And then the massacres after that, ritual killings, always the same, all these bodies skinned alive. That hotel room they showed me? There are dozens like that. The same carnage, the same rituals. Different props, different circumstances, spontaneous, but always the same, as if something is reaching through from the other side and making it happen…

That scares the people in charge. It doesn't make sense…

Something is happening…

They have to do something…

That's when they call the Squad.

* * *

LIEUTENANT (voice over): I lean over the bow, watching the waves, as the tramp steamer cruises towards its destination. I'm hoping to see dolphins.

But of course anything that can sense what we're carrying, it's already fled miles away.

DIEGO: You shouldn't be alone. Captain's orders. It's not safe,

She looks at him and smiles.

LIEUTENANT: I'm okay.

LIEUTENANT (voice over): The Captain has decreed that no one on the ship can be alone. We're on a buddy system now, what with the disappearances and the suicides.

Only the Captain is alone, hanging on in the bridge with his hexes and his Gris Gris, bible pages plastered over every surface that isn't an instrument. He peels back pages to see out the bridge windows. He sleeps there now.

The rest of the crew is haunted. They know something is very wrong. They tell stories of things walking the deck at nights. Their dreams are full of disturbing images so they don't sleep. Instead they numb themselves with drugs. They say some of the suicides aren't really suicides. That some of the disappearances aren't just bodies lost overboard to the sea.

They don't know what's on board with them. Supposedly it's contained. Three times a day, the Lieutenant check the locks on the shipping containers. They haven't been tampered with. So if they're getting out, she don't know how. But they'll get out if they want to, that's who they are.

But even if they aren't getting out, you can feel them. The stench of them, the corrosion of their presence. Even if you don't know they're there... you know something is here.

When she met him, Diego was young, horny and exuberant. They hooked up, and the sex was wild. Now he's haunted like the rest of them. At night, he clings to her like a drowning man.

When they set out from New Orleans, there were thirty in the crew.

Now there are fifteen. They're short-handed now.

She's trying to keep him alive.

The Lieutenant's trying to keep them all alive, at least until they reach destination. If they can get off the ship after that, they have a chance. That's all she wants, for them to have a chance.

She keeps checking the locks.

But they're getting out anyway.

She can't save anyone.

* * *

LIEUTENANT (voice over): Before the Panama Canal, Puerto San Miguel had been a thriving town, transshipping from the Pacific to the Atlantic by a creaky railroad, with crude river and road access to the interior. But the Canal had come along, the bottom dropped out of the local economy, and it had slipped into senescence as a forgotten backwater.

The Captain is dead. The bridge is locked. There is no one left alive except for her. The Captain was the last to die, finally giving up as the ship cruised into harbour. The ship is steaming into port at full speed. Harbour boats are alongside, she can hear angry shouting from megaphones.

The Lieutenant ignores it, compulsively checking the locks on the container. Still secure. The ship lurches and there's a loud crunching sound, she goes flying, and end up bracing against a railing. She knows, without having to look that the ship has overtaken one of the tugboats trying to corral it, plowing it under and breaking it in half. Everyone on the tug is probably dead.

Hand over hand along the railings the Lieutenant pulls herself towards the back of the ship, towards the crew area. She can feel the ship listing as it lurches to the left, towards the docks. The collision with the tug must have damaged the hull, it's probably taking on water. But in a few minutes that won't matter. Her pry bar goes skittering along the deck, and she grabs it quickly, taking comfort in the length of cold heavy metal.

The ship is just minutes from the docks. She needs to secure herself. Collision is imminent. Engines running, the ship sweeps aside tugboats battling futilely to direct it, crashing into the docks, shipping containers flying, fires breaking out. The derelict ship, pushed by runaway engines, thousands of tons of steel, begins to crumple as it tears through the wood and concrete, shoving its way up onto land.

The old wooden docks and piles splinter under the impact of ten thousand tons of steel. The metal gantries crumble, steel twisting like spaghetti. The shock of impact crumples the already damaged hull, but the momentum of the engines drives it forward, climbing the slope of the shore.

Then it happens, the noise is indescribable, a series of booms and cracks. The ship lurches hard 40 degrees to the side, she feels the bow lifting. Somewhere metal is screaming as it's pulled apart like toffee, and concrete breaks apart with a series of booms. The Lieutenant is sliding along the deck of the ship, to the thunderous sound of containers breaking free of their moorings and tumbling into the water. She hooks the pry bar against a pipe, arresting her tumble and nearly tearing her shoulders out of joint.

The ship's engines, one propeller exposed, whine like demons. She hears the distant sound of sirens. But the ship keeps moving forward, bucking as it scrapes some kind of massive concrete abutment, lurching even further. From the periphery of her vision, she sees fragments of wooden pilings twenty feet long and a foot and a half thick flung into the air like toothpicks.

Then it's all still and motionless, and she's picking her way through the wreckage.

Abruptly, the ship lurches one more time, hard, and stops suddenly, flinging her around, but she's anchored by the pry bar. Suddenly, all is motionless. She can still hear sirens, and now screaming, and the sound of metal groaning and wood splintering. There's a great splash, one of the shipping containers going over.

Climbing to her feet on the twisted deck, the Lieutenant peers over the rail. Fires are already starting. The ship must have plowed through fuel lines as it struck the docks and climbed halfway up the harbour. No sign of fire trucks or rescuers but they're only minutes away.

She slips, and goes sliding across the dock, swinging around wildly for purchase, about to tumble onto the rocks below. At the last minute, something catches her. A gloved hand. Blue overalls.

The Lieutenant looks up into the almost featureless corpse mask, shorn of all humanity, gazing at me with bland indifference. Michaels.

She can't see his eyes in the mask.

You can't ever see their eyes in their masks, just a kind of emptiness. They only ever wear masks.

His grip on her forearm is like iron. His other hand holds his knife, a long serrated blade. The Lieutenant wonders if this is the moment she dies. She grips her pry bar tightly, ready to bash him with it. You can escape them, sometimes, if you're quick and ruthless.

LIEUTENANT: I'm all right, asshole. Let me go.

Surprisingly, Michaels lifts her to her feet and releases her. She braces herself to move, to pull free, to evade, to strike. But she can feel it, his attention is drifting away from her. Whatever accident or impulse put him in position to save her life, it's evaporating away.

LIEUTENANT: This is all your fault.

The Lieutenant doesn't know why she felt she had to tell him, to assign blame. None of them care. He's already turning away. She thinks about checking the container, seeing if it's still secure. But it doesn't matter. They will not be contained, these.

There are more sirens, the shriek of fire trucks. Michaels and the others can take care of themselves. Perhaps they'll just disappear the way they do and reassemble for the next stage with no one having to die. Or perhaps the emergency rescue will find nightmares waiting for them. Not her problem, and not anything she can do about.

She needs to focus on getting off the ship and to the rendezvous point.

They can take care of themselves.

It's the town that's in danger.

* * *

Puerto Miguel is burning, Murdoch doesn't care. Last night a tramp steamer plowed into the docks at full speed. The ship tore through the ancient infrastructure, crawling half way up the harbor before finally rolling over on its side, tearing through gas lines and water mains. Everyone in town heard the thunderous series of booms and cracks as if the world was ending, had come rushing down to see the disaster.

Then the fires had started, broken and ruptured gas lines going up in a dozen places. Fire and ambulances had been caught up in the traffic jam of onlookers and amateur rescuers. With the water mains down, the fire rescue had nothing to pump. The fires leaped from one wood frame building to the next, catching people caught in the middle. In some places, the fire had been so intense that gasoline in cars' fuel tanks spontaneously erupted.

People burn, others trample each other in the rush to escape, some trying to rescue their own property were killed as looters. Others were killed by looters seeing their opportunity. In the chaos, there are knives, scores are settled, chances seized. For every person who sees disaster, there are others who see opportunities.

It's been nine hours and no end in sight. The hospital collapsed when an out of control fire truck laden with burn victims plowed into the building. The interruption in gas, or possibly fire reaching transformers had caused power to go out. The citizens of Puerto Miguel continue their desperate losing battle to save their homes, the ones who care anyway.

Murdoch doesn't care. It's not his job to care.

Truthfully, he despises Puerto Miguel. The town lost its reason for existing when the Panama Canal opened. In the last couple of decades, it found a new lease on life as a shipment point for the Cartels and their dirty money spreading corruption. Beneath the surface of this sleepy, friendly little town, there are drug dealers and pistoleros, whores and brothels, human trafficking, select marshes where bodies are regularly deposited, and endless filthy dark secrets.

As far as he's concerned, the whole town can die. Or maybe it's already dead. The disaster at the docks and harbor is massive, more massive than the government is able, or the cartels are willing, to repair. The cartels will take their money elsewhere and Puerto Miguel will slip away, unmourned into history.

Not his problem. Murdoch has his assignment, he's to meet up with and help guide a Special Forces team to Modovar's stronghold. It's a fool's errand, but it's the assignment.

As Murdoch and his local asset, Jesus Echeverria, drive the massive truck over bumpy roads to the rendezvous point, he sees something strange.

They pass a man. But what a man. The figure is huge, tall and massive with a barrel chest, a hulking figure, dressed in ragged dark overalls, simply standing by the side of the road. The strangest thing is that the man seems to be wearing a mask of some kind.

Murdoch opens his mouth to mention it to Jesus, but immediately changes his mind. The young Colombian has his hands full wrestling the vehicle as it lurches over the bumpy, winding dirt road.

In the side mirror, Murdoch sees the man in the mask turn his head, his unfathomable gaze tracking the motion of the truck, then his body moves smoothly following. Then he's lost to sight, and Murdoch forgets about him entirely, except for a vague sense of unease.

* * *

LIEUTENANT: You're late.

Murdoch pauses and looks back at his sidekick, Jesus. Al Hambre on the outskirts of Puerto Miguel barely rates as a ghost town. Settled at the beginning of the 20th century by Lebanese immigrants, they'd built a little community slowly whittled away by disease, departure and age until there was nothing left. Since then, it had been sporadically occupied and abandoned, re-occupied and abandoned again. What had been a mosque had become a Christian church, then a tavern, then a brothel, briefly a local headquarters for some cartel before they'd completely corrupted the neighboring town, then a storage depot for whatever the cartels shipped back and forth, then a torture camp, before finally being abandoned again.

The Lieutenant sits at a table with a bottle of whisky and some glasses, looking for all the world like she's simply having a drink in a tavern. Which is basically what it is, provided you ignore the crude pornographic murals lining the walls, or the hooks and chains hanging from the decaying ceiling rafters where human beings were hung and disemboweled. Or the dead body in the corner. Or the bloodied iron pry bar on the table with the blood-spattered drinking glasses, next to the aviator's helmet.

Murdoch can smell the sickly sweet smell of fresh blood, overlaying the suffocating reek of decay. The doors are closed, only high windows and gaps in the ceiling allow light or air through, and not much of either. It's unbearably hot, here in the still air, Murdoch can hardly breathe. He desperately wants to get out. The locals say the village is cursed, to Murdoch, it's just a hole, a latrine, and all he wants is to go away and find a shower.

MURDOCH: We're early. And anyway, this wasn't the original mission.

The original instructions were to meet the steamer in port, and take delivery of a shipping container 'Trojan Horse,' transport said container to Al Hambre, where the content thereof would disembark, and proceed by truck and boat into the interior. Hours before the collision, Murdoch had received new orders. Since then, since the crash, he's been wondering.

They had to know what was coming to change his orders.

Which implies the collision and destruction of the town was deliberate?

But that made no sense. Why? Why the pointless destruction. It could only attract unwanted attention.

Murdoch tries not to think about it. His job is to take orders.

But it bothers him.

Jesus is already nervous. Murdoch knows better than to show uncertainty in front of an asset. Despite that, they both clutch their firearms.

Word is, the cartels used to feed their victims to the feral swine left behind by the Lebanese. The swine, the story goes, developed a taste for human flesh. The cartel sometimes hadn't bothered to make sure their victims were dead before they went to the pigs, and so the swine had learned not to be fussy. Meat was meat, even if it was walking around, or running away.

Stories of man-hunting pigs were a major reason why Al Hambre, literally over the hill from Puerto Miguel, is abandoned.

Its certainly one of the reasons you don't stand around outdoors in the empty hamlet. Even a decaying tavern, redolent with its history or murder and perversion, reeking of must and decay, light streaming in from holes in the roof was preferable. You wanted a solid door and solid walls between you and whatever might be lurking out there.

Confidently, Murdoch motions Jesus to follow. He walks over to the table where the Lieutenant is sitting. He knows who she is, he's been briefed, she's part of the dossier he reviewed and destroyed. You can't show fear to these types. You can't let the deep scary spooks rattle you.

MURDOCH: Do you mind?

The Lieutenant shrugs.

LIEUTENANT: Suit yourself.

She's not that scary. He's worked with the sort of animals that made their bones in Bagram or Guantanamo Bay, dead eyed men with thousand yard stares and no moral limits. The Lieutenant is creepy, but she isn't in that class, he tells himself.

Murdoch pours himself a whisky. He glances at the pry bar laying on the table, next to the whisky bottle and the glasses. He notes the end of the pry bar is covered with gore, still fresh. There are clumps of human hair sticking to it. Jesus is trying not to stare at it. The young man sits uneasily.

The Lieutenant is calm, far too calm for Murdoch's tastes. He wonders if she's some kind of psychopath. Special Forces, Covert Ops. You meet some pretty disturbing personalities. Or disturbed personalities.

Murdoch jerks a thumb to the body in the corner. Even through the musk and decay, he can still smell the man's fresh blood, the stink of loosened bowels, the fluids slowly running out of him. There's a piece missing from the skull.

MURDOCH: Who is that?

LIEUTENANT: Someone who shouldn't have been here.

The Lieutenant isn't any more forthcoming. Beside him, Jesus clutches his rosary. Murdoch can almost hear him reciting the Lord's Prayer over and over. The boy's eyes are wide, the whites showing. They remind Murdoch of the eyes of a horse with a broken leg he'd seen as a boy on his parent's farm, wild and terrified. Jesus is sweating even more than the heat demands. His father had killed it with a sledgehammer to the head, it had taken three blows.

Murdoch pours the boy a glass and commands him to drink.

LIEUTENANT: Who is this?

MURDOCH: Jesus. Local asset.

LIEUTENANT: You brought a civilian?

There's just a hint of reproach in her voice. A trace of contempt. Murdoch bristles.

MURDOCH: You want to go into the interior? You need someone local, born on the rivers who knows them. Jesus can drive a truck, pilot a boat, and he knows all the villages and tribes along the way.

The Lieutenant just stares. Murdoch and the boy glance uncertainly at each other. Murdoch puts a hand on Jesus' knee, and turns to stare hard at her.

MURDOCH: I know Jesus, I trust him with my life. You, on the other hand? I don't know you at all.

He keeps his eyes on the Lieutenant. You can't show any weakness to these types. Eventually, she shrugs and looks away. Murdoch feels a little more confident.

MURDOCH: Mission status?

LIEUTENANT: Going ahead.

Somehow, he expected it. But he's still mildly surprised.

MURDOCH: Really? After that colossal fuck up in town? This was supposed to be a stealth operation.

LIEUTENANT: It is.

MURDOCH: You're kidding me right? You blew up or burned half the town. That's not stealth. I could have rented advertising on a blimp and it would have been stealthier. You think Modovar doesn't have people here? That they're not going to pay attention? Those fucks are paranoid as hell, and you just sent up flares.

The Lieutenant shrugs again, as if this whole conversation has bored her.

LIEUTENANT: The mission is on, that's all you need to know. Either of you.

MURDOCH: The mission is fucked. I don't even know how you made it out of that mess. Or the rest of your team. Unless you weren't even on the steamer? It was a diversion?

Murdoch wonders suddenly how much of his briefing is real. In this line of work, everyone lies to everyone about everything. Maybe the real mission is not what they told him. But that opens a door to questions.

The Lieutenant gives nothing. She doesn't acknowledge Murdoch's curiosity. She shows no interest, she just sits there, indifferent. Flies buzz around, attracted by the sickly sweet smell of the dead man. One of them lands on a clump of gore and human hair clinging to the pry bar and becomes stuck. They watch it struggle.

Finally, Murdoch speaks, challenging.

MURDOCH: Where's your team?

LIEUTENANT: They're around.

MURDOCH: I'd like to meet them.

And suddenly, somehow, the Lieutenant is alive. For a moment, the eerie blankness of the psychopath gives way, and something human is looking out her eyes. The change is unnerving. She's looking at Jesus and Murdoch now, and they can both feel the change. Suddenly, she's... compassionate, afraid, sad. He can't place the emotions he's seeing.

LIEUTENANT: No. No, you don't want to meet them. If you're lucky, you'll never meet them. You'll do your job, and you'll look the other way when they're around, because the worst thing you can do is look at them, because they'll look back. And if you're very, very, lucky, you'll get to walk away and keep walking and never ever stop walking and never look back.

Then it's gone. Whatever that human flash was, it shuts down, is locked away. Murdoch is startled and off balance. For just an instant, he thinks about that man on the side of the road, but then the memory is gone. He's frightened and he's not sure why.

MURDOCH: All right.

He's blinking, uncertain and disturbed. He decides he needs to be defiant.

MURDOCH: You don't have to be a bitch about it.

No response from the Lieutenant, the mask of psychopathy is firmly in place. Murdoch pours another whisky and takes a drink. He swears.

MURDOCH: Jesus!

JESUS: Yes?

* * *

They sit in the Tavern for an hour and a half. The Lieutenant makes them wait. So they just sit there sweating. The heat is unbearable, and minute by minute the stench of the corpse grows more pervasive. There's almost no conversation. At one point Murdoch asks about the flight helmet. The answer is curt, "souvenir," brooking no further questions. There are sounds outside. Sudden squeals of feral pig that make Jesus and Murdoch clutch their weapons, they've heard too many stories not to be nervous if Al Hambre's man-eating swine are nearby.

Then there's a sound of screaming almost as if from a human, but there's all kinds of sounds in the jungle. It's probably not human. Just a howler monkey having sex or something. Or maybe one of the Al Hambre swine they've heard so much about, but it's hard to imagine what would make a pig scream like that.

At some point, Jesus starts to pray, clutching his rosary, whispering the Lord's Prayer over and over again in accented Spanish. Neither the Lieutenant nor Murdoch object.

Strangest of all, the sound of a motor, as if from a lawn mower or a chain saw. An alien mechanical sound that doesn't belong. Murdoch listens to it rise and fall for a minute, then stop. He wonders if he imagined it. He wonders if he should mention it. But Jesus is terrified already, and the Lieutenant... gives nothing. Murdoch shuts his mouth, he can't imagine the conversation leading to anything he wants to know.

At the end of the hour and a half, Murdoch is restless. Daylight is passing. No one dares drive the jungle roads at night. They're already behind schedule.

The Lieutenant announces it's time. She leads them out to the truck.

There's no sign of the Special Forces unit. But the canvas flaps on the box of the truck are all down, covering the rear. They weren't that way before, he's sure. He almost mentions it, but decides not to.

The Lieutenant is inspecting the truck, everything but the box. She ignores that. Instead, she focuses on the tires, the axles. She bends down on her knees to examine the gas tank. She has Jesus pop the hood so she can check the battery and wires.

Jesus protests. He's gone over the truck himself.

The Lieutenant has one word, that doesn't mean anything to either of them.

LIEUTENANT: Vernon.

Finally, she has to go through the cab meticulously, before she'll let them in. Another half hour gone for nothing, Murdoch thinks. But there is no arguing with the Lieutenant. And again, he's got this feeling that perhaps if he does argue, he might learn something he didn't want to know, maybe end up knowing something that he can't un-know.

He feels a suffocating dread, even beyond the ceaseless pervasive heat. He tells himself its all spy craft, espionage bullshit, need to know, want to know, all the garbage that becomes part of your life as a field agent.

Nothing more than that.

Finally, they're ready to go. None of them look to the box as they enter the cab. Murdoch isn't sure why, he's aware he doesn't want to look. But he doesn't want to examine the feeling.

Jesus pops the clutch, the truck lurches into gear. None of them look back.

* * *

The day passes without incident. Jesus drives, piloting the lurching vehicle over the uneven muddy, broken cattle paths that pass for a road. On quiet stretches Murdoch takes over. A few times they have to downshift into four or six wheel drive, pitching their way through stretches of bog or mud, struggling and slow but never quite getting stuck.

There is no conversation. The driver needs to focus on the road. The passengers sometimes call out obstacles. But the Lieutenant has nothing to say. Bored, Murdoch fiddles with the radio. A lot of the stations are awash with news of the disaster at Puerto Miguel. Body counts, tales of survivors, atrocities, looters. The disaster has brought out the worst in people. There is a story of a man wearing a pig's head, another about a man with a hook for a hand, both murdering children.

LIEUTENANT (softly, almost whispering): Godel and Soames.

Murdoch glances at her, disturbed, unsure if she's really spoken. The radio is talking about another hooded figure and a series of arsons. Murdoch searches up and down the frequencies, eventually settles on an evangelical program. A harsh voice in American accented Spanish rants about hellfire and damnation. He recognizes it, a mad evangelical pastor, fled his flock in America because of certain excesses with children, retreating to the middle some nowhere town on the coast to preach to the airwaves. A nameless little man, in a dingy hotel room with an AM transmitter.

Towards the end of the day they come to a hamlet, one of the nameless little farming communities or communes of the interior. They pull into the clearing, stopping so Jesus can check the radiator. As Jesus pokes around under the hood, Murdoch gets out to stretch his legs. The Lieutenant follows.

No one comes out to greet them. There's no sign of life. But it's hot, people are probably visiting, or sleeping. Or just watching. Murdoch feels watched.

LIEUTENANT: Is it safe?

MURDOCH: Safe enough. We're outside the territory of CRAC or Modovar's Cartel.

LIEUTENANT: CRAC?

MURDOCH: Colombian Revolutionary Alliance Confederation. Radical communists, back in the fifties and sixties they left the universities and went into the jungle to spread revolution among the natives and overthrow the government. You know, typical socialist revolution; that was the thing back then. But it didn't happen.

LIEUTENANT: But they're still around?

Murdoch is mildly surprised. This is relevant background, it should have been in her briefing. He can't imagine it getting left out. But he can't imagine her being sloppy and not reading it, she seems too... meticulous. Is he being tested?

MURDOCH: They just ended up staying in the jungle, using their guns and ideology to set up these crazy little hermit kingdoms in the interior. They couldn't take over, the army couldn't root them out, so they just stayed and got weirder and weirder. CRAC, FARC and a few other splinters, they ended up controlling half of Colombia's territory, just hidden away from the world.

LIEUTENANT: Until the cartels?

MURDOCH: Yeah. The cartels spread so much money around, they were happy to get in bed. Modovar especially. They say he's got his tentacles in them, private armies. He's got his own Khmer Rouge loons, just waiting to rain down on the rest of us.

Murdoch kicks at a rock, watching the row of scarecrows propped up on sticks on the side the road. Idly, he counts them: Eight. Funny number. Funny places to put scarecrows, he thinks.

He decides to challenge her. If she's testing him, he needs to push back.

MURDOCH: You should know this stuff. Didn't you go over the mission briefings?

LIEUTENANT: Not really. I don't really care, it's not important to the mission. That stuff, it's just tourism to me, you know.

For a moment, Murdoch is speechless. It's as if the Lieutenant had started speaking in Latin. The words came out, but they made no sense. How could she not know about this? More important, how could she not care? How do you have a mission if you don't understand the target?

He glances at the Lieutenant, and notices the flight helmet casually hanging from her hip. Air force? Marines? Her manner is casual. She's not messing with him. She really doesn't care.

He has the image of a pilot in an airplane, dropping a bomb. There's no need for history or context if you're just delivering death. For a moment, he's filled with unasked questions about who she is, and who her unseen Special Forces team is and what their real mission is.

He doesn't want to ask.

Instead, he looks around and notices something. It's been minutes now. Still nothing.

MURDOCH: There's no one here.

LIEUTENANT: What?

MURDOCH: There's no one here. People should have heard us coming. They should have been coming out of their houses to see us. But there's no one.

He scans the handful of huts.

MURDOCH: Some of the vehicles are missing. I guess they left...

Around one house, chickens are scratching. A goat is tethered near another. Somewhere a cow moos. Farm instruments lean against a shed, as if placed casually for a moment.

MURDOCH: Left in a hurry.

Jesus has shut the hood of the truck and walked over to join them. Murdoch notices that the boy is very careful to look away from the big box of the truck and its canvas framework covering. They all are. It's not deliberate, but a subconscious avoidance. Murdoch realizes whenever he glances in that direction, his gaze slides away, the gnawing unease jolts inside him. One way or the other, he'll be glad when the mission is over.

Jesus crosses himself.

JESUS: Protection against evil.

MURDOCH: What?

JESUS (points at scarecrows): Traditional magic. Protection against evil spirits. There and there, you see the Gris Gris-men? And the signs on the houses? You smell the witch fire? It's an herb the old women burn when evil is around.

There's a bittersweetness in the air, a trace of smoke, a roughness. But it's faint as if the fires have burned down. Murdoch kicks himself for not noticing before. But the rain forest is full of smells and sounds, cloying heat and oppressive humidity. It's hard to concentrate when sweat is running down your face, sliding down your spine.

JESUS: Lots of protections against evil. Then they ran away. Like evil was coming, but they couldn't stop it, just… confuse it, slow it long enough to escape.

LIEUTENANT: Modovar? Is the cartel stretching out?

JESUS: Everyone knows Modovar, the cartels, CRAC? They're just men. This is something else.

Murdoch doesn't mention it, but this far in the interior, villages have come to accommodations with Modovar and other horrors. Villagers aren't accessories or collaborators, they just… coexist. He wonders if the Lieutenant is aware of these nuanced relationships in the interior. Then he realizes that she doesn't care.

LIEUTENANT: I don't know. Modovar is pretty fucked up. There's something more going on there. There was some strange things in the file, something beyond…

MURDOCH: So you did read the briefing?

Murdoch's heart is pounding suddenly, and he feels a cold sweat trickling down his back. His briefing wasn't complete. Large sections on Modovar were redacted, disturbing things, reading between the lines, around the edges, the parts he was allowed to see and the parts he could figure out painted a disturbing picture, one that his rational mind would not accept. It had kept him up nights afraid to sleep for fear of the dreams that would come.

Had she read the whole thing? Those parts he'd been denied. Was this why she seemed so strange, so damaged?

MURDOCH: Do you think we're compromised? Modovar knows?

Murdoch is almost excited at the thought. The mission's blown. They can turn around and go, too bad, so sad. One of those things. No one can blame them.

The Lieutenant seems to think it over.

LIEUTENANT: It doesn't matter.

Murdoch is aware that he should be shocked. And he's aware that he isn't. If you're compromised, you scrub the mission. Enemy knows you're coming, is ready for you? You don't go. Standard protocol. Scrubbing the mission, that's what should happen.

But Murdoch is coming to realize, this isn't an ordinary mission. The rules don't apply. This is more like a guided missile proceeding to destination. Because whatever is in the back of the truck, he knows that's not regular Special Forces.

That's not any kind of Special Forces...

It's with a sense of shock that Murdoch is suddenly aware of how intensely he wasn't thinking about the Special Forces, or whoever or whatever that was in the back. How rigorously he'd forced the awareness from his mind, until, now that he'd actually focused on it, it was like a bath of ice water. He felt assailed by waves of formless dread, as if even awareness of the things in the truck was toxic and corrosive. He tightened his grip on his pistol. The thought flitted through his mind, how soothing, how restful it would be to put the tip of the pistol under his chin and pull the trigger, how it would free him from this awful nameless, formless feeling of dread.

He glanced at Jesus, clutching his rosary. He liked the boy, and with a sudden flush of human sympathy, decided to do him a favor. He'd shoot the boy first, and then himself. Yes.

The Lieutenant was staring at him, giving him her awful blank, empty look. But there was something odd in it, far in the back, as if from a great distance. Something human.

The spell was broken.

MURDOCH: We had a stop scheduled here.

The Lieutenant seemed to think it over.

LIEUTENANT: No. We don't stop here. No one goes into those houses. We come to a place like this, no one goes in. We keep going. Come night, we'll make camp.

She turns around, and heads back for the truck. The words come back to them.

LIEUTENANT: We keep going.

At they leave, Murdoch stares out the passenger window, staring in the side mirror, at the seven scarecrows, the Gris Gris men. Something about them bothers him, but then it slips away.

* * *

The sun goes down and it is completely dark. It's still hot though, and humid. The day sounds fade away, and a strange new symphony of clicks and whistles and howls take its place. Somewhere near the water, something groans loudly, and there's a splash.

The Lieutenant insists that they not leave the cab, despite the suffocating heat and the stench of their own sweat, so they sleep in their seats. The Lieutenant puts on her flight helmet, Murdoch can see that the visor is mirrored and cracked. He wondered where she'd gotten it, why she seems so attached to the broken piece of equipment.

She leans back with her pry bar across her lap and goes to sleep. He listens to her soft snores, and takes comfort. To Murdoch it's the first truly human sound she's made. In the darkness, a lion roars, but she does not wake.

Jesus clutches his rosary and softly, quickly, recites the Lord's Prayer. His voice was comforting. After a while, Murdoch places his hand on Jesus, their fingers tangling together in the prayer beads and joins him in the whispering benediction. His body pressed against Jesus', the sweat drenched fabric of their shirts and trousers mingling and he found he was hard. The two of them hold each other, reciting the prayer over and over until he falls asleep.

Murdoch's dreams are strange and awful, about stumbling desperately through the darkness, unseen shadowy presences stalking him, he dreams of suffocation and drowning. He knows he's dreaming and desperately wants to wake up. When he does, he can't remember any of it, just a vague sense of terror.

* * *

Half way through the morning, they are stopped. Murdoch is mildly surprised, but only mildly. Satellites had showed the road clear, so this checkpoint is new. CRAC extending its reach. The revolutionary army did that from time to time, changing its positions, advancing, retreating, or simply moving, staying ahead of the Colombian Army.

This far out, sometimes you could get away with an explanation, or a bribe, or you might end up robbed, or simply abused for amusement until they decided to let you on your way.

Or they'd simply rob you, execute you, and leave your bodies to rot on the side of the road.

Armed, uniformed soldiers surround the truck, aiming their assault rifles, barking out commands. Jesus halts the truck, and turns off the engine. All three in the cab raise their hands, making no movements.

Murdoch considered their options and didn't like them one bit. He counted nine, no officer visible, but there would be one. He didn't see a vehicle but there would be at least one nearby and camouflaged. Probably a heavy weapon too, possibly a fifty caliber, or an RPG. There was a tree overlooking them, possibly what passed for a sniper was hidden in the foliage.

Two pistols: Hers and his. Two rifles: His and Jesus'. She had that damnable pry bar. No fighting their way out.

One of the soldiers is screaming at them, Murdoch had enough Spanish to know they were being ordered out.

The Lieutenant nods her head as if to comply but doesn't move. She keeps her hands on her head. On his side of the truck, one of the soldiers stepped up on the runner, and reaches for the door handle. It clacked. Locked. The soldier shouts orders.

Murdoch moves slowly to comply.

LIEUTENANT: No.

MURDOCH: What?

LIEUTENANT: No. Don't open the door. Don't do anything. Keep your hands on your head, and just keep looking forward. You know tunnel vision, just do that, stare into the tunnel. Make it as narrow as you can. Don't look anywhere else.

Shouting from the back. A burst of gunfire. More shouting.

A scream. The truck rocks slightly, as if something is climbing on, or getting out.

LIEUTENANT (whispering): This is very important. Don't look. No matter what you hear, don't look. Don't look out the windows, or in the mirrors. Don't look to the side, not for any reason. Just stare straight ahead. Don't speak, don't talk, don't move. Don't make any noise. Just stare straight ahead, no matter what.

Murdoch's heart is racing. His pistol hangs at his hip, but he keeps his hands on his head, too afraid to reach for it. From the corner of his eye, he can see Jesus, lip trembling, ashen, too frightened to pray.

LIEUTENANT (whispering): Don't look at them. Just look ahead. It will be over soon.

Murdoch wants to say something, but is afraid to speak. The terror from his nightmare is back, half remembered, but vivid. His mouth is dry, he can feel cold sweat running down his back, his guts are knotting. He's terrified, but he's not sure whether he's scared of the soldiers or whatever it is in the back of the truck. Two words flitter through his mind: "It's out!"

There are more screams. More bursts of automatic fire. From the tree, there's a series of muzzle flashes. The truck rocks again, and again. On the periphery of his vision, he sees soldiers running, shouting, firing weapons. Perhaps running towards something. Perhaps fleeing, he's not sure. The minutes drag on to howls of pain, and weapons fire growing desultory and infrequent, and at one point a soft muted 'floof' that might be a muffled explosion.

And then there's no more weapons fire. Just the sound of screams and sobbing. Then just silence punctuated by sobbing. Occasional broken begging.

LIEUTENANT (whispering): Don't move. It's almost over.

There's a tap at the window. Murdoch and Jesus both jump in their seats, but they don't look. Tap. Tap. Soft.

Murdoch stares straight ahead with more intensity than he's ever felt in his life. But despite it, he's vividly aware that there's something outside his window. Something standing on the runner, just as the soldier had, but something taller and larger and more dangerous, something is standing there looking at him.

Something that wants him to look back.

Tap. Tap. This sound is harsher, not tapping with a finger, but something hard: wood perhaps, or metal... or bones. Murdoch blinks and swallows.

LIEUTENANT (whispers tensely): Don't.

Murdoch doesn't move. He focuses on a speck on the windshield, the remains of a dead insect. He makes that his whole world, refusing to look away, to even look past. Just focusing on the speck.

Eventually, the presence seems to move away.

Suddenly, there's a childlike giggle. The Lieutenant gasps. Murdoch almost looks at her, his heart pounds suddenly in his chest, as he realizes that the Lieutenant is as terrified as they are.

But it doesn't repeat.

It's just quiet.

After fifteen minutes, the Lieutenant speaks.

LIEUTENANT: It's okay. We can go now. Start up, and let's start driving.

They put their hands down gingerly, Murdoch's shoulders are on fire. His body is a mass of stress, as if he's run a marathon. Over in the driver's seat, Jesus is shaking like a leaf, the boy looks like he's about to burst into tears.

MURDOCH: Are you sure? Should we get out and...?

LIEUTENANT: No. Don't get out. Just drive.

Her voice is unsteady.

MURDOCH: But....

LIEUTENANT: No.

The engine roars to life. The truck lurches into gear. Murdoch breathes deeply, realizing he's been practically holding his breath all this time. The cabin stinks of acrid fear sweat, it's almost overpowering. He doesn't even think of opening a window.

The truck rumbles along, bouncing on the rough path. Murdoch holds himself as steady as he can, staring straight ahead. Finally, when he can't contain it any more, he asks the question.

MURDOCH: What the hell was that?

But the Lieutenant doesn't answer. Murdoch won't give up.

MURDOCH: How did you know? How did you know when it was safe to go?

There's a long pause.

LIEUTENANT: I can feel them.

She pauses.

LIEUTENANT: And you're starting to feel them too, a little.

When he dares, he glances out the passenger door window.

Someone has painted a big smiley face on the outside of the window.

In blood.

* * *

LIEUTENANT: I thought I saw a tiger!

Murdoch follows her pointing finger, sees the flash of orange and black stripes disappearing into the jungle. The windows are rolled down slightly, the bottom of the smiley face is obscured. It's still unbearably hot and humid, but the movement of air makes it bearable. The reek of fear that had filled the cabin has diminished.

MURDOCH: It's a tiger all right.

The truck grinds to a halt as Jesus throws it into neutral, and cranes his neck, trying to catch a glimpse.

LIEUTENANT: How can that be? Tigers aren't native to South America?

The psychopathy has cracked and a human being is peaking out. She sounds... normal. Murdoch allows himself to relax a little.

MURDOCH: Cartels.

He takes a breath. Jesus is listening too, the youth obviously interested. Murdoch collects his thoughts.

LIEUTENANT: Cartels? Was that in the briefing? Tell you what, let's just park here for a while, I'd like to hear about this.

MURDOCH: Are you sure? I think we're just a half hour out from the next village. We can go in, get something to eat, I'll tell you about it then.

She seems to think about it, and shakes her head.

LIEUTENANT: I just now saw a tiger. I think I'd like to hear about it while it's fresh.

Murdoch shrugs, willing to cater to her while she's being human.

MURDOCH: I think the first cartel. Pablo Escobar? Remember him. The thing is, these guys running things, they'd have more money than god. Insane amounts of money. They'd just do anything. So Escobar decided he wanted a personal zoo, right in the middle of the Colombian jungle. And if he wanted...

LIEUTENANT: So it's from Escobar's zoo? What, thirty or forty years ago. How long do tigers live?

MURDOCH: That's the thing. It was a big zoo. He had a lot of money, an unbelievable amount. So he didn't get just one animal. He'd pick up a few, two or three, a dozen. Male and female. Pairs would breed. Anyway, Escobar died. His animals, probably some of them were killed or sold. But it's the middle of the jungle and no one is paying to retrieve them, or maintain them where they are. A lot of them ended up in the wild, released or escaped. That tiger you saw, probably second or third generation.

JESUS: It's actually pretty cool.

MURDOCH: Sort of. Not so cool if one starts hunting you. Some of the animals, mountain goats or camels, probably didn't fare so well in the jungle. But a lot of them, like the tigers, survived and fit right in. I hear that there may even be a few wild elephants; not many of those though. The worst ones are the hippos.

LIEUTENANT: Hippos? Hippopotamus? Like on African Safari at Disney? They're cute.

MURDOCH: They're vicious, bloodthirsty animals, and they kill more humans in Africa than all other animals combined. They live in water or dense brush, they're huge and powerful, almost impossible to stop. They have no predators. Escobar's zoo released a small herd.

Jesus nodded.

MURDOCH: The jungle here suits them perfectly, they can hide in the rivers and streams. You don't see them until they're on top of you. They've been reproducing and expanding their range every year. They're actually quite dangerous, not afraid of humans. There have been more and more reports of attacks each year.

LIEUTENANT: Why doesn't the government do something? Or the locals? Cull the population?

MURDOCH: The government barely controls the territory, if it does at all. If it can't handle CRAC and Modovar, I don't think it's going to spend any effort on hippos. And the beasts are mean enough that no one goes hunting.

LIEUTENANT: Interesting.

MURDOCH: I guess. Shall we get going? We're close to the next phase.

The Lieutenant shakes her head and yawns.

LIEUTENANT: You know what? Let's take a break. Wait a bit. Stretch our legs.

That's when Murdoch notices. He glances at Jesus to be sure, notes the ease with which he sits, the lack of tension. He examines his own absence of dread, the suffocating weight that has enveloped him this whole mission is lifted. Not entirely gone, and he realizes suddenly, it will never go away, it will be with him for the rest of his life, he's marked, contaminated. But the overpowering sense of it, that's lifted.

Murdoch adds it up.

MURDOCH: They're not here. I can feel it. They've gone up ahead, haven't they?

The Lieutenant stares carefully at him. Jesus watches them both, only half understanding. Finally, she speaks.

LIEUTENANT: Yes.

Nothing more. Murdoch stares at her, watches her eyes, her hands.

MURDOCH: You're different. The way you've been, that's because they were around, isn't it? But now, they're not here. So....

LIEUTENANT: Yeah.

She looks out the window, not meeting his eyes. Earlier, she could have stared emptiness into him for days on end. Murdoch takes a deep breath. He gathers his thoughts.

MURDOCH: Modovar, he knows we're coming. He's probably got something waiting up at the landing. That's why they've gone ahead.

The Lieutenant shrugs.

LIEUTENANT: Probably. (Sighs) I know, protocol is when surprise is lost, scrub the mission. But we both know this isn't a normal mission. It didn't really matter. We figure that with whatever he's got, he'd know we were coming. His Intel has been better than ours. That's why he runs rings around law enforcement. This... group? There's no hiding them. We figured he'd know something was coming, just maybe not exactly what.

Murdoch absorbs this without comment. He's figured out this much already.

Jesus is watching them carefully, comprehension dawning. The boy will have to be managed, one way or the other. Sooner or later, he'll come to the obvious question, the one that Murdoch is wrestling with.

Suddenly, he wonders if they'll have to kill the boy. He tries to push the thought away, repelled by it. Jesus is innocent, he's done nothing, he doesn't deserve... whatever is going on. How can he even think like this? The boy knows nothing. He knows nothing.

But at some point, both of them might. Murdoch decides he shouldn't press any further. No more questions, especially not in front of the boy. No answers that they won't be allowed to live with. But he can't help himself.

MURDOCH: So this... so called Special Forces Team?

LIEUTENANT: The Squad. We call them The Squad. Squad Thirteen.

MURDOCH: The Squad? Who the fuck are they? What the fuck are they? Are they even human? If I went back there, what would I have seen? Horns? Raptors? Tentacles?

Murdoch is mildly shocked by his own questions, by the assumptions under it. It's been in his mind, but to speak things like that out loud?

But he's felt the cloying claustrophobic darkness of their presence. He hasn't seen them, but he's felt it. It's not anything human.

The Lieutenant shrugs, there's something forlorn in the gesture.

Abruptly, an image crystallizes in Murdoch's mind, the hulking man in the mask and tattered overalls by the side of the road. Suddenly, he's very sure he knows what at least one member of the Squad looks like.

LIEUTENANT: We don't know.

MURDOCH: What the fuck?

Murdoch is frustrated, particularly because he feels she's trying to be honest. Murdoch pauses, tries to get his head around it, reframe his thoughts. Come at this from another angle.

MURDOCH: What's your part in this? You're in charge, he wants to demand. How do you not know, if you're in charge? How do you not bother to read briefings? Do you think this is tourism? How do you kill a man with a pry bar and just leave pieces of his brain on it? Why do you carry the thing? Are you one of them?

The Lieutenant looks out the window, not to lie, Murdoch decides, but to organize her thoughts, focus herself.

LIEUTENANT: I'm what they call a 'Final Girl.'

Murdoch absorbs this. Finally, he speaks.

MURDOCH: I have no fucking idea what that means.

LIEUTENANT: I guess. (Nods to herself). Do you know anything about anthropology? Mythology? Masks? Since humans began, there have been masks. And the thing is, when people put on masks, they change, they're different. The folklore is that they get possessed, they let spirits into them. Or maybe the masks lets something out of them. It takes away the face. Identity gets lost, or maybe the spirit leaks away, and there's something empty left. I don't know.

LIEUTENANT: Sometimes, once in a while, there's something. There's a man and a mask, and it's not human. It's like some death god or something.

JESUS: What the fuck are you talking about? This isn't Christian talk. Death gods?

Murdoch is surprised at Jesus swearing. But he holds his tongue.

LIEUTENANT: We think that it's always been around, the phenomena. Comes and goes, ebbs and flows. But if you look at history and myth, and you know where to look, you'll find them.

Murdoch glances at Jesus, they share a look, an acknowledgment that the woman is insane. All this talk of masks and myth in the middle of the sweltering jungle. Except that they've felt the presence of whatever had been in the back of the truck.

The Lieutenant pauses, licks her lips, and continues.

LIEUTENANT: Anyway, back in the nineteen-seventies and eighties, they started to appear, mostly in out of the way places. The bodies would pile up, and they'd disappear, except that they'd show up again later, and more bodies. After a while, there were a lot of them. Things with leather masks, or hoods, or Halloween masks, helmets, faces made from human skin, they're just... unstoppable, bulletproof. Stab them, shoot them, blow them up, nothing stops them.

Murdoch nods carefully, watching her. She's not looking at them. He can tell she believes what she's saying. He waits.

LIEUTENANT: Eventually, you know, law enforcement, the military, the intelligence community, starts to notice a pattern. So it goes looking for these men in masks.

MURDOCH: And?

LIEUTENANT: Doesn't go well. Bodies, lots of bodies. They can't really be stopped. You can maybe get away, or slow them down. If you're a Final Girl, you can survive. Everyone else? Dead.

MURDOCH: So how does there get to here? What, you sent them all Draft letters? And they showed up?

LIEUTENANT: Someone finally had a bright idea. Put them together, and use them. Point them at really fucked up shit, and let them do it. Really fucked up shit. Things you can't imagine. Vampires? Aliens? Things we don't even have names for. You wouldn't believe the shit I've seen.

MURDOCH: What's in it for them?

LIEUTENANT: I don't know. They don't talk to us. There's no communication. I suppose they get to kill, that's what they do. We send them, but we don't get in their way.

MURDOCH: And you?

LIEUTENANT: Final Girl. I'm good at staying alive around them. I can point them at things... sometimes.

MURDOCH: They're pointing them at some fucking run of the mill drug lord?

LIEUTENANT: Modovar's not run a run of the mill drug lord. He's fucked up shit. Ever hear of Crimson?

Both men nodded.

LIEUTENANT: It's not just a drug. It's some kind of supernatural or metaphysical virus, or maybe coding or something, it programs users to carry out these weird escalating blood rituals. Ritual mass murders all over the Eastern Seaboard. You heard of those?

MURDOCH: No. I don't follow that crap.

LIEUTENANT: Well, it's happening, and it goes back to Modovar, or whoever is dealing for him, or making product for him. It doesn't matter. Maybe it's Modovar, or just someone close. But there's a wizard or a demon, or maybe some alien with blood tech, or a D&D nerd who stumbled onto something real. We don't care. It's all just fucked up shit and it's going to keep getting more fucked up, unless we do something. So here we are, and there they are.

Murdoch was quiet for a few moments reflecting on it. If they were back in Puerto Miguel, he'd have no hesitation in saying it was insane. But now on the road, with an abandoned village, and a slaughtered guerilla unit, and whatever it had been that had been tapping on the window... that had drawn a smiley face in blood... the definition of what was insane had drifted.

Maybe he was insane. Maybe it was just her, carrying some kind of infectious insanity, and he and Jesus had caught it. Maybe it was all smoke and mirrors, and there was nothing in the back except whatever she'd convinced them of.

He didn't believe it for a second.

But there was a sane part to the story, something that wasn't a feeling, or some cryptic glimpse from the corner of your eye. Something real and concrete. The man they were heading towards.

MURDOCH: You realize, this fucker, Modovar. He's got a fucking army. Hell, add CRAC, he's got two fucking armies. Three if he wants to buy Colombia's. I don't care what these fuckers are, he can put as many guns between them and him as he needs to. If he's that bad, nuke him from orbit. Fly a plane over, fuel air explosive, whatever. Just obliterate him.

LIEUTENANT: Some kinds of fucked up shit, that doesn't work for.

Murdoch nodded slowly. Of course. Because we've all lost our minds, and doing something sensible doesn't work. He had the sense that they'd left the real world, somehow found their way into a world of nightmare logic.

Then it struck him, a moment of insight. A certainty.

MURDOCH: Modovar knows you're coming.

She nodded.

LIEUTENANT: It won't matter.

Murdoch's expression didn't change, but his eyes widened.

MURDOCH: That confident? Okay.

Murdoch looked over at Jesus, deliberately shifting his attention.

MURDOCH: What do you say, amigo? Is this the most fucked up thing you've heard? What's your take?

Jesus blinked at suddenly being included in the conversation, he blushed and leaned forward, clutching the steering wheel.

JESUS: I think... I think... We should turn around and go home. Leave this 'Squad' to Mr. Modovar. This isn't for people like us. No good will come of it.

MURDOCH: I agree. I think they're close enough to Modovar, especially as he knows. I say leave them to it. Time to go home.

He paused.

MURDOCH: While they're gone, we can leave. They're not here, we can feel them when they're here. We can't feel them now. We could go. Leave them behind. They can just go ahead without us.

LIEUTENANT: You can't.

Murdoch's lip quirked. Somehow he knew she'd say that. He notices her fingers tightening slightly on the pry bar. He remembers the first time he'd seen it, the end of it, caked with human gore and clumps of hair. It occurs to Murdoch that she's not telling the whole truth. Maybe there's an omission. Maybe she forgot to mention that sometimes it's Women in Masks. He glances at Jesus, willing him to speak.

JESUS: Why not?

LIEUTENANT: Because you'll die.

While she's speaking to Jesus, Murdoch allows his hand to rest on the pistol. It's not even a movement really, not noticeable at all. His fingers curl around the grip. He tenses.

LIEUTENANT: I'm sorry, but you've felt them, you've felt what they're like. There's no going back, they'll just find you and kill you. No running. No hiding. You'll only draw their attention. The only way is forward. We follow the path to the end, stay in the eye of the hurricane. It's the only way to survive.

She puts her hand on Jesus' as it rests on the steering wheel. Murdoch feels... something, jealousy, concern for the boy. There's something wrong with her, and he doesn't like her touching Jesus. It's as if she's contaminated.

LIEUTENANT: I'm sorry you're in this. I'll do my best, I'll try to make sure you both come out of this alive and safe. But there's no choice. We have to go through to the end.

Murdoch's eyes narrow.

MURDOCH: So just stay close to you?

LIEUTENANT: Close as you can. You won't be safe no matter what. But the farther you get, the more danger. They're watching. If you're out of my sight…

There's a clean shot, she's not even looking at him. She can't see, Jesus is in her way. Unless she's faster than any human possibly could be, it is muzzle to her head, pull trigger, game over.

Jesus will scream, after all a woman's head's blown off right in front of him. But he'll know it was necessary, he'll accept it.

The trouble is that deep down, more certainly than he's known anything in his life, he knows she's telling the truth. He's felt those things, felt their presence, and more than that, felt their attention. She's the only thing that's kept them alive in their presence. That attention won't go away.

Maybe the better thing would be to just put the pistol in his mouth. There's a fleeting impulse there, a residue of their presence, that surprises him.

His hand slips from the pistol.

MURDOCH: Sounds like we're pretty fucked.

LIEUTENANT: I'll do my best.

* * *

LIEUTENANT (voice over): There's no one left alive in O'Heirs Landing when we finally arrive of course. No conversation as we drive in. Murdoch and Jesus look pretty shook up. But that's not surprising. I'm impressed that Murdoch figured as much of it out as he did.

O'Heirs Landing used to be a Catholic mission, founded by an Irish priest, on a clearing by the junction of the Oricali River. The river had given access to a huge swath of the Colombian interior, to the tribes and settlers. A trading post had grown up, and then a little mission school. The Catholics had gone home, but the little town, now established, had carried on, weathering the rise and fall of drug lords and revolutionary movements.

LIEUTENANT (voice over): And more impressed that he was prepared to blow my brains out. Or at least, prepared to try. I hope they survive.

They pull up into what passes for the town square. On one side, the river. On the other, a large white building, walls covered with stucco, mounted on piles. The doors are open. It's dark inside. Around it a handful of smaller buildings, dwellings. Chicken coops, gardens, some derelict vehicles.

Nothing is moving.

The truck pulls into the square, sweeps around before it stops and they disembark. To the left, not visible from the road, several trucks are clustered together under the shelter of one of the great trees, behind a pile of sandbags and earth. A makeshift fortification. The Lieutenant turns around, trying to spot the owners.

The boy shivers.

JESUS: They're here, I can feel them watching.

There's no sign of the Squad. Jackson, Vernon, Michaels, Sawyer, Hopkins any of them. That's not a surprise. Mostly, you only see them when they want to be seen, when they show themselves.

LIEUTENANT: It's not that they can turn invisible. It's just that they're good at not being where you are looking. Even when you know they're there, even when you're running from them, you just keep looking where they're not, right up until the moment they're right there.

MURDOCH: I feel it too. Is it always like this?

His hand is tight on his pistol.

LIEUTENANT: It's hard to feel them when they're on their own. Not unless you're sensitive or tuned in, and even then not necessarily.

She pauses.

LIEUTENANT: Like Mansfeld up in Oregon, Mister Christmas, they called him. Our latest recruiting effort. Killed half the team, no one saw him, no one felt him coming. Just that stupid little giggle. He's settled in with the rest. But he still scares me.

Murdoch absorbs this quietly.

She's scared of them too.

LIEUTENANT: But we can feel them when they're together. I've been wondering about that. Are they letting us feel them, deliberately broadcasting? Is this something they can dial up or down, or shut off? Or is this just a factor of them being together? The more of them, the stronger it gets?

Her voice trails off. She's not sure what to think. Or more accurately, every line of thought leads to disturbing places. If only the R&D people could stay sane long enough to come up with some answers.

Murdoch keeps to the open areas, he steps over to a derelict pickup truck, pulling away a tarp and prying into the back. He pulls a long object out. She recognizes it. Military ordnance.

MURDOCH: RPG. Rocket Propelled Grenade. Someone was waiting for us. Paramilitary.

A dog runs past carrying a child's arm in its jaws, the hand waving jauntily at them. The dog glances towards the trio and skitters off. Murdoch thought it had the decency to look ashamed.

JESUS: Is everyone dead? Everyone? No one is left?

The Lieutenant shrugs.

LIEUTENANT: Probably. They don't usually leave anything alive. It doesn't matter.

Jesus points to the wall of a stucco building. The school house? She can't tell. There's some kind of design on it, so hastily and sloppily painted, that she can see smears and runs.

JESUS: A ward against evil. Like in the village. Maybe some of them knew what was coming?

The Lieutenant doubted it.

JESUS: I know this place. When I was young, we used to come out here, to trade, when my father wanted a knife or an axe, or when mother wanted cloth. I never saw buildings so big, I stared and stared. We would come sometimes for holy services, the Priest, he had a projector and he would show movies after, always the same ones. But it was like magic.

Murdoch and the Lieutenant glance at each other. She feels a sudden wave of sympathy. After a while in this job, it all blends together, every place is every other place. But this was part of his life. It makes her uncomfortable.

JESUS: When I was a boy, Mother got sick. We came here for her. We all lived here a month, but the medicine man, he tried, but he said there was nothing he could do. We tried a witch too. But they both told us, go to the city.'

MURDOCH: Puerto Miguel.

JESUS: Didn't help. She died. We stayed there after.

At that point, something cried out. It sounded like a baby. They all looked at each other.

LIEUTENANT: No.

Jesus and Murdoch looked at each other. She could tell what they were thinking.

JESUS: You said they don't leave anything alive?

LIEUTENANT: They don't, not usually.

They could tell she was lying. The truth is, they like to leave a survivor, sometimes a couple, to carry the word. Or as a lure.

Somewhere up ahead they can hear the sound of an infant wailing, sobs of irritation or hunger. Imagine a child in its crib, crying, scared, alone. If that is a baby. Maybe it is, maybe it isn't. Some of them like tricks.

LIEUTENANT: We have a mission. We need to get going.

JESUS: The dog was alive. Back at the village we saw a goat.

He's trying to convince himself. She shouldn't allow that. Not if she want to keep him alive.

MURDOCH: You said probably. Should we search? We should search.

Search? The Lieutenant shudders at the thought of what they might find. The wind shifts bringing a stench of blood and excrement.

LIEUTENANT: Even if it is a baby, what are we going to do with it? Bring it on the mission? Leave it. Someone else will be along, they'll take care of it.

She curses herself even as the words come out. The Lieutenant can't believe she sounds so cold blooded. Part of her wants to cringe from the way they look at her. She want to protest. To reassure them that she's human too. That she has feelings. But as awful as it sounds, she knows it's just not safe.

LIEUTENANT: You can feel them can't you? All around us. This sense that something is wrong. It's a feeling, like dread, or weight. You can't see them, but you know they're there, watching us, waiting to see what we do. Maybe that's a baby? Maybe they missed it? Or maybe they left it on purpose? Ask yourself: Why? Maybe there's no baby, maybe they just want you to go in there?

Murdoch nods. He understands. Maybe he'll live.

JESUS: I'll go in, just to look. And I'll come right back out. You can watch from the doorway.

The crying goes on, little sobs, choking one after another, building up steadily to an infant's anguished heartbreaking wail, and then starting all over again.

MURDOCH: It's not a baby.

JESUS: I have to see. I'll just go, I'll come right back.

Murdoch swallows.

MURDOCH: I'll go with you.

LIEUTENANT: I'm only going to say this once. If we split up, you're both dead. Whatever is going on with me that keeps me alive, it doesn't extend to you. The minute you're out of my sight, you're dead.

The Lieutenant can tell looking at them, they know she's right. They know she's telling the truth. But the damned baby is crying and crying and none of them can turn away. It's not a baby. But if it is, she imagines it alone in the blood drenched room, crying and crying. No one to change it, no one to feed it. Wallowing in its own filth. Slowly starving, dehydrating. Crying and crying, not understanding why it's dying and no one is coming.

Or perhaps a dog or a jaguar will come, something attracted by the sound. The crying ends suddenly with a crunching of soft bones.

Or maybe, death will appear from the window, a flutter of wings, then perching on the crib and plucking at the hapless squirming body. She imagine a crow, its head darting towards the squirming crying baby, a wail of suffering, and suddenly the crow lifts its head, an eyeball in its beak.

Or worst of all: One of them, doing the things they do. One of the masks, patient and empty and dark.

She sighs and gives up.

Stupid to go in there.

But she can't turn away, none of them can.

LIEUTENANT: We'll go in together. We stay close. Anything happens, run for the dock. One of the boats. Or just swim, they don't like water.

MURDOCH: What if there are crocodiles?

She shrugs.

LIEUTENANT: Take your chances.

They stand facing the building. The Lieutenant legs don't want to move. But Jesus, bless him, steps forward, and Murdoch follows and so she goes along.

Climbing the wooden steps are like climbing Everest. They can feel the psychic weight of the others presence like mountains weighing them down. The charnel house reek of blood and shit and split intestines pours outside. It flows at them like a river in the hot humid air, surrounds us, immerses, and suddenly they feel like they're swimming in decaying flesh.

In the bright light, they can't see anything but darkness inside, yawning, a hungry void waiting to devour them.

This close, they can see the signs of damage. Blood spatters on the steps, a bloody hand print on a door jam. The doors are gone, one side ripped out by the hinges, on the other side a single long splinter of wood hangs from a twisted hinge.

Inside the fucking baby is crying.

All the Lieutenant wants to do is run. She's not special. She's not superhuman. She is frail and mortal, a bag of blood and organs and twisted fragile bones, stumbling and gurgling full of wet sounds. She knows she is not safe from them, not immune. The Division thinks she has some kind of influence, some control, because they haven't killed her yet.

But no one knows what they are or what they do.

Sooner or later she's going to die.

They're at the doorway, and they can sort of see inside. There are bodies everywhere. Dismembered. Posed. Hung. Everyone they've killed in this village, they brought here.

They take another step. They're inside. The stench is unbelievable. In the suffocating heat it is a physical presence, like walking into a wall. The Lieutenant's eyes water. Murdoch is gagging.

There's something right in the center. They stare at it, not really understanding what they're seeing.

Then Jesus speaks, and just like that, it clicks into focus.

JESUS: It's a Christmas tree.

And that's when they hear it.

A giggle.

And that's when the Lieutenant turns around and runs. Rushing down the stairs, Murdoch and Jesus are right behind her. She gets a dozen steps and then vomits. Behind them, the baby cries on, but she doesn't care. None of them are going back.

LIEUTENANT (speaking rapidly): We follow the mission. We take a boat, we go upriver. They won't go in the boat. They don't like water. It blocks them. But they'll follow along the banks.

MURDOCH: Look.

He's pointing.

They see it. Over by the trees, a tall figure in dark blue overalls, standing still as a statue. His face is a corpse mask, handsome bland features, leprous white. He doesn't move. Doesn't acknowledge them. But they know he's watching. Michaels. The Lieutenant nods, acknowledging him.

LIEUTENANT: Time to go.

Concentrate on the Mission, she think. Focus on that. Don't think about what's inside. Don't think about it. Forget the baby. Forget the Christmas tree.

She has a flash of insight. The baby is real, it's alive and it's in there, she's absolutely certain. That's how they work. But she also knows, that if they'd gone in, they'd all die. She doesn't tell the others, she just leaves the baby to its fate, hating herself for it, another step on the path of damnation.

* * *

INTERROGATOR: A Christmas tree? You saw a Christmas tree in there?

MURDOCH: It was and it wasn't. It was made of bones, tied together with ribbons of skin and sinew, so it looked like a tree, trunk and branches. Strips of flesh hanging off. In places, you could see the parts of the body they'd used to be.

MURDOCH: It was green, it was wet and sticky and dripping, it was that fresh. Someone had shredded leaves from outside, and the leaves were sticking to the meat, so it was green and red, streaks of white, I don't know what that was from. It looked festive, like a Christmas tree in a picture book, just like that, until you looked hard, and the more you looked the worse it became.

MURDOCH: The garlands were intestines, they were slick and shiny. So shiny. I saw them pulse with systolic motion, the flesh was dead, but the fluids, the mulch inside was slowly oozing downwards as they hung, and it made them move.

MURDOCH: At the top, instead of a star, there was this bouquet, this crest of eyeballs and tongues tied together. Someone had made a Christmas tree out of children.

The interrogator stares. Finally, he licks his lips, his voice is tremulous.

INTERROGATOR: How do you know it was children?

Murdoch's eyes are haunted and empty. He stares at the Interrogator.

MURDOCH: Because he used their faces for ornaments. He hung them all over the tree.

* * *

LIEUTENANT (voice over): We abandon the truck of course. We grab what food and water we can, working as quickly as possible. Murdoch takes the RPG he'd found, he insists on grabbing as many weapons as we can find. All the time, Michaels stands there in the shadows. He doesn't move once, doesn't twitch. He's like a statue, except when we look up, he is gone.

There were only a few boats on the dock, fewer than expected. As they approach, the Lieutenant look for signs. Places where something might rise out of a pile of leaves, or step out of a shadow. She looks for boards half sawn, ropes half cut, tripwires, splashes of blood, personal objects dropped in a scuffle.

There's a wooden post by the dock, reaching up some twelve feet, a light crudely nailed on top of it, with a line leading down into the earth, presumably to a generator shed. The door of the shed is torn half off. Flies buzz around it.

They glance at each other, but we don't look inside. There's nothing in there they'd want to find. But as they work, we make sure to keep an eye on it, just in case there's something waiting in there that they don't want to find.

Murdoch keep thinking of the baby crying. He wonder if it's still crying. He wonder if they went back he'd hear it. Or if he stopped right now and listened hard. He pauses, listening.

It might have been a baby after all, Jesus wonders. The Men in Masks like to play sometimes, leave a survivor, they might have let one live.

They might have let them walk in and take it, the Lieutenant thinks. They do that sometimes. She thinks it amuses them.

They don't want to think about it. But they can't help it., none of them. They know they can never be forgiven for this.

Against the pole, a chair is leaning back on two legs. The dirt under it is disturbed, high up the pole, about seven feet, there's a gouge in the wood and a red splash.

The Lieutenant can see in her mind's eye how it happened. Someone sitting, watching the river, casually leaning back against the pole.

And then… and then, afterwards, when the body had been disposed of, one of them had carefully put the chair back, because some of them are obviously fastidious.

At the dock, they find more boats sunk into the waters. Canoes with holes in them. Most of the boats that are floating have water in the bottom. The marks are there, bloodstains, a steering wheel torn off. None of these are for them, they'd get a mile up the river before they started to fall apart.

There is an intact motorized river skiff, with a little cabin at the back, fully fueled, as if waiting for them. Of course.

The smell from inside the school clings to them. She can feel it, she knows the others do too.

They can all hear the baby in their heads.

They don't talk about it. They just load up, and set off.

Jesus is in the cabin, piloting the boat. Murdoch told her that he was born on this river. That's why he was recruited. A poor boy, from the rivers come to the big city, Puerto Miguel, marveling at paved streets and buildings two and three stories tall, and so many stores and shops they made a row of them. He'd been an easy recruit for Murdoch. Poor bastard.

JESUS: Back there, there weren't as many boats or trucks as I expected? There should have been more? I think some of them left, you know? Remember the wards they painted? I think some people felt something coming, and they left, they got away?

Jesus' voice rises to a question at the end of each statement. He's trying to convince himself. They let him talk. He needs to talk. Murdoch has no words. There's nothing for the Lieutenant to say.

The Lieutenant tries not to think of the Christmas tree. The image keeps forcing itself into her mind. You can't ever forget how awful they are. But some things…

JESUS: Out here, it's not like the city. People can tell. That first village. I think they felt something coming, they put up their wards at first, but they knew to run away. No one died there. I'm sure of it?

MURDOCH: Maybe.

JESUS: They were all in the truck, the ones with us. They couldn't get there first. No one died there.

The Lieutenant feels guilty now. She doesn't think they escaped. No one ever gets away from them, not unless they want to leave a survivor.

MURDOCH: The cartel transits a lot of product different ways. Planes mostly, helicopters. But there's a dozen routes out. They keep it quiet. The ones at the checkpoint in the jungle, at O'Heirs, they were waiting for something. Modovar, he knows something is coming.

Murdoch pauses.

MURDOCH: Modovar put them there. It was an ambush. But he doesn't know, doesn't understand what it is. Or he'd have done more, a lot more. I dunno. He'd have napalmed us, sent tanks, helicopters.

He stares at the water.

MURDOCH: He doesn't know. I didn't know. If I knew, I wouldn't. I wouldn't. I just wouldn't.

Murdoch is losing it. Jesus and the Lieutenant simply stare at him.

MURDOCH: When I was a kid my father took me to a movie. I was young, I don't remember much, not even the name. Just some guys going down a river. It was funny, I laughed. I think that was because I was young. But I remember this one guy, he said that he was afraid of being in some place so dark and evil that if he died there, his soul would never be able to find its way out to heaven, that it would be lost there, forever.

He looks up at them.

MURDOCH: I can still feel them. Not like in the truck. But I can feel them, they're out there.

Jesus looks up, his eyes searching the shore. The Lieutenant glances at him.

LIEUTENANT: Stick to piloting. We don't need to run aground because you get distracted. Murdoch will keep an eye on the shores. I'll keep watch up front.

She is harsher than she mean to be. But what can she say? That they'll live through this? At some point, that becomes a threat, not a promise.

The Lieutenant makes her way to the front of the boat, sitting at its bow. There's nothing to watch out for. The river is high, and they're going down the center. It's not as if there's a sand bar to hit. At least she's away from them. It's hard to bear up under their stares. It's hard to promise they'll live.

* * *

GENERAL: Free neutrons.

LIEUTENANT (voice over): I glance at the old man, all dress uniform, wearing his salad proudly. None of those military decorations helped in the end.

LIEUTENANT: What?

GENERAL: That's what radiation is. Radium, Polonium, Curare. It's just unbalanced atoms, not symmetrical, too large. So they shed a neutron. It goes wandering, and if it hits another big unbalanced atom, then it knocks a neutron loose there. That's all it is, just unstable decomposing atoms, losing neutrons, knocking other neutrons loose. You put enough of them together, all those free neutrons start knocking each other, you get a chain reaction.

The Lieutenant wipes away a film of sweat from her brow, and flicks her hand at the river, watching sweat drops making tiny splashes. She's so tired.

LIEUTENANT: I've had a long day. What the fuck are you on about?

GENERAL: We figured it out you see. We worked it all out, came up with atomic theory, did the math. We made a chain reaction, an atomic pile, an atomic bomb, we did it deliberately. We knew what we were doing.

LIEUTENANT: Maybe you could tell me something useful for once. Like how to cope with them? Oh no! You can't. They fucking killed you. So it turns out, you didn't know fuck all. You were as stupid as the rest of us.

GENERAL: But what if we didn't know what we were doing? What if we were just monkeys? We didn't have theory, we didn't have math. We just thought, hey, that uranium sure is shiny, let's pile a whole bunch of it together!

She decides to ignore him and just stare out at the water. On the shore, some crocodiles slip into the water. Were they crocodiles? She try to remember the briefings she hadn't bothered with. There was another name. Caimans? Fuck it. Alligators, crocodiles, whatever. Who cares?

GENERAL: What would that be like? A whole bunch of stupid monkeys, piling uranium together enjoying the pretty sparkle, not understanding why their hair is falling out, why they're dying, why everything is dying? Until.... BOOM!

She looks behind her. Jesus and Murdoch are talking quietly at the back of the boat. They glance up at her, and she looks away.

GENERAL: You ever stop to think maybe we're the monkeys? We don't understand what they are, where they came from, what they're made of, what principles they operate under. We just thought, hey, let's weaponize this, and we started sticking them together. Like plutonium. We didn't even think about it.

LIEUTENANT: Maybe if you assholes had thought about it, you'd still be alive?

He laughs.

GENERAL: Maybe we made a mistake.

LIEUTENANT: No shit Sherlock. You know, I don't mind you showing up, but maybe some time, you could give me something I could use? If I wanted to hear stupid Alzheimer's stories that don't relate to anything, I could just go see my Dad at the care home.

GENERAL: He's dead.

The Lieutenant gives him her darkest blank look. He laughs and looks out over the waters.

GENERAL: You stress out too much. Where you came from is bad, where you're going is worse. But right now? This is pretty nice. It reminds me of going fishing on the Coyahoga River with my grandson. You should just enjoy the river while you can.

The Lieutenant grins.

LIEUTENANT: You just made a mistake, asshole.

GENERAL: How so?

He looks bemused. She casts her gaze out over the river, smiling.

LIEUTENANT: The Coyahoga River? That's real or it isn't. The real General went there, or he didn't. He had a grandson, or he didn't. They went fishing on the river, or they didn't. I don't know any of these things, I absolutely don't. I can't. But I can check up on that, that's verifiable.

GENERAL: And?

LIEUTENANT: And if it doesn't pan out, then I know you're a hallucination, some diseased part of my rotting brain talking to itself, spewing useless Chinese fortune cookie wisdom.

GENERAL: Or?

LIEUTENANT: Or it checks out, it verifies. Which means you're a ghost, haunting me, with useless meandering Alzheimer bullshit.

The General chuckles.

GENERAL: You're tough, I'll give you that. I'm glad we picked you, I'm glad they let you live. You're not going to last much longer though, you know that, right?

LIEUTENANT: I know.

GENERAL: They're watching you talk to yourself.

He nods towards the back of the boat.

LIEUTENANT: They can go fuck themselves.

LIEUTENANT (voice over): Just then, I notice something in the waters ahead, a disturbance, a ripple, and suddenly a great broad gray curving mass breaks the water. At first I don't understand what I'm seeing. At first it looks unnatural, perhaps some pieces of driftwood or canvas pushed up by a bubble of air. But more and more of it breaches. It's immense, bigger than I imagined, like the back of a whale. But a whale in the river?

LIEUTENANT (voice over): Then the massive head lifts up, and I know what it is. I've never realized how enormous they were. How huge. You see one at the zoo, but it's not the same thing as seeing them in the wild. It's a goddamned hippopotamus!

LIEUTENANT: Hey!

But the General is gone. She calls to the back of the boat, her voice human with excitement.

LIEUTENANT: Hey, check it out! You were right. Hippos!

* * *

At first Murdoch welcomes the change in the Lieutenants personality. This new Lieutenant is human at least, a far cry from the psychopath with the thousand yard stare and a pry-bar caked with human hair and brains.

Her eyes are different, there's someone in there looking out. A responsiveness, as if she's relating to them, not looking at a pair of bugs. There's warmth, humanity, compassion.

And fear.

Until she starts talking to herself, animated angry conversations, sarcastic rejoinders to an unseen companion. Sometimes she glares at an empty spot in the air, or smiles or sneers at an unheard remark.

She tries to hide it at first, but there's no hiding it on the small boat. It disturbs Murdoch.

Jesus crosses himself frequently and avoids her as much as he can on the small boat. He's not sure she's actually talking to herself.

Murdoch doesn't like to think that way, it poses questions as to who or what is talking to her.

Murdoch and Jesus can only watch.

What disturbs Murdoch more, is that the Lieutenant is afraid. She tries not to show it, but Murdoch can spot the signs. The hesitations in speech, the moments of uncertainty in her body language. The brutal purpose and confidence of the psychopath is gone now. She seems nervous, unsure of herself. She scans the waters and shores over and over.

She's terrified, and lost and afraid, just like them.

Murdoch and Jesus have whispered conversations about turning the boat around and going back. Can they persuade her? They discuss beaching her on the shore with food and water, to continue on her own. Or just hitting her with an oar and pitching her into the water. They have their guns, they can just shoot her, no one would know.

But her pry-bar is always near her hand, and Murdoch can't shake the image of the first time he saw her with it: brains and hair clinging to the hook at the end.

If it was just her, they'd chance it. But Murdoch has seen the psychopath version, and he's not sure that's not the real her. And of course the others are out there. They can all feel them, their lurking presences, the suffocating dread ebbs and flows, but it never quite goes away.

He can tell when they're close, the Lieutenant clutches her pry-bar tightly, the psychopathic version of her seems to slide back into place, all relentless certainty and thousand yard stare.

There's no going back.

* * *

There is the sound of a helicopter. Jesus pilots the boat closer to a riverbank, protected by the jungle canopy and idles the engine. They wait, looking up into the green, as the sound passes overhead and then recedes.

LIEUTENANT: We can go now.

The engine cycles up, and they continue.

MURDOCH: We're running out of water.

And food and fuel.

They're staying off the main river, making their way along tributaries, picking their way along the banks. They've almost beached on sand bars twice. This isn't the first helicopter to sweep along the river.

LIEUTENANT: We'll restock. There are villages up ahead.

How does she know? Murdoch wonders. Then answers it for himself. She doesn't. It's just bullshit. She doesn't know the river, she didn't read the briefings or the charts. All that matters to her is the target.

But Jesus nods in agreement, and Murdoch will take that over her. Something catches his eye and he points to the shore.

MURDOCH: Look.

One of them is sitting on the shore with a fishing pole. The overalls are rolled up, exposing bare knees and bare arms. It's found a straw hat from somewhere. Jesus angles the boat further out into the water away from it. It looks for all the world like something out of Mark Twain. Huckleberry Finn fishing for catfish on the bank of the Mississippi.

Except instead of a face, there's a mask, bulging cheeks and forehead, a baby's face. It waves cheerfully.

LIEUTENANT: That's Vernon. Don't wave back.

They have names, Murdoch has learned. They don't answer, they don't respond, but they've been assigned names rooted in local folklore. Jackson, the behemoth he saw by the road. Michaels, the sexton and his corpse masks, filling graveyards. Sawyer, Otis, Hart, Mansfeld. They all have their particular styles, their tools, their methods of play. Vernon is the trickster.

Vernon's fishing pole jerks. With a pantomime of excitement he leaps to his feet, and begins to wrestle with the pole with exaggerated motions. As it jerks up and down, Vernon pretends to struggle heroically, lifting the pole higher and higher, the wood bending.

At the end of the line a human corpse rises half way out of the water. The line snaps, it plunges back in. Vernon falls on his ass and flings down his straw hat in a faux display of frustration.

As they pass around the bend, Vernon waves cheerfully.

Then he's gone from sight.

* * *

MURDOCH: She's talking to herself again.

Murdoch speaks quietly, sitting at the back with Jesus. He's spelling off, piloting the boat while the younger man eats and rests. Jesus glances up and crosses himself.

JESUS: She's talking to someone.

MURDOCH: Them?

But as soon as Murdoch says it, he knows it's wrong. She's too human right now, not as psychopathic. And their presence, even to Murdoch and Jesus' dull awareness, feels attenuated. Faint. They're there, but not close.

MURDOCH: No. No, she's not talking to Them. Or anyone. She's just crazy.

JESUS: She's not right.

Jesus pauses.

JESUS: We should go, leave her behind and go.

Murdoch isn't surprised. He's thought of it too, working it out in his head. It's not the first time either of them has thought about it. Or talked about it.

He's thought about killing her. Shooting her. Cutting her throat as she sleeps. He wouldn't hesitate with the psychopath version of her. But he thinks about it even when she's most human, when she's friendly, conversational. Do it then, a voice whispers, it's the best chance.

He's even thought about enlisting Jesus, knowing the boy would never truly agree, but wondering if he might.

He watches her sometimes, seeing opportunities slip away one after the other. Sometimes, she looks directly at him, as if she knows what he's thinking. The thing that bothers him most, is that she doesn't seem to care.

MURDOCH: Then what? We can both feel them out there, waiting. They're watching.

Murdoch hasn't seen any of them since Vernon. But every now and then, there's something. Footprints on the shore, or an empty spot where there should be crocodilians or birds congregating, or a movement in the bush. Jesus nervously scans the river bank – Murdoch suspects they've shown themselves to the youth. But he's not sure. Neither of them will talk about their sightings.

JESUS: Put her on shore, and then go down the river. She said they don't go on water. Maybe they'll stay with her. We can get away.

MURDOCH: And if they don't?

There's no answer.

MURDOCH: I don't think we can run. I think we have to follow it to the end.

On the river bank, there's a rustling as birds take off and crocodilians slither into the water. The brush seems to part, and for a second, Murdoch almost sees the suggestion of a shape. He looks up quickly, and the Lieutenant has abandoned her conversation with the unseen and is staring at the same spot.

For a moment, Murdoch feels overwhelming dread. The feeling passes, to be replaced by a sudden impulse to take the gun and put it to the soft spot just behind his chin, or to drench himself with fuel and light it, or to give himself to the jaws of crocodilians. It creeps over him regularly now, a morbid hunger, an almost subliminal urge to end himself.

Jesus is pale and shaking, the boy staring at the jungle as well. The urge to extinction passes so quickly that Murdoch doesn't remember having it. Instead, he feels a wave of compassion and sympathy, a warmth that enfolds them both.

MURDOCH: I'm sorry. I'm so sorry I brought you into it. But there's nowhere to go.

* * *

They pass by a small herd of hippos basking on the opposite bank. They've seen lone animals in the water, but this is the first time they've seen a group, or seen them out of the water. The animals range from huge males with massive swinging heads, to smaller females and calves. There's something beautiful and bucolic about them.

The hippos gaze warily as the boat chugs past, the two groups keeping an eye on each other, but not disturbed. Some of the larger hippos yawn at them, immense three foot long heads splitting wide, gaping almost a hundred and eighty degrees into a pink maw five feet wide, exposing massive jagged teeth, culminating in canines like tusks, a foot and a half long.

Murdoch shudders and clutches his gun, but the animals show no more interest. The yawns subside, they drift away casually, paying the boat no mind. He relaxes.

Escobar's Zoo: The other day, they saw an anteater the size of a calf. Jesus swears he glimpsed a chimpanzee.

The shores are thick with crocodiles, the trees alive with birds and monkeys, the green is endless.

It's beautiful, even with the stultifying heat, Murdoch could almost forget the mission. Perhaps they should forget the mission. Perhaps they'll get lost here in the endless maze. Perhaps they're already lost. Would that be so bad? Wandering the green rivers endlessly, like the Flying Dutchman? You can almost fall into that fantasy.

Except they're running out of food and water and gasoline. They're being hunted. And out there in the jungle all around them, things are pacing them, things with human shapes and masks, and wherever they go, there is endless dread.

An hour after the hippos, they come to a village, little more than a collection of huts. Everyone is dead, of course.

They're there, somewhere around. The sense of dread is overpowering. Perhaps they're watching and waiting. Or maybe they've already moved on, their work done, leaving corpses and a psychic residue behind.

They spend a little time ashore scavenging a few cans of gas, huddling close together. They try not to stare at the extravagantly posed corpses, the woman impaled all the way up at the top of a flagpole, the children dangling hung from a clothes line like the day's laundry, a man stretched and elongated to impossible dimensions, suspended between four posts.

The Lieutenant picks her way on a rickety wooden walkway over a marsh, she presses on a railing and it gives way. Bending down, she examines the careful cut in just the right place.

LIEUTENANT: Don't go into any of the huts. Don't touch anything you don't have to.

MURDOCH: They're waiting for us in there?

LIEUTENANT: Vernon was here, he likes to set traps.

Jesus wanders over to a garden, kneeling down to examine the growing plants.

JESUS: It's dead.

MURDOCH: We know, everyone's dead. Let's just get what we can and get out.

JESUS: No. I mean the garden is dead.

Curious, Murdoch joins him. The young man reaches out, touches a vine.

MURDOCH: It's green.

JESUS: But it's dead. It's still green, but it's dead.

He squeezes his hand on the leaves, and they crumble. Murdoch takes a step back, horrified. Jesus points to the ground.

JESUS: See there? Beatles. Ants. They're just dead. The garden is dead.

He lifts a broad leaf, there's a field mouse beneath, lying on its side.

JESUS: See? It's just dead. Their presence, it's not just a feeling that comes with them around. Their presence does this. They are evil and things die in their presence. Life extinguishes.

Murdoch steps away from the garden, he turns towards a tree, reaches up for a low hanging branch. The tree is green with leaves, but as Murdoch tugs on the branch, the leaves come away, crumpling in his hand. He turns to the Lieutenant, who is watching him. She shrugs.

LIEUTENANT: We keep them out in the desert, at an irradiated nuclear test site. There's not much that grows out there. But yes. Plants die, bugs die. Things just die around them, some sort of area effect of their combined presence. We don't understand it.

MURDOCH: But... but you knew about it? About the effect?

LIEUTENANT: Yes.

For a moment, Murdoch is speechless, overcome by the enormity of it, by the thought of an evil so overpowering and pervasive that life simply withers and dies in its presence. By the wanton hubris of thinking that something like that could be managed and used, and what it said about those who would do such a thing...

MURDOCH: You're no better than they are. Maybe... worse.

LIEUTENANT: Fuck off.

There is no force to her words. Murdoch has the feeling that, in that moment, she agrees with him. That within the humanity, there is a pit of self-loathing at what she does, at what she's made to do.

Perhaps that's it, he thinks, she's stuck here, and her humanity is being eroded away, until eventually, there won't be anything left to her but the psychopath he's seen. Maybe she knows it. She sees it in a mirror. She's horrified by what's happening to her. But there's nothing she can do about it.

JESUS: This is an unholy place now. Profane. God cannot see it. We should burn it.

LIEUTENANT: No.

JESUS: Burn it all.

He looks to Murdoch. But the Lieutenant speaks first.

LIEUTENANT: Grow up. Modovar is sending helicopters out. He's probably already got detachments waiting for us. So by all means, let's send out a giant smoke signal for him to find us. We're not going to burn it. We're just going to leave.

She hesitates.

LIEUTENANT: Or you can stay here... with them.

The Lieutenant is practical. But Murdoch thinks she's just as scared as they are.

As they leave, they hear the frenzied shrieking yelps of a dog in terrible agony. They don't look back.

Maybe it is a dog.

Maybe it isn't.

* * *

The next village is absolutely empty and silent, no bodies, no animals alive or dead, no wreckage or ruins. As they stand in the village center, there's complete unearthly silence, no sounds of birds or insects. It's as if everyone calmly walked into the forest and vanished.

Not even Jesus will pretend the inhabitants might have escaped.

The helicopters are frequent now. They avoid the main river, sailing up narrower tributaries where the tree canopy offers concealment.

They stop in the evenings, mooring out on the river, away from shore, tossing a heavy anchor overboard to hold their place. Each morning the three of them must struggle to retrieve. Murdoch is terrified that they'll lose it, that it will get caught up in something down below and they'll have to cut it loose.

Because then, if they lose that anchor, they'd have to moor along the banks, close to them.

Sleeping on the boat is awkward and uncomfortable, there's no respite from the endless oppressive heat, or the insects. Sweat drenches their clothes and makes films of slime on their body no matter how often they wipe it away. Sleep is fitful and full of formless nightmares. They wake up sore and aching each morning, but Murdoch remembers her remark that water seems to block them in some way.

Each night, Murdoch tries to ignore the ceaseless insects, the choking humidity. He listens to Jesus constant prayers, and the Lieutenant's whispered conversations with the air. He tries not to sleep, knowing the dreams that wait for him. But each night, sooner or later, he sleeps.

Early in the morning, before dawn, they hear the sounds of gunfire not far up the river. It goes on, sporadically for hours. They wait until the Lieutenant says it is safe to proceed.

The camp when they find it, was well concealed. 'Was' being the operative word. The concealment and camouflage is torn away. Everyone is dead of course. They were not allowed to die easily or well. It was not gentle or quick.

They take whatever supplies they can find and go.

The next day they encounter the hippos.

* * *

JESUS: I count twenty-four animals... Including the calves.

MURDOCH: Fuck me. How many of the damned things did Escobar import?

Jesus is idling the boat's motor low, so as not to disturb the animals. The tributary they are traveling is shallow and narrow. Up ahead, the herd of hippopotami bask, eating the river vegetation beneath the waters. Diving and breaching, mounting up the shallow banks.

LIEUTENANT: They seem pretty peaceful. Do you see a path through?

The others don't bother to reply. The animals are dispersed randomly from one bank to the next. They yawn frequently, giant gaping maws large enough to swallow a man whole, punctuated by fangs the length of a forearm, literal tusks. Despite the yawns, the animals are placid enough.

Slowly the boat swings sideways in the river current.

They speak in hushed tones.

LIEUTENANT: We could wait, see if a path opens up?

MURDOCH: We could do that. Or maybe just go back, find another way through.

LIEUTENANT: No. We go back, we die. No options.

MURDOCH: Even you?

LIEUTENANT: There are rules. Go back, die. Even me.

MURDOCH: Your job really sucks.

LIEUTENANT: Tell me about it.

JESUS: Maybe we could make a big noise, with the guns and stuff? Scare them away.

MURDOCH: Those are pretty big damned animals. I don't think they scare.

LIEUTENANT: I'd rather not make noise if we can help it. That camp we passed through back there, the one we almost stumbled into? Someone is going to come looking for payback.

MURDOCH: I checked. The radio was wrecked. I don't think they got a call out.

LIEUTENANT: Doesn't matter. They would have been checking in regularly. If they go silent, someone will notice, assume something went wrong, and they'll send out a mission in force. They'll know someone was through, and approximately when. Then they'll sweep, serious sweeps with boats, not just helicopters, until they find us.

Murdoch nods.

MURDOCH: Makes sense. How much of a head start do you figure we have?

The Lieutenant shrugs.

LIEUTENANT: Depends on when the call-in times were, I'm assuming a morning call-in, but they might not worry. Second call-in, probably noon. Miss that, they'll figure something is up. Take a few hours to put together reconnaissance in force, and then figure out how far someone could travel by boat or foot from that point in a given period of time. The further away we get, the more ground they need to cover, the harder we are to find.

Murdoch absorbs this.

MURDOCH: What about your 'friends'? They've been pretty good clearing the path for us. Why won't they clear the ones who come hunting the same way? Was it the water? They can't cross water or something, like vampires?

LIEUTENANT: They're not my friends. And they weren't clearing a path for us.

JESUS: What then?

The Lieutenant waves back the way they came.

LIEUTENANT: It's just what they do. That's all. They're not here to do us favors. If they were going to do this... they'd have done it.

JESUS: You can't ask them?

LIEUTENANT: Can't ask. Can't even talk to them, really.

MURDOCH: Fuck them, so they don't help, they just kill... including us. And the clock is ticking before violent assholes come looking for us. And we've got a herd of hungry, hungry, hippos. So here we are, stuck in the middle, deeper and deeper. I don't know. (sighs) Jesus, do you figure you can pilot us through? Slow and easy, don't rile them up?

JESUS: I don't know.

The doubt in his voice is genuine. The three of them look back and forth.

MURDOCH: Fuck.

LIEUTENANT: I don't think we've got a choice. Arm up, we get low. We don't provoke them. We just pass through.

JESUS: I don't know

The Lieutenant shakes her head.

LIEUTENANT: They're just animals. Everything else we're dealing with is so much worse.

Murdoch checks one of the pistols, hands it to the youth.

MURDOCH: Hang onto this in the cabin. You got the rifle there? Is it ready?

Murdoch catches Jesus's glance at the Lieutenant, he understands and nods ever so slightly.

JESUS: I keep it ready.

LIEUTENANT: That's my pistol.

MURDOCH: Yeah, you're on rifle duty with me. Besides, you have that pig-sticker. This is going to be just like the Jungle Cruise at Disneyland.

Jesus retreats to the small cabin. As the engine revs and the boat swings around the Lieutenant and Murdoch crouch in the bow.

The hippos look up curiously as the boat put-puts towards them. A cow moves away. The boat swings left towards an empty space in the water, away from another cow and two juveniles. On the shore, a bull stares and then yawns, its ears flicking angrily.

It chugs carefully a dozen feet, twenty, then lurches hard to the right to avoid a bull that seems disinclined to move. Only the back and eyes of the immense animal are visible. To Murdoch it's eyes seem to burn with hatred and madness as the boat slowly moves away from it.

MURDOCH (whispers): Just animals. That's all.

They're in the middle of the herd now. Jesus idles the engine, the boat barely holding its place in the current, as he tries to gauge the next step forward. The animals are spooked now, aware of the boat in their midst, their natural movements shift. Some are moving away. The more aggressive ones begin drifting toward the interloper.

A gap opens up, Jesus deliberately paces the boat in that direction, the chugging picks up. The noise rouses the already nervous beasts. Murdoch glances towards the cabin, through the dirty window he can see the youth's intense concentration. His gaze shifts towards the Lieutenant. They exchange nods. They're going to make it.

That's when he goes flying, an impact sending him rolling across the boat, tearing the rifle from his hands, as he hurls into the Lieutenant. There's a bellowing in his ears like thunder, and an echo, no answering bellows. For a moment, a huge head appears over the bow, as it swings wildly to the left. Murdoch glimpses a mouth like pink hell, four curving tusks erupting within it, a gaping nightmare to swallow him, and then it snaps shut.

It's a cow, one with a calf, that has charged the boat, and now the other hippos are converging. Jesus staggers in the tiny cabin, almost losing his grip. He opens the throttle wide, and the boat surges ahead.

There's a crash, and the bow lurches upwards, Murdoch's rifle sliding back. He's not sure if they've crashed, or another one charged.

LIEUTENANT (screaming): Jesus! Get us out of here!

Jesus screams something back in Spanish. Murdoch isn't paying attention. The Lieutenant pushes him off and he's scrambling to recover his rifle. Water is pouring in, the timbers of the starboard hull are broken and pushed in. As Murdoch lays hands on the rifle, the boat lurches again, and he's hurled backwards toward the port side. The boat lurches again, and helpless, he rolls starboard. Paws and shoulders appear above him, four tons of weight dragging the boat back. The largest jaws he's ever seen open wide yawning a horror of pink gaping maw and giant tusks, close enough to seize him and drag him under.

Murdoch screams and throws himself backwards, emptying the rifle's clip into the gigantic maw, watching blood and gore fountain, and then the monster head drops and the creature falls away, the boat lurching and splashing.

The sound of gunfire is loud in his ears. The Lieutenant has managed to brace herself, and is firing controlled bursts at the approaching hippos, first one, then the other, as they sink leaving red blooms in the brown water.

Murdoch tries to fire, but his rifle clicks empty. He's used up the entire magazine. He reaches for his pistol, trying to steady his aim. A section of the side splinters away, the wood torn like match sticks as another Hippo rears up, smashing against the boat, titanic jaws snapping murderously. Murdoch puts three pistol shots into its forehead, point blank and the animal breaks off its attack.

The boat lurches again, this time the bow rising up in the air. Jesus screams, and Murdoch turns to see a hippo, lunging up against the aft section, literally climbing half onto the boat. It's four or five tons of weight unbalancing the entire craft. Jesus fires three shots, and the creature collapses heavily on its side. The boat pitches to the shifting weight, leaning hard left, and the creature slides into the water.

Murdoch is up to his calves in water. The boat is ruptured, water pouring through. Smoke is pouring from the sputtering, coughing engine. Murdoch imagines being trapped in the water with these animals, and the sudden terror eclipses the suffocating dread of the presences. It's almost welcome, if he wasn't so scared he was pissing himself.

MURDOCH (screaming): Jesus! Get us to fucking shore!

He doesn't know if Jesus heard or understood, but the boat turns about, the dying engine roaring, gunning for the bank. Behind it are the wild bellows of the enraged hippos, and the steady measured volleys of the Lieutenant as she picks off the closest animals with controlled bursts.

Despite the chaos Murdoch clutches his pistol like a holy talisman. There's a spare clip in his belt but he can't find his rifle. The bank is coming up fast, and he tries to brace himself.

Murdoch goes flying through the air as the boat slams into the bank. For a moment, in free fall, Murdoch feels surprise, he expected the boat to mount up the river bank, but instead it plowed into the mud and vegetation, the bow splintering and collapsing. As he tumbles, he glimpses the Lieutenant, thrown as well, and feels odd satisfaction at her hapless humanity. The momentum of the crash sends Jesus tumbling the length of the boat, smashing across the wrecked structure.

Then Murdoch lands hard on his back, sinking into grass and soil, all the breath goes out of him, his vision goes spotty, and for a second, he has no idea where he is or who he is.

Murdoch sucks air, thrashes trying to get his bearings. He reaches for his pistol and can't find it. Forcing unwilling limbs to move, he rolls over onto his side.

The boat's on fire.

When had that happened? Had he lost consciousness? How long? A burning slick from the boat stretches across water, a barrier against which the angry hippos bellow but do not approach.

The Lieutenant is dragging Jesus from the boat towards him. Murdoch pulls himself laboriously together and staggers forward to help.

Suddenly, the bushes part, and a massive gray shape is hurtling towards him, its hulking sides' slick with blood. There's a bellow and giant gaping maw of pink, yawning impossibly wide, full of tusks and teeth, is rushing towards them. One of the hippos came up on the bank on the other side of the fire and is charging. All three of them freeze. Murdoch's heart stops dead cold as he sees death bearing down on him. The immense jaws open five feet wide, the tusks protruding out a foot and a half. In that instant, Murdoch knows he's dead, they're all dead.

A figure steps in front of it, and is seized in its monstrous jaws, pierced by tusks, picked up, swung like a rag doll and thrown in pieces. In the next instant, the hippo collapses, dead, a piece of rebar sticking out from its skull. Murdoch stares in mute incomprehension. They all stare.

MURDOCH: Fuck.

Murdoch's mind isn't working, he knows it should work, that he should say something useful, that he should have thoughts, articulations, suggestions, ideas, plans or even comments. He's got nothing.

MUDOCH: Fuck.

LIEUTENANT: Everyone all right?

JESUS: Yeah. I think so.

MURDOCH: Fuck.

There's movement from the corner of his eye. Murdoch tracks it. He's having trouble thinking.

LIEUTENANT: The rest of the gas is going to blow, and whatever munitions. When it goes, it's going to be a giant red flag. We need to get moving and put some distance from it.

For a moment, the words make no sense to Murdoch, they're simply sounds, disconnected from each other. He almost has to physically attach meaning. He's distracted by the movement.

In the grass yards from the dead hippo, is one of Them, torn in half, torso separated from legs by ropes of intestine. And yet still alive, on its back, its head moves side to side, the arms flounder in the air, as if begging for help. The face turns towards him, it's the baby-doll mask. Vernon.

Vernon seems to stare at him, reaches an outstretched hand, the fingers trembling. Clearly in agony, clearly dying, the strength draining out even as Murdoch watches. A dying man, begging for human connection as the dark closes in.

LIEUTENANT (visibly exhausted): Oh fuck you. I'm not in the mood for your bullshit. Pull yourself together, we're not falling for your act.

She sighs.

LIEUTENANT: Or you know, just lay there and wait for whoevers. I'm sure that someone will be along for you to play with.

Vernon's struggles grow more plaintive, the life ebbing out of him.

JESUS: He's fucking torn in half.

The Lieutenant sighs. She picks up her pry-bar from the grass. Retrieves the helmet, straps it to her hip. There's a pistol in the grass, Murdoch's pistol. She picks it up, checks the magazine and then tosses it away. She looks at Murdoch.

LIEUTENANT: Can you walk?

Murdoch stares at the pry-bar, he remembers the blood and gore clinging to it. They're not on the water any more. The barrier that allowed her to be human is gone. The psychopath is back. They're disposable.

MURDOCH: Yeah.

LIEUTENANT: What about him?

She points at Jesus. He's covered with blood, and his arm is funny. Dislocated shoulder, Murdoch thinks. Possible scalp wound. Concussion. Otherwise minor. He can't allow her to decide he's useless.

MURDOCH: He'll be okay. I'll help.

LIEUTENANT: Then we move.

Anger flares in Murdoch, he wants to push back.

MURDOCH: You're kidding? We're fucking lost. We don't even know where we're going.

Psychopathic eyes glitter down at them, her fingers tighten around the pry-bar. Murdoch notices her absently, casually stroke the flight helmet dangling at her hip. Why does she carry that thing? He wonders. He's almost never seen her wear it. It's not even the right kind of helmet for this mission.

LIEUTENANT: I know where to go.

Murdoch gives up.

MURDOCH: All right, fine. Let's go.

He pulls himself painfully upright, steps towards Jesus, reaching out for the young man. Over by the river bank, the flames are climbing higher and higher. There's a crack of ammunition detonating, followed by popping sounds as it begins to cook off. They look over.

LIEUTENANT: Not much time.

Jesus' good arm lays over Murdoch's shoulders. The boy weighs almost nothing. They stagger off. As they pass by, Vernon finds the strength to reach out one trembling arm in supplication. Murdoch hesitates.

LIEUTENANT: Don't encourage him. He's just fucking with you.

Murdoch looks away.

LIEUTENANT: We have to get moving.

They walk.

* * *

Middle of the day, the Lieutenant allows them to stop so Murdoch can pop Jesus' arm back into place. The boy is ready to pass out. He accepts the relocation with barely a grunt. Jesus is out of it. Murdoch checks his pupils, dilated but even.

MURDOCH: He needs to rest for a few minutes.

Psychopath eyes watch. Dread surrounds them. Murdoch stares back, he doesn't care. Finally, the Lieutenant relents.

LIEUTENANT: Fine.

They sit on the forest floor. It's surprisingly dry. The ground is spongy. Jesus simply sits, waiting numbly. Murdoch tries to collect his thoughts.

Above them, there's the sound a helicopter passing overhead. None of them look up, the forest canopy is too thick. They're invisible, protected. The Lieutenant tilts her head.

LIEUTENANT: They'll assume that the hippos got us, or the fire. They'll find Vernon, but past that, they won't be looking hard. We'll be safe.

Murdoch doesn't know if she's saying it for his benefit, or if she actually believes it. He has the sense she doesn't care. He's noticed with the passing of the helicopter, that he doesn't hear anything. No birds, no monkeys, no insects, just silence.

She hesitates.

LIEUTENANT: Besides, Vernon will play with them. They'll have their hands full.

Not for the first time, Murdoch suspects that beneath the psychopathy, there is simple insanity. The one she calls Vernon was torn in half, top and bottom held together only by a loop of intestine, dying as they watched. He's not going to be playing with anyone. They'll find a corpse, that's all.

He hopes.

MURDOCH: How do you know where you're going?

LIEUTENANT: Because I can feel it now. I can feel where we need to go, it's like a pull.

MURDOCH: You feel it?

Murdoch is openly sceptical. The Lieutenant merely shrugs.

LIEUTENANT: You can feel them.

He can. He can feel the dread weight of their presence hanging over them. Away from the protection of the water, the feeling is suffocating. He strokes the grass next to where he's sitting, it's green, but it crumples. He remembers what Jesus said.

Everything dies around them.

MURDOCH: So you feel it, where to go, and you go there? And they follow? How does it all fucking work?

LIEUTENANT (shrugs): I don't know. We don't know what they are or how it works. There's bits and pieces. Guesses. I'm the Final Girl, I'm part of what happens, some kind of key.

MURDOCH: So if you knew where to go, where to lead them, what the hell did you need us for?

LIEUTENANT: It's just how it works.

MURDOCH: That sounds so fucked up.

The Lieutenant laughs suddenly. There's no humor in it, only despair. The sound surprises Murdoch.

LIEUTENANT: Yeah, tell me about it.

And there it is again, that glimpse of rapidly eroding humanity, almost buried completely under the psychopathy.

JESUS: Hey?

They look at him. He's staring and pointing. Slowly, they turn to follow his gaze.

A jaguar sits watching them. The cat is huge, resplendent. Murdoch realizes he has no idea how long the big cat has been there. It could have killed them at any moment. But it's just been sitting and watching. They stare at it.

JAGUAR: This place is not for you. These are sacred lands, not for your kind. Go back. Gods walk here. They are jealous.

For a moment, they're all stunned speechless.

MURDOCH: Is that fucking cat talking to us?

Then it's gone. Vanishing into the brush.

MURDOCH: Radio transmitter. It must have had some kind of transmitter, maybe a tiny one, buried under its skin. At its throat, I bet, so when it goes off, it triggers the muscle. Makes the jaw work so it looks like its talking.

The Lieutenant looks at Murdoch. He's shaken. He doesn't believe his own words. Jesus looks distraught, something like religious terror cutting through his fatigue and injuries.

She sighs.

LIEUTENANT: Welcome to my world. Are we ready to go?

* * *

After that, there are no more talking jaguars or hippos or cannibal pigs. There are no more emptied villages, or unspeakable monuments. Or screams in the night. There's no more bumpy truck ride across rutted roads, or boat down the river. There's no up or down, or back or forth. Every direction is the same, everything is the same.

There's just the jungle.

There's just the jungle, the endless, exhausting trudging beneath the silent canopy. And the dead silence. It's eerie. He can hear his own breathing, and Jesus' grunts and moans, he can hear their footsteps and gasping. The crunch of leaves and grass underfoot, still vibrant green, but already dead and crumbling.

There's just the endless oppressive heat that never varies, that's the same day or night, in sun or shade, that surrounds and swallows. Sweat builds up in films on their bodies, sometimes trickling wetly down their bodies, sometimes dropping, sometimes pooling in crevices and corners. They feel the irregular trickles, moments when a bead of sweat has gathered sufficient wet mass that it begins its slide across their skin. Sometimes it just sits forming a slimy film until they wipe it away, and it's back an instant later.

But nothing else. No birds. No monkeys. No bugs. He finds he misses the swarming, buzzing, biting things, misses their constant presence. The absence is disturbing. It's like they're walking through a bubble of dead space.

Once in a while, they hear a helicopter passing overhead. They don't even bother to look up. The canopy is too thick, they can't be seen, and they can't see it. So why bother? It's an alien sound from an alien world, passing over, leaving no trace, signifying nothing.

Murdoch is too tired to care anymore. Fatigue drenches him, it's like a thick goo wrapped all around him, seeping into him. He's more tired than he's been in his life. He hurts everywhere. It hurts to breathe. His right arm clicks when he moves it, he feels a stabbing pain in his elbow. He's hungry and thirsty, he can't remember the last time he drank. Was it back at the boat? Was that yesterday? Two days ago? It would be unbearable, except for the exhaustion. Jesus is worse off than he is. He practically drags the boy along.

The Lieutenant walks like a machine, her two legs pistoning relentlessly as she moves forward, smooth as a metronome. The vegetation does not cling to her, the soft mucky soil does not drag at her footsteps. She doesn't seem to tire. She doesn't seem human.

Sometimes, she wears her flight helmet, she's started doing that now. And when she does, Murdoch feels an existential terror overcoming him.

She will stop, if they beg. But only for a few minutes, and then the marching resumes. Up and down, up and down, through the low hills and valleys. Through the brush, sometimes around if it's thick enough, but she is relentless. Across streams and marshes. Her sense of direction is absolute.

The only time her path diverges is when they come to an obstacle, a river or tributary. Then they walk along it, stumbling across the muddy ground, as she searches for a place to cross. Then she splashes into the water, crocodilians fleeing from her presence, and the other two follow in her wake.

Murdoch and Jesus stumble after her, dragged along by her wake, struggling through a kind of hell.

He can feel Them. The others, the silent watchers, the presences.

They don't see them, not any of them. None of them show themselves, or give any sign of their presence. In the few minutes the Lieutenant allows them to rest, he listens for them. The sound of heavy breathing not their own, a footstep, a snapped twig, a tapping or a giggle. Nothing. Just the cursed bubble of silence. No sign of them, no sound.

But Murdoch knows they're there. He can feel Them, the weight of their existence, the unstoppable sensation of dread. Out on the water, the effect was reduced, he could almost ignore it. But here it is full force, their awful presence that seems to somehow distort the fabric of reality. It is almost unendurable.

He can see in Jesus' eyes that the young man feels it too. The look in them is beyond haunted, it's the look of the damned, of despair beyond hope.

Only the Lieutenant seems immune, plodding on mechanically. Even the glittering psychopath in her eyes seems worn away, flattened or suppressed by whatever is calling her. Her identity is simply the march, caring for nothing else.

They don't speak at all now, any of them, except when he demands rest and they pause, and then moments later when she abruptly orders they march on.

Murdoch can't go on. He wants to stop, to sit there, to lay down and die.

But he can't.

He knows that if he stops, she'll just keep going. She'll leave him behind, drawn by her compulsion.

She'll just keep walking until she's out of sight. Vanished. Gone.

And then he'll be alone.

And They will come.

Whatever bubble of safety there has been in her presence will be gone.

Instead, he'll be alone with Them. And They will come.

Murdoch is so exhausted, so worn, pushed past his limits, starving and dehydrated, stumbling on his last reserves, mentally and physically broken, that he doesn't care about dying.

But he's very afraid that if he stops to die, They will come.

And so he stumbles along after her, dragging Jesus with him, because the boy doesn't deserve whatever it is that they are.

Eventually, of course, they are captured.

* * *

LIEUTENANT (voice over): In hindsight, I am amazed that we managed to get as close as we did before they caught us.

Quite suddenly, they surrounded by guns. Men are shouting at them.

She puts up her hands carefully. Murdoch and Jesus look like they're ready to drop. The gunmen are in uniform, green fatigues, not camouflaged, carrying standard AK-47s. There's no insignia of rank, and no visible order among them. They're excited and angry, but not disciplined. Revolutionaries? Bandits? Drug lord army? Who knows? They jab their weapons at them. A man with a beard gets in the Lieutenant's face and jabbers wildly.

For a fraction of an instant, she has an image of her hooking the pry-bar into his mouth, the claw piercing upwards through the palate, using his jaw as lever point. His eyes bulging with surprise and horror as she yanks and his face tears off. After that, the rest of them...

Then it's gone, and she has a very important realization.

She doesn't speak Spanish.

The Lieutenant almost wants to laugh out loud. Here they are, in the middle of a mission in the middle of Colombia to kill an insane drug lord, and she doesn't speak even a little bit of Spanish. She hasn't needed to, up to now. It didn't even occur to her that she'd need to.

She supposes she just assumed that Jesus would get them through that, if it ever came up.

Jesus falls to his knees, then topples face first, in that limp way that tells you they were gone before they fell. He doesn't even put his hands up, just falls, plop. There's no faking that. Maybe that's why they don't shoot him.

The Lieutenant is vaguely surprised he's managed to last this long.

"¿Speekee Inglis?" she asks. But there's no comprehension.

Murdoch's the field agent. She's willing to bet he speaks the language. She turns her head to him, trying to catch his eye. He's not far from going like Jesus, but she needs him to hang on a little longer. She speaks calmly and clearly.

LIEUTENANT: Murdoch.

He lifts his head, staring blankly in the Lieutenant's direction. Good enough.

LIEUTENANT: Can you talk to them? Do you understand what—

Her head pitches forward in whiplash, she feel this explosion of blunt pain. The Lieutenant's vision is stars.

And black.

* * *

As the Lieutenant falls unconscious from the rifle butt smashing into the back of her head, several things happen.

Murdoch sees one of the soldier's heads fall off. It rolls gently to lay in front of the Lieutenant, their lips almost touching. Its eyes widen. The head seems surprised.

Another soldier notices there's something wrong with his shirt. Something odd sticking out of it, like a piece of lint or a peculiar bug. Staring, he flicks at it with his fingertip, feeling the ting of steel. It seems to be the end of a machete, but that makes no sense. He's aware that his legs are no longer long enough to reach the ground, which is strange. But the mystery of the machcte occupies him. If this is a machete... where's the rest of it? Where's the handle? Somewhere behind him?

Then he's dead.

Jackson lets the corpse slide off his machete. His head calmly swivels from right to left, choosing his next victim. His gaze fixes, he moves.

The soldiers are backing away, shouting instructions, their AK-47s' raised. An old man in a Hawaiian shirt and flip flops and nothing else snaps orders.

Murdoch whips his head around. Where did he come from? Why isn't he wearing pants? Or shorts? Murdoch is certain he wasn't there before. He glances at Jesus. The young Colombian is lifting his head wide eyed, the sudden excitement cutting through his exhaustion.

JESUS: He says 'shoot the ghost.'

At that moment, there's an eruption of firepower, all of them discharging their AK-47s at Jackson from point blank range. The hulking figure is caught mid-stride, machete raised, it seems to dance, jigging and shuddering as bullets tear through it. Then it takes a step back. The firing goes on.

Murdoch thinks they're making the same mistake he did with the hippo. Emptying their clips. Short controlled bursts, that's what they need.

Impossibly, Jackson is still standing. His body is smoking, his overalls are shredded with bullet holes. He raises his machete, and falls backwards, crashing like a tree. For a second, there's absolute silence.

The soldiers are panting. None of them think to reload. Jackson begins to rise, sitting up.

The old man in the Hawaiian shirt with no pants is already there, smearing a thick red goo on his torso. Jackson grabs the old man's arm. But the man is chanting and chanting, guttural meaningless syllables. He slaps a palm full of red goo on Jackson's hand, and the hand falls away. He dips his fingers and draws three streaks down Jackson's mask, chanting all the while.

Jackson's not finished. His body twitches, his back arches, his limbs flail, but the old man sits on top of him, squatting on his chest, chanting away relentlessly, drawing lines and circles and spirals of red ooze all over Jackson's frame, until slowly the twitches die away.

When the body is completely inert, he steps away, reaching for a sack. From it, he draws what seems to be an endless length of leafy vine dotted with tiny flowers. He barks orders.

JESUS (whispering): He says its sleep won't last, he's telling them to bind the ghost with consecrated vine.

Several of the soldiers rush to the old man's bidding. Satisfied, the old man turns and looks down at the Lieutenant. He nudges the severed head away from her face. She makes no response, still unconscious. Finally, he nods. Next, he turns to Murdoch and spits in his face.

Just before everything goes black, Murdoch has an instant to realize that he can't feel Them anymore. It's a relief.

* * *

LIEUTENANT (voice over): I wake up to a splitting headache, taste copper and blood in my mouth. The rhythmic noise is overwhelming, chop-chop-chop. I can barely think. The first thing I realize is that I'm in a helicopter. Nobody ever realizes how loud these things are. The second is that I probably have a concussion.

LIEUTENANT (voice over): I'm sitting up, bent over. My wrists are tied behind me. Zip ties I think. The movement makes flashes of light go off in my vision, but I lift my head. Murdoch is sitting opposite me, wrists tied behind, staring blackly at me. He speaks. I can't hear him, but I know the lip movement.

MURDOCH: Fuck you.

LIEUTENANT (voice over): Okay. I guess I had that coming. Jesus is beside him, slumped over. My head is pounding from the movement, and the noise is driving almost every thought out of my head. But no one has cracked me with a rifle butt again, so I take a chance and look around.

LIEUTENANT (voice over): It's windy on the chopper, we're flying through the air, the immense helicopter blades cutting away. The noise is overwhelming, but it's also cool. The air is still warm, still that overpowering South American heat. But it's away from the sun, the humidity of that damp march across the jungle floor. It feels refreshing. My clothes are still drenched with sweat, clammy on my body, but now the wetness feels cold.

LIEUTENANT (voice over): The interior is huge, which surprises me. You always expect helicopters to be cramped. This must be one of the military transports the US government sold to the Colombian army, and the Colombian army immediately turned around and gave to the Cartel… because hey, they needed it more. Shipping, don't you know?

LIEUTENANT (voice over): There are a half dozen goons in here with us, sitting on the floor of the chopper. Are there some new faces? Not all the same crew that caught us then. They were probably called in. They all have the same uniforms, no insignia, but sloppy discipline. Their rifles are beside them, unsecured, again poor discipline.

LIEUTENANT (voice over): Big deal. What am I going to do, snap my cuffs, rush them, grab a rifle and commandeer the helicopter? They're not worried. I can understand that.

LIEUTENANT (voice over): They're not talking, just sitting there in patient miserable silence. Not their first rodeo. They've been on this ride before.

LIEUTENANT (voice over): Some of them are looking at me, watching with flat disinterest. I meet their gaze. They don't care. I'm just where they're looking, that's all. I remind myself not to be fooled by the sloppiness and apparent lack of discipline. These are all very dangerous men, they're field soldiers, which means that they know what to do when it needs to be done.

LIEUTENANT (voice over): I look back the other way, down the cargo hold. There's a fortune in cocaine there, packed in plastic bags, sealed behind netting.

LIEUTENANT (voice over): I wonder if cocaine is good for headaches. I have a splitter. Maybe if I asked they'd let me?

LIEUTENANT (voice over): Randomized thoughts, free association, another sign of concussion. I'll have to watch that.

LIEUTENANT (voice over): They interrupted a drug run, just to pick us up? I guess we're important. I feel very special. I wonder where it was going. Probably not Puerto Miguel, that place is trashed. Sorry about that. You know how the boys are when you let them off the leash. Except they're never really on the leash, are they?

MURDOCH: Fuck you.

LIEUTENANT (voice over): I almost heard that as his lips move. He's staring daggers. Probably blames me for everything bad in his life. He's got a point. Wait, I was on to something. Something about leashes. Boys on leashes.

LIEUTENANT (voice over): How did we get captured in the first place?

LIEUTENANT (voice over): That's a good question, come to think of it. They were all over, keeping pace with us, so close I could feel them individually. They were killing everyone in the way, before we even got to them. No way those paramilitaries should have just been able to walk up to us.

LIEUTENANT (voice over): Unless They allowed it. Unless the paramilitaries were allowed to catch us.

LIEUTENANT (out loud): What the fuck?

GENERAL: Things happen for reasons. There are steps to go through. Sequences. Just because you don't know the reasons doesn't mean that they don't exist.

LIEUTENANT: Do you know something? Is there something you can tell me? Or is this just bullshit guessing.

Sitting next to Murdoch, the General spreads his hands in a gesture of emptiness. He looks around, taking it all in.

GENERAL: This brings me back. Remember the war. I loved helicopters. They were so... efficient. Transporting a prisoner you didn't need, just over the side, you didn't even have paperwork. There's just something clean about throwing people out of helicopters.

LIEUTENANT: I'm not sad that they killed you. But I wish I could have gotten to know you better, so that I could have enjoyed it more.

MURDOCH: Fuck you.

LIEUTENANT (voice over): I don't think he heard me or made out what I said. He just assumed I was speaking to him. Honestly, Murdoch's conversation is getting a little tiresome. I hope he gets over it soon. I hope they decide all three of us are worth keeping for the full ride.

GENERAL: I speak a little Spanish. From my time with the Contras.

She nods.

LIEUTENANT: Are you going to share a little? Maybe be helpful?

MURDOCH: Fuck you.

GENERAL: Of course not.

She nods again.

LIEUTENANT: Typical.

MURDOCH: Fuck you.

LIEUTENANT (voice over): I can't say I blame him.

LIEUTENANT (voice over): Jesus doesn't rouse, doesn't move. I hope he's all right. I didn't see them hit him or anything. But then, I might have missed some stuff. I move my head, feel dizziness and dried blood. A lot of dried blood, all down my back. They split the scalp when they clubbed me.

LIEUTENANT (voice over): Damn this headache. Maybe I should ask for some Advil?

* * *

LIEUTENANT (voice over): There isn't much to see on the way in. I don't have a window seat. So it's just Murdoch and the paramilitaries, and Murdoch has pretty much run out of things to say and switches to glowering.

Jesus regains consciousness, sort of. At least, he becomes aware, not that that's any great shakes

They feel the chopper bank as it swoops around. They must be close. Modovar has an elaborate complex according to the briefing, the parts she bothered to read.

The helicopter lands, the soldiers or whatever they are, stand and grab their gear. They move smoothly, no wasted motion, no surprise. They know what they're doing. The doors peel open, The Lieutenant and her companions are grabbed and dragged out like so much baggage. She goes limp and lets them, they don't need cooperation so she doesn't bother. Murdoch struggles briefly until they hit him. Jesus allows himself to be dragged.

The sun is very bright. Too bright after the time under the jungle canopy, it hurts her eyes. Or is that the concussion? Her lips are cracked, parched. Maybe at some point, they'll give them some water?

They're dragged two dozen feet from the helicopter towards a large building. The Lieutenant decides it's some kind of hangar, or maybe a warehouse. In front of it, they wait. Heat waves rise from the tarmac, where their bodies touch the pavement it burns, but they're all too broken to care. The Lieutenant look longingly at a patch of shade from a building. It's just a few feet away, a clear line dividing the scorching tarmac from blessed relief. But there is no relief.

A pickup truck comes along, they're made to stand and piled into the back, then it lurches off. From the corner of her eye, she sees the Helicopter taking off, resuming its interrupted drug run.

That's when she realizes, she can barely feel them. They're practically absent. She sighs, a mixture of pleasure and happiness, and allow a slight smile. The concussion makes smiling hurt. The Lieutenant doesn't care. It's a beautiful day after all, despite the blood and pain, she resolves to enjoy it while it lasts.

She knows it won't.

The soldiers in the box of the truck with us stare at her blankly as she smiles at them.

They don't understand.

When they do, it will be too late.

$$* * *$$

LIEUTENANT (voice over): We drive by a Ferris wheel. It towers up out of the jungle, a crazed spider web of steel and colored lights and gaily painted boxes, towering over the trees, turning slowly. I gawp. We all turn our heads to keep it in sight.

SOLDIER: It's for the kids. They love it.

LIEUTENANT (voice over): That's all he says. He's not interested in speaking further, and the message is clear; at least one of them understands English, so no games for us. Fine. They don't seem to mind us looking around, which probably isn't a good sign. So I crane my head and play sightseer. Why not enjoy the day?

LIEUTENANT (voice over): The compound is huge. Even with my limited view I can see that. It sits astride a huge lake. The place is a polyglot, no rhyme or reason. There are prefab steel buildings, shipping containers, mobile homes scattered around everywhere, alongside more modern or conventional construction.

LIEUTENANT (voice over): Some of the buildings look old, decaying wood frame construction. Pablo Escobar's summer home from decades ago? Relics of previous cartels? I have no idea. Maybe there's a brochure?

LIEUTENANT (voice over): Or maybe even older? From the early 20th century, when this place was awash with the rubber boom, and the Indians were kidnaped from their villages and chained and caged to work in the rubber plantations, work so brutal ninety per cent of them died.

LIEUTENANT (voice over): Dirt roads and paved roads mingle. We pass a huge 19th century Catholic Church, converted to a mansion. A steel frame processing lab, looking like some big box superstore, white coated technicians and hazmat suits mingling outside, having a smoke during the coffee break. They watch us go by without a trace of curiosity.

LIEUTENANT (voice over): We circle around a tall sharply sloping hill overgrown with vegetation, sitting in the middle of the camp, and I realize, it's some sort of pyramid, covered over by the jungle.

LIEUTENANT (voice over): That's when I take a second look at the geography around us, and I realize it's far too regular and systematic.

This place was a temple complex a thousand years ago, abandoned and returned to nature, lost in the rain forest, taken over by howler monkeys. I look down, and in the erratic mix of dirt and paved roads, there are stretches of ancient stone pathways.

LIEUTENANT (voice over): Aztec? No. Maya? No, that's Central America. Who was in Colombia? Some lost, abandoned culture, somewhere between the Andes and Meso-America. Modovar has re-occupied an ancient city, clearing what he needs, sitting in the middle of jungle covered ruins. In a mound of rubble, I see the remains of ancient statuary. Later on, there's a figure of some leering demon god casting a shadow over us as we drive past. Was it always there and now restored, or is imported from somewhere else? I have no idea.

LIEUTENANT (voice over): There's too much to take in, everything is glimpses and fragments. What looks like a Las Vegas chorus girl, in full sequined regalia and ostrich-feather head-dress, leads a donkey resplendent, its eyes glazed over from an overdose of viagra. Elsewhere, a painted clown hands out balloons to naked brown children, and they cheer as he does juvenile magic tricks. A sidewalk vendor in a dirty apron stands by his cart, selling hot dogs. There are soldiers of course, men in uniforms, Colombian army, US Marines, CRAC paramilitary, drug soldiers. But every kind of person, men and women, dressed every which way. And guns, guns everywhere.

LIEUTENANT (voice over): Then the ride is over, we're at Modovar's private compound. Inside an immense mansion circled by shipping containers wedged together as a fence, gold painted statues of naked women in pornographic poses in rows around the top. Classy. On the final approach, we pass a series of gibbets on either side, corpses rotting in them. I want to meet his designer.

LIEUTENANT (voice over): Deep inside, I feel something, a vibration, a thrum. I think of an insect caught in a spider's web, its struggles shaking a strand, telling the spider where it is, telling the spider to come and eat it.

LIEUTENANT (voice over): I'm here, I realize. I'm where I'm supposed to be.

LIEUTENANT (voice over): And now they know where to go.

* * *

Murdoch runs out of things to say. His story ends. Sweat drips from the end of his nose, it slides down his back and pools at the base of his spine, flowing down his cheeks. He ignores it.

The soldier in the corner simply stands there, watching with stony faced attention. Murdoch suspects that the man speaks no English, has no idea what has transpired.

That's how he'd do it. You don't need to understand the language to shoot someone. Better that you didn't speak it, you might end up knowing something you shouldn't, something that you'd need killing for.

The Interrogator watches Murdoch for a while, waiting to see if there's more. Then he reaches into his pocket, pulls out a pack of cigarettes. With careful deliberation, he pulls one, lights it, and smokes it.

They don't speak at all.

When it's almost finished, he drops it to the floor, but doesn't bother to stub it out. He takes another cigarette out. Lights it, and takes several deep drags.

He passes it to Murdoch, who takes it, puts it to his lips and inhales. Murdoch leans back against the wall, and exhales slowly, watching the smoke curl in the air in front of him.

INTERROGATOR: That's quite a story.

MURDOCH: Yeah.

INTERROGATOR: Suppose that I believe you. Let's suppose that. That it's true. Why would you tell me this?

Murdoch takes another draw on the cigarette.

MURDOCH: You know, I used to believe. We all believe. We say we don't, we're all grown up. But down basic, we believe – good and bad, right and wrong, good and evil. We fuck around a lot. But yeah, we believe.

The Interrogator waits.

MURDOCH: I thought I knew, I thought I understood. But now, I've met them. Felt them... I mean, you're only a drug dealer. That's all. I mean, in the big picture, so what? That's practically harmless. But them...

A long silence. Murdoch doesn't even smoke. The cigarette slowly burns down.

MURDOCH: I'm sorry.

The Interrogator pulls his pistol. Murdoch doesn't move. He presses it to Murdoch's forehead. Murdoch just stares, not hard, surprisingly mildly, the Interrogator thinks. Not defiance, or even acceptance, just... indifference. He cocks the hammer. Nothing, no reaction at all. Not even interest.

He puts the pistol away.

INTERROGATOR: You're going to die.

MURDOCH: Yeah.

Not even interest.

INTERROGATOR: Later. When the time is right.

MURDOCH: Okay.

INTERROGATOR: We'll come for you.

MURDOCH: I'll wait here.

The Interrogator leaves.

Murdoch leans back and closes his eyes and dreams of breezes. It's the closest he can come to the idea of heaven.

* * *

There is a swimming pool in the middle of the living room. That's the first thing the Lieutenant registers as she's dragged through the gaping doors. In the cathedral space above the pool is a gigantic multicolored chandelier rotating slowly. Despite it all, the pool is dwarfed by the immensity of the room, multiple levels with dining tables, couches and love seats, gaudy painted statuary of every possible style, ancient relics and a series of hot tubs filled with naked boys and girls. Everything is some combination of gold, chrome or red velvet.

There is an upper level, a huge balcony overlooking the living room and the pool, with grotesquely wide marble staircases running up on either side. From the center of the balcony's edge, there's a waterfall, or perhaps an immense waterspout, descending into what must be a deep pit on the other side of the swimming pool, given the complete absence of splashing.

It's as if God gave Donald Trump an unlimited budget to redesign his own rectum.

The Lieutenant is dragged past the pool, up one of the marble staircases to the upper level of the main chamber.

Against the back wall, set high up there's a gigantic golden statute of a naked woman. Beneath porn-star looks, her belly is swollen, her legs up, and from between her spread thighs dangles a half born child. Beneath them, more tumbling babies connected by umbilical cords, over and through all of which gushes an endless stream of water from the distended vagina, flowing down into an artificial brook which runs the length of the balcony to flow out a spout beneath the far railing, overlooking the pool, where it becomes the waterfall. The brook is crossed here and there by small ornate bridges.

The Lieutenant gapes. It's quite possibly the most tasteless thing she's seen in her life.

The rest of the upper level is similarly bizarre. The decor fluctuates wildly between Aztec primitivism, futuristic gothic, and weirdly pedestrian comfort. She spies computer workstations, a refrigerator, couches, tables, an immense waterbed on a pedestal half enclosed by a semi-circular viewing gallery, a small forest of dangling harnesses, an inexplicable air hockey table, and things she has no name for. Along the walls are ancient weapons, spears, a collection of Aztec war clubs, flattened maces of hardwood lined with flint along the edges, a conquistador's armor.

There are people, men and women, some clearly ornamental by their states of undress and lingerie, others clearly occupied with work at computer stations or phone banks. Both groups ignore her utterly, as if she doesn't exist.

The Lieutenant looks around wildly, as she is frog-marched to an ancient stone Altar, near the golden statue. Her captors bend her over it. Two guards hold her down, almost dislocating her shoulder.

On a level above the Altar, almost even with the eyes of the giant statue, is a bench on which three people sit. On the left is a heavy middle-aged woman, face pockmarked by some tropical disease, wearing a distaff uniform. To the right is an elderly man, half naked, covered in shells and beads, and a robe that's barely strips of fabric.

Modovar sits in the center, a late middle aged balding man, with a brush mustache and a very expensive suit, open at the crotch and exhibiting the largest genitalia she's ever seen.

Modovar rises from the bench, descends the six steps to the Altar. He grabs her by the hair and lifts her head, looking into her eyes.

MODOVAR: Is this the one? She reeks. You should have given her a bath first.

SOLDIER: We did. He told us to. A special bath in oils drown her magic, that's why she smells.

This close, she can see his monstrous genitalia is clearly a codpiece held around his trousers by heavy leather straps. A face has been etched into the glans of the fake penis. It winks at her.

Modovar turns to the old man. He's incredibly ancient, his skin like parchment, his body covered by tattoos. He walks with the aid of a staff. When the robe moves, she can see that he has no genitals at all.

The Priest reaches out a shaking bony hand, skeletal fingers stroke her hair and then yank a few strands loose. The priest puts them in a toothless mouth, makes a show of chewing and then spits the wadded mass into her face. He rakes fingers down her face, pulls the underside of her eyelid down, hooks a finger into her lips and examines her gums. Her mouth is forced open, and he reaches in to tug at each of her front teeth.

MODOVAR: Well?

PRIEST: There's magic in her, but not much. A little witch. Tiny. Just enough to draw attention from the spirit world. Ghosts follow her. Big ones, little ones, but merely ghosts. She helps them wrap in flesh. They're little things to cause so much trouble.

MODOVAR: Is this what you felt?

WOMAN: They caused a lot of trouble. They left a trail of bodies through the jungle, everywhere they went.

PRIEST: Not them. The ghosts that followed.

MODOVAR: Can you handle them? The other ghosts.

PRIEST: No need. It's hard for ghosts to keep attention. They fade and wander. They are drawn, like moths to a flame, to her, to us. But there is no substance. Without her to give them form, they fade. We are wind to their dust, I scatter them to nothing.

LIEUTENANT: Can I say something?

Her head is slammed down on the Altar. Her nose breaks, she feels blood surging out. Her head is forced flat. One of the soldiers whispers in her ear.

SOLDIER: You don't talk to them, they don't talk to you. They have people whose job is to talk to you, so that they don't have to, and so they don't have to hear you. You don't have the right to listen to them, we should cut your ears off. You don't even rate to look at them, so be glad we didn't take your eyes. Now shut up.

The Lieutenant acknowledges with the barest grunt. The trio give no sign that they've heard. Modovar doesn't even acknowledge her. It's as if she hadn't spoken, the guard hadn't slammed her, as if nobody even heard the soldier speak to them.

MODOVAR: So if there's nothing to them, let's just give them to the Eaters. They're always hungry.

PRIEST: Not Eaters. The Great and Hungry Devourers. Address the Gods by their respectful titles.

Modovar barely holds back from rolling his eyes.

MODOVAR: Yes, yes. The hungry, hungry ones.

WOMAN: Give them to the Gods. Feed them to the ritual.

PRIEST: That is what was meant to be. The fates have brought them for this purpose. They will feed the Hungry Gods, their bodies and their souls.

WOMAN: What about the ghosts? What about that thing we caught?

PRIEST: Gods eat ghosts. They are a delicacy.

MODOVAR: Honestly, I expected more. Something more significant. This hardly seems worth the time. Yes. Fine. Now, moving on...

One of the soldiers lifts the Lieutenant's head high. She feels what's coming and tries to resist, arching her back, stiffening her neck. But the soldier is too strong, and smashes her head hard on the unyielding stone of the Altar. She feels another painful crack in her nose, a fresh gout of blood, a tooth loosens, for a moment her head is filled with stars. The world spins crazily.

LIEUTENANT (thinking): Not another concussion.

Then black.

* * *

Murdoch is crammed into the back of a transport truck with a couple of dozen other people, so tightly they can only stand. The vehicle stinks of human misery, of men and women in despair and terror. A guard is shouting something in Spanish, a gun fires. He doesn't understand, he just goes with the flow.

The truck stops, and they're unloaded, harried with sticks and kicks and curses down an ancient enclosed stone tunnel. Someone kicks Murdoch, he stumbles but doesn't fall, rushes along, and bumps and stumbles into other people.

Then suddenly, he's blinking under harsh blinding white light. He and the others are standing, stunned on an alabaster plaza. Behind him, around him, rising up are ascending rows of seating in a rough semicircle. Above the entrance where they came out is a platform on which a half dozen figures in exotic headdresses stand ready. On the other side of the small plaza is a circular pool.

It's a Cenote. A sacrificial pool of the Mayan civilization. Murdoch remembers this from his Pre-Colombian studies degree, from simpler more innocent times. These aren't Maya, and he recalls the sacrificial pools were vaguely associated with sink holes in the Yucatan peninsula's limestone. But it doesn't matter, he knows a Cenote when he sees one. Particularly when he's waiting to be sacrificed at one. He's not alone, over two dozen people have been dumped here with him. Men, women and children, all ages, jabbering away in Spanish. Behind him, a pair of massive wooden doors reinforced with steel bands close, sealing the tunnel they came from.

Behind Modovar's mansion, near the drug labs and helicopter pads, away from the airstrip and the golf course, the Cenote borders the lake. It's an ancient construction, restored, a circular pool, three quarters complete, the circle opening onto the lake, stairs descending into the sacrificial pool, rising up a sort of walled courtyard, and beyond to a semicircular amphitheater already filled with the faithful here to watch the sacrifices.

Around the Cenote, ancient carved native megaliths, lovingly restored and reset in their original places, alternate with giant gold plated statues of impossibly statuesque women in vulgar poses.

The whole thing is illuminated by stadium lights mounted high on steel frames, like a baseball field. The Cenote is bright as daylight, the waters glistening, the arena, made harsh by stark LED light.

Murdoch stands in the courtyard between the surrounding amphitheater and the Cenote pool, it's almost circular, except for the big bite taken out by the pool.

In the center is Jackson, the immense hulking brute twists futilely against the bonds. Jackson's still wrapped in the flowered leafy vines, but someone has thought to add heavy chains. Murdoch can't help but agree with the sentiment. It's faint, but whatever Jackson is, he can feel it rolling off him. The other prisoners keep their distance as well.

He looks at the steps leading down into the water. Conceivably, if you were brave enough, or fast enough, you could run down the steps, dive into the water, swim the length of the Cenote out into the adjoining lake to freedom.

Nobody tries, so he assumes that there's a reason. Instead, he focuses on the people around him, looking for Jesus and the Lieutenant. He finds them easily enough. The Lieutenant seems out of it, unfocused, as if she can't steady her head. She keeps looking at Jackson as if she can't understand what she's seeing. She vomits all over herself but doesn't seem to care.

MURDOCH: Lieutenant?

When she looks at him, her pupils are two different sizes. Her face is slack and empty. Murdoch recoils. She's useless. Over her shoulder, he sees Jesus. The boy stands confused, listless. He walks up and squeezes his tender shoulder. The slight pain focuses the boy.

JESUS: Hey?

MURDOCH: You with us? I think the Lieutenant is done. It's just us.

Jesus looks over Murdoch's shoulder to see her swaying there, corpse-like, vomit soaking her front. He nods.

JESUS: They're going to sacrifice us to the four Gods.

Around them, people are praying, wailing. Someone is shouting angrily up at the Amphitheater as the crowd jeers back. Jesus seems... indifferent. Murdoch understands. They've both spent too much time in the soul eroding proximity of them. Being sacrificed to God doesn't mean much after that, nothing means much after that.

MURDOCH: Well...

He's not sure what to say next. But he doesn't have to, because fireworks go off, loudspeakers blare, the crowd roars and the ceremony begins.

Murdoch can see the ceremonial platform from where he is, the figures on it. He can even hear them, although he can't understand what they're saying. There are a half dozen men and women on it. Most of them old. He recognizes the old man without pants, he's still without pants, but now he wears an immense headdress of jade and feathers. It looks so heavy, Murdoch is surprised the old fart can stand.

They all wear head dresses, chains and amulets. There's an ugly middle aged woman, some form of modesty has led her to wear an undershirt, camouflage pants and combat boots. Another ancient woman, skin like leather, teats sagging. A fat old man, naked under his robes.

The leader seems to be a middle aged man he recognizes as Modovar from the briefing pictures, heavy set with a brush mustache and a monstrous codpiece that looks like the maker started out intent on genitalia and switched to dragon at the last minute. The eyes in the head of the codpiece blink and it twists to look at him before its attention is drawn somewhere else.

They chat idly. Murdoch isn't sure what about. It could be some arcane theological point, or drug lord shop talk, local gossip, or last night's baseball game. They speak to each other with a sense of ease and familiarity. Not their first sacrifice, they've done it a lot, the magic has worn off, it's all pretty standard stuff by now.

The old Priest steps forward. He spreads his arms wide, and begins a speech. Or perhaps it's an invocation. The crowd falls silent. His voice is unnaturally loud. There's a measured cadence to his words. He takes a ceremonial knife and cuts at his breast, Murdoch glimpses the healed scars of many such cuts on the Priest's body.

Now that he sees it, he spots scars on all of them. They've all been cutting for a long time. Themselves? Each other? Doesn't matter.

The Priest smears blood running down his chest onto his palm and holds it out, first up to the sky, then out to the waters, and then in a sweeping circular motion. With each movement, he gives an ululating cry.

The Priest's voice rises and falls, it breaks into chanting, then back to invocations. At times, others join in, sometimes counterpoint, sometimes all of them chanting together. There's more cutting from each of them.

Somewhere along the way, Murdoch realizes he can understand. The words make sense. Invocations to the spirits, the forces of nature, invocations and entreaties to the guardians of life, the hungry, the devouring, taking and giving. For just an instant, he wonders if they've switched to English for some unknowable reason, and realizes that they haven't. The language isn't English or even Spanish. It's ancient, primordial.

The Priest steps back, and then it's the old woman. Then Modovar. Then the next. But each time, the old Priest returns to the center, chanting invocations.

The waters ripple.

The eyes and snout of a huge Hippo surface from the green waters in center of the Cenote. Behind it, flanking it, come two more, and then a fourth at the rear. The waters are so impenetrable, that there is no sign of the immense creatures beneath. These are not ordinary animals, the creatures gaze at Modovar and his crew at the Altar.

Modovar looks at the native priest.

MODOVAR: What's wrong?

The priest shook his head.

PRIEST: The Gods are displeased.

MODOVAR: The Deus are always pissy. What is it now? They're like spoiled children, it's tiresome. Who worshiped them before me? What servant did they have before I came along? Naked savages worshiping bush pigs? Fuck them.

PRIEST: You should not profane the Gods.

MODOVAR: All I'm asking for is a little respect, that's all. A little consideration. Is that too much to ask? A little professionalism.

PRIEST: You blaspheme.

MODOVAR: I give them what they need, which is why they talk to me and not you. But seriously, does every little thing have to be drama? They're such whiny diva bitches.

The Hippos begin to swim into the Cenote.

* * *

The Lieutenant watches without comprehension. Her mind is full of clouds, and she finds it hard to focus through the blinding pain that criss-crosses her skull. There's something wrong with her body, she sweats profusely, but it's not the heat, overpowering as it is. Her muscles don't seem to work right, the world tilts. She's vaguely aware of having vomited on herself, her bladder voided long ago.

A glimmer of light catches her attention. She watches the water. The Hippos move forward, swimming smoothly, leaving ripples in their wake. Two dozen feet away, the first head rises from the water, and rises and rises. Green water and slime sluice from its hide as it lifts higher. For a second, the Lieutenant's mind seizes up and she can't comprehend what she is seeing.

The General is standing beside her.

GENERAL: Magnificent beasts, aren't they?

LIEUTENANT: What the fuck?

Everything feels broken and unreal to the Lieutenant, as if in a fractured dream. She's vaguely aware of her environment, of savage head blows. Multiple concussions definitely. Maybe skull fracture.

Maybe she's dying? That would be good.

The lead Hippo's body continues to rise out of the water, standing upright, forelimbs at its sides. It advances, towering higher with every step. It begins to ascend the stairs.

Behind it, the others also rise up, their bodies contorted into manlike proportions, walking erect. Their torsos remained barrel chested, the legs short, the limbs heavy. They're Hippopotamuses, the proportions of Hippos, bent and twisted to stand upright and walk like men.

The sight is so unearthly, that it draws the Lieutenant through her fog of pain.

LIEUTENANT: What the fuck?

Suddenly, the General is beside her, or perhaps he's been beside her all along and she hasn't cared.

GENERAL: You know the Houngan from Vodun? Priests who let the Loa spirits possess their bodies? These things here are nature spirits that normally possess animals to ride around in. The trouble they have is animals that live here, jaguars, tapirs, monkeys can resist them. Hard to get into, easy to be shaken off. It was hard to possess them, the local animals had resistance, acquired an immunity to the local supernatural. There has to be a willingness to possession, an acceptance or an opening to them, and that's difficult to achieve without the right ceremonies. So the local priests, they got good at helping the spirits inhabit critters.

The fog is clearing, the pain in her broken skull coming into sharper relief. She finds she can ignore it. Around her, people are kneeling, praying, screaming. Some have run back to press themselves against the wall, even trying to climb it to get into the Amphitheater.

GENERAL: But then Escobar comes along, he brings in all these new animals without immunity to the local supernatural. The spirits could slide right into them without any resistance at all. They could go beyond possession, merge completely so that one is the other. Those nature spirits, they just naturally gravitate to the biggest, most powerful animals. If you're going to ride around in something, you wanted something strong. All that power, natural and supernatural available to them, and those spirits in their new homes, they were hungry.

Water drains off them as they climb out of the lake rising to a height of four meters. The second's hide is streaked with red in sheets and trickles, as if sweating blood. The third covered with mats of green algae. The last, bluish with streaks and patches of blinding white like clouds across its hide.

They look around, gazing upon their worshipers. They seem to grin, pleased with the devotion. One of them lifts up his arms over his head.

His jaws yawn wide and he bellows. The others, one by one, do the same.

GENERAL: They're all so very hungry.

The crowd goes wild.

The Great Devourers, the Gods, have arrived.

* * *

The lead Hippo, the great gray one, largest of the four, climbs up onto the platform. Everyone in the courtyard is cringing away from it, except for Jackson, tied to his post, writhing slowly as he struggles in his bonds.

The Hippo stares at Jackson with unconcealed distaste. It looks up at the Priests gathered at the Altar. Its mouth opens in a sneer, there is a flash of tusks.

GREAT HIPPO: YOU BRING US… ABOMINATION???

The Lieutenant is shocked. She hasn't expected it to speak. But the words rang out from a massive barrel torso and cavernous throat. They are booming sounds, bellows, human words from an inhuman throat. The language, the sounds, are alien, but that doesn't matter. The words also ring inside her head, its voice in her thoughts, meaning and intent slap at her in massive waves. The effect is overwhelming.

MODOVAR: It's a ghost wrapped in bacon. They tell me it's like candy to you people. Pastry. Enjoy!

GREEN HIPPO: YOU ARE DECEIVED. THIS IS NO GHOST. THIS IS AN ABOMINATION. THIS THING IS OPPOSITE TO LIFE.

Modovar turns to the old Priest, whispering.

MODOVAR: You said it was a fucking ghost?

He shouts out to the Hippos.

MODOVAR: Yeah, well sorry. My guy's bad. Look, there's plenty of other kibble, eat up. You want more? You want something special? You just say the word.

The Hippos glare at the Priests. Psychic waves of displeasure seem to roll off them in pulses, the Priests on the dais, even the spectators, seem to cringe away from their anger. Modovar's knees buckle, but he holds himself upright.

MODOVAR (weakly): Mi Casa Su Casa, you know that. I'm sorry, honest mistake. You know me. Anything you want. We good?

The great gray Hippo turns to the bloody red one.

GREAT HIPPO: CRUSH THE ABOMINATION. WE WILL TEACH THE PRIESTS TO REGRET THEIR OFFENSE.

The red raw Hippo-creature, the savage God, its blood red eyes blazing, advances on Jackson as he slowly struggles to free himself. The creature wastes no time, it simply kicks, shattering the pillar. Jackson makes no sound but simply goes flying, tumbling like a rag doll and landing with an awkward bone shattering crunch.

The prisoners scream and huddle against the wall as the other Hippos stride past them, approaching the platform where the Priests cower. They seem to grow in size, until their faces are level with the Priests.

Unhurried, the red monster strides forward. Jackson is struggling to rise when the thing kicks him onto his back. It takes a step and plants a massive hoof in the center of Jackson's chest, and puts its weight, some five metric tons, grinding down.

Even from this distance, the Lieutenant can hear the brittle cracking of Jackson's bones breaking as his chest caves in. The big man makes no sound, he never makes a sound, but his hands claw desperately, futilely at the foot crushing down on him. As the weight bears down, forcing him into the earth, he simply writhes like a bug pinned to a board. The Hippo bears down with its weight, grinding.

Above him, the red raw creature does not even look down. Instead, it gazes off into the distance, examining the throngs filling the amphitheater, eyes filled with cold fire, an ancient God surveying its world. It barely deigns to notice Jackson squirming helpless under its massive foot.

Casually, it lifts its foot. Impossibly, Jackson is still moving, albeit barely. It kicks again and once again, Jackson flies through the air, tumbling end over end, bonelessly as a rag doll. He lands on his head, and there's a sickening crack.

With casual strides, the monster advances on Jackson. It picks up the shattered remains of the pillar handling it like a toy, and reaching Jackson, smashes it down, using it like a hammer. Through it all, Jackson makes no sound, beyond bones breaking and wet pulping noises. Black fluid spurts and squelches as the thing pounds his body. The remnants of the pillar break, and it hammers with giant fists instead.

The Lieutenant is horrified. She's gotten used to Jackson being indestructible. The members of the Squad seemed immutable, less beings than some kind of personification of unknown fundamental force of nature, Jackson more so than the others.

The other three loom over Modovar, looking down as if on a misbehaving child.

GREAT HIPPO: WE ARE EATERS OF FLESH AND SOULS. WE ARE THE GREAT DEVOURERS. YOU OFFER US TAINTED MEAT. THIS THING IS DISEASED!

The words are booming, but there's another force behind them, like the roar of a psychic jet engine, the God's voice in their minds so loud and overpowering in their heads it blocks everything out.

Modovar is bleeding from his eyes and mouth. He falls to his knees, swaying with each syllable of the God's voice. His head-dress is fallen, his codpiece detaches and struggles to crawl away.

The words are alien, the syllables guttural and unearthly.

The Lieutenant can hear things that sound like Spanish, strange inflections of English syllables, and a babble that might be fragments of native dialects, or perhaps the speech of things that existed before humans. Yet, she understands it clearly.

The sounds are utterly unnatural, the meaning blooms in her mind, she understands the words.

All but one, 'diseased.' There it seems to flicker, a dozen different meanings writhe in her head, infection, infestation, unnatural, a sense of something that does not belong in this world, in this universe.

There's no right word. But beneath, she senses the monsters' revulsion.

The other priests on the platform are screaming. One seems to be doing a jig, standing in place, twitching, vomiting up blood. Another rolls around in epileptic convulsions. They weep, they beg. The old Priest, holding his head in his arms, rushes behind the ugly woman, and as she struggles to retain her balance, kicks her off the platform toward the monsters.

The great gray monster snatches her out of the air. She has time to scream as it raises her to its mouth and bites her head off. It hands the corpse, now luminous with St. Elmo's fire, to the Sky Hippo companion, who solemnly bites the torso off the at the rib cage, and then passes to the Green Hippo, who accepts it as liver and intestines spill away. The Green Hippo holding the legs together, tears off the pelvis, and lets the remaining pieces drop away as it wipes its mouth.

The thoughts of the giant gray monster boom in her head.

GREAT HIPPO: CONTRITION IS DEMONSTRATED, THE LESSON IS LEARNED.

As the word 'monster' passes through her, one of the Hippos turns its massive head to look directly at her.

VOICE: NOT MONSTERS.

The words appear in her head like thunder on a horizon. She can't tell which one of them has spoken to her, or of there is even a distinction between the creatures...

VOICE: GODS.

The Lieutenant knows these are not her thoughts, but the creature somehow addressing her.

VOICE: KEEPERS OF THE WORLD. GUARDIANS OF LIFE. DEFENDERS AND GATEKEEPERS AGAINST...

...and here the concepts grow indistinct, as if there is no human concept...

Taking mortal flesh and blood, mortal souls, and building a great barrier against...

...and again the concepts elude her. Against something awful, something alien, a void. An emptiness underlying and contiguous with everything.

There is a timeless pause, she has the sense of something immense peering at her, and she's afraid. It's as if there is a cyclopean eye hovering directly above her, over her head. An eye a thousand yards wide, staring unblinking, translucent pupil and an endless presence behind it, a God's attention, terrifying and unrelenting.

VOICE: YOU ARE TAINTED.

The words appears in her mind, a final judgment.

All three of the Hippos have turned their head to look at her. A sense of consensus, of agreement. They have all seen and weighed her, and now she is judged. The Green Hippo separates from the others, bearing down on her. The Lieutenant backs away, but there's nowhere to run.

Suddenly, the Red Hippo bellows, and she feels a wave of psychic shock, of attention torn away from her. While the others are judging her, the red monster picks up Jackson's shattered body, lifting the limp broken form to its mouth to bite its head off. But suddenly Jackson stiffens in the creatures hands, grabbing a massive lower tusk in the gaping maw.

For a moment, even the Gods stare with mute incomprehension. The Red Hippo holds Jackson's body like a doll, its jaw gaping, but for all its size and power, it cannot move the tiny figure it holds. They're frozen together. Jackson pulls his other arm free and wraps both hands around the tusk. Blood-sweat trickles down the monster in rivulets, dripping, its muscles straining, ears gone flat, eyes glittering madly, as Jackson forces its jaw wider.

The tusk snaps off in Jackson's hands with an audible crack. The Lieutenant feels a sudden psychic shock of pain and outrage, presses a hand to her own jaw in sympathetic pain. Anger and outrage explode in her head. Jackson slashes at the creature's snout as it bellows its outrage. Then a second later, it hurls him with all its might.

Everyone gasps as Jackson's body tumbles through the air, high over the amphitheater. The Blood-Red Hippo, radiating waves of mad rage, tracks the body through the air and then tears off in that direction, smashing through the enclosure wall, climbing through the amphitheater, indifferently crushing screaming onlookers.

That's when they hear the other screams, and above it, the sound of a chain saw. Up at the top of the amphitheater Sawyer appears wearing his mask of human skin, waving his chain saw high over his head, his hips thrusting obscenely. Sawyer thrusts the saw into the face of a nearby person and blood and brains burst into the air like a fountain. He swings gaily, and more blood spurts from terrified screaming spectators.

In the stands, there is panic. People are falling over themselves to escape Sawyer, but there's nowhere to go. They panic, packing close, trying to climb over each other, trampling each other. Sawyer, now drenched red, swings and swings, the chain saw tearing through packed squirming humanity.

VOICE: ABOMINATIONS!!!

Even the Red Hippo pauses in its pursuit of Jackson, to stare up at the carnage.

Guards and soldiers are trying to fight through the packed fleeing throng to reach Sawyer. Others, more sensible, are trying to shoot him from a distance, but their shots, if they hit, have no effect.

A wave of loathing and contempt rolls outward from the Blood-Red Hippo, its thoughts drip with blood.

BLOOD HIPPO: BROTHERS, DESTROY THE NUISANCE. I WILL HAVE MY REVENGE.

Then it turns and proceeds, leaving the guards and others to deal with Jackson, its mind full of curt dismissal. The others are confused and angry, their thoughts, unshielded and radiating rage without focus. Their attentions flicker from Sawyer, to the appalling screaming humans and their shrieking filthy mindless terror, like a noisy stain, to the assembled Priests whose mission is to maintain order.

GREAT HIPPO: FALSE PRIEST! TRAITOR! YOU HAVE PROFANED THE HOLY TEMPLE. YOU

HAVE WELCOMED ABOMINATIONS INTO SACRED SPACE!

MODOVAR (to the Hippo): Hold on, this is just a misunderstanding. We're good, you and I. (Shouting out to the guards) Someone shoot that asshole! We don't need this shit! (To the Hippo) Look, calm down, that's an order. We'll take care of it.

The Hippos break down the walls around the amphitheater, striding into the screaming crowds, crushing humans underfoot in their path, kicking them aside, reaching down sometimes throwing, sometimes rending limb from limb, or biting. They roar constantly, great jaws opening wide, tusks exposed, creatures of mad belligerence.

GREAT HIPPO: THERE MUST BE ATONEMENT! ABOMINATIONS AND THEIR TAINT MUST BE PURGED!

MODOVAR: Back the fuck off. Who do you think you're talking to? You work for me!

GRAY HIPPO: BLASPHEMERS!!!

It slams a fist against the side of the platform. Concrete shatters, steel rebar bends and deforms. Modovar pulls a pistol and fires uselessly at the Gray monster.

The Sky Hippo roars in irritation, it picks up a worshiper, bites her head off and throws it away, never taking its mad gaze from the capering figure and its chain saw.

SKY HIPPO: ABOMINATION!!!

That's when the lights go out.

* * *

An eerie calm falls over the Lieutenant. She can feel Them again. The throbbing clusters of pain, the disorientation and nausea, the struggle to even hold her balance, all fade away. The awful weight of their presence enfolds her like a cloak, smoothing away all human feeling. It brings lucidity.

The Lieutenant closes in on herself, a sensation as if she was shutting windows and locking doors, unplugging wires. She steps back and back, people around her oblivious to her presence. The crowd closes around her like a blanket, concealing her in the boiling turmoil of their minds. She feels the awful force of attention concentrated on her dissipating, losing focus, wavering and uncertain.

The Gods are furious, she feels their rage as they bellow and stamp, their fury is like a hurricane, waves of raw emotion buffeting the hapless humans. Men and women fall and thrash, bleeding from their eyes and mouths. The guards trying to shoot Sawyer clutch their heads, curling into balls. The Sky Hippo crushes worshipers, flinging broken bodies aside like dolls in its fury.

The Green Hippo pauses before the huddling cornered mass of human sacrifices, confused. Carefully, it picks up a young boy of no more than thirteen. The child is terrified, compliant and passive. The Hippo sniffs him carefully, then tears him in half, tossing away the remains. The child doesn't have time to scream. The creature peers down at the rest of them, its eyes searching. It reaches out.

Its gaze passes over the Lieutenant without recognition, even as its head swivels back and forth. She realizes that it can't see her. No that's wrong. It can see, but whatever psychic or metaphysical way they perceive, it is blind to her. They called her tainted, they zeroed in on that. But now, although it knows she's there, it can't find her.

The old woman Priest falls from the platform, already dead. Her body splats in the darkness in the crowd right in front of the Lieutenant, ancient bones snapping like a nest of twigs. The Lieutenant kneels, feeling the broken neck, the cooling leathery flesh long past any normal life span. Hands patting blindly across robes and limbs, she comes to a belt, and in the belt an obsidian knife. It will do.

An instant later the man directly in front of her is picked up by his head. With a casual flick of its wrist, the Green Hippo tears off the head, the body jerking spastically as it falls back into the screaming throng. The green nature God continues its search, blindly fumbling for her. The Lieutenant works her way backwards among the struggling bodies.

* * *

Murdoch touches his hand to his nose. It comes away red. He can feel the Gods raging in his head, it's like being pressed up against a giant bass speaker, an overpowering primordial sensation that makes his soul vibrate. The lights go back on, halogen LED's blinding everyone, people clutching their eyes. He sees the Blood Red Hippo standing, head swinging angrily, looking for its next target. Up in the stands, the Sky Hippo is reaching for Sawyer, who is backing away, swinging the saw. The Gray Hippo roars his fury at the Priests above, on their knees supplicating it.

The Green Hippo kicks at squealing sacrifices, somehow obsessed with terrorizing a hapless crowd of cornered humans, as if searching for someone. Picking up one, he places the thrashing victim completely in his mouth and bites savagely, the scream cuts off as severed arms and legs rain down with splashes of blood. The creature tosses its head and spits the mangled torso.

At least it's not paying attention to them. Murdoch pulls Jesus to him. The young man is almost catatonic, ceaselessly reciting the Lord's Prayer, the words a monotonal rush. The wailing from other sacrificial victims around them is constant, some are screaming.

Others, their minds blasted, articulate the tonal roars of the gods. There's nothing in their eyes. The power of the Gods shines out, drowning out their human identities.

Murdoch is surprised that he's still thinking, perhaps the corrosive effect of the Others has given him a degree of immunity. He notices two thing: Jackson is vanished, the hulking manlike thing took the full violent fury of the Blood God, and now he's gone. Not ripped apart, not crushed or dismembered, just gone, as if he simply got up and walked away. The Red Hippo, is gone too, following, although he can feel the lingering trace of its outrage and fury, as it sheds blood-sweat with each step.

Murdoch doesn't care, though he knows he should. It's all about triage. The Green Hippo is rampaging, and everyone with faculties left to move is scurrying this way and that, trying to avoid the monster. There are breaches in the wall where the monsters broke through, wreckage and rubble. If they can reach it, get through the breach, maybe there's a way out of there.

The idea of following in the path made by one of those things, coming behind them, as they're all so close by, makes Murdoch want to shit himself. Behind them, the Green Hippo lifts up a man and a woman, one in each hand, raising them up high, their arms and legs kick like dolls, they scream and beg. It slams them down, first one, then the other, so hard their bodies burst like rotten melons. Murdoch clutches Jesus wrist, as they work their way along the wall. He steps on something wet and soft, but doesn't bother to look, he knows it's someone. Keep moving, he thinks.

Because there's also the other thing he's noticed. In a pocket of shadow, where shadows should not be, a tall man in dark blue overalls stands, his mask a neutral corpse white face. Michaels. He's not doing anything, just watching.

The lights go off again. There's the sound of a helicopter.

* * *

For a moment, everyone, everything, goes still. Even the Gods pause.

Everyone except for Murdoch and Jesus, as Murdoch leads him through the gap in the wall. Murdoch stumbles on broken rubble, half falls, smashing his knee, cursing helplessly. He refuses to look back.

At first, with the death of the halogen stadium lights, everything is pitch black, everyone pauses, as if consumed by void. But then, measured through heartbeats, vision returns. First the stars, then the vague shape of the amphitheater, the flickering of light on the waters of the Cenote. Humans are dark shapes. The Gods are great pools of darkness looming over them.

There's the sound of a helicopter overhead. Murdoch identifies it as one of the massive cargo carriers that he rode in after capture. He looks up, the aircraft hovers high above, invisible, a looming black shape against the stars.

A beam of light, a searchlight stabs down on the alabaster plaza, and moves left, illuminating the Green Hippo in a circle of incandescent steaming light. It lifts its head, shielding its eyes with a forelimb in a disturbingly human gesture. All around, its impending victims scatter like mice, making for the holes in the wall, for the now gaping tunnel entrance while the God is transfixed. Murdoch hopes some of the poor bastards make it.

Then something happens, there's a stutter in the even sound of the helicopter's rotors. A 'floof' sound. A jet of flame surges out from the side of the helicopter, briefly illuminating it. Suddenly, the whole helicopter is on fire, a massive hovering fireball, the rotors creating a wondrous bloom as the fire spreads out like a flower and down into a narrow stem.

It falls then, plunging into the waters of the Cenote, sending a wave capped with froths of burning fuel up onto the Cenote plaza, washing around the waists of the Red and Green Hippos, and drawing screaming human victims back into the water for waiting crocodilians.

* * *

The Lieutenant is walking through an ancient stone tunnel. When they brought her, she thought there was only one tunnel. But now, after escaping the Green Hippo with the other survivors, she realizes that there is a labyrinth underground, passageways curving like serpents, merging, branching, an ancient underground labyrinth created to connect ceremonial sites, growing more elaborate with each generation.

She has no idea where she is or where she's going, but she finds she walks with certainty, as if her feet know the way. This doesn't bother her.

She should be huddled semiconscious in some corner, going in and out of delirium, slowly dying. But the pain in her head has subsided entirely, the ringing, the flashes of light are gone. She feels fine. She feels lucid, focused, filled with purpose.

She doesn't question this. Why bother?

The sections she walks are strung with wires, lit with electric lights. In wider passages, there's storage, rows after rows of wooden boxes, in one section cots and a portable refrigerator. There's something wrong with the power, the lights keep going on and off. She hears cries and screams, but nothing near her.

The Lieutenant passes a man impaled on a steel pole sticking out of the wall. His head brushes the top of the passage, his feet dangle a foot and a half from the ground. He wears a Simpson's T-shirt and shorts. The pool of blood below him extends all the way to the other side of the passage. When the light flickers on, it shines like oil.

She does not even slow down, there's nothing of interest.

Voices up ahead, she slows, clutching the obsidian knife. It feels insubstantial, she craves something heavier, the weight of a length of cold steel. She feels naked, she wishes she had her flight helmet. She felt safe, looking out through the visor.

There are two men, gunmen, both cartel, not paramilitary. They're naked except for trunks, boots and bandoleers. There's no circulation down in the tunnels, and although it's not as cripplingly hot as above, the temperature and still air takes its toll. Their bodies almost gleam with sweat. One speaks urgently into a satellite phone, the other watches him.

The phone crackles with desperate words. There's something going on at the Ferris Wheel, she overhears, though it's not clear what.

"They're taking families" comes the cry. "Help us!" The are other voices on the line, promising help, demanding back-up, complaints of being needed elsewhere, demands for information.

The Lieutenant waits patiently for the lights to go off. When they do, she steps up to cut the watcher's throat. Arterial blood spurts in the face of the man on the satellite phone, panicking he grabs his pistol putting shot after shot into his companion as she walks the dying man into the gunfire. When she's close enough she lets him drop, sweeping the other's pistol away with her free hand, and plunging the obsidian knife into his rib cage walking it down in descending order - left right left right left right, past the ribs her slash opens his intestines, and a final flourish cuts through his shorts, severing his penis.

The man drops like a sack, staring up at her, trying to breathe through multiple sucking wounds in his chest, one hand futilely holding his intestines in. The Lieutenant retrieves his gun, discards the clip and replaces it with a fresh one. He watches her, eyes pools of horror. She glances down, uninterested, his death is already slipping over him.

She ignores the phone. There's nothing coming out of it but screaming and incomprehensible fragments of speech. She catches frantic babbling about something done at the Ferris Wheel, or on it, or to it. She's not surprised, when They come, the horror always runs wild. It doesn't matter, it's not part of the mission, just a distraction, and she's not concerned with distractions.

She glances down at him without interest, his eyes have gone dim there's nothing left, and continues on her way. Behind her, on the phone, cutting through the sound of screams and the chug of a diesel motor, someone is begging for mercy.

She ignores it.

The General clears his throat to draw her attention. He's just there, of course. He never appears or disappears, sometimes he's there, sometimes he isn't. She's not interested. But there he is.

GENERAL: Those things, the monsters we've come to kill, bad as they are. You know they're the good guys? You know that right?

LIEUTENANT: It doesn't matter.

GENERAL: I suppose not.

LIEUTENANT: I keep wondering about you. Are you real? Or are you just figments of my brain rotting inside my skull? Gears slipping loose, just one of the malfunctions that come from being around those things?

GENERAL: Why does it matter?

LIEUTENANT: Maybe I want to know if there's something else afterward? Heaven or Hell? Or just something?

The figure beside her seems to pause, as if thinking about it.

GENERAL: If there is a Heaven, then just being near them means you'll never get there.

LIEUTENANT: Hell then?

GENERAL: If that exists, then no. You won't go there either. Because of them. They're a stain on the fabric of existence. Whatever they are, it goes down to subatomic levels, quarks, gluons, it goes past that. Quantum foam, whatever time and space are made of. We don't even know what they are.

LIEUTENANT: I keep hoping you might be real, because then maybe some time you could be useful. But all I ever get is fortune-cookie gibberish.

The General laughs.

LIEUTENANT: Any useful advice?

GENERAL: We're past that.

The Lieutenant sighs.

LIEUTENANT: I suppose we are.

GENERAL: There's not much of you left.

* * *

The Blood Red Hippo roars, red sweat dripping across its body in rivulets, dripping in its path, as it Stocks through the motor pool. It passes a repair shop, walking between buses and transport trucks that dwarf it, kicking aside motorcycles and ATVs.

Its rage is overpowering, a maelstrom, a hurricane, fuelled by pain from its torn tusk socket, the slashes across its muzzle. It bellows again, not caring that its roars can be heard by its prey. There is no thought in its mind, only the overpowering reckless intent of a God, a will as relentless and void of thought as an earthquake. Pure existence and purpose, unmediated.

The Blood Red God smacks at a massive fist at a military transport as it passes, overturning the heavy twelve-ton vehicle. It turns its head, searching, the great jaws yawn wide, exposing the awful tusks, and it bellows its challenge to the night.

It wants nothing to do but tear apart the small manlike abomination that offends it so. It can feel the thing, vaguely, a node of absence, a pocket of unreality and anti-life. Despite the brutal pounding, Jackson walks unharmed, apparently unconcerned.

The hulking man in the broken sports mask steps out from between two military transports. His mask is cracked, bits of plastic and metal barely holding together and stained with blood and filth, his overalls torn. There are no eyes visible behind the mask. Jackson has found a machete.

The Man in the Mask stands, patient, relentless, dwarfed by the raging, monstrous bulk of the four meter tall monster.

From somewhere, there's an ear splitting shriek of tortured metal that goes on and on, the lights all over the camp flicker wildly, off and on. Over the loudspeakers, a festive calliope melody blares, there's a buzz of static, and then the opening strains of a pop song. In the distance, a new screaming begins.

The two figures ignore it all, distant, irrelevant. They simply stare at each other, two giants facing off. The man in the mask and his machete, blank, empty, impersonal and relentless, and the Blood Red

God, full of fury and passion, eyes blazing, rage and pain, brimming with life.

Then the God roars and charges.

* * *

Murdoch is struggling futilely to hot-wire a pickup truck, it has a fifty-millimeter machine gun mounted in the back. It reminds him of other places, other wars, the dry heat of North Africa, and working with revolutionaries bounding across the desert in Toyota trucks with heavy machine guns bolted in the box.

Suddenly he hears the roar of the Blood Red Hippo, altogether too close by. He can smell the creature, its red sweat a mixture of blood and spices in the air. Its psychic presence overpowers the feeling of dread that seems to never leave him. It's like shouting in his head, an earthquake in his mind, physically shaking his thoughts. His hands shake helplessly.

Beside him, Jesus cries out and falls to his knees clutching at his head. Perhaps his native ancestry makes him more sensitive to the emanations of these Gods.

The lights go off again, plunging the compound in darkness. He can't hot wire the truck, and the creature is too close. There's a mighty crash. Whatever it's doing in its rampage, they don't want to be anywhere near. He grabs Jesus' shoulder, forcing the young man to look at him, and gestures.

The night is full of the sounds of gunfire. Individual shots, like pops, staccato bursts. Somewhere someone screams.

MURDOCH: We have to get out of here.

JESUS: Where?

MURDOCH: Doesn't matter. Just keep moving.

Boats, Murdoch thinks. Find the dock, steal a zodiac, or a speedboat, or a fucking canoe. Get in the water, away from Them. Water blocks Them, Murdoch thinks.

JESUS: The Gods, they are of the river. River of Life. Born from the River Mother.

Murdoch squints. Had he spoken out loud? His head feels funny, as if the psychic backwash of the Gods is breaking down the barriers of the mind, thoughts bleeding from one person to another. He touches a hand to his lip. His nose is bleeding.

As he does so, Jesus makes an identical gesture, his fingers come away red

The youth is babbling, a mixture of English, Spanish and more ancient tongues, the litanies of the Gods are going through both their minds. Jesus focuses and looks at Murdoch.

JESUS: Find the dock, steal a zodiac...

MURDOCH: Yes.

Together they stumble through the night.

The lights flash back on. Britney Spears' "Toxic" begins to play over loudspeakers, but the sound is distorted, slowing down and speeding up.

They come to a main street, open and empty. Jesus steps out, but Murdoch drags him back. There's a clatter of metal, a shriek of steel beams twisting and rivets popping. The Ferris Wheel, somehow unmoored from its mountings rolls by, full of screaming passengers. The wheel wobbles, one of the carriages swings wildly, flinging a woman loose. Her body strikes one of the metal struts on the way down, cutting off her scream and slicing her in half.

The wheel rolls past them, wobbling to the left, it turns a corner, its speed unimpeded. Then it's gone, even its noise is barely perceptible. Just another sound of screaming and chaos in the ongoing carnage, punctuated by Britney Spears and shrieking metallic guitars.

For a moment, Murdoch stands there, unable to think, his mind locking up, wondering if it even happened?

But the body of the woman lies in the street. She's native, gray haired, thick bodied as some women become late in life. Her wrists are tied, he notices, as are her ankles.

Someone did this to her. Abducted her, tied her, placed her in the Ferris Wheel carriage. Did this over and over for each carriage. And then... set the wheel loose? How would you set a Ferris Wheel loose? Even if you could somehow manage to kidnap all those people and fill all the carriages? How could you tie people to the spokes? Wouldn't someone stop you? And the Ferris Wheel was going so fast, how was that possible? And it turned, almost as if it was guided…

The Ferris Wheel lights were on as it rolled past them filled with screaming passengers. How was that even possible? It wouldn't have independent lights, the electricity would be tied to the framework.

His mind wants to seize up, the details, the implications are inconceivable.

Murdoch looks at Jesus helplessly.

MURDOCH: What the actual fuck?

JESUS: Keep moving, that's all, keep moving.

MURDOCH: Yeah.

At least it can't get any worse.

* * *

Murdoch stops, gaping in astonishment, holding Jesus by the wrist. He's standing in front of a pile of bodies. No, not bodies. Body parts. A great mound of chopped flesh, human and animal, cows, chickens, goats. Limbs and paws, intestines and innards.

Something blurs at the edge of his vision. His eye tracks it. It strikes the mound with a soft wet plop near the top, and rolls down, tumbling to face them. It's a child's severed head. Murdoch and Jesus stare numbly at it.

Then they look up.

A few dozen feet away, two figures stand.

One is a grotesquely fat man in bib overalls, no shirt, no shoes. His body is covered with hair and warts, a hand with overgrown spade-like fingernails clutches the largest meat cleaver Murdoch's ever seen. He wears the severed, half hollowed out head of a pig as a mask, the pig's broken jaw wobbles as his head turns.

The other appears to be a boy, at perhaps twelve, perhaps fourteen, wearing blue jeans torn open at the knees, and a red-t shirt with the logo of some band. He has a bath towel tied around his neck, like a cape. His mask is a crudely woven, oversized balaclava. His hands are stained red up to the elbow, and he is holding a woman's head, prepared to throw.

They turn to look at Murdoch and Jesus, and he can feel the weight of their attention. No surprise, no interest, simply the relentless, remorseless attention of sharks.

Murdoch has never seen either of them, never dreamed of them, at best he's only felt them from a distance. But here and now in this moment, he knows they are every fear and every nightmare he's ever had or will ever have in his life.

The lights go off, and they're plunged into darkness.

Jesus doesn't wait. He runs blindly through the darkness. His touch, the sense of his movement, sends Murdoch stumbling after him in the darkness.

As he runs, there's a soft muffled boom, immensely loud, like a nuclear bomb wrapped in swaddling cloth. As he looks up, a few thousand yards away, illuminated by starlight, a white cloud rises up into the air spreading out like a mushroom.

* * *

PISTOLERO: Don't kill me, please don't kill me, don't kill me!

The gunman babbles, tears streaming from his eyes, as he lifts up his pistol. He is a narco, a drug soldier, easily distinguished by his brightly coloured shirt and casual clothes. He and his fellows are standing behind three kneeling, bound men, soldiers by their uniforms, paramilitary, from CRAC.

The Lieutenant watches from the shadows, they don't notice her. She feels unnaturally calm. Some part of her wonders if it's an effect of the concussions. At least she's not throwing up. She found a pry-bar near some sort of workman's site. It's not her bar, but it comforts her.

She's also taken a pistol off a dead body, it's her third pistol, this one has a full clip. It doesn't comfort her nearly as much. Only seven bullets. You can't do much with that. But she knows she'll find other pistols, or take them.

As nearly as she can work out, the eruption at the Cenote has shattered whatever fragile alliance existed between the drug cartel and the revolutionary paramilitary. Firefights are breaking out all over the camp, their speed and viciousness suggesting that one group was already preparing to do the other one in. There are bodies everywhere.

The revolutionaries have had the worst of it. Now three captured soldiers kneel in front of a pit, waiting for their bullets. But something is wrong, they're all babbling, the words are each other's thoughts, flushing uncontrollably from their mouths.

Overlaid, far too loud, a distorted version of Britney Spears' 'Toxic' staggers unevenly through its beats, on crackling speakers.

Beyond them, also standing in shadows, is a man in tight fitting leather and latex, his body covered in straps, wearing a gas mask. One arm is wrapped in a heavy gauntlet of thick cow hide, covered in studs and spikes, with lengths of long razored chains depending from each finger.

They watch as the Pistolero, still babbling, marches from one kneeling man to the next, firing the pistol into the back of their heads. They flop over like dolls, one after the other.

Bored, the Man in the Mask retreats back further into the shadows, intent on his own purposes.

PISTOLERO: It won't stop. Why won't it stop?

The Pistolero holds his head. As he turns, he catches sight of the Lieutenant. His eyes widen.

PISTOLERO: I can't feel you.

At that moment, there's a muffled boom, like an atom bomb wrapped in swaddling. They feel the shockwave passing through. The Pistolero and his companions turn. A white cloud is rising up into the air.

When they turn back, the Lieutenant is gone.

* * *

The Blood Red Hippo has picked up an ATV and is using it as a club. An outward swing catches Jackson mid-stride, sending him tumbling end over end through the air. Like a freight train, the Red God, bleeding from a dozen wounds, marches down on Jackson and uses the ATV to pound the struggling figure, roaring all the while. Blood-sweat almost fountains from its thick skin, flung by its frantic exertions.

It kneels over the struggling figure, roaring sheer fury, smashing the ATV down again and again, for all the world like a toddler in a tantrum, stubbornly trying to smash a useless toy.

Abruptly, the monster stiffens and screams, trying to stand and falling steadily to one side with the uncontrolled gracelessness of a tree toppling. It rolls desperately, struggling to climb to its feet, bracing against the side of a transport. The ATV crashes and rolls away, both it and its victim forgotten.

Reaching down, it finds a knife stuck in the back of its left knee. Angrily, it pulls the blade out, and flings it away, snarling.

Michaels, with the patient dignity of a gravedigger, steps out of the shadows and picks up the knife, his blandly handsome, inexpressive corpse mask staring with empty indifference.

The Bleeding Monster snarls, cornered.

The ATV tumbles and Jackson sits up. Michaels doesn't bother to look, simply stares at the Bleeding God.

Jackson stands, his machete ready.

Neither of the men in masks acknowledge the existence of the other. But somehow, at the same moment, they move in.

This is how a God dies.

* * *

Suddenly, they're walking through a white fog. Murdoch feels the numbness on his lips and tongue, and immediately knows what it is. Murdoch tears off his shirt to make a makeshift mask, wetting it from a puddle.

They hear sounds of laughter and sobbing, screaming. Indistinctly, they see bodies staggering and collapsing. Murdoch can feel grit in his eyes, every time he blinks. The breath in jury-rigged mask is moist. The white fog is fine dust, it settles on their skin, mingling with the sweat. When Murdoch wipes his brow, he can feel the dust particles congealing together with the sweat, like fine gravel under his fingers.

MURDOCH: Don't breathe. This is cocaine. That thing that went up, that mushroom cloud was all coke. We're walking through it. Jesus, I can't imagine how much they had stored away to make a cloud of this.

Jesus follows his example, pressing a wet cloth to his face. As Murdoch watches, the cloth covering Jesus' mouth stains red from the inside. He's still suffering the residue of the God's power.

They run past a man bent over, vomiting uncontrollably.

MURDOCH (muffled): We have to get out of here.

JESUS: I know, we're walking through poison dust.

MURDOCH: No, no. I grew up in wheat country. I was a kid, when the grain silo blew. It's just particles, flammable aerosolized particles. Once a particle ignites, they all go, the fire spreads, it's everywhere, it eats up all the oxygen. Like a fuel air explosive.

JESUS: What do we do?

MURDOCH: Get inside somewhere, find someplace airtight. All it takes is a spark. We need to hide, it's only a matter of time.

JESUS (understanding): Not much time.

* * *

As simple as a match struck, a cigarette puffed, a candle flame, a cooking stove, a pistol shot. It doesn't matter where the spark comes from, only that there is a spark.

Tiny particles of cocaine suspended in humid air ignites, the heat of ignition triggers the chain reaction spreading faster than the speed of sound, the entire cloud turns to fire. Cascades of electrons polarise, sending lightning bolts surging within and through the fireball, grounding wherever they touch. The lightning fast fire consumes all oxygen within grasp, superheated air cycling upward, sucking more oxygen in.

The fireball turns into a fire pillar, glowing and surging, the incandescent column of heated gases sucking air in from all directions, creating maelstroms, spontaneous whirlwinds, that collapse buildings and send vehicles tumbling and fling screaming victims into the sky.

Everyone caught in the fireball dies horribly, their skins burned away, their lungs incinerated from within, eyeballs bursting and melting. The last taste is of their own frying flesh. They stagger and fall as the fire clings to their skin, eating away at layers of fat, muscle turning to charcoal. Some are electrocuted by lightning bolts, flash fried where they stand, in deaths almost merciful.

Everyone caught in the fireball dies horribly. The lucky ones die instantly.

Most aren't lucky.

* * *

The Sky Hippo staggers, coughing heavily. Its eyes are bleeding, and it rubs at them, half blinded, struggling to see. Its ears, half burned away are roaring. Its massive head swings around, dimly taking in the charred corpses, some of them still squirming. It retches, vomiting up ropes and lumps of blackened goo.

The creature straightens, trying to draw air into charred lungs, coughing and snorting soot stained mucus. Patches of its blue and white hide are burning, but one by one, the fires go out as it draws on inner reserves. It is a God, after all.

The roar of a chainsaw comes as a shock, unbearably, impossibly near. The Sky Hippo swings its massive head, looking for the source. It turns...

Unbearable pain arches up between its legs as the relentless buzz of the saw changes pitch. Agony stabs deep. It feels its bowels, bleeding and shredded spilling down its thighs.

Panicking, the monster tries to run, lunging and staggering. But the pain, the roar of the saw only follows, tearing and pushing deeper. Bellowing, it turns to swing, trying to shake away the horror devouring it, but it can't reach.

It falls to one knee, and then rights itself standing through sheer desperate force, as the chain saw drives deeper, ravaging flesh. Its life is spilling out between its legs, muscles contract and convulse in useless spastic agony, expelling intestines and organs in wads of shredded gore.

The sound of the chain saw is entirely muffled now, but the agony of the creature redoubles. It screams in horror as it feels a new weight inside, bracing against its pelvic girdle. It feels the vibration of the muffled saw, the tremors shifting with each movement as it psychically radiates its torment.

All of the dying humans and animals within a hundred yards are snuffed out instantly by the sudden psychic wave of its shock and terror. The tortured tissues of the humans in range are momentarily aflame one last time, blood vessels rupturing, tissues turning to slurry ejecting like geysers from every orifice before collapsing.

The Sky Hippo vomits blood, falling to knees and then all fours. Through sheer will, it climbs to its feet, staggering in a half circle, looking down at itself in horror as the saw tears through two inch thick hide, poking out its belly.

Desperately, the Sky God grabs the end of the chain saw, uncaring as the whirling saw-chain rips its paws to the bone. But its agony and desperation are such that it refuses to let go. It tightens its grip even as the saw tears into bone, fighting to pull it physically out of its body. Through sheer effort, it pulls two feet of whirring chain saw out of its body, a fine red mist spraying out as its hands disintegrate, the sound of the chainsaw engine now hideously loud inside it, before its paws are so ruined it can no longer grip.

The saw vanishes back inside it, and thrusts upward.

The Sky Hippo throws its head back and howls in mind shattering misery and agony as blood spurts up like a fountain from its throat.

Desperately, shredded paws, now sticks of bone and broken muscle, lumps of gore claw at itself, tearing open its flesh, ripping its guts further, spilling fragments of intestines and organs.

It takes a step. Its psychic cry rings out with its bellow.

SKY HIPPO: HELP ME! BROTHERS! PLEASE! ANYONE! HELP ME! HELP ME!

It takes another step, continuing to tear away, reaching higher. Inside, the thing is bracing against its ribs, climbing them like a ladder, the saw thrusting and swinging inside. It claws at its chest, hide sloughs away, revealing banded muscle.

Its bellows stall out as its lungs are sliced away to confetti. Spastic muscle reflex forces some chunks and shreds up its throat, it coughs, choking. The rest slides down its innards, spilling out in puffy pink gobbets, falling or trickling down its legs as it staggers.

The psychic blast goes on and on, radiating outwards, now barely more than pure mindless horror and fear at the desecration of its body.

SKY HIPPO: HELP ME! PLEASE! PLEASE! SOMEONE! ANYONE! PLEASE!

It stops, spreading its arms wide, its head facing skywards, it opens its jaws wide as if for one last scream.

SKY HIPPO: IT HURTS!

The chain saw pokes out of the back of its mouth, slicing away its tongue.

SKY HIPPO: PLEASE!

The chain saw darts upwards, through the roof of the mouth, tearing through flesh and bone to the brain cavity.

Another God dies.

The saw goes on and on, from the center of the forehead it pokes out, then withdraws. Then it roars again, tearing through the neck. A forelimb flops as flesh is cut through.

Sawyer climbs out. The saw goes still. Sawyer, in his mask made of human faces, looks around curiously, almost expectantly. There are fires everywhere. Mostly small, but some of them are starting to spread. There's nothing alive within sight.

Behind, there's the trail of gore, blood and spilled organs, intestines and fluids left behind as the Sky Hippo staggered through its death throes.

Sawyer steps up onto a splayed limb, climbing until he's standing on top of the corpse. He pulls the cord, and the chain saw begins its rasping raucous song once again.

Holding the roaring saw above his head, waving it triumphantly, Sawyer begins to dance.

"Toxic" plays on, broken and blaring, from ruined loudspeakers.

Sawyer dances to it.

* * *

PISTOLERO: Don't move, fuckers.

Murdoch and Jesus freeze, holding up their hands, palms out. There are four of the cartel soldiers, all heavily armed. Murdoch notes that they're all staring at them, not behind them. He feels relief. At least it means that the others, the Men in the Masks, are not standing behind them.

PISTOLERO: You're not CRAC. Who the fuck are you? And how are you alive?

MURDOCH: We're just trying to stay alive, just like you. We're buyers, in from the States. America.

The Pistolero stared levelly at them.

PISTOLERO: Bullshit.

MURDOCH: We're just buyers, man. From up north. We were just here to do business when the shit hit the fan. That's all.

One of the other cartel soldiers barks a stream of Spanish. The Pistolero must be the only one with English, Murdoch thinks. Jesus answers back in Spanish, which prompts a skeptical retort and then a back and forth too fast for Murdoch to follow with his limited field lingo.

PISTOLERO: Fuck you. You're the assholes that we took when we grabbed the Witch and that big fucker with the mask. I got close to him, he fucking smelled like a corpse. And you smell of him.

For a moment, Murdoch wonders if he's just talking shit, or if somehow the presence of the others, all the time they traveled with them, has left some sort of stain on his soul, a taint that some people can sense and perhaps mistake for a smell.

Murdoch wonders if he's damned.

If simply having been in their presence was enough.

Stick to the lie, he reminds himself.

MURDOCH: Just buyers. We have money, we brought it down with us.

Was that how it worked? How did money move? Would buyers bring suitcases of money?

MURDOCH: We brought shit for Modovar. Gifts and shit. It was business, you know. You bring money and shit and stuff.

The Pistolero's not buying it.

PISTOLERO: No. You're with the Witch and the Corpse-smell Fucker. You're tied up in this. We're going to bring you to El Jefe, maybe it will help him sort this out. Everything's fucked, it's unbelievable.

Murdoch and Jesus look at each other. There are no good options. But there are things out there.

MURDOCH: Yeah, sure. But listen, can we go now? We think some... things… are following us.

Even at gunpoint, he can't help himself. He looks over his shoulder. Still nothing. But that's not reassuring. They're out there. They're all out there.

PISTOLERO: Fuckers that look like people... but wear masks?

Jesus says something in Spanish. The Pistolero responds in kind, joined by some of the other gunmen. There's another rapid fire exchange. Murdoch can follow just enough to know they're talking about Them.

PISTOLERO: Let's get out of here. We're taking you in. I'm tired of this shit.

They're lead to a transport truck, singed, the paint scoured off, but still working. To Murdoch's vague surprise, all six men, the four cartel soldiers and their two prisoners climb into the cab. There isn't even a consideration of anyone getting in the back, it's as if the box of the truck isn't there at all. Murdoch notices wet red stains oozing from the seams.

The interior is impossibly cramped, it reeks of male sweat and stale smoke, the scent so thick you can cut it with a knife. The windows are rolled up, the heat of the day combined with their bodies, and the still air, lack of circulation is suffocating. Jesus is panting. The transport lurches into motion. The smell of fried pork is overpowering. But at least with the windows closed, the blare of the dying, stuttering public address system and its perverse pop music is muffled.

Murdoch decides to chance it.

MURDOCH: What's in the back?

The others, including the driver, ignore him, but the Pistolero frowns.

PISTOLERO: My men.

MURDOCH: What happened?

The Pistolero stares at him, as if thinking it over. Finally he pulls out a cigarillo, lights it up.

PISTOLERO: I should have thought of this before. Helps with the smell.

The Pistolero waves the cigarillo. Says something in Spanish. A couple of the other cartel gunmen laugh bitterly.

PISTOLERO: Those CRAC fuckers. You could tell, they were always sniffing around, looking into things. They were lining up to take us out. All the time, friendship, allies, all that bullshit. Couldn't talk to them though, it's just fucking bourgeois this and capitalism that and proletariat and analysis. They didn't mind the whores, just like the rest of us. But even then, they never stopped.

He took a puff.

PISTOLERO: Like I said, all smiles and friendly hand, but a knife behind their back. They were going to try, we knew it. We were just waiting for their move, to take them all out.

He smiled.

PISTOLERO: El Jefe, he fed the CRAC bitch to the Gods. That's when we all knew. Time to move. They were ready, they were fast. But we hit them hard everywhere. Rolled the fuckers all up. I capped the bitch's captains myself, pop, pop, pop.

Murdoch nodded.

MURDOCH: So what went wrong?

PISTOLERO: The fuckers prepared. They blew the cocaine. That big white cloud? Coke. Would you believe it? Blew it all up. But what they did next…

MURDOCH: What?

PISTOLERO: Atom bomb.

Murdoch's eyes widened. He didn't dare look at Jesus, but just pressed a hand against his knee, hoping to keep him silent.

MURDOCH: What?

PISTOLERO: They blew an Atom bomb. They said they had one, I never believed. Fucking bullshit, they were always bullshitting you know. But I guess they had one, we had them, they lost, but I guess there were a few of them left. They blew it up. The damn dirty bastards blew us all to hell.

JESUS: Fuck.

PISTOLERO: Yeah. We were inside the cab when the Atom bomb blew. It protected us. But we had a full crew in back of the truck, out in the open. Thirty men. They were caught in the bomb.

He paused, mournfully.

PISTOLERO: Thirty men, caught in the open by the Atom bomb. It killed anyone who was caught out in the blast, radiation, you know. The men in the back, they were protected a little, but not enough. The truck stopped dead, everything was fire outside, we didn't know what was going on and then the fire was over. Just like that. One second, the world is fire, truck rocking like there's a hurricane outside. Then nothing. When it was safe, we stepped out. Everyone was dead, burned alive. That's when we heard it.

The man crossed himself reflexively. Jesus repeated the gesture.

PISTOLERO: Madre de Dios, I never heard anything like that before. If I live a hundred years, I never want to hear sounds like that again. We look in the back. They're charred. Flesh black, falling off. Some of them, pressed against each other, they were melted together. They were all alive, mostly. But burned worse than anything. Eyes melted. Fucking tongues charred, like to break off. Saw someone cough, black syrup came out. They were dead, but living in pain, horrible pain, you never heard or saw anything like it.

MURDOCH: What did you do?

But he didn't have to ask. He already knew.

PISTOLERO: Fucking killed them. We had to climb in there and do it. These men were my brothers. Couldn't stand outside and shoot them, might not do it. And we might set off something - all their gear was with them, contaminated by radiation, who knows? So we had to go in. Shot them till we were out of bullets. Then I had to use my knife.

The gunman's eyes were haunted.

PISTOLERO: Some of them, they could still talk. They called out to me. To me! Their eyes and ears burned off, their skin… you touched it, like charcoal, pieces flaking off, and underneath, all melted. They called out to me, begging my help, and I'm standing right in front of them, but they can't even tell I'm there. Just crying out. Only one way to help them, and they don't even know it's me.

MURDOCH: I'm sorry, man.

Jesus said something in Spanish. The gunman nodded.

PISTOLERO: So that's why you're not in the back. Because they're there. After this is over, we'll treat them right - Christian burials.

He sighed.

PISTOLERO: What a fucked up night. You know, the Gods come and walk among us, you can feel their holy thoughts, you can feel your mind bleeding out, other people's thoughts swimming in your head, and that's when those CRAC assholes decide to do all this. Assholes. Profane assholes.

He lifted his head.

PISTOLERO: I think those assholes in masks you saw are with them. CRAC specials. Or they're with the Witch. Or maybe they're all in it together, CRAC, the Witch, the Masks, you can never tell. Maybe you're in it too.

Jesus said something in Spanish. The Pistolero replied back.

PISTOLERO: You say that. Maybe. But what do I know? We were getting reports all night, strangers walking around. Strange reports, like you wouldn't believe. Men walking around without faces. A man whose face was a mirror. Some asshole in an executioner's hood, tight pants, no shirt, like a fucking cartoon. You wouldn't believe.

Jesus spoke again, rapid Spanish. The gunman shook his head.

PISTOLERO: No. We didn't see those assholes. But I'll tell you one. We get a call at the schoolhouse.

MURDOCH: You have a schoolhouse?

PISTOLERO: Fuck you, you stuck up Yankee bastard! Yes, we have a schoolhouse. We get called, there's this Santa Claus fucker creeping around. We go - and fuck me, there he is, right there in the doorway. He's wearing these big rubber wading boots, like the fishermen have, and those big rubber gauntlets. But he's got a red coat, and a red hat, and damn me to hell, he's wearing this cheap plastic Santa Mask.

MURDOCH: What did you do?

PISTOLERO: Plugged the fucker up. We all opened fire. You see a guy looking like that, you don't have to ask any questions, you just go ahead and shoot him. You see. But here's the fucked up thing, you went inside, for the children. You know what we found? The whole place was decorated. But such decorations…

JESUS: A Christmas Tree… made out of children.

The Pistolero stared at them.

PISTOLERO: Now how the fuck would you know that?

MURDOCH: Because we're running from him, and the ones like him.

The Pistolero's eyes narrow, as if he doesn't quite believe them.

PISTOLERO: Maybe I should just save everyone time, take you out by the side of the road and shoot you both.

He seemed to think it over, and shook his head.

PISTOLERO: I'll leave it to El Jefe. You know the most fucked up thing? We turned around, looking for the body, it wasn't there. It was like someone took him. Or he walked away. (sighs) I'll say one thing, those creepy fuckers did us one good favour. We were all armed up on alert for them, when the fucking CRAC made their move - we were ready because of that, and so put them down. We won…

Murdoch looked out the smeared window at the devastated burning ruins of the compound. It doesn't look like any kind of victory. Wisely, he keeps his mouth shut.

The Gunman pauses reflectively.

PISTOLERO: Except for the Atom Bomb. I guess it's true what they say, no one wins with the Atom Bomb.

The truck pulls up in front of an immense mansion.

PISTOLERO: We're here, fuckers. Now we'll see what's what.

He stubs out his cigarillo. He looks up suddenly, catching Murdoch's glance.

PISTOLERO: No smoking inside the house.

* * *

The Priest is still in his regalia from the ceremony at the Cenote, the Lieutenant notes. How much time has passed since then? An hour? Less?

Somehow he survived the fireball. Protected by his magic, she wonders? More likely, he was inside somewhere safe and reasonably airtight, perhaps inside a vehicle, or some kind of ceremonial chamber.

She imagines the Priest in some underground sanctum, burning powders and herbs, spilling blood, chanting and dancing, trying to supplicate Gods or spirits while the end of the world broke over them.

The Priest's eyes narrow.

PRIEST: Witch!

LIEUTENANT: Where's your boss?

There is a moment of flickering incomprehension in the Priest's eyes. She realizes that he didn't see Modovar as his boss. He probably saw him as a subject, or pawn, or plaything. They all think they're really in charge, the Lieutenant thinks.

The Lieutenant almost laughs. It is all so random. Spirits and drug dealers, half senile hedge shamans, jungle revolutionaries, all thinking they're in charge, rulers of their tiny little worlds, bouncing off each other, hooking up, building each other into something powerful and terrible, all the while each of them maintaining the illusion that they were in charge, the ultimate power, the ultimate ruler. Each of them insecure, still hungry for more and more power. Each of them no more than a heartbeat from betraying the others. All of them just continually climbing higher and higher on the rickety structure of delusions and betrayal and ambition they'd built together.

They'd created Gods, and thought they controlled them.

It was all doomed from before the first moment, from literally before Modovar started buying off local villages by co-opting Shamans, before they cast a spirit into a Hippo, or made a deal with revolutionaries.

The Squad hadn't been needed at all. Collapse was inevitable.

The miracle was that it had all lasted this long.

PRIEST (snarling): There's no need, Witch. I am your Judgment. You think you can betray the spirit world? Your trickery will come to nothing. The spirits have seen your like, and the like of the things you serve.

The Priest takes up his rattle and waves it in a figure eight, shaking it and chanting.

PRIEST: You are bound!

The Lieutenant didn't feel bound.

She could almost see who he'd been before this all started. Some little village charlatan, dancing, chanting, speaking in riddles. Trying to do whatever good he could with his limited knowledge of actual folk medicine and whatever skills he had as a counselor. Petty and jealous in the way such men are, self-serving and foolish. Alternately venerated and tolerated. It must have been an uneasy life, leavened only by belief in his own bullshit. That and just enough brushes with the fringes of the supernatural to validate his narrow self-absorbed world view.

He could have lived and died and never mattered at all. But somehow, he'd found himself on this strange path, architect and victim both, hollowed out until all that was left was the mad empty shell before her.

PRIEST: We are the guardians of life, of the cycles of death and rebirth, of the circle of the world. The spirits of life rise up to defend me. They shall overcome the unclean, the abomination, so it has been and will always be.

The Lieutenant rolls her eyes and thinks about simply shooting him and being done with it. Instead, she clutches her pry-bar and takes a step.

LIEUTENANT: I don't care.

The Priest pales, glancing down at the pry-bar.

PRIEST: You bluff! That is not your Talisman! There's no power in it. (sneering) I have your Talismans, I have their power, I have your soul you locked within it. You are bound to me now. My magic is great—

The Lieutenant swings overhand, driving the claw of the pry-bar down into his forehead. There is a momentary crunch of bone as the metal claw punched through, deep into frontal lobes and down into the suborbital arches.

The Priest goes still, standing motionless, face gone slack. For a moment, she watches the irises of his eyes expand wide, and then turn red as the eyeballs fill with blood.

Then she twists and lifts the bar, the hook jerking forward, taking out the Priest's eyes and forehead. The eyeballs pop out and fall to the ground, a section of forehead flopping forward, still connected by skin, hanging off and concealing the lower part of his face.

The body stands for an instant longer. Then it trembles and drops to the ground.

The Lieutenant wipes flecks of blood from her face, smearing them. She feels tired. She wishes she had her flight helmet with her. That always makes her feel... complete.

She stares at the body of the Priest. Had she just done that? It was just a second ago. She remembers it clearly, but it almost felt like someone else, like she'd been someone else, or something else. Again, there is a sensation, like a craving for the helmet, a feeling of incompleteness, of not being entirely whole. She shakes her head, pushing it away.

The Lieutenant glances down at the body again. She feels she should say something. She wishes that the General was here, he'd have something useless to offer.

LIEUTENANT: You stupid superstitious fucker. It's not a talisman. There's no magic. That's all bullshit. It's just a piece of metal.

She pauses. Something more is needed.

LIEUTENANT: Asshole.

Then she sees it, a few feet beyond the Priest, mixed in with his gear, his feathered shaking sticks, and his sashes and Gris Gris. There's the pry-bar she carried. It doesn't matter, she's already got one, and one's as good as another.

The helmet. A battered helicopter flight helmet, the visor cracked. She stares wanting it, but now that it's in front of her she finds she's a little afraid of it.

The Priest called it a Talisman, claimed it contained her soul. He was full of shit, it's just an object, no magic in it, just junk. A good luck charm, no more significant than a rabbit's foot.

For a second, she thinks about leaving it behind, but the impulse isn't serious, she wants it badly.

She doesn't need it, she tells herself.

But reaches for it anyway, her hands trembling.

When she touches it, there's no electric charge, no energy, it's just inert molded plastic and metal, like its always been. There's no magic in it. The Priest was full of shit.

When she puts it on, she's relieved to feel that she's no different.

That disturbs her, because she feels now, that perhaps something… She searches for a word. Intangible? Something intangible has been slipping away from her for a while.

But the world through the cracked visor is no different. She shakes her head.

There is a mission. Focus on that. She needs to stick to the mission.

A moment later, she finds the Priest's driver, and kills him too. He never sees her coming. To her it's like squashing a bug.

She forgets him as she passes.

* * *

Murdoch and Jesus walk in with the gunmen surrounding them. Murdoch is agog as he stares at the giant swimming pool that dominates the center of the room, the waterfall descending from the upper levels, the hot tubs, the whirling multicolored chandelier high above in the cathedral ceiling. The water is steaming, there is something wrong, some acrid smell burns his nose

The PA system finally died sometime on the way over. Murdoch is grateful for that.

As he passes by one of the hot tubs, he glimpses a pair of skeletons beneath the surging waters. Some sort of grisly Halloween decoration? A macabre prank by Modovar? He doesn't have time to think about it, the entire place reeks of discordant excess and bad taste.

They march up the right hand staircase. Half way Murdoch thinks he glimpses a figure at the bottom of the left staircase, he tries to turn to see, but someone shoves him forward. He forgets about it as he stumbles. Worry about the Pistolero with the gun at your head, not the one doing flunky work.

As they climb to the top, Murdoch's step falters, and his eyes almost pop. He hears Jesus gasp beside him.

At the back of the massive upper level, there is a cheesy, gold plated, gigantic statue of a nude porn star. He actually recognizes the porn star, and the seminal pose from posters and centerfolds and magazine covers, breasts thrust proudly, legs spread, vulva on display. The only difference is the swollen belly, and the succession of infants descending from her. A literal river gushes from between her legs, filling a winding stream crossed by bridges, running all the way to the balcony's edge, where the water passes beneath the railings and becomes a waterfall.

Jesus swears, a phrase he's never heard. Then he switches to English.

JESUS: Mother of the River, the source of all life!

Murdoch has no idea what he's talking about. He can't take his eyes off the statue, alternately hideous and beautiful, gauche and holy. It is the gaudiest thing he's ever seen in his life. And yet, beside him, Jesus is almost trembling at the sight, and Murdoch realizes that as tawdry as it is, this over the top, ludicrous, vulgar effigy strikes a chord in his companion. That there's some deeply powerful allusion to the myths and mythology Jesus has grown up with. But it's just so godawful tasteless.

MODOVAR: Who are these assholes?

Someone shoves Murdoch hard and he stumbles forward. He falls to his knees, but before he can fall completely on his face, someone grabs him. He's hustled past an antique stone Altar. An Altar? But before he can do more than glimpse it, he's standing in front of Modovar and his lieutenants, and forced to his knees again. Jesus grunts with pain, his knee cracks with audible impact as he too is forced down beside him.

Modovar is wearing cargo shorts, and he's ditched the elaborate head-dress, and there's a stain on the shorts to match the departed cod-piece. But in most other respects, he's dressed in the regalia that he was wearing at the Cenote. Some of his companions are still wearing the ceremonial trappings, including the head-dresses. One is in an ersatz uniform, not of CRAC, not of any army. Another wears a leisure suit.

Murdoch feels a moment of profound disorientation. That feels like it was ages ago, eons, some forgotten antique time of stories, when the world made sense, when it wasn't all blood and gore and burning and even the Gods and Monsters were orderly.

MODOVAR: Who are these assholes?

There's no recognition at all in Modovar's face. Surely he saw pictures when they were captured? How long was he in a cell? It's almost insulting not to be recognized.

PISTOLERO: I guess they're not buyers.

MODOVAR: What the fuck are you talking about? You're wasting my time. The world is going to shit, half my town is burning, I've got fucking bodies everywhere I look, the goddamned Monsters are on the rampage. The fucking US Air Force is bombing us. What the fuck?

PISTOLERO: We caught these Pendejos sneaking around. They were with the Witch.

That gets Modovar's attention.

MODOVAR: The Witch? And that big smelly fucker with the mask, the one the Priest said was a ghost wrapped in meat?

He stares.

MODOVAR: Do you have anything to with that fucker with the chain-saw we saw back there?

Murdoch nods. Might as well come clean.

MURDOCH: There's a bunch of them. There's something wrong with them, all of them. You can feel it, the wrongness.

MODOVAR: I've been getting reports. The Priest said they were just ghosts, without the Witch, they'd just unspool. Evaporate away. Those guys made the Monsters crazy like I never saw. What are they?

MURDOCH: I don't know.

Modovar rubs his chin.

MODOVAR: How do you stop them?

Before Murdoch can answer, a new question occurs to Modovar.

MODOVAR: How do you control them? I want them. I want to own those fuckers.

MURDOCH: I don't know, I don't think anything controls them.

MODOVAR: Can you talk to them? Can I talk to them?

MURDOCH: They don't talk.

MODOVAR: What about the Witch? Is she the key?

MURDOCH: I don't know.

Modovar backhands him. Murdoch's ears ring from the blow, the next punch sends him sprawling, teeth loosened.

MODOVAR: You're fucking useless.

Modovar turns to Jesus, there's a rapid conversation in Spanish, the words flowing back and forth, faster than Murdoch can follow. Modovar grabs a pistol from the man in the leisure suit and holds it to Jesus's temple. He shouts. Jesus shouts back, then closes his eyes, pressing his head against the pistol, he starts to recite the Lord's Prayer. Modovar slaps the boy, stepping over and putting his foot on Murdoch's back, pointing the gun. Jesus replies, and then starts to recite his prayer.

MODOVAR: Both fucking useless.

Modovar looks up at his men.

MODOVAR: I want the Priest and I want the Witch, both of them. Get the word out, anyone and everyone that's left.

He pauses, and glances at the prisoners.

MODOVAR: And kill those fuckers.

The man in the fake army outfit steps forward, pulling a luger. Modovar's eyes widen.

MODOVAR: Are you stupid? You want the mess in here? Don't go and shit where I eat. Kill them outside. What the fuck? You get raised in a barn?

Murdoch feels hands pull him roughly to his feet. For a moment he looks up into the grinning face of the Pistolero.

PISTOLERO: Game over, Pendejos.

Murdoch is terrified. From the corner of his eye, he sees Jesus pale with fear. But he finds, he almost welcomes death. He feels their psychic oppression hanging heavy upon them, as if they were close by. The taint they've left on his soul weighing him down. Better to die, than live in their presence.

That's when they all hear it. The massive heavy footfalls. The sound of marble cracking with each step. The feel of an immense psychic presence enfolds them like a blanket.

MODOVAR: Holy shit (wonderingly). One of the fuckers is coming here? The fucker's here!

He glances at the Pistolero.

MODOVAR: Change of plans. Maybe these stupid Pendejo fuckers aren't useless after all. I can talk to these Gods, they respect me. We got an Altar here, we can deal with them. I might need some sacrifices in a hurry, so have them ready. If not, take the Pendejos out and shoot them later.

There's a hasty whispered discussion in Spanish. Modovar sneers and waves them silent.

MODOVAR: You have to know how to talk to them. I'll have him eating out of my hand. All I got to do is feed him a couple of souls.

He glances at the prisoners.

MODOVAR: Or more.

As the grey head of the Great Hippo rises above the stairs, its eyes glittering with fury, their heads fill with its anger and its relentless purpose.

Modovar steps forward, spreading his arms wide.

MODOVAR: Oh Great Lord Devourer, Timeless as Stone, Master of the Earth, First of the Four Children of the River Goddess, Chief of Blood, Sky and Nature, welcome. We serve thee!

GREAT HIPPO: BLASPHEMERS! APOSTATES! ASSHOLES! WHERE IS MY PRIEST!

* * *

The Great Gray Hippo advances on the group of hapless humans cringing beneath the psychic onslaught. Only Modovar stands straight, but he backs away.

MODOVAR: We serve thee my lord, as the covenant dictates. We offer thee sacrifices as of old, flesh and souls of your enemies. We obey the old ways.

GREAT HIPPO: OUR TEMPLES ARE PROFANED!

MODOVAR: Sacrifices! We offer sacrifices!

Murdoch and Jesus lay flat on the floor. The others cringe or crawl or kneel, the creature's voice overwhelming them, filling their minds. Only Modovar stands, and he's shaking under the psychic onslaught.

From where he's lying, from the direction, he thinks he sees someone else standing. It's in his peripheral vision, just the impression of a figure. He turns his head to see better, but somehow the figure just moves smoothly into the edges of his vision, and waits.

GREAT HIPPO: ABOMINATIONS WALK IN HOLY PLACES. THE UNCLEAN CONTAMINATION BEFOULS.

MODOVAR: Yes, we are working on that. We will make it right. We have sacrifices, right now. Sacrifices to your hunger and your glory.

GREAT HIPPO: PARASITE! THEY ARE YOUR FAULT! YOU BROUGHT THEM!

Modovar steps back, catches himself, and then from some hidden reserve straightens up. He stares defiantly at the Monster and screams.

MODOVAR: Back the fuck off! It's not my goddamned fault you whiny bitch.

There's a sudden pause in the psychic storm, a kind of freezing, a re-ordering of reality, as the thing's anger and frustration folds in on itself and re-aligns. As if suddenly, it focuses on Modovar for the first time, all that attention coalescing upon him like a microscope zeroing in on a bug. Modovar's eyes and nose starts to bleed, a red stain spreads from inside his cargo shorts but he ignores it all, standing his ground.

GREAT HIPPO: YOU DARE?

Murdoch steps forward, suddenly flushed. His orifices are all bleeding but he pays no attention. Murdoch can see that his skin is bright crimson, and realizes that blood is seeping through Modovar's pores. The man must be in agony. But he stands defiant, knowing that any hesitation, any weakness, his God will simply eat him.

MODOVAR: Fucking right I dare. Someone's got to talk sense to you, and the Priest isn't here. We didn't bring those fuckers... (pauses) What do you call them?

GREAT HIPPO: ABOMINATIONS.

MODOVAR: Yeah, those. Abomination-things. We didn't bring them. Why would we? Why would we want to insult our Gods? What does disrespect bring us? They're poison to you. Poison to us. We don't want them any more than you do. We want rid of them. You see all this shit? Why would we want that? We serve the Lords. Think it through.

The focus continues, the vast anger shifts again, refolding itself, re ordering itself.

The figure which maddeningly stands on the periphery of his vision is moving, but still in the periphery somehow, still gray and indistinct. It is carrying something, something long and sharp. Moving more quickly now.

GREAT HIPPO: WE REQUIRE SACRIFICE. A SHOW OF FAITH.

The voice in their heads is calmer, less rage and fury, an ancient narcissism reasserts itself.

MODOVAR: Got them right here!

Pleasure and gratification. Then irritation.

GREAT HIPPO: ONLY TWO? TWO ARE NOT SUFFICIENT RESTITUTION.

MODOVAR: Tip of the iceberg, buddy. We'll get you more. All you want. An all you can eat buffet, you and your pals.

Something hungry and greedy surges through their minds, the naïve cleverness of a greedy child, as its attention washes over the others.

GREAT HIPPO: MORE?

Greed. In mind's eye Murdoch finds himself imagining endless throngs of screaming victims stretching to the horizon in all directions as the Gods walk among them, feeding randomly.

MODOVAR: Lots more. Mountains of sacrifices. But not these other guys, they're mine, I still need them. Just the two and then more later. Good?

Modovar indicates his men, the Pistolero and gunmen, the coterie of advisors and henchmen. The God's eyes pass over them, the massive head nods ever so slightly. Then the drug lord waves at Murdoch and Jesus.

MODOVAR: These two HERE, as appetizers. Trouble makers.

Contemplation.

Acquiescence.

GREAT HIPPO: ACCEPTABLE. BUT MORE LATER, MANY MORE.

The jaws part, preparing to yawn in that terrifying gape, the massive tusks visible in the pink mouth. The Great Hippo reaches out for Jesus, who cries out in sheer naked terror.

Then the figure is running, absolutely silent, like a ghost, crossing his field of vision. Vernon, with his baby face mask, is moving. Vernon, who had been torn in half the last time he had seen him. For a second, as it passes by, Vernon glances down at him. Murdoch looks up into blackness where eyes should be. The figure puts a finger to the lips, quiet. And then it passes, silently swinging its killing blow.

The Great Hippo turns and seizes Vernon in one mighty paw, lifting him up in the air. Bones crack as it squeezes. The Aztec war club falls from nervous fingers, clattering on the floor. The Great Hippo stares at the figure squirming in its paw, its eyes luminous with rage. Its massive head swings to look down on Modovar, visibly shrinking as he backs up.

MODOVAR: Hey, that's... that's....

But it's futile. Murdoch can feel the Grey God's rage unfolding and unfolding, arcs and angles, opening up in all directions, blossoming, growing all consuming.

GREAT HIPPO: YOU LIE!!!

The Great Hippo hurls Vernon with all its might into the fertility goddess, shattering the cheap plaster beneath the golden cladding. Water roars through the rupture in the statue, the flow redoubling its pressure, the artificial brook overflows its banks as water spills across the floors. Vernon bounces from the statue, landing on an impossibly large waterbed which ruptures immediately, sending a wave across the floors. The head of the porn-star Goddess, almost intact, the face surreally recognizable from DVD covers, rolls and is pushed by the wave until it's almost facing towards them.

The God turns back to its worshiper, snorting audibly, ears flat like a cat. The great jaws gape wide. But Modovar is already backing rapidly away, shoving his followers in front of him.

MODOVAR: Someone kill that thing! Shoot it!

Rifle and pistol fire pepper its frame as it roars with fury. It steps forward, grabbing a pool table and flipping it, obliterating a man. Another is bitten in half, the pieces flung in opposite directions. The Pistolero fires, but the snap of massive jaws takes his arm. Everything is upheaval. While the monster is killing, Murdoch and Jesus scramble across suddenly shattered furniture and debris, intent on hiding.

MODOVAR: Get the fucking rocket launcher!

As if in answer, there's the roar of a rocket propelled grenade. Even from hiding, Murdoch's lungs are burning and the smell of accelerants fills the air. The rocket hisses and an instant later, the front of the mansion explodes outward. There's a scream, mercilessly ended with the sound of wet tearing as the victim literally comes to pieces in the monster's paws.

Then Modovar screams as he's lifted up high into the air, no more words, just wild incoherent terror.

Modovar lands on his back, within their frame of sight.

The God walks ponderously past them, looming over the terrified drug lord. It looks down at him from the full height of over four meters, and places one of its massive feet on his chest. A single word, both spoken and thought rings out, filling their awareness.

GREAT HIPPO: TRAITOR!

Then it presses down, and Modovar bursts like a grape, blood and organs squirting in every direction.

For an instant, neither Jesus nor Murdoch can breathe. Their hearts pound, and Murdoch is terrified at how loud that sound is. They hear the creature's soft breathing, and an impossible, overpowering stillness... and the sound of clapping.

* * *

Slowly the Great Hippo turns its head.

On the other side of the flooding brook, opposite one of the ornamental bridges, Vernon stands, no worse the wear. He pauses for a moment to brush a bit of plaster off, his child's doll mask looking down. Then he resumes clapping.

The Great Hippo lowers its head, its ears flattening. Its nostrils flare as it snorts, spraying mucus. The lips curl, exposing the massive tusks. As its jaws part, it seems to grin.

GREAT HIPPO: ABOMINATION!

Vernon continues to clap deliberately.

The creature swings its massive bulk to face Vernon, moving towards him deliberately, each step redoubling speed until within four steps it is charging. Nine thousand pounds of raging, furious monster hurtle towards the man. The God roars its fury.

As it reaches the swollen brook, it steps up on the ornamental bridge. The bridge collapses under it. The monster falls awkwardly, bellowing and thrashing, but somehow it's tangled in the bridge which has come unmoored. As the Great Hippo struggles to right itself it slips again and again, the water rushing past pushing it down the length of the brook. Try as it might, the creature cannot seem to find its footing, it flounders in the rushing water, twisting as it moves faster and faster towards the gap for the waterfall.

Then suddenly it hits the railings, which shatter against its impact. It bellows twisting wildly, scrabbling for any kind of hold.

Then it's gone.

From below comes a massive splash, and a blood curdling shriek of absolute agony. There's a hiss, and splashing, and more screams, and the acrid smell is in the air. Murdoch's mind shifts a gear, and he recognizes the smell from when he came in, remembers the bleached skeletons in the hot tub, the apparent steam, now fumes, rising from the pool. It was filled with acid.

Down below, the screams and thrashing continue. Vernon, finished clapping, notices a box with a red button by his feet. He picks it up pretending to study it. Experimentally, he presses the red button.

And suddenly, the huge multi-colored whirling chandelier is falling, Vernon appearing not to notice, presses again and again. A thousand weighted, jagged pieces of crystal cut their way through the air descending towards the God as it writhes in an agony of broken bones and dissolving flesh.

Vernon shrugs innocently, tossing the box with its red button away. He saunters over to the ruins of the balcony railing to peer over.

Vernon stands at the lip of the broken balcony, hands in pockets, looking down watching the smoke rise and listening to the screams and moans of the dying creature from beyond the ledge, broken, cut to ribbons, its flesh hissing as the acid eats away. The sounds of gasping agony and cries of torment rise and fall far below them.

He pulls an object from his pocket. It's a lighter. For a moment, Vernon amuses himself, flicking the lighter on and off, on and off. Finally growing bored, he tosses it over the balcony, watching its progress as it tumbles down.

When it touches the fluid in the pool it ignites, sending a column of flame all the way up to the balcony level. The Monster's screaming had been dwindling as it succumbed to its injuries, but now it redoubles, rises in pitch, finding new dimensions of agony. Its mind is shattered, but they can feel the endless roiling psychic residue of its unending pain and suffering.

Hidden by the wreckage, Murdoch and Jesus watch. Jesus has his arms wrapped around Murdoch, his hand on his mouth to keep him from screaming. Neither of them move. They pretend to be dead.

Out of the line of sight, the Pistolero moans in pain. He tries to move, and they hear the sudden intake of breath from the pain of broken bones being jostled.

Vernon lifts his head, and turns it towards the sound. For a moment, he's motionless, as if thinking things over. Then he steps away to the left, passing from the field of vision, heading towards the wall of weapons.

He crosses back across their frame of sight, carrying one of the heavy Aztec blades, then he's gone. The Pistolero moans, they hear scrabbling sound, pained curses, a final shouted word in Spanish, and then a meaty slap.

There's a clatter. The sound of an Aztec club being tossed aside casually. And then footsteps descending the marble stairs, with the sound of an occasional two step.

After a long wait, Murdoch dares to look around. Moving as silently as possible, Murdoch and Jesus first crawl, then stand, picking their way around the wreckage, careful not to make a sound.

Murdoch carefully approaches the lip of the balcony, to see what lies below, in case anyone or anything is lying in wait. He stares at the rail where the Great Hippo went over.

He notices the rail posts were cut half through, so they'd snap easily.

What had the Lieutenant said?

Vernon is all about tricks and traps. Don't go into a house if Vernon's been there.

* * *

Broken by the fall, dropped in acid, pierced by crystal shards, set on fire, the Gray God still lives, but it's dying. The creature's supernatural vitality is eroding away bit by bit. It's not even screaming any more, or moving, it barely whimpers.

Vernon sits on edge of the pool, cheerfully swinging his legs, not bothered by the smoldering fire or toxic fumes. Somehow he's found a straw hat, just like the one before. He watches the dying God burn alive slowly.

Murdoch and Jesus pick their way down the stairs slowly. They're not quite sure why or how they're still alive. But they know that they can't stay. Vernon seems distracted by the roasting God. With luck, none of the others are close by.

As they reach the bottom Vernon turns and reaches out, palm up, fingers outstretched, trembling, begging, supplicating. Murdoch recognizes it. It's the exact gesture of pleading Vernon made, out there in the jungle, after he'd been torn apart.

Murdoch keeps Jesus behind him, and backs away carefully.

Vernon shrugs indifferently, and begins to mount a pair of human eyeballs on an unstrung wire coat hanger, holding them over the burning carcass of the dying Hippo, for all the world like a child roasting marshmallows.

* * *

The troop transport still has its keys in it. Murdoch and Jesus waste no time. Ignoring the suffocating smell of roasted decaying human flesh or the steady red dripping from the back and sides, Jesus piles into the driver's seat of transport cab, so familiar, and hits the door lock, Murdoch crawling up the passenger side.

They both roll up the windows, remembering the fireball. Seal the cab, that's first thing on their minds. Check the mirrors. Scan the surroundings. Nothing.

They're alone in a landscape of dead bodies and spreading fires, in a scorched truck filled with charred, bleeding corpses, thickening blood oozing and dripping from the sides of the box. Flies are everywhere. There are no signs of Gods or Monsters.

They're safe. Murdoch exhales. It's not much safety, given what they've seen, and it may not last long. It may be a mere illusion. But it's enough. It feels like he's been holding his breath for years, it finally comes with such relief.

For a moment, they both flash on the beginning, the same images playing in their minds, as if from a lingering trace of the psychic communion of the Gods, of meeting the Lieutenant in the decaying ghost village, driving the together down dirt roads, the truck empty, not understanding that the unspeakable was following them.

JESUS: It's like it was all a thousand years ago.

MURDOCH: Yes.

Jesus turns the key, to their relief, it starts immediately. He guns the engine. The RPM needle on the dashboard swings up, they feel the vibration, the muted roar of the engine. It's comforting, an assertion of sanity, of a world of physics and chemistry rather than Gods and Monsters.

He looks over at Murdoch.

JESUS: Where do we go?

They stare at each other, unsure. Murdoch's voice is slow and tentative.

MURDOCH: Airfield, maybe? I'm rated for single engine. I might be able to fly something? I don't know? If there's anything there? If they're not there? If they haven't destroyed it?

He pauses.

MURDOCH: Maybe the docks? A boat? Something? Anything that floats? I don't know. We don't know.

He thinks.

MURDOCH: Anywhere we go, they might be waiting for us. But we can't stay here.

The windshield of the truck is smeared with soot, vision muddy. But they can see corpses in their field of view. In that strange communion, they both wonder without speaking, how many dead?

JESUS: Maybe people got away?

MURDOCH: Yeah.

Neither of them believe it.

They stare outwards, smoke is rolling across, they can smell it. There are a dozen large fires now, and more building.

MURDOCH: The fires are spreading. This place is going up fast. I think we can get to one, the airfield or the docks, but after, we may not be able to make it to the other. We need to pick one.

JESUS: The docks. They can't cross running water. If we can get on the water, we're safe.

Murdoch remembers Vernon dancing across the brook on the balcony. He's not sure that's true. He suspects it might be an affectation for them.

MURDOCH: Yeah.

He hesitates.

MURDOCH: What about the things, those... Gods?

JESUS: What about them?

Jesus laughs, or maybe he weeps. They've both seen the Men in the Masks, felt the dreadful corrosive presence of the Men in Masks, they've seen their works, and they've seen them. Risk the Men in the Masks, or risk the Gods? There's really no choice at all.

MURDOCH: Yeah. Fuck them.

Jesus half smiles.

JESUS: They're on their own.

Murdoch barks, a humourless sound that could be a laugh.

Jesus throws the engine into gear, it lurches ahead. He stops.

JESUS: Hey, if we see someone....

MURDOCH: Yeah?

JESUS: We try and save them. Doesn't matter who. Just try and save someone.

Murdoch thinks about it.

MURDOCH: Yeah.

But neither of them really believes that there's anyone else left.

* * *

Navigating through the fires is hellish. Smoke is everywhere, visibility is poor. They've had to turn several times, the path being blocked by spreading fires.

They drive through chaos. There's charred rubble everywhere, vehicles overturned and flung outward by the blast, or sucked in by the inversion. Many of the buildings survived the blast, but almost none of them intact, walls and roofs torn away, mobile homes tumbled. What could catch fire is often burning. Charred corpses are flung everywhere, tangled in the rubble.

On the way to the waterfront, their road is blocked by a massive twisted arch of contorted metal, bodies of women and children dangling from it in distorted poses, in some places only arms or legs dangle. Around it metal struts are sticking out wildly in every direction, more corpses and torn shreds of corpses are tied with barbed wire and festive streamers. Impossibly, a few coloured lights wound against the structure continue to blink cheerfully.

It takes Murdoch a second to recognize it as the remains of the Ferris Wheel, half unspooled before them.

As they watch, one of the bodies tied to the arch, arms outstretched in a parody of crucifixion, legs half dangling, twists on its own. They can't make out a face, or recognize a sex, anything identifiable has been charred away. The figure is blind, its eyes burned out. There's no way that it can tell they're there. It coughs and vomits red and black, and keeps twisting against its bonds.

Murdoch and Jesus simply stare at it for a moment. Then without saying a word, Jesus shifts gears, the transmission grinds, the truck lurches into reverse, and they turn around. They find it hard to look at each other after that.

At some point, they drive through some pool of viscous burning liquid that clings and now one of the back tires is burning. No matter how or where they drive, it won't stop burning, the flames dying down and then rising up again. It's only a matter of time before the fire spreads into the back of the truck, and eventually reaches the gas tanks.

Murdoch hopes that the wooden frame of the box is sufficiently blood soaked, the charred wet corpses filling the back are sufficiently damp that maybe the fire will not catch and crawl. He doesn't want to have to get out of the truck. The fire makes him think of the corpses, and the corpses make him think of the Ferris Wheel.

JESUS: What we saw? Back there?

What they saw? Murdoch is incredulous. They saw Gods. They saw horrors. But he knows what Jesus is talking about.

He can't stop thinking about the writhing charred body, twisting on the wreckage of the Ferris Wheel.

MURDOCH: There was nothing we could do. They were already dead. There was no way to help.

Murdoch hopes that is true. In his mind's eye, the crucified figure twists in agony, coughing up blood, sightless eyes look to them, begging for salvation, for mercy.

MURDOCH: Don't think about it. Just keep driving.

He knows they've damned themselves. They could have stopped, could have tried to help. But they didn't. Just like the baby back in the empty village. He thinks of the Pistolero, having to shoot his own dying men, that was mercy. He's not that brave, not that strong.

In the rear view mirror on his side, Murdoch watches the burning tire, turning round and round every time they slow, a circle of flame when they go a little faster. The fire has spread to the box, climbing up the wooden side. The bloodied, burned corpses in back aren't slowing it, their only effect is to redouble the stench of burning flesh.

He knows the fire is spreading to the undercarriage as well.

Murdoch wonders where the gas tanks are? How close they are to the back? How much time before the fire slowly crawls to the tanks?

How much time do they have left? Before the Men in the Masks come for them.

He doesn't want to leave the truck. But he doesn't want to burn in it either.

There's a wall of flame in front of them. Jesus halts the vehicle.

JESUS: Maybe we can just get through it.

MURDOCH: Remember Vernon?

The Trickster. Vernon who innocently sets traps. Drive through a wall of flame, only to bust your axles in a pit. If not Vernon, then one of the others. They can't see through the fire, not well enough.

MURDOCH: We find another way.

JESUS: Look!

Murdoch looks. There's a man watching them, not bothered by the billowing gusts of smoke. Not bothered by the proximity to the fire. He's dressed like a scarecrow, he wears a burlap sack for a hood, and he holds in each hand the blades of a broken pair of gardening shears. He's simply watching them, through the single hole in his sack.

The hole is in a place where no human shaped head would have an eye. And yet, it watches through the hole.

MURDOCH: Move!!!

Murdoch's shout shakes Jesus from his paralysis. He guns the transport into reverse, pulls back in a wide circle, and roars out of there, taking a wide berth, smashing a pickup truck out of the way. Jesus accelerates, the man is left far behind. They glimpse shapes in the smoke, and don't slow down. Instead, Jesus goes faster and faster blazing through the wreckage.

Then suddenly, a God appears in front of them.

* * *

The screaming in the cab is so loud that Murdoch feels his eardrums bursting. He can't tell if it's himself or Jesus screaming, or something else shrieking psychically inside their heads.

The Green behemoth, the Nature God, looms up in front of them out of nowhere. It's gigantic, overpowering. He can feel a psychic wave of surprise, as the truck turns the corner at high speed, bearing down on it. Then a snap of anger.

At the moment of impact, it lashes out. And then Murdoch is smashed against the windshield like a bug. All they can hear is the sound of shredding and tearing metal, the crash of impact lacing in their incoherent shouts and screams. The Nature God masses maybe six thousand pounds. The transport truck is rated thirty tons. But the Green Hippo is a God, its strength is incalculable.

The transport truck goes flying, Murdoch and Jesus free fall in the cab as it turns over in the air, battered against the interior, and then it hits the ground, slides, rolls onto its side. The charred bloody corpses in the back fly off in every direction.

The cab is full of blood. Some of it drips onto his face. Murdoch blinks in the unnatural silence.

Murdoch is astonished to discover that he's alive.

Jesus weeps.

Outside, a couple of dozen feet away, the Nature God lies on its back, one of its hind limbs twisted even more unnaturally than before. It's bleeding. It groans painfully, and rolls over, trying to rise. It cannot.

The Lieutenant is standing in front of it.

Murdoch doesn't understand why she's wearing her helmet.

* * *

The great Green Hippo, the last God, lies there, in a spreading pool of its own blood, gasping for breath. It watches as the Lieutenant approaches.

GREEN HIPPO: YOU DO NOT KNOW WHAT YOU DO!

The Lieutenant simply stares. The creature is reflected in the dark surface of her helmet's visor. There's no trace of expression on what can be seen of her face. No body language, only stillness.

GREEN HIPPO: WE ARE THE HOPE, THE LAST HOPE. WITHOUT US, WHO WILL HEAL THIS BROKEN WORLD? WHO WILL BRING LIFE BACK TO THIS DYING PLANET? WITHOUT US WHAT HOPE? … WITHOUT—

The Lieutenant fires her luger into the left eye of the creature. It jerks and spasms, and then goes still. She keeps firing into the eye socket, the bullets chewing up flesh and bone.

She steps forward and rams the sharp end of her pry-bar into the cavity in its skull. There's a moment of resistance as she breaks through the final layer of bone into the brain, plunging it deep and twisting it around and around inside the skull, turning the gray matter into mush. It makes a slurping noise.

Satisfied, she pulls the pry-bar out and turns around.

* * *

Murdoch is standing there in front of her, his arm outstretched, pistol pointed at her forehead.

Behind him, Jesus staggers towards the docks. There's a zodiac boat moored.

JESUS: Come on, we can make it.

Murdoch doesn't move. He just stares at the Lieutenant, pistol almost touching the visor of her helmet. Behind the mirrored plastic, he can just barely see her eyes staring at him. They're empty. He waits. He waits for her to speak, to say something. To justify, to excuse, to demand or complain. He waits to see whether she'll be the person he knew on the river, or the psychopath on the road, or anyone at all.

She simply stares back.

He pulls the trigger. The hammer clicks. Nothing. He pulls again and again.

Click. Click. Click.

The Lieutenant doesn't speak at all. She just walks past him, and walks away.

Murdoch stares at her as she vanishes into the smoke. He coughs a bit, his lungs irritated by the heated gases. He hurts, everything hurts, he can feel his injuries catching up with him. He can feel his blood, trickling under his clothes. He is so tired. He drops the useless pistol.

Then he turns back to follow Jesus.

THE END

Squad Thirteen, Worse than Death – Page 289

More Books by the Author

If you've skipped to the end, looking for an apology, well... Sorry? Also, no refunds.

Thank you for taking the time out to read my little book. If you've made it all the way here, then I'm just going to assume you liked it.

What else do I have to offer? Well, there's as a trilogy of collections of horror stories, another trilogy of collections of alternate history stories, two collections of funny fantasy stories for a change of pace, a two part alternate history novel, and a fantasy murder mystery.

For non-fiction, I have three kick-ass *Doctor Who Pirate Histories,* *LEXX Unauthorized*, the chronicle of a cult sci fi series, and *Starlost Unauthorized and the Quest for Canadian Identity*.

If you liked this, could I suggest you leave a review? Mention it on your blog? Or Facebook? Say nice things. Just toss me a couple of stars? A little appreciation is a wonderful thing. But there's more: It's about trying to get out there. There are a lot of people writing a lot of books, and it can get hard to get noticed. Reviews help.

And hey, check out my Website,

www.denvaldron.com

HEARTS IN DARKNESS

A Trilogy of Horror Collections

Giant Monsters Sing Sad Songs – The connection between the author of the Necronomicon and a boy in Providence; a girl who meets the last Sasquatch, a poet who shares abandoned Tokyo with a Kaiju, and more…

What Devours Also Hungers – The unkillable killers in masks are recruited into the army, vampires and their hunters, clever monsters, ghosts and more…

There Are No Doors in Dark Places – A childlike cancer that talks to its owner; A single mother drawn into dark magic; A man who turns into a different monster each night; a vampire that twists lives; a pregnant woman finding her body being stolen from her; and many more

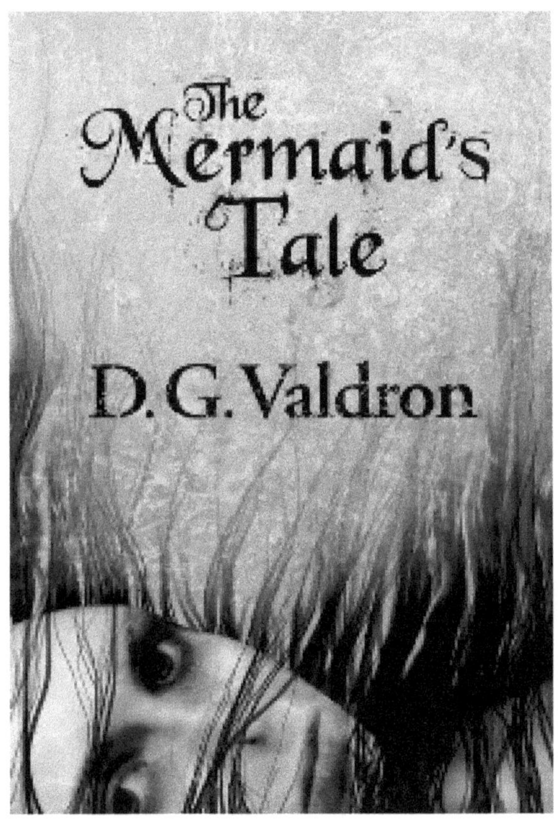

A Dark Fantasy of Murder and Redemption

There's a City where all the races come together uneasily, descending into civil war.

There's a Mermaid, murdered cruelly her people distraught and crying out for justice.

There's an Orc, the lowest and the worst, her mission: Solve the murder, before it all comes crashing down.

She finds something else... the world's first serial killer.

Drunk Slutty Elf
and Other Stories

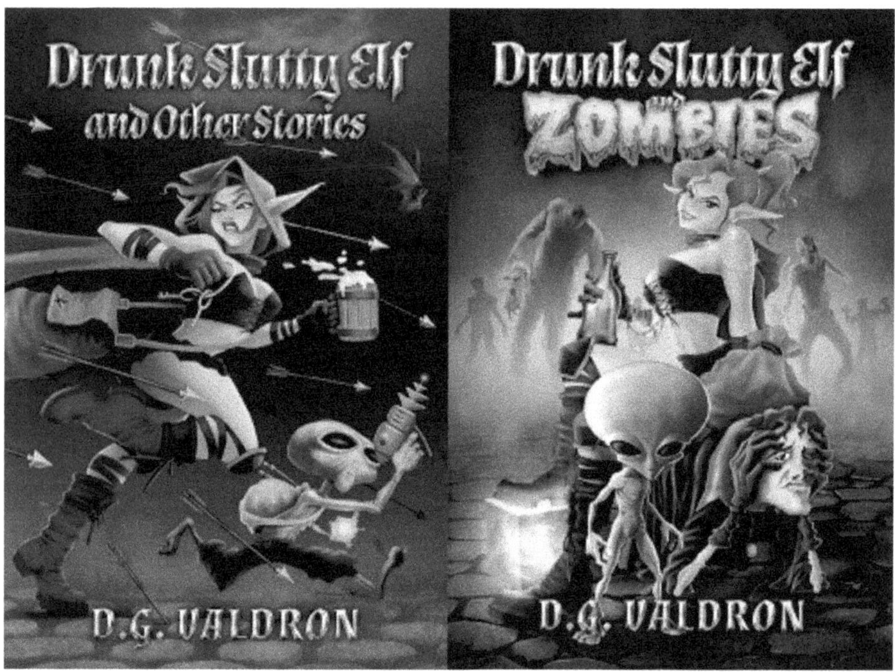

Drunk Slutty Elf and
Zombies

Hilarious Science Fiction and Fantasy

Two volumes of savage, satirical, subversive wicked, funny, frantic science fiction and fantasy. Demented ghost hunters, frustrated aliens, horny giants, drunken elves, sneaky ghosts, wayward barbarians and many more.

AXIS OF ANDES

NEW WORLD WAR

An Alternate History of WWII in South America

Berlin, 1937, Adolph Hitler and his cabinet meet with a strange delegation from Ecuador. The delegates from the small South American nation beg for help, fearing an impending invasion from their rival, Peru. What happens at that meeting sets in motion a chain of events that lights the entire continent on fire. By the time it's done, millions are dead, nations are in ruins, and the map of Latin America will be changed beyond recognition.

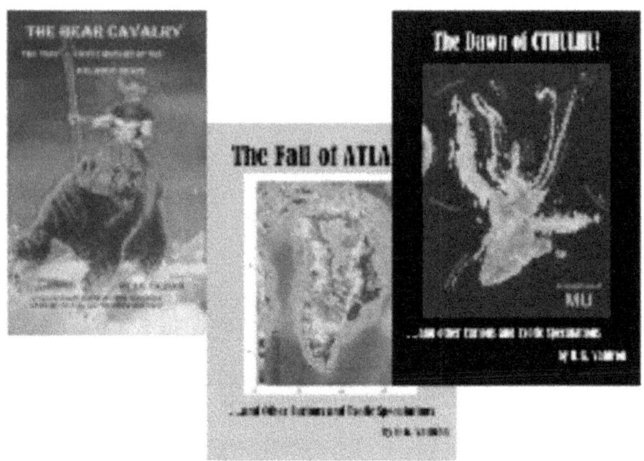

ALTERNATE REALITIES

A Trilogy of Strange New Worlds

The Dawn of Cthulhu - The Secret History of H.P. Lovecraft's Cthulhu Cult; Lost Continents Found – real and legendary; The Monsters of Sesame Street, is a light hearted examination of Muppets as if they were actual animals.

The Fall of Atlantis – Retroverse, An Accidental Cinematic Universe of 50's Sci Fi movies, Greenland Without the Ice, Rome Crosses the Atlantic, and the Rise and Fall of Atlantis, an ecological catastrophe.

The Bear Cavalry, the True (Not!) History of the Icelandic Bears, an off the wall, short novel about the Viking domestication of bears, their evolution into a medieval cavalry Bonus novelette, The Sharebear Apocalypse.

TWILIGHT OF ECHELON from AT BAY PRESS

Explore the surreal retro-sci fi universe of Echelon, from the mind of Artist Robert Pasternak, inspiring remarkable stories written by D.G. Valdron, as well as Blaise Moritz, Alex Passy and Lovern Kindzierski.

STARLOST was a 1973 sci fi series produced in Canada, and created by Harlan Ellison. But before it ended, Ellison was flaming the show and it was cancelled after sixteen episodes, going down in infamy as *'the worst Sci Fi series ever!'*

But there was another side to the story, overlooked until now. Starlost, came along during the wave of Canadian nationalism, and its stories were an overlooked and brilliant exploration of the issues and ideas of a nation struggling to find itself. A brilliant reappraisal of an unjustly maligned television series.

The Pirate Histories!

What's a Pirate's History, you ask? It's the things they don't want you to know about, or that they don't care about, things that are great and marvellous and intriguing... but unapproved. It's a history of secret and forgotten corners of the Whoniverse. The first woman Doctor, the first black Doctor, animations, audios, the stage plays and fan films.

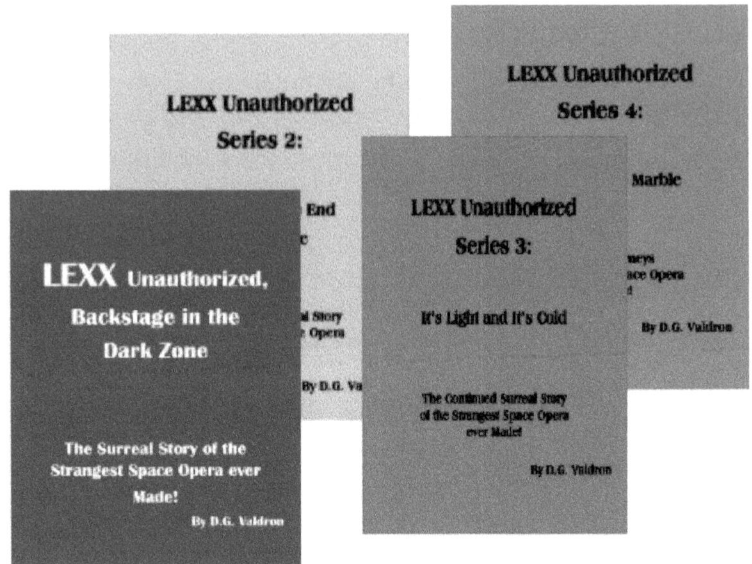

LEXX UNAUTHORIZED

LEXX Unauthorized about the making of a show about a giant space bug that blows up planets, the cowardly security guard who is its captain, and the undead assassin, runaway love slave, and robot head who form its crew.

Originally billed as 'Star Trek's Evil Twin,' the cultiest of cult sci fi, LEXX's forte was black humor, startling visuals, big ideas, and a sensibility that had more to do with surrealists like Jodorowsky or Bunuel than mainstream science fiction. And, as unconventional as it was onscreen, the story of how it came to be is even more bizarre.